WORLD WAR II

A Political and Diplomatic History of the Modern World

WORLD WAR II

Edited by Alisha Bains

IN ASSOCIATION WITH

Published in 2017 by Britannica Educational Publishing (a trademark of Encyclopædia Britannica, Inc.) in association with The Rosen Publishing Group, Inc. 29 East 21st Street, New York, NY 10010

Copyright © 2017 by Encyclopædia Britannica, Inc. Britannica, Encyclopædia Britannica, and the Thistle logo are registered trademarks of Encyclopædia Britannica, Inc. All rights reserved.

Rosen Publishing materials copyright © 2017 The Rosen Publishing Group, Inc. All rights reserved.

Distributed exclusively by Rosen Publishing.
To see additional Britannica Educational Publishing titles, go to rosenpublishing.com.

First Edition

Britannica Educational Publishing
J.E. Luebering: Executive Director, Core Editorial
Anthony L. Green: Editor, Compton's by Britannica

Rosen Publishing
Alisha Bains: Editor
Nelson Sá: Art Director
Matt Cauli: Designer
Cindy Reiman: Photography Manager
Bruce Donnola: Photo Researcher

Library of Congress Cataloging-in-Publication Data

Names: Bains, Alisha.
Title: World War II / edited by Alisha Bains.
Other titles: World War 2 | World War Two
Description: First edition. | New York : Britannica Educational Publishing in association with Rosen Educational Services, 2017 New York. | Series: A political and diplomatic history of the modern world | Audience: Grades 7 to 12. | Includes bibliographical references and index.
Identifiers: LCCN 2016003769 | ISBN 9781680483604 (library bound : alkaline paper)
Subjects: LCSH: World War, 1939–1945—Juvenile literature.
Classification: LCC D743.7 .W6713 2017 | DDC 940.4—dc23
LC record available at http://lccn.loc.gov/2016003769

Manufactured in China

Contents

INTRODUCTION   11

CHAPTER 1
THE ORIGINS OF WORLD WAR II, 1929–39   20

Political Consequences of the Depression   21
Failures of the League   25
The Rise of Hitler and Fall of Versailles   29
    Failure of the German Republic   29
        Mein Kampf *("My Struggle")*   32
    European Responses to Nazism   34
    Italian Aggression   40
    The First German Move   41
British Appeasement and American Isolationism   44
    The Rationale of Appeasement   44
    The Civil War in Spain   46
    The Return of U.S. Isolationism   48
        Good Neighbor Policy   49
    Japan's Aggression in China   50

CHAPTER 2
THE OUTBREAK OF WAR   54

The German-Austrian Union   54
The Taking of Czechoslovakia   57
    Munich Agreement   59
    Blitzkrieg   64
Technology, Strategy, and the Onset of Hostilities   67
    Rearmament and Tactical Planning   67
    Poland and Soviet Anxiety   71
    Hitler's War or Chamberlain's?   76

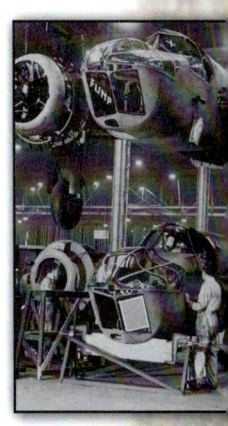

CHAPTER 3
THE WAR IN EUROPE, 1939–41   79

Forces and Resources of the European Combatants, 1939   79

The Campaign in Poland, 1939   82

The Baltic States and the Russo-Finnish War, 1939–40   85

The War in the West, September 1939–June 1940   87

    The Invasion of Norway   89

    The Invasion of the Low Countries and France   91

    The Evacuation from Dunkirk   97

    Italy's Entry Into the War and the French Armistice   100

    Free French   102

The Battle of Britain   105

Central Europe and the Balkans, 1940–41   108

CHAPTER 4
OTHER FRONTS, 1940–41   115

Egypt and Cyrenaica, 1940–Summer 1941   115

East Africa   118

Iraq and Syria, 1940–41   119

The Beginning of Lend-Lease   120

The Atlantic and the Mediterranean, 1940–41   122

    Convoy System   123

German Strategy, 1939–42   126

Invasion of the Soviet Union, 1941   128

The War in the Pacific, 1938–41   136

    The War in China, 1937–41   136

    Japanese Policy, 1939–41   137

    Pearl Harbor and the Japanese Expansion, to July 1942   141

        The "Back Door to War" Theory   143

The Fall of Singapore   147
  The Chinese Front and Burma, 1941–42   151

CHAPTER 5
DEVELOPMENTS FROM AUTUMN 1941 TO AUTUMN 1943   153

  Allied Strategy and Controversies, 1940–42   153
  Libya and Egypt, Autumn 1941–Summer 1942   156
  The Germans' Summer Offensive in Southern Russia, 1942   160
  The Allies' First Decisive Successes   162
   The Pacific and Other Fronts, July 1942–May 1943   162
   Burma, Autumn 1942–Summer 1943   166
   Montgomery's Battle of el-Alamein and Rommel's Retreat, 1942–43   167
   Stalingrad and the German Retreat, Summer 1942–February 1943   169
   The Invasion of Northwest Africa, November–December 1942   172
   Tunisia, November 1942–May 1943   174
   The Atlantic, the Mediterranean, and the North Sea, 1942–45   177
   Air Warfare, 1942–43   179
    Casablanca Conference   181
   Casablanca and Trident, January–May 1943   182
   The Eastern Front, February–September 1943   183
   The Southwest and South Pacific, June–October 1943   184

CHAPTER 6
THE FINAL SOLUTION   187
  Changes in Policy   188
    Wannsee Conference   189

Nazi Anti-Semitism and the Origins of the Holocaust   192
   Nürnberg Laws   193
From Kristallnacht to the "Final Solution"   197
   Non-Jewish Victims of Nazism   198
   Nazi Expansion and the Formation of Ghettos   199
The Einsatzgruppen   201
Extermination Camps   202

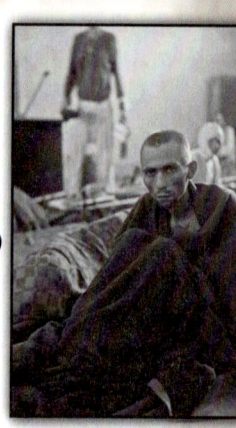

CHAPTER 7
DEVELOPMENTS FROM AUTUMN 1943 TO SUMMER 1944   209

Sicily and the Fall of Mussolini, July–August 1943   209
The Quadrant Conference (Quebec I)   211
The Allies' Invasion of Italy and the Italian Volte-Face, 1943   212
   Katyn Massacre   214
The Western Allies and Stalin: Cairo and Tehran, 1943   216
German Strategy, from 1943   218
The Eastern Front, October 1943–April 1944   220
The War in the Pacific, October 1943–August 1944   222
   The Encirclement of Rabaul   223
   Western New Guinea   224
   The Central Pacific   224
The Burmese Frontier and China, November 1943–Summer 1944   228
The Italian Front, 1944   230

CHAPTER 8
DEFEAT OF THE AXIS POWERS   233

The Allied Invasions of Western Europe, June–November 1944   234

The Eastern Front, June–December 1944   240
Air Warfare, 1944   242
Allied Policy and Strategy:
    Octagon (Quebec II) and Moscow, 1944   244
The Philippines and Borneo, from September 1944   245
Burma and China, October 1944–May 1945   249
The German Offensive in the West, Winter
    1944–45   251
The Soviet Advance to the Oder,
    January–February 1945   253
Yalta   255
    The Last Big Three Summit   257
The German Collapse, Spring 1945   259
Potsdam   263
The End of the Japanese War,
    February–September 1945   264
  Iwo Jima and the Bombing of Tokyo   264
  Okinawa   266
  Hiroshima and Nagasaki   267
  The Japanese Surrender   268
    The Decision to Use the Atomic Bomb   269

CHAPTER 9
COSTS AND AFTERMATH OF THE WAR   273
  Killed, Wounded, Prisoners, or Missing   273
  Human and Material Cost   274
    Europe   274
    The Far East   276
  Postwar Developments   277
    The Marshall Plan   278
    War Trials and Peace Treaties   280
    The Problem of Germany   281

Nürnberg Trials 282
The Problems of Austria and Trieste 285
Postwar Problems in Asia 286
Buildup to the Cold War 287

CONCLUSION 289
GLOSSARY 291
BIBLIOGRAPHY 294
INDEX 298

INTRODUCTION

Along with World War I, World War II was one of the great watersheds of 20th-century geopolitical history. It resulted in the extension of the Soviet Union's power to nations of eastern Europe, enabled a Communist movement to eventually achieve power in China, and marked the decisive shift of power in the world away from the states of western Europe and toward the United States and the Soviet Union.

The war involved virtually every part of the world during the years 1939–45. The principal belligerents were the Axis powers—Germany, Italy, and Japan—and the Allies—France, Great Britain, the United States, the Soviet Union, and, to a lesser extent, China. The war was in many respects a continuation, after an uneasy 20-year hiatus, of the disputes left unsettled by World War I. The 40,000,000–50,000,000 deaths incurred in World War II make it the bloodiest conflict, as well as the largest war, in history.

By the early part of 1939 the German dictator Adolf Hitler had become determined to invade and occupy Poland. Poland, for its part, had guarantees of French and British military support should it be attacked by Germany. Hitler intended to invade Poland anyway, but first he had to neutralize the possibility that the Soviet Union would resist the invasion of its western neighbour. Secret negotiations led on August 23–24 to the signing of the German-Soviet Nonaggression Pact in Moscow. In a secret protocol of this pact, the Germans and the Soviets agreed that Poland should be divided between them, with the western third of the country going to Germany and the eastern two-thirds being taken over by the U.S.S.R.

Having achieved this cynical agreement, the other provisions of which stupefied Europe even without divulgence of the secret

A World War II memorial in Washington, D.C., honours the millions of Americans who contributed to the war.

protocol, Hitler thought that Germany could attack Poland with no danger of Soviet or British intervention and gave orders for the invasion to start on August 26. News of the signing, on August 25, of a formal treaty of mutual assistance between Great Britain and Poland (to supersede a previous though temporary agreement) caused him to postpone the start of hostilities for a few days. He was still determined, however, to ignore the diplomatic efforts of the Western powers to restrain him. Finally, at 12:40 PM on Aug. 31, 1939, Hitler ordered hostilities against Poland to start at 4:45 the next morning. The invasion began as ordered. In response, Great Britain and France declared war on Germany

Introduction

on September 3, at 11:00 AM and at 5:00 PM, respectively. World War II had begun.

How could the Axis powers have imagined that they might win the war, given their narrow base of land area, population, and production and the size and strength of the enemies they themselves forced into the war? The answer was blitzkrieg, which involved more than simply a set of tactics for mobile combat but was rather an encompassing theory of total war. The theory posited a strategically mobilized and organized economy meant to avoid a repetition of the war of attrition that wore Germany down in 1914–18. By overrunning their neighbours one by one in swift assaults, the Germans constantly added to their own manpower and resource base while shrinking that available to the enemy. In addition, armament in breadth rather than depth provided the flexibility necessary to shift production from one set of weapons to another depending on the needs of the next campaign, and it permitted constant innovation of weapons systems. Most tellingly, blitzkrieg shifted the burdens of war from Germany to the conquered peoples. By June 1940 the British were unable to budge a Nazi empire that drew on the resources of the entire continent. But Hitler also realized by late 1940 that all the resources of the United States would eventually be made available to Britain, hence his decision to break the stalemate by unleashing blitzkrieg against the Soviet Union. Soviet survival, however, turned the blitzkrieg into a gigantic war of attrition after all, one in which Germany could never prevail.

Cut off from foreign sources of capital, Germany paid for World War II through taxes and ruthless exploitation of occupied regions. Levies on conquered peoples amounted to 40 percent of the income raised by internal taxation, and 42 percent of that tribute came from France. The number of slave labourers deployed by various arms of the regime peaked at 7,100,000 in 1944; this figure included prisoners of war and "racial enemies" condemned to slavery until death in camps run by the SS, the black-uniformed elite corps and self-described "political soldiers" of the Nazi Party.

Seen only in cold economic terms, Nazi genocide against Jews and other groups, racially or ideologically or otherwise defined, was the height of irrationality. As early as January 1939 Hitler gave vent to his pathological hatred and fear of the Jews before the Reichstag: "If the international Jewish financiers… succeed in plunging the nations once more into a world war the result will be the obliteration of the Jewish race in Europe." The war gave Hitler the opportunity to seek a "final solution." In 1939–40 the Nazis considered using Poland or Madagascar as dumping grounds for Jews. But the invasion of the U.S.S.R. emboldened Hitler, Nazi Party leader Hermann Göring, and SS leaders Heinrich Himmler and Reinhard Heydrich to decide instead on mass extermination in camps at Belzec, Majdanek, Sobibor, Treblinka, and Auschwitz. Large numbers of SS troops, as well as railroads and rolling stock, were absorbed in capturing, transporting, and putting to death as many as 12,000 Jews per day. The total by war's end would reach 6,000,000, almost half from Poland, and some 2,000,000 others including Gypsies, clergy, Communists, and other resisters. SS troops accompanied the regular army into the Soviet Union in 1941 and made racial war on the Slavs as well in order to prepare the farmlands of Ukraine for German settlement.

News of the Holocaust reached the West slowly but surely, although Auschwitz was able to keep its monstrous secret for more than two years after the first gassings in May 1942. Reports appearing in Western newspapers inspired the Allies to make a declaration on Dec. 17, 1942, condemning "this bestial policy of cold-blooded extermination," and on January 22, 1944, U.S. President Franklin Roosevelt established a War Refugee Board "to forestall the plan of the Nazis to exterminate all Jews and

Introduction

other minorities." But the Allies were unable to take direct action of any sort until the capture of Italy brought Allied bombers within range of the camps. Jewish leaders were then misled by hints that the Germans might negotiate about the Jews. Finally, after June 1944, when escapees confirmed the existence and nature of Auschwitz, the World Jewish Congress requested bombing of the gas chambers. But the Allied Bomber Command judged that its efforts should be directed only at military targets and that the best way of helping the Jews was to hasten the defeat of Nazi Germany.

Allied strategic bombing was the most deadly form of economic warfare ever devised and showed another side of the indiscriminateness of industrial war. But in mid-1941 the British Chiefs of Staff soberly concluded that morale, not industry, was Germany's most vulnerable point and ordered Sir Arthur Harris of the Royal Air Force (RAF) Bomber Command to concentrate on "area bombing" of cities. British Prime Minister Winston Churchill's scientific adviser Professor L.A. Lindemann of Oxford (later Lord Cherwell) concurred in April 1942 that one-third of all Germans could be rendered homeless in 15 months by strategic bombing of cities. The Royal Air Force accordingly assigned its new Lancaster four-engine bombers to a total war on German civilians. After attacks on Lübeck and the Ruhr, Harris sent a thousand planes against Cologne on May 30–31 in an attack that battered one-third of the city. In 1943, after an interlude of bombing German submarine pens, the Lancasters launched the Battle of the Ruhr totaling 18,506 sorties and the Battle of Hamburg numbering 17,021. The fire raids in Hamburg killed 40,000 people and left a million homeless. The Royal Air Force then hit Berlin (November 1943 to March 1944) with 20,224 sorties, avenging many times over all the damage done by the Luftwaffe to London.

By early 1943 the U.S. 8th Air Force joined in the air campaign but eschewed terror bombing. Its B-17 Flying Fortresses and B-24 Liberators conducted daylight precision bombing of industrial targets. As a result, they suffered heavy losses that climaxed in October 1943 over the Schweinfurt ball-bearing plants, when the United States lost 148 bombers in a week. The Army Air Forces suspended daylight sorties for months until the arrival of a long-range fighter, the P-51 Mustang. Bombing then resumed and concentrated on the German oil industry, creating a serious shortage that virtually grounded the Luftwaffe by the time of the D-Day invasion in 1944. The effectiveness of strategic bombing is a subject of great debate, since German war production actually increased over the years 1942–44. German engineers became masters at shielding equipment, restoring it to operation in a matter of days, or even moving plants underground. Nor did the German people crack under British devastation of their towns and homes. But the air offensive did force the Germans to divert as many as 1,500,000 workers to the constant task of rebuilding and established the Allied mastery of the air that permitted the success of the Normandy landings.

In 1944, as the cold, wet season advanced, the Allied drive slowed down. Aided by the bad weather, the Germans launched a surprise counterattack on December 16. The main attack came south of Aachen in the Ardennes. The Battle of the Bulge, as this attack was called, ended in final German defeat in this region. The year ended with the Allied forces in the west and east ready to throw their weight into the drive that would crush Nazi power.

After driving the Germans from the Ardennes bulge the Allied armies advanced into Germany. By the end of March 1945 the Americans and British had advanced halfway across Germany. The Germans also collapsed on other fronts. Budapest fell to the Soviets in February and Vienna in April.

Introduction

In Italy Mussolini was caught and shot by partisans on April 28. The next day the Germans in Italy surrendered unconditionally.

Despite the utter hopelessness of the German cause Hitler remained defiant in his underground Berlin bunker. The Soviets attacked Berlin on April 21. To escape capture by the Soviets Hitler committed suicide the night of April 30. Now all attention turned to the Far East.

Japan's strategy was similar to Germany's blitzkrieg in that the swift conquest of isolated territories was designed to create a self-sufficient empire capable of withstanding any blow from without. Once again, precise operational planning permitted Japan to increase weapons production steadily from the inception of a full war economy in 1942 to early 1945, when U.S. bombing intensified. By 1944, naval ordnance production was more than five times that of 1941 and aviation more than four and a half times. The Japanese, like the Nazis, exploited their conquered peoples and even more than the Nazis subjected prisoners of war to slavery or death. But the fact that attacking Pearl Harbor would "awaken a sleeping giant" was lost on Japanese planners. By 1944 military expenditures absorbed 50 percent of the Japanese GNP, a degree of concentration second only to that of the Soviet Union. Yet the United States, with half its effort diverted to Europe, still overwhelmed the Co-Prosperity Sphere.

By April 1944, Japan lay open to direct assault by land as well as air and sea. How could the United States bring Tokyo to surrender? Three means suggested themselves: invasion, inducement, and shock. The first would involve a lengthy, brutal campaign in which, it was estimated, hundreds of thousands of American and perhaps 2,000,000 Japanese lives would be lost. Yet the Joint Chiefs had no choice but to prepare for this eventuality, and by May 25 they had instructed General Douglas MacArthur to plan Operation

"Olympic," an invasion of Kyushu, for November 1. The second means, inducement, was clearly preferable, and on May 8, the day after the German surrender, President Harry S. Truman tried it. Unconditional surrender, he said, would mean "the termination of the influence of the military leaders who have brought Japan to the present brink of disaster," but did not mean "the extermination or enslavement of the Japanese people," who would be free to "return to their families, their farms, their jobs."

The third means of achieving a surrender—by shock—had become a possibility on Dec. 30, 1944, when General Leslie Groves, head of the Manhattan Project, reported that it was "reasonably certain" that a gun-type atomic bomb equivalent to 10,000 tons of TNT and an implosion-type bomb would be ready for testing by the summer of 1945. Soon after Truman's accession to the presidency, Secretary of War Henry L. Stimson formed an Interim Committee of statesmen and scientists to debate how the bomb should be employed. On May 31 and June 1 the committee received scientific briefings and held discussions on whether to share the secret with the Soviets, how long it would take other nations to develop their own atomic bomb, how international control might be achieved, whether the U.S. monopoly might help Washington in its relations with Moscow, and whether the bomb would be a universal blessing or a Frankenstein's monster.

In the matter at hand, however, the committee concluded that the bomb should be used to end the war as soon as possible; that it should be dropped on a military-urban target so as to demonstrate its full force; and that a demonstration or warning should not be made beforehand, lest the bomb lose its shock value.

A specially equipped B-29, the Enola Gay, dropped an atomic bomb on the military port of Hiroshima on Aug. 6,

Introduction

1945. The heat and blast effaced everything in the vicinity, burned 4.4 square miles, and killed some 70,000 people (lingering injuries and radiation sickness brought the death toll past 100,000 by the end of the year). Two days later the U.S.S.R. declared war on Japan and invaded Manchuria. On August 9 the second atomic bomb fell on Nagasaki, killing 39,000 people. On Sept. 2, 1945, General MacArthur received the Japanese surrender on the battleship *Missouri* in Tokyo Bay, and the greatest war in history came to a close.

When World War II ended many countries throughout the world had to rebuild their war-damaged cities and lands. Some of the nations who won the war suffered almost as much as those who lost it.

The western Soviet Union and Poland had undergone as much war damage as Germany. Britain, France, and the Netherlands were as battered as Italy. In China and the Philippine Islands the losses were as great as in Japan.

The losses in life, money, resources, and production were so great they can only be estimated. In addition throughout Europe and eastern Asia death by famine and disease threatened the lives of people who had survived the war.

The political consequences of World War II, like those of World War I, altered the course of 20th-century world history. The war resulted in the Soviet Union's dominance of the countries of eastern Europe and eventually enabled a Communist movement to take power in China. It also marked a decisive shift of power away from the countries of western Europe and toward the United States and the Soviet Union. The tense rivalry between those two countries and their allies, known as the Cold War, would influence events throughout the world for the next 50 years.

CHAPTER 1

THE ORIGINS OF WORLD WAR II, 1929–39

The 1930s were a decade of unmitigated crisis culminating in the outbreak of a second total war. The treaties and settlements of the first postwar era collapsed with shocking suddenness under the impact of the Great Depression and the aggressive revisionism of Japan, Italy, and Germany. By 1933 hardly one stone stood on another of the economic structures raised in the 1920s. By 1935 Adolf Hitler's Nazi regime had torn up the Treaty of Versailles and by 1936 the Locarno treaties—which guaranteed peace in western Europe—as well. Armed conflict began in Manchuria in 1931 and spread to Abyssinia in 1935, Spain in 1936, China in 1937, Europe in 1939, and the United States and U.S.S.R. in 1941.

The context in which this collapse occurred was an "economic blizzard" that enervated the democracies and energized the dictatorial regimes. Western intellectuals and many common citizens lost faith in democracy and free-market economics, while widespread pacifism, isolationism, and the earnest desire to avoid the mistakes of 1914 left Western leaders without the will or the means to defend the 1919 order. This combination of demoralized publics, stricken institutions, and uninspired leadership led historian Pierre Renouvin to describe the 1930s simply as "la décadence."

The militant authoritarian states on the other hand—Italy, Japan, and (after 1933) Germany—seemed only to wax stronger and more dynamic. The Depression did not cause the rise of the Third Reich or the bellicose ideologies of the German, Italian, and Japanese governments (all of which pre-dated the 1930s), but it did create the conditions for the Nazi seizure of power and provide the opportunity and excuse for Fascist empire-building. Hitler and Italian prime minister Benito Mussolini aspired to total control of their domestic societies, in part for the purpose of girding their nations for wars of conquest, which they saw, in turn, as necessary for revolutionary transformation at home. This ideological meshing of foreign and domestic policy rendered the Fascist leaders wholly enigmatic to the democratic statesmen of Britain and France, whose attempts to accommodate rather than resist the Fascist states only made inevitable the war they longed to avoid.

Political Consequences of the Depression

The debate over the origins of the Great Depression and the reasons for its severity and length is highly political, given the implications for the validity of theories of free market, regulated, and planned economies and of monetary and fiscal policy. It is usually dated from the New York stock-market crash of October 1929, which choked the domestic and international flow of credit and severely damaged global trade and production. Wall Street prices fell from an index of 216 to 145 in a month, stabilized in early 1930, then continued downward to a bottom of 34 in 1932. Industrial production fell nearly 20 percent in 1930. Unlike previous swings in the business cycle, this financial panic did not eventuate in the expected period of readjustment but rather defied all governmental and private efforts to restore prosperity for years until it seemed to a great many that the system itself was breaking down.

Mutual recriminations flew across the Atlantic. Americans blamed the Europeans for the reparations tangle, for pegging their currencies too high upon the return to gold, and for misuse of the American loans of the 1920s. Europeans blamed the United States for its insistence on repayment of war debts, high tariffs, and the unfettered speculation leading to the stock-market crash. Certainly all of these factors contributed. More tangibly, however, a sudden contraction of international credit in June 1928 made an international emergency likely. Since the Dawes Plan of 1924, which was based on a report by American financier Charles G. Dawes on question of German reparations for presumed liability for World War I, Europe had depended for capital and liquidity on the availability of American loans, but increasingly American investors were flocking to the stock market with their savings, and new capital issues for foreign account in the United States dropped 78 percent, from $530,000,000 to $119,000,000. Loans to Germany collapsed from $200,000,000 in the first half of 1928 to $77,000,000 in the second half and to $29,500,000 for the entire year of 1929. A world crisis was also brewing in basic commodities, a market in which prices had been depressed throughout the decade. Mechanization of agriculture stimulated overproduction, and Soviet dumping of wheat on the world market to earn foreign exchange for the First Five-Year Plan compounded the problem.

The Smoot–Hawley Tariff, the highest in U.S. history, became law on June 17, 1930. Conceived and passed by the House of Representatives in 1929, it may well have contributed to the loss of confidence on Wall Street and signaled American unwillingness to play the role of leader in the world economy. Other countries retaliated with similarly protective tariffs, with the result that the total volume of world trade spiraled downward from a monthly average of $2,900,000,000 in 1929 to less than $1,000,000,000 by 1933. The credit squeeze, bank

Unemployed workers wait in a long line at a soup kitchen in New York City during the Great Depression.

failures, deflation, and loss of exports forced production down and unemployment up in all industrial nations. In January 1930 the United States had 3,000,000 idle workers, and by 1932 there were more than 13,000,000. In Britain 22 percent of the adult male workforce lacked jobs, while in Germany unemployment peaked in 1932 at 6,000,000. All told, some 30,000,000 people were out of work in the industrial countries in 1932.

The Depression naturally magnified European bitterness over the continuing international obligations, but the weakest link in the financial chain was Austria, whose central bank, the Creditanstalt, was on the verge of bankruptcy. In

March 1931, German foreign minister Julius Curtius signed an agreement with Vienna for a German–Austrian customs union, but French objections to what they saw as a first step toward the dreaded Anschluss—the political union of Austria with Germany—provoked a run on the Creditanstalt and forced Berlin and Vienna to renounce the union on September 3.

The panic then spread to Germany, rendering the Reichsbank unable to meet its obligations under the Young Plan of 1929, the second renegotiation of Germany's World War I reparation payments. President Herbert Hoover responded on June 20, 1931, with a proposal for a one-year moratorium on all intergovernmental debts. Short of a general recovery or global agreement on the restoration of trade, however, the moratorium could only be a stopgap. Instead, every country fled toward policies of protection, self-sufficiency, and the creation of regional economic blocs in hopes of isolating itself from the world collapse. On Sept. 21, 1931, the Bank of England left the gold standard, and the pound sterling promptly lost 28 percent of its value, undermining the solvency of countries in eastern Europe and South America. In October a national coalition government formed to take emergency measures. The Ottawa Imperial Economic Conference of 1932 gave birth to the British Commonwealth of Nations and a system of imperial preferences, signaling the end of Britain's 86-year-old policy of free trade.

The Lausanne Conference of June–July 1932 took up the question of what should be done after the Hoover Moratorium. Even the French granted the impossibility of further German payments and agreed to make an end of reparations in return for a final German transfer of 3,000,000,000 marks (which was never made). The United States, however, still insisted that the war debts be honoured, whereupon the French parliament willfully defaulted, damaging Franco-American relations.

Failures of the League

Panicky retrenchment and disunity also rendered the Western powers incapable of responding to the first violation of the postwar territorial settlements. On Sept. 10, 1931, Viscount Cecil assured the League of Nations that "there has scarcely ever been a period in the world's history when war seemed less likely than it does at the present." Just eight days later officers of Japan's Kwantung Army staged an explosion on the South Manchurian Railway to serve as pretext for military adventure. Since 1928, China had seemed to be achieving an elusive unity under Chiang Kai-shek's Nationalists (KMT), now based in Nanking. While the KMT's consolidation of power seemed likely to keep Soviet and Japanese ambitions in check, resurgent Chinese nationalism also posed a threat to British and other foreign interests on the mainland. By the end of 1928, Chiang was demanding the return of leased territories and an end to extraterritoriality in the foreign concessions. On the other hand, the KMT was still split by factions, banditry continued widespread, the Communists were increasingly well organized in remote Kiangsi, and in the spring of 1931 a rival government sprang up in Canton. To these problems were added economic depression and disastrous floods that took hundreds of thousands of lives.

Japan, meanwhile, suffered rudely from the Depression because of her dependence on trade, her ill-timed return to the gold standard in 1930, and a Chinese boycott of Japanese goods. But social turmoil only increased the appeal of those who saw in foreign expansion a solution to Japan's economic problems. This interweaving of foreign and domestic policy, propelled by a rabid nationalism, a powerful military-industrial complex, hatred of the prevailing distribution of world power, and the raising of a racialist banner (in this case, antiwhite) to justify expansion, all bear comparison to European Fascism. When the parliamentary government in Tokyo divided as to how to confront this complex of crises, the Kwantung Army acted on its own. Manchuria, rich in raw materials, was a prospective sponge for Japanese emigration (250,000 Japanese already resided there) and the gateway to China proper. The Japanese public greeted the conquest with wild enthusiasm.

China appealed at once to the League of Nations, the organization for international cooperation established by the victorious Allied powers at the end of World War I. The League called for Japanese withdrawal in a resolution of October 24. But neither the British nor U.S. Asiatic fleets (the latter comprising no battleships and just one cruiser) afforded their governments (obsessed with domestic economic problems) the option of intervention. The tide of Japanese nationalism would have prevented Tokyo from bowing to Western pressure in any case. In December the League Council appointed an investigatory commission under Lord Lytton, while the United States contented itself with propounding the Stimson Doctrine, by which Washington merely refused to recognize changes born of aggression. Unperturbed, the Japanese prompted local collaborationists to proclaim, on Feb. 18, 1932, an independent state of Manchukuo, in effect a Japanese protectorate. The Lytton Commission reported in October, scolding the Chinese for provocations but condemning Japan for using excessive force. Lytton recommended evacuation of Manchuria but privately believed that Japan had "bitten off more than she can chew" and would ultimately withdraw of its own accord. In March 1933, Japan announced its withdrawal instead from the League of Nations, which had been tested and found impotent, at least in East Asia.

The League also failed to advance the cause of disarmament in the first years of the Depression. The London Naval Conference of 1930 proposed an extension of the 1922 Washington ratios for naval tonnage, but this time France and Italy refused to accept the inferior status assigned to them. In land armaments, the policies of the powers were by now fixed and predictable. Britain and the United States deplored "wasteful" military spending, especially by France, while reparations and war debts went unpaid. But even Herriot and Briand refused to disband the French army without additional security guarantees that the British were unwilling to tender. Fascist Italy, despite its financial distress, was unlikely to take disarmament seriously, while Germany, looking for foreign-policy triumphs to bolster the struggling Republic, demanded equality of treatment: Either France must disarm, or Germany must be allowed to expand its army. The League Council nonetheless summoned delegates from 60 nations to a grand Disarmament Conference at Geneva beginning in February 1932. When Germany failed to achieve satisfaction by the July adjournment it withdrew from the negotiations. France, Britain, and the United States devised various formulas to break the deadlock, including a No Force Declaration (Dec. 11, 1932), abjuring the use of force to resolve disputes, and a five-power (including Italy) promise to grant German equality "in a system providing security for all nations." On the strength of these the Disarmament Conference resumed in February 1933. By then, however, Adolf Hitler was chancellor of the German Reich.

A common impression of Herbert Hoover is that he was passive in the face of the Depression and isolationist in foreign policy. The truth was almost the reverse, and in the 1932 campaign his Democratic opponent, Franklin Roosevelt, was the more traditional in economic policy and isolationist in foreign policy. Indeed, Hoover bequeathed to his successor two bold initiatives meant to restore international cooperation in matters of trade, currency, and security: the London Economic Conference and the Geneva Disarmament Conference. The former convened in June 1933 in hopes of restoring the gold standard but was undermined by President Roosevelt's suspension of the gold convertibility of the dollar and his acerbic message rejecting the conference's labours on July 3. At home, Roosevelt proposed the series of government actions known as the New Deal in an effort to restore U.S. productivity, in isolation, if need be, from the rest of the world. The Disarmament Conference came to a similar end. In March, Ramsay MacDonald proposed the gradual reduction of the French army from half a million to 200,000 men and the doubling of Germany's Versailles army to the same figure, accompanied by international verification. But a secret German decree of April 4 created a National Defense Council to coordinate rearmament on a massive scale. Clearly the German demand for equality was a ploy to wreck the conference and serve as pretext for unilateral rearmament.

Negotiations were delayed by a sudden initiative from Mussolini in March calling for a pact among Germany, Italy, France, and Britain to grant Germany equality, revise the peace treaties, and establish a four-power directorate to resolve international disputes. Mussolini appears to have wanted to downgrade the League in favour of a Concert of Europe, enhancing Italian prestige and perhaps gaining colonial concessions in return for reassuring the Western powers. The French watered down the plan until the Four-Power Pact signed in Rome on June 7 was a mass of anodyne generalities. Any prospect that the new Nazi regime might be drawn to collective security disappeared on Oct. 14, 1933, when Hitler denounced the unfair treatment accorded Germany at Geneva and announced its withdrawal from the League of Nations.

The Rise of Hitler and Fall of Versailles

The origins of the Nazi Third Reich must be sought not only in the appeal of Hitler and his party but also in the weakness of the Weimar Republic. Under the republic, Germany boasted the most democratic constitution in the world, yet the fragmentation of German politics made government by majority a difficult proposition. Many Germans identified the republic with the despised Treaty of Versailles and, like the Japanese, concluded that the 1920s policy of peaceful cooperation with the West had failed. What was more, the republic seemed incapable of curing the Depression or dampening the appeal of the Communists. In the end, it self-destructed. The first Depression-era elections, in September 1930, reflected the electorate's flight from the moderate centrist parties: Communists won 77 seats in the Reichstag, while the Nazi delegation rose from 12 to 107. Chancellor Heinrich Brüning, unable to command a majority, governed by emergency decree of the aged president, Paul von Hindenburg.

FAILURE OF THE GERMAN REPUBLIC

The National Socialist German Workers' Party (Nazis) exploited the resentment and fear stemming from Versailles and the Depression. Its platform was a clever, if contradictory, mixture of socialism, corporatism, and virulent assertion in foreign policy. The Nazis outdid the Communists in forming paramilitary street gangs to intimidate opponents and create an image of irresistible strength, but unlike the Communists, who implied that war veterans had been dupes of capitalist imperialism, the Nazis honoured the Great War as a time when the German Volk had been united as never before. The army had been "stabbed in the back" by defeatists, they claimed, and those who signed the Armistice and Versailles had been criminals; worse, international capitalists, Socialists, and Jews continued to conspire against the German people. Under Nazism alone, they insisted, could Germans again unify under *ein Reich, ein Volk, ein Führer* and get on with the task of combating Germany's real enemies. This amalgam of fervent nationalism and rhetorical socialism, not to mention the charismatic spell of Hitler's oratory and the hypnotic pomp of Nazi rallies, was psychologically more appealing than flaccid liberalism or divisive class struggle. In any case, the Communists (on orders from Moscow) turned to help the Nazis paralyze democratic procedure in Germany in the expectation of seizing power themselves.

Brüning resigned in May 1932, and the July elections returned 230 Nazi delegates. After two short-lived rightist cabinets foundered, Hindenburg appointed Hitler chancellor on Jan. 30, 1933. The president, parliamentary conservatives, and the army all apparently expected that the inexperienced, lower-class demagogue would submit to their guidance. Instead, Hitler secured dictatorial powers from the Reichstag and proceeded to establish, by marginally legal means, a totalitarian state. Within two years the regime had outlawed all other political parties and co-opted or intimidated all institutions that competed with it for popular loyalty, including the German states, labour unions, press and radio, universities, bureaucracies, courts, and churches. Only the army and foreign office remained in the hands of traditional elites. But this fact, and Hitler's own caution at the start, allowed Western observers fatally to misperceive Nazi foreign policy as simply a continuation of Weimar revisionism.

Adolf Hitler recounted in *Mein Kampf*, the autobiographical harangue written in prison after his abortive putsch of 1923, that he saw himself as that rare individual, the "programmatic

Deputy party leader Rudolph Hess stands in the foreground as Adolf Hitler gives the Nazi salute from a car at a parade in Weimar in 1936.

thinker and the politician become one." Hitler distilled his Weltanschauung (literally, a "view of the world") from the social Darwinism, anti-Semitism, and racialist anthropology current in prewar Vienna. Where Marx had reduced all of history to struggles among social classes, in which revolution was the engine of progress and the dictatorship of the proletariat the culmination, Hitler reduced history to struggle among biologic races, in which war was the engine of progress and Aryan hegemony the culmination. The enemies of the Germans, indeed of history itself, were internationalists who warred against the purity and race-consciousness of peoples—they

MEIN KAMPF ("MY STRUGGLE")

Mein Kampf (German "My Struggle") is a political manifesto written by Adolf Hitler. It was his only complete book and became the bible of National Socialism (Nazism) in Germany's Third Reich. It was published in two volumes in 1925 and 1927, and an abridged edition appeared in 1930. By 1939 it had sold 5,200,000 copies and had been translated into 11 languages.

The first volume, entitled *Die Abrechnung* ("The Settlement [of Accounts]," or "Revenge"), was written in 1924 in the Bavarian fortress of Landsberg am Lech, where Hitler was imprisoned after the abortive Beer Hall Putsch of 1923. It treats the world of Hitler's youth, the First World War, and the "betrayal" of Germany's collapse in 1918; it also expresses Hitler's racist ideology, identifying the Aryan as the "genius" race and the Jew as the "parasite," and declares the need for Germans to seek living space (*Lebensraum*) in the East at the expense of the Slavs and the hated Marxists of Russia. It also calls for revenge against France.

According to Hitler, it was "the sacred mission of the German people...to assemble and preserve the most valuable racial elements...and raise them to the dominant position." "All who are not of a good race are chaff," wrote Hitler. It was necessary for Germans to "occupy themselves not merely with the breeding of dogs, horses, and cats but also with care for the purity of their own blood." Hitler ascribed international significance to the elimination of Jews, which "must necessarily be a bloody process," he wrote.

The second volume, entitled *Die Nationalsozialistische Bewegung* ("The National Socialist Movement"), written after Hitler's release from prison in December 1924, outlines the political program, including the terrorist methods, that National Socialism must pursue both in gaining power and in exercising it thereafter in the new Germany.

In style, *Mein Kampf* has been appropriately deemed turgid, repetitious, wandering, illogical, and, in the first edition at least, filled with grammatical errors—all reflecting a half-educated man. It was skillfully demagogic, however, appealing to many dissatisfied elements in Germany—the ultranationalistic, the anti-Semitic, the antidemocratic, the anti-Marxist, and the military.

Postwar German law banned the sale and public display of books espousing Nazi philosophy. Moreover, the copyright for *Mein Kampf* had been awarded to the German state of Bavaria, which refused to grant publishing rights. However, foreign publishers continued to print the work, an act that brought condemnation both in Germany and in the countries where the book was published, not least because of its popularity with neo-Nazi groups, especially those that arose in Germany in the 1990s. There also was great concern in some circles over the availability of the book from Internet-based booksellers. On January 1, 2016, the copyright for *Mein Kampf* expired, and the book entered public domain. Shortly thereafter Munich's Institute for Contemporary History published a heavily annotated edition.

were the capitalists, the Socialists, the pacifists, the liberals, all of whom Hitler identified with the Jews. This condemnation of Jews as a racial group made Nazism more dangerous than earlier forms of religious or economic anti-Semitism that had long been prevalent throughout Europe. For if the Jews, as Hitler thought, were like bacteria poisoning the bloodstream of the Aryan race, the only solution was their extermination. Nazism, in short, was the twisted product of a secular, scientific age of history.

Hitler's worldview dictated a unity of foreign and domestic policies based on total control and militarization at home, war and conquest abroad. In *Mein Kampf* he ridiculed the Weimar politicians and their "bourgeois" dreams of restoring the Germany of 1914. Rather, the German Volk could never achieve their destiny without *Lebensraum* ("living space") to support a vastly increased German population and form the basis for world power. *Lebensraum*, wrote Hitler in *Mein Kampf*, was to be found in Ukraine and intermediate lands of eastern Europe. This "heartland" of the Eurasian continent (so named by the geopoliticians Sir Halford Mackinder and Karl Haushofer) was especially suited for conquest since it was occupied, in Hitler's mind, by Slavic *Untermenschen* (subhumans) and ruled from the centre of the Jewish-Bolshevik conspiracy in Moscow. By 1933 Hitler had apparently imagined a step-by-step plan for the realization of his goals. The first step was to rearm, thereby restoring complete freedom of maneuver to Germany. The next step was to achieve *Lebensraum* in alliance with Italy and with the sufferance of Britain. This greater Reich could then serve, in the distant third step, as a base for world dominion and the purification of a "master race." In practice, Hitler proved willing to adapt to circumstances, seize opportunities, or follow the wanderings of intuition. Sooner or later politics must give way to war, but because Hitler did not articulate his ultimate fantasies to the German voters or establishment, his actions and rhetoric seemed to imply only restoration, if not of the Germany of 1914, then the Germany of 1918, after Brest-Litovsk. In fact, his program was potentially without limits.

EUROPEAN RESPONSES TO NAZISM

European reaction to the rise of Nazism was cautious, but not at first overtly hostile. The Four-Power Pact and a concordat with the Vatican (July 20, 1933), negotiated by the Catholic Franz von Papen, conferred a certain legitimacy on the Nazi regime. (Hitler sought to end Vatican support for the Catholic Centre Party while he proceeded to subordinate the churches and to corrupt Christianity into a state-centred form of neo-paganism. Pope Pius XI, like every other European statesmen after him, thought that he could appease and moderate the Nazis.) On Jan. 26, 1934, Hitler shocked all parties by signing a nonaggression pact with Poland. This bit of duplicity neutralized France's primary ally in the east while helping to secure Germany over the dangerous years of rearmament. The new Polish foreign minister, Józef Beck, was in turn responding to the dilemma of Poland's central position between Germany and the U.S.S.R. He hoped to preserve a balance in his relations with the two giant neighbours (Poland signed a three-year pact with Moscow in July 1932) but feared the Soviets (from whom Poland had grabbed so much territory in 1921) more than the still-weak Germans. The pact with Germany was meant to run for 10 years.

France was the nation most concerned by the Nazi threat and most able to take vigorous action. But fear of another war, the defeatist mood dating from the failure of the Ruhr occupation, the passivity engendered by the Maginot Line (the elaborate defensive barrier in northeastern France, due for completion in just five years), and domestic strife exacerbated by the Depression and the Stavisky scandal of 1933 all served to hamstring French foreign policy. As in the Weimar Republic, Communists and monarchists or Fascist groups like the Croix de Feu and Action Française battled in the streets. In February 1934 a crowd of war veterans and rightists stormed the parliament, and the Édouard Daladier Cabinet was forced to resign to head off a coup d'état. The new foreign minister, Louis Barthou, had been a friend of former French prime minister Raymond Poincaré and made a final effort to shore up France's security system in Europe: "All these League of Nations fancies—I'd soon put an end to them if I were in power. . . . It's alliances that count." But alliances with whom? The French Left was adamantly opposed to cooperation with Fascist Italy, the Right despised cooperation with the Communist Soviet Union. Britain as always eschewed commitments, while Poland had come to terms with Germany. Nevertheless, the moment seemed opportune; both Italy and the U.S.S.R. now made clear their opposition to Hitler and desire to embrace collective security.

To be sure, Mussolini was gratified by the triumph of the man he liked to consider his younger protégé, Hitler, but he also understood that Italy fared best while playing off France and Germany, and he feared German expansion into the Danubian basin. In September 1933 he made Italian support for Austrian Chancellor Engelbert Dollfuss conditional on the latter's establishment of an Italian-style Fascist regime. In June 1934 Mussolini and Hitler met for the first time, and in their confused conversation (there was no interpreter present) Mussolini understood the Führer to say that he had no desire for Anschluss. Yet, a month later, Austrian Nazis arranged a putsch in which Dollfuss was murdered. Mussolini responded with a threat of force (quite likely a bluff) on the Brenner Pass and thereby saved Austrian independence. Kurt von Schuschnigg, a pro-Italian Fascist, took over in Vienna. In Paris and London it seemed that Mussolini was one leader with the will and might to stand up to Hitler.

Joseph Stalin, secretary-general of the Communist Party of the Soviet Union, meanwhile, had repented of the equanimity with which he had witnessed the Nazi seizure of power. Before 1933, Germany and the U.S.S.R. had collaborated, and Soviet trade had been a rare boon to the German economy in the last

Adolf Hitler (right) stands with Benito Mussolini, who would be his ally during the war.

years of the Weimar Republic. Still, the behaviour of German Communists contributed to the collapse of parliamentarism, and now Hitler had shown that he, too, knew how to crush dissent and master a nation. The Communist line shifted in 1934–35 from condemnation of social democracy, collective security, and Western militarism to collaboration with other anti-Fascist forces in "Popular Fronts," alliance systems, and rearmament. The United States and the U.S.S.R. established diplomatic relations for the first time in November 1933, and in September 1934 the Soviets joined the League of Nations, where Maksim Litvinov became a loud proponent of collective security against Fascist revisionism.

Thus, Barthou's plan for reviving the wartime alliance and arranging an "Eastern Locarno" began to seem plausible—even after Oct. 9, 1934, when Barthou and King Alexander of Yugoslavia were shot dead in Marseille by an agent of Croatian terrorists. The new French foreign minister, the rightist Pierre Laval, was especially friendly to Rome. The Laval–Mussolini agreements of Jan. 7, 1935, declared France's disinterest in the fate of Abyssinia in implicit exchange for Italian support of Austria. Mussolini took this to mean that he had French support for his plan to conquer that independent African country. Just six days later the strength of German nationalism was resoundingly displayed in the Saar plebiscite. The small, coal-rich Saarland, detached from Germany for 15 years under the Treaty of Versailles, was populated by miners of Catholic or social democratic loyalty. They knew what fate awaited their churches and labour unions in the Third Reich, and yet 90 percent voted for union with Germany. Then, on March 16, Hitler used the extension of French military service to two years and the Franco-Soviet negotiations as pretexts for tearing up the disarmament clauses of Versailles, restoring the military draft, and beginning an open buildup of Germany's land, air, and sea forces.

In the wake of this series of shocks Britain, France, and Italy joined on April 11, 1935, at a conference at Stresa to reaffirm their opposition to German expansion. Laval and Litvinov also initialed a five-year Franco-Soviet alliance on May 2, each pledging assistance in case of unprovoked aggression. Two weeks later a Czech-Soviet pact complemented it. Laval's system, however, was flawed; mutual suspicion between Paris and Moscow, the failure to add a military convention, and the lack of Polish adherence meant that genuine Franco-Soviet military action was unlikely. The U.S.S.R. was in a state of trauma brought on by the Five-Year Plans, the slaughter and starvation of millions of farmers, especially in Ukraine, in the name of collectivization, and the beginnings of Stalin's mass purges of the government, army, and Communist Party. It was clear that Russian industrialization was bound to overthrow the balance of power in Eurasia, hence Stalin was fearful of the possibility of a preemptive attack before his own militarization was complete. But he was even more obsessed with the prospect of wholesale rebellion against his regime in case of invasion. Stalin's primary goal, therefore, was to keep the capitalist powers divided and the U.S.S.R. at peace. Urging the liberal Western states to combine against the Fascists was one method; exploring bilateral relations with Germany, as in the 1936 conversations between Hjalmar Schacht and Soviet trade representative David Kandelaki, was another.

Italy and Britain looked askance at the Franco-Soviet combination, while Hitler in any case sugar-coated the pill of German rearmament by making a pacific speech on May 21, 1935, in which he offered bilateral pacts to all Germany's neighbours (except Lithuania) and assured the British that he, unlike the Kaiser, did not intend to challenge them on the seas. The Anglo-German Naval Agreement of June 18, which countenanced a new German navy though limiting it to not larger than 35 percent the size of the British, angered the French and drove a wedge between them and the British.

ITALIAN AGGRESSION

The Stresa Front collapsed as soon as Paris and London learned the price Mussolini meant to exact for it. By 1935 Mussolini had ruled for 13 years but had made little progress toward his "new Roman Empire" that was to free Italy from the "prison of the Mediterranean." What was more, Il Duce, as Mussolini was called, concluded that only the crucible of war could fully undermine the monarchy and the church and consummate the Fascist revolution at home. Having failed to pry the French out of their North African possessions, Mussolini fixed on the independent African empire of Abyssinia (Ethiopia). Italy had failed in 1896 to conquer Abyssinia, thus to do so now would erase a national humiliation. This spacious land astride Italy's existing coastal colonies on the Horn of Africa boasted fertile uplands suitable for Italy's excess rural population, and Mussolini promised abundant raw materials as well. The conquest of Abyssinia would also appear to open the path to the Sudan and Suez. Finally, this landlocked, semifeudal kingdom seemed an easy target. In fact, Emperor Haile Selassie had begun a modernization program of sorts, but this only suggested that the sooner Italy struck, the better.

The Italian army was scarcely prepared for such an undertaking, and Mussolini made matters worse by ordering ill-trained blackshirt brigades to Africa and entrusting the campaign to a Fascist loyalist, Emilio De Bono, rather than to a senior army officer. The military buildup at Mitsiwa left little doubt as to Italian intentions, and Britain tried in June to forestall the invasion by arranging the cession of some Abyssinian territories. But Mussolini knew that the British

Mediterranean fleet was as unready as his own and expected no interference.

De Bono's absurdly large army invaded Ethiopia from Eritrea on Oct. 3, 1935. Adwa, the site of the 1896 debacle, fell in three days, after which the advance bogged down and Mussolini replaced De Bono with Marshal Pietro Badoglio. The League Council promptly declared Italy the aggressor (October 7), whereupon France and Britain were caught on the horns of a dilemma. To wink at Italy's conquest would be to condone aggression and admit the bankruptcy of the League; to resist would be to smash the Stresa Front and lose Italian help against the greater threat, Germany. The League finally settled on economic sanctions but shied away from an embargo on oil, which would have grounded the Italian army and air force, or closure of the Suez Canal, which would have cut the Italian supply line. The remaining sanctions only vexed Italy without helping Abyssinia. Germany, no longer a League member, ignored the sanctions and so healed its rift with Rome.

In December, Laval and Sir Samuel Hoare, the British foreign secretary, contrived a secret plan to offer Mussolini most of Abyssinia in return for a truce. This Hoare–Laval Plan was a realistic effort to end the crisis and repair the Stresa Front, but it also made a mockery of the League. When it was leaked to the press, public indignation forced Hoare's resignation. The Italians finally took the fortress of Mekele on November 8, but their slow advance led Mussolini to order a major offensive in December. He instructed Badoglio to use whatever means necessary, including terror bombing and poison gas, to end the war.

THE FIRST GERMAN MOVE

Hitler observed the Abyssinian war with controlled glee, for dissolution of the Stresa Front—composed of the guarantors of Locarno—gave him the chance to reoccupy the Rhineland with minimal risk. A caretaker government under Albert Sarraut was in charge of France during a divisive electoral campaign dominated by the leftist Popular Front, and Britain was convulsed by a constitutional crisis stemming from King Edward VIII's insistence on marrying an American divorcée. On March 7, 1936, Hitler ordered a token force of 22,000 soldiers back across the bridges of the Rhine. Characteristically, he chose a weekend for his sudden move and then softened the blow with offers of nonaggression pacts and a new demilitarized zone on both sides of the frontier. Even so, Hitler assured his generals that he would retreat if the French intervened.

German reoccupation and fortification of the Rhineland was the most significant turning point of the interwar years. After March 1936 the British and French could no longer take forceful action against Hitler except by provoking the total war they feared. Why did the French, especially, not act to prevent this calamity to their defensive posture? They were not taken by surprise—Hitler's preparations had been noted—and Sarraut himself told French radio listeners that "Strasbourg would not be left under German guns." Moreover, the French army still outnumbered the German and could expect support from Czechoslovakia and possibly Poland. On the other hand, the French army commander, General Maurice Gamelin, vastly overestimated German strength and insisted that a move into the Rhineland be preceded by general mobilization. The French Cabinet also concluded that it should do nothing without the full agreement of the British. But London was not the place to look for backbone. Prime Minister Stanley Baldwin shrugged, "They might succeed in smashing Germany with the aid of Russia, but it would probably only result in Germany going Bolshevik," while the editor of *The Times* asked, "It's none

Mounted German troops ride down a street in Heidelberg after Germany retook the Rhineland.

of our business, is it? It's their own back-garden they're walking into." By failing to respond to the violation, however, Britain, France, and Italy had broken the Locarno treaties just as gravely as had Germany.

The strategic situation in Europe now shifted in favour of the Fascist powers. In June, Mussolini appointed as foreign minister his son-in-law Galeazzo Ciano, who concluded an agreement with Germany on July 11 in which Italy acquiesced in Austria's behaving henceforth as "a German state." The Rome–Berlin Axis followed on November 1, and the German–Japanese Anti-Comintern Pact, another vague agreement ostensibly directed at Moscow, on November 25. Finally, Belgium unilaterally renounced its alliance with France on October 14 and returned to its traditional neutrality in hopes of escaping the coming storm. As a direct result of the Abyssinian imbroglio, the militant revisionists had come together and the status quo powers had splintered.

Meanwhile, on May 5, 1936, Italian troops had entered Addis Ababa and completed the conquest of Abyssinia, although the country was never entirely pacified, despite costly and brutal repression. The Abyssinian war had been a disaster for the democracies, smashing both the Stresa Front and the credibility of the League. As the historian A.J.P. Taylor wrote, "One day [the League] was a powerful body imposing sanctions, seemingly more effective than ever before; the next day it was an empty sham, everyone scuttling from it as quickly as possible." In December 1937, Italy, too, quit the League of Nations.

British Appeasement and American Isolationism

It is time to explore the roots of democratic lethargy in the face of Fascist expansionism in the 1930s. British policy, in particular, which Prime Minister Neville Chamberlain would proudly term "appeasement," conjures up images of naive, even craven surrender to Nazi demands. In the minds of British statesmen, however, appeasement was a moral and realistic expression of all that was liberal and Christian in British culture.

THE RATIONALE OF APPEASEMENT

First, 1914 cast a dark shadow on the opinion leaders of the 1930s, who determined this time to shun arms races and balance-of-power and commercial competition and so to spare the world another horrible war. Second, the overextended British Empire lacked the resources to confront threats from Japan in Asia, Italy in the Mediterranean, and Germany in Europe all at once. Wisdom dictated that Britain come to terms with the greatest and closest to home of its potential adversaries, Germany. Third, the British public was understandably provincial about central Europe and had no desire (in the popular French phrase) "to die for Danzig." This sentiment was even more pronounced in the British dominions. Fourth, many Tory and Labour leaders, while put off by Hitler's ideology and brutality, shared his antipathy to Versailles and urged "fair play" in cases where German nationals were separated from the fatherland. Thus, national self-determination, as advocated by former U.S. president Woodrow Wilson, perversely made the Nazis appear to be on the side of principle. Fifth, the appeasers also presumed that the Nazis would become less rambunctious once their grievances were removed. Sixth, some demoralized Englishmen believed the propagandistic claim that Fascism was the only bulwark against the spread of Bolshevism. Seventh, domestic opinion in Britain favoured a passive reliance on the League of Nations somehow to prevent another catastrophe—Baldwin's policy of sanctions without war in Abyssinia, as the chief case in point, earned his party a huge electoral victory in November 1935. Nor had pacifism flagged since 1933, when the Oxford Union "Resolved that this house refuses to fight for King and Country."

Voices of dissent existed. Some Left-Labourites warned that Fascism must be stopped sooner or later, while a few Tory backbenchers led by Winston Churchill demanded rearmament. In the mid-1930s a source in the Air Ministry leaked data to Churchill suggesting that Germany's air force was rapidly overtaking Britain's. Fear of the Luftwaffe only provided another excuse for appeasement, however, for aviation had developed to the point that theorists like the Italian Giulio Douhet could argue that air bombardment would win the next war in 48 hours by leveling enemy cities. In an air age, the English Channel no longer sheltered Britain from destruction.

Many of these same considerations afflicted French policy: fear of another total war and of destruction from the air, apathy toward eastern Europe, and ideological confusion. The election of May 3, 1936, brought victory for the Popular Front, which formed a cabinet under the Socialist Léon Blum, but his economic policies threw France into a turmoil of strikes, capital flight, and recrimination. "Better Hitler than Blum," said some on the right.

THE CIVIL WAR IN SPAIN

The Spanish Civil War highlighted the contrast between democratic bankruptcy and totalitarian dynamism. In 1931 the Spanish monarchy gave way to a republic whose unstable government moved steadily to the left, outraging the army and church. After repeated provocations on both sides, army and air force officers proclaimed a Nationalist revolt on July 17, 1936, that survived its critical early weeks with logistical help from Portugal's archconservative premier, António Salazar. The Nationalists, rallying behind General Francisco Franco, quickly seized most of Old Castile in the north and a beachhead in the south extending from Córdoba to Cádiz opposite Spanish Morocco, where the insurrection had begun. But the Republicans, or loyalists, a Popular Front composed of liberals, Socialists, Trotskyites, Stalinists, and anarchists, took up arms to defend the Republic elsewhere and sought outside aid against what they styled as the latest Fascist threat. Spain became a battleground for the ideologies wrestling for mastery of Europe.

The civil war posed a dilemma for France and Britain, pitting the principle of defending democracy against the principle of noninterference in the domestic affairs of other states. The ineffectual Blum at first fraternally promised aid to the Popular Front in Madrid, but he reneged within a month for fear that such involvement might provoke a European war or a civil war in France. The British government counseled nonintervention and seemingly won Germany and Italy to that position, but Hitler, on well-rehearsed anti-Bolshevik grounds, hurriedly dispatched 20 transport planes that allowed Franco to move reinforcements from Morocco. Not to be outdone, Mussolini sent matériel, Fascist "volunteers," and, ultimately, regular army formations. The Italians performed miserably (especially at Guadalajara in March 1937), but German aid, including the feared Condor Legion, was effective. Hitler expected to be paid for his support, however, with economic concessions, and he also saw Spain as a testing ground for Germany's newest weapons and tactics. These included terror bombing such as that over Guernica in April 1937, which caused far fewer deaths than legend has it but which became an icon of anti-Fascism through the painting of Pablo Picasso. International aid to the Republicans ran from the heroic to the sinister. Thousands of leftists and idealistic volunteers from throughout Europe and America flocked to International Brigades to defend the Republic. Matériel support, however, came only from Stalin, who demanded gold payment in return and ordered Comintern agents and commissars to accompany the Soviet supplies. These Stalinists systematically murdered Trotskyites and other "enemies on the left," undermined the radical government of Barcelona, and exacerbated the intramural confusion in Republican ranks. The upshot of Soviet intervention was to discredit the Republic and thereby strengthen Western resolve to stay out.

The war dragged on through 1937 and 1938 and claimed some 500,000 lives before the Nationalists finally captured Barcelona in January 1939 and Madrid in March. During the final push to victory, France and Britain recognized Franco's government. By then, however, the fulcrum of diplomacy had long since shifted to central Europe. The Nationalist victory did not, in the end, redound to the detriment of France, for Franco politely sent the Germans and Italians home and observed neutrality in the coming war, whereas a pro-Communist Spain might have posed a genuine threat to France during the era of the Nazi–Soviet pact.

THE RETURN OF U.S. ISOLATIONISM

The extreme isolationism that gripped the United States in the 1930s reinforced British appeasement and French paralysis. To Americans absorbed with their own distress, Hitler and Mussolini appeared as slightly ridiculous rabble-rousers on movie-house newsreels and certainly no concern of theirs. Moreover, the revisionist theory that the United States had been sucked into war in 1917 through the machinations of arms merchants or Wall Street bankers gained credence from the Senate's Nye Committee inquiries of 1934–36. U.S. isolationism, however, had many roots: liberal abhorrence of arms and war, the evident failure of Wilsonianism, the Great Depression, and the revisionism of American historians, who were among the leaders in arguing that Germany was not solely responsible for 1914. Nor were isolationists restricted only to the Great Plains states or to one political party. Some members of Congress favoured punctilious defense of U.S. interests in the world but rejected involvement in the quarrels of others. Some were full-fledged pacifists even if it meant surrendering certain U.S. rights abroad. Left-wing isolationists warned that

> ## GOOD NEIGHBOR POLICY
>
> The Good Neighbor Policy was the popular name for the Latin American policy pursued by the administration of the U.S. president Franklin D. Roosevelt. Suggested by the president's commitment "to the policy of the good neighbor" (first inaugural address, March 4, 1933), the approach marked a departure from traditional American interventionism. Through the diplomacy of Secretary of State Cordell Hull, the United States repudiated privileges abhorrent to Latin Americans. The United States renounced its right to unilaterally intervene in the internal affairs of other nations at the Montevideo Conference (December 1933); the Platt Amendment, which sanctioned U.S. intervention in Cuba, was abrogated (1934); and the U.S. Marines were withdrawn from Haiti (August 1934).
>
> The policy's success was measured in part by the rapidity with which most Latin American states rallied to the Allies during World War II. After the war, however, U.S. anticommunist policies in Europe and Asia led to renewed distrust in the Americas and the gradual lapse of the Good Neighbor Policy.

another great war would push the United States in the direction of Fascism. Conservative isolationists warned that another great war would usher in socialism.

These factions disputed among themselves over the wording of legislation, but their collective strength was enough to carry a number of bills designed to prevent a recurrence of the events of 1914–17. The Johnson Act of 1934 forbade American citizens to lend money to foreign countries that had not paid their past war debts. The Neutrality acts of 1935 and 1936 prohibited sale of war matériel to belligerents and forbade any exports to belligerents not paid for with cash and carried in their own ships. Thus, the United States was not to acquire a stake in the victory of any side or expose its merchant ships to submarines. The effect of these acts, however, was to preclude American aid to Abyssinia, Spain, and China and thus hurt the victims of aggression more than the aggressors.

The United States did take steps in the 1930s, however, to mobilize the Western Hemisphere for the purposes of fighting the Depression and resisting European, especially German, encroachments. Roosevelt gave this initiative a name in his first inaugural address: the Good Neighbor Policy. Building on steps taken by Hoover, Roosevelt pledged nonintervention in Latin domestic affairs at the Montevideo Pan-American Conference of 1933, signed a treaty with the new Cuban government (May 29, 1934) abrogating the Platt Amendment, mediated a truce in the Chaco War between Bolivia and Paraguay in 1934 (with a peace treaty following in July 1938), and negotiated commercial treaties with Latin-American states. As war approached overseas, Washington also promoted pan-American unity on the basis of nonintervention, condemnation of aggression, no forcible collection of debts, equality of states, respect for treaties, and continental solidarity. The Declaration of Lima (1938) provided for pan-American consultation in case of a threat to the "peace, security, or territorial integrity" of any state.

JAPAN'S AGGRESSION IN CHINA

The first major challenge to American isolationism, however, occurred in Asia. After pacifying Manchukuo, the Japanese turned their sights toward North China and Inner Mongolia. Over the intervening years, however, the KMT had made progress in unifying China. The Communists were still in the field, having survived their Long March (1934–35) to Yen-an in the north, but Chiang's government, with German and American help, had introduced modern roads and communications, stable paper currency, banking, and educational systems. How might Tokyo best round out its continental interests: by preemptive war or by cooperating with this resurgent China to expel Western influence from East Asia? The chief of the operations section of the Japanese general staff favoured collaboration and feared that an invasion of China proper would bring war with the Soviets or the Americans, whose economic potential he understood. Supreme headquarters, however, preferred to take military advantage of apparent friction between Chiang and a North China warlord. In September 1936, when Japan issued seven secret demands that would have made North China a virtual Japanese protectorate, Chiang rejected them. In December Chiang was even kidnapped by the commander of Nationalist forces from Manchuria, who tried to force him to suspend fighting the Communists and to declare war on Japan. This Sian Incident demonstrated the unlikelihood of Chinese collaboration with the Japanese program and strengthened the war party in Tokyo. As in 1931, hostilities began almost spontaneously and soon took on a life of their own.

An incident at the Marco Polo Bridge near Peking (then known as Pei-p'ing) on July 7, 1937, escalated into an undeclared Sino-Japanese war. Contrary to the Japanese analysis, both Chiang and Mao Zedong vowed to come to the aid of North China, while Japanese moderates failed to negotiate a truce or localize the conflict and lost all influence. By the end of July the Japanese had occupied Peking and Tientsin. The following month they blockaded the South China coast and captured Shanghai after brutal fighting and the slaughter of

Chinese guerrilla fighters equipped with dadao *swords gather during the Second Sino-Japanese War.*

countless civilians. Similar atrocities accompanied the fall of Nanking on December 13. The Japanese expected the Chinese to sue for peace, but Chiang moved his government to Han-k'ou and continued to resist the "dwarf bandits" with hit-and-run tactics that sucked the invaders in more deeply. The Japanese could occupy cities and fan out along roads and rails almost at will, but the countryside remained hostile.

World opinion condemned Japan in the harshest terms. The U.S.S.R. concluded a nonaggression pact with China (Aug. 21, 1937), and Soviet-Mongolian forces skirmished with Japanese on the border. Britain vilified Japan in the League, while Roosevelt invoked the Stimson Doctrine in his "quarantine speech" of October 5. But Roosevelt was prevented by the

Neutrality acts from aiding China even after the sinking of U.S. and British gunboats on the Yangtze.

On March 28, 1938, the Japanese established a Manchukuo-type puppet regime at Nanking, and spring and summer offensives brought them to the Wu-han cities (chiefly Hank'ou) on the Yangtze. Chiang stubbornly moved his government again, this time to Chungking, which the Japanese bombed mercilessly in May 1939, as they did Canton for weeks before its occupation in October. Such incidents, combined with the Nazi and Fascist air attacks in Spain and Abyssinia, were omens of the total war to come. The United States finally took a first step in opposition to Japanese aggression on July 29, 1939, announcing that it would terminate its 1911 commercial treaty with Japan in six months and thereby cut off vital raw materials to the Japanese war machine. It was all Roosevelt could do under existing law, but it set in train the events that would lead to Pearl Harbor.

CHAPTER 2
THE OUTBREAK OF WAR

Heightened assertiveness also characterized foreign policies in Europe in 1937. But while Hitler's involved explicit preparations for war, Britain's consisted of explicit attempts to satisfy him with concessions. The conjuncture of these policies doomed the independence of Austria, Czechoslovakia, and Poland and set Europe on a slippery slope to war.

The German-Austrian Union

By the end of 1936, Hitler and the Nazis were total masters of Germany with the exceptions of the army and the foreign office, and even the latter had to tolerate the activities of a special party apparatus under the Nazi "expert" on foreign policy, Joachim von Ribbentrop. Nazi prestige, bolstered by such theatrics as the Berlin Olympics, the German pavilion at the Paris Exhibition, and the enormous Nürnberg party rallies, was reaching its zenith. In September 1936, Hitler imitated Stalin again in his proclamation of a Four-Year Plan to prepare the German economy for war under the leadership of Hermann Göring. With the Rhineland secured, Hitler grew anxious to begin his "drive to the east," if possible with British acquiescence. To this end he appointed Ribbentrop ambassador to London in October 1936 with the plea, "Bring me back the British alliance." Intermittent talks lasted a year, their main topic being the return of the German colonies lost at Versailles. But agreement was impossible, since Hitler's real goal was a free hand on the Continent, while the British hoped, in return for specific concessions, to secure arms control and respect for the status quo.

Meanwhile, Stanley Baldwin, having seen the abdication crisis through to a finish, retired in May 1937 in favour of Neville Chamberlain. The latter now had the chance to pursue what he termed "active appeasement": find out what Hitler really wants, give it to him, and thereby save the peace and husband British resources for defense of the empire against Italy and Japan. By the time of Lord Halifax's celebrated visit to Berchtesgaden in November 1937, Hitler had already lost interest in the talks and begun to prepare for the absorption of Austria, a country in which, said Halifax, Britain took little interest. Hitler had also taken measures to complete the Nazification of foreign and defense policy.

On November 5, Hitler made a secret speech in the presence of the commanders of the three armed services, War Minister Werner von Blomberg, Foreign Minister Konstantin von Neurath, and Göring. The Führer made clear his belief that Germany must begin to expand in the immediate future, with Austria and Czechoslovakia as the first targets, and that the German economy must be ready for full-scale war by 1943–45. On November 19, Hitler replaced Schacht as minister of economics. Two months later he fired generals Blomberg and Werner von Fritsch in favour of the loyal Walther von Brauchitsch and Wilhelm Keitel and replaced Neurath with Ribbentrop. Historians have debated whether the November 5 speech was a blueprint for aggression, a plea for continued rearmament, or preparation for the purges that followed. But there is no denying that the overheated Nazi economy had reached a critical turn with labour and resources fully employed and capital running short. Hitler would soon have to introduce austerity measures, slow down the arms program, or make good the shortages of labour and capital through plunder. Since these material needs pushed in the same direction as Hitler's dynamic quest for *Lebensraum*, 1937 merely marked the transition into concrete time-tables of what Hitler had always desired. Nazification of the economy, the military, and the foreign service only removed the last vestige of potential opposition to a risky program of ruthless conquest.

German intrigues in Austria had continued since 1936 through the agency of Arthur Seyss-Inquart's Nazi movement. When Papen, now ambassador to Vienna, reported on Feb. 5, 1938, that the Schuschnigg regime showed signs of weakness, Hitler invited the Austrian dictator to a meeting on the 12th. In the course of an intimidating tirade Hitler demanded that Nazis be included in the Vienna government. Schuschnigg, however, insisted that Austria remain "free and German, independent and social, Christian and united," and scheduled a plebiscite for March 13 through which Austrians might express their will. Hitler hurriedly issued directives to the military, and when Schuschnigg was induced to resign, Seyss-Inquart simply appointed himself chancellor and invited German troops to intervene. A last-minute Italian demarche inviting Britain to make colonial concessions in return for Italian support of Austria met only "indignant resignation" and Anthony Eden's irrelevant complaints about Italy's troops in Spain. A French plea for Italian firmness, in turn, provoked Ciano to ask: "Do they expect to rebuild Stresa in an hour with Hannibal at the gates?" Still, Hitler waited nervously on the evening of March 11 until he was informed that Mussolini would take no action in support of Austria. Hitler replied with effusive thanks and promises of eternal amity. In the nighttime invasion, 70 percent of the vehicles sent into Austria by the unprepared

Wehrmacht broke down on the road to Vienna, but they met no resistance. Austrians cheered deliriously on the 13th, when Hitler declared Austria a province of the Reich.

The Taking of Czechoslovakia

The Anschluss outflanked the next state on Hitler's list, Czechoslovakia. Once again Hitler could make use of national self-determination to confuse the issue, as 3,500,000 German-speakers organized by another Nazi henchman, Konrad Henlein, inhabited the Czech borderlands in the Sudeten Mountains. Already on February 20, before the Anschluss, Hitler had denounced the Czechs for alleged persecution of this German minority, and on April 21 he ordered Keitel to prepare for the invasion of Czechoslovakia by October even if the French should intervene. Chamberlain was intent on appeasing Hitler, but this meant "educating" him to seek redress of grievances through negotiation, not force. He issued a stern warning to Germany during the spring war scare while pressuring Czech president Edvard Beneš to compromise with Henlein. Germany, however, had instructed Henlein to display obstinacy so as to prevent agreement. In August a worried British Cabinet dispatched the elderly Lord Walter Runciman to mediate, but Henlein rejected the program of concessions he finally arranged with Beneš. As the prospect of war increased, the British appeasers grew more frantic. In the spring the editor of the leftist New Statesman thought "armed resistance to the dictators was now useless. If there was a war we should lose it." General Edmund Ironside, ruing the prime minister's reluctance to rearm, sneered that "Chamberlain is of course right. . . . We cannot expose ourselves now to a German attack. We simply commit suicide if we do." And a shocking *Times* editorial called for the partition of Czechoslovakia, a view shared

Adolf Hitler (centre back) *talks to British Prime Minister Neville Chamberlain during the 1938 Munich Conference.*

by Hitler at the Nürnberg party rally, where he condemned "Czechia" as an "artificial state." Chamberlain then journeyed to Berchtesgaden and proposed to give the Germans all they demanded. Hitler, nonplussed, spoke of the cession of all Sudeten areas at least 80 percent German and agreed not to invade while Chamberlain won over Paris and Prague.

The French Cabinet of Édouard Daladier and Georges-Étienne Bonnet agreed, after the latter's frantic pleas to Roosevelt failed to shake American isolation. The Czechs, however, resisted handing over their border fortifications to Hitler until September 21, when the British and French

MUNICH AGREEMENT

On Sept. 30, 1938, Germany, Great Britain, France, and Italy reached an agreement that permitted German annexation of the Sudetenland in western Czechoslovakia. After his success in absorbing Austria into Germany proper in March 1938, Adolf Hitler looked covetously at Czechoslovakia, where about three million people in the Sudeten area were of German origin. It became known in May 1938 that Hitler and his generals were drawing up a plan for the occupation of Czechoslovakia. The Czechoslovaks were relying on military assistance from France, with which they had an alliance. The Soviet Union also had a treaty with Czechoslovakia, and it indicated willingness to cooperate with France and Great Britain if they decided to come to Czechoslovakia's defense, but the Soviet Union and its potential services were ignored throughout the crisis.

As Hitler continued to make inflammatory speeches demanding that Germans in Czechoslovakia be reunited with their homeland, war seemed imminent. Neither France nor Britain felt prepared to defend Czechoslovakia, however, and both were anxious to avoid a military confrontation with Germany at almost any cost. In mid-September, Neville Chamberlain, the British prime minister, offered to go to Hitler's retreat at Berchtesgaden to discuss the situation personally with the Führer. Hitler agreed to take no military action without further discussion, and Chamberlain agreed to try to persuade his cabinet and the French to accept the results of a plebiscite in the Sudetenland. The French premier, Édouard Daladier, and his foreign minister, Georges Bonnet, then went to London, where a joint proposal was prepared stipulating that all areas with a population that was more than 50 percent Sudeten German be returned to Germany. The Czechoslovaks were not consulted. The Czechoslovak government initially rejected the proposal but was forced to accept it reluctantly on September 21.

On September 22 Chamberlain again flew to Germany and met Hitler at Godesberg, where he was dismayed to learn that Hitler had stiffened his demands: he now wanted the Sudetenland occupied by the German army and the Czechoslovaks evacuated from the area by September 28. Chamberlain agreed to submit the new proposal to the Czechoslovaks, who rejected it, as did the British cabinet and the French. On the 24th the French ordered a partial mobilization; the Czechoslovaks had ordered a general mobilization one day earlier.

In a last-minute effort to avoid war, Chamberlain then proposed that a four-power conference be convened immediately to settle the dispute. Hitler agreed, and on September 29, Hitler, Chamberlain, Daladier, and Italian dictator Benito Mussolini met in Munich, where Mussolini introduced a written plan that was accepted by all as the Munich Agreement. (Many years later it was discovered that the so-called Italian plan had been prepared in the German Foreign Office.) It was almost identical to the Godesberg proposal: the German army was to complete the occupation of the Sudetenland by October 10, and an international commission would decide the future of other disputed areas. Czechoslovakia was informed by Britain and France that it could either resist Germany alone or submit to the prescribed annexations. The Czechoslovak government chose to submit.

Before leaving Munich, Chamberlain and Hitler signed a paper declaring their mutual desire to resolve differences through consultation to assure peace. Both Daladier and Chamberlain returned home to jubilant welcoming crowds relieved that the threat of war had passed, and Chamberlain told the British public that he had achieved "peace with honour. I believe it is peace for our time." His words were immediately challenged by his greatest critic, Winston Churchill, who declared, "You were given the choice between war and dishonour. You chose dishonour and you will have war." Indeed, Chamberlain's policies were discredited the following year, when Hitler annexed the remainder of

Czechoslovakia in March and then precipitated World War II by invading Poland in September. The Munich Agreement became a byword for the futility of appeasing expansionist totalitarian states, although it did buy time for the Allies to increase their military preparedness.

made it clear that they would not fight for the Sudetenland. Chamberlain flew to Bad Godesberg the next day only to be met with a new demand that the entire Sudetenland be ceded to Germany within a week. The Czechs, fully mobilized as of the 23rd, refused, and Chamberlain returned home in a funk: "How horrible, fantastic, incredible it is that we should be digging trenches and trying on gas masks here because of a quarrel in a far-away country between people of whom we know nothing." But his sorrowful address to Parliament was interrupted by the news that Mussolini had proposed a conference to settle the crisis peacefully. Hitler agreed, having seen how little enthusiasm there was in Germany for war and on the advice of Göring, Joseph Goebbels, and the generals. Chamberlain and Daladier, elated, flew to Munich on September 29.

The awkward and pitiful Munich Conference ended on the 30th in a compromise prearranged between the two dictators. The Czechs were to evacuate all regions indicated by an international commission (subsequently dominated by the Germans) by October 10 and were given no recourse—the agreement was final. Poland took the opportunity to grab the Teschen district disputed since 1919. Czechoslovakia was no longer a viable state, and Beneš resigned the presidency in despair. In return, Hitler promised no more territorial demands in Europe and consultations with Britain in case of any future threat to peace. Chamberlain was ecstatic.

Why did the Western powers abandon Czechoslovakia, which, by dint of its geography, democracy, military potential (more than 30 divisions and the Škoda arms works), and commitment to collective security, could rightly be called "the keystone of interwar Europe"? No completely persuasive answer is possible, but this height of appeasement can be accounted for by politics, principles, and pragmatism. There is no question that the Munich settlement was extremely popular. Chamberlain returned to London claiming "peace for our time" and was greeted by applauding throngs. So was Daladier. The relief was so evident even in Germany that Hitler swore he would allow no more meddling by "English governesses" to cheat him of his war. Of course, the euphoria was not universal: Aside from the Czechs, who wept in the streets, Churchill spoke for a growing minority when he observed that the British Empire had just suffered its worst military defeat and had not fired a shot.

Could Czechoslovakia have been defended? Or was Munich a necessary evil to buy time for Britain to rearm? Certainly British air defenses were unready, while France's scarcely existed, and the strength of the Luftwaffe, so recently discounted by the British Cabinet, was now exaggerated. The French and Czech armies still outnumbered the German, but French intelligence also magnified German strength, while the army had no plans for invading Germany in support of the Czechs. The Munich powers were criticized for ignoring the U.S.S.R., which had claimed readiness to honour its alliance with Prague. The U.S.S.R., however, would hardly confront Germany unless the Western powers were already engaged, and the ways open to them were few without transit rights across Poland. The West discounted Soviet military effectiveness in light of Stalin's 1937 purge of his entire officer corps down to battalion level. The Soviets were also distracted by division-scale fighting that broke out with Japanese forces on the Manchurian border in July–August 1938. At best, a few squadrons of Soviet planes might have been sent to Prague.

Of course, the moral cause of liberating the Sudeten Germans was ludicrous in view of the nature of the Nazi regime and was far outweighed by the moral lapse of deserting the doughty Czechs. (French ambassador André François-Poncet, upon reading the Munich accord, choked, "Thus does France treat her only allies who had remained faithful to her.") That betrayal, in turn, seemed more than outweighed by the moral cause of preventing another war. In the end, the war was delayed only a year, and whatever the military realities of 1938 versus 1939, the appeasement policy was an exercise in self-delusion. Chamberlain and his ilk did not begin their reasoning with an analysis of Hitlerism and then work forward to a policy. Rather, they began with a policy based on abstract analysis of the causes of war, then worked backward to an image of Hitler that suited the needs of that policy. As a result, they gave Hitler far more than they ever gave the democratic statesmen of Weimar and, in the end, the freedom to launch the very war they slaved to prevent.

Hitler had no intention of honouring Munich. In October the Nazis encouraged the Slovak and Ruthene minorities in Czechoslovakia to set up autonomous governments and then in November awarded Hungary the 4,600 square miles north of the Danube taken from it in 1919. On March 13, 1939, Gestapo officers carried the Slovak leader Monsignor Jozef Tiso off to Berlin and deposited him in the presence of the Führer, who demanded that the Slovaks declare their independence at once. Tiso returned to Bratislava to inform the Slovak Diet that the only alternative to becoming a Nazi protectorate

BLITZKRIEG

The concept of blitzkrieg was formed by Prussian military tactics of the early 19th century, which recognized that victory could come only through forceful and swift action because of Prussia's relatively limited economic resources. It had its origins with the *Schwerpunktprinzip* ("concentration principle") proposed by Carl von Clausewitz in his seminal work *On War* (1832). Having studied generals who predated Napoleon, Clausewitz found that commanders of various armies had dispersed their forces without focused reasoning, which resulted in those forces being used inefficiently. So as to eliminate that wasteful use of manpower, he advocated for a concentration of force against an enemy. All employment of force should have an effective concentration in a single moment, with a single action, Clausewitz argued. Clausewitz called that concentration the *Schwerpunkt* ("centre of gravity") where it was most dense, identifying it as the effective target for attack.

For historical generals, from Alexander the Great of ancient Macedonia to Frederick II of 18th-century Prussia, their armies functioned as the centre of gravity. If the army was destroyed, the commander would be considered a failure. In smaller countries or countries engaged in internal strife, according to Clausewitz's reasoning, the capital becomes the centre of gravity and should be identified as the *Schwerpunkt*. Beginning in the 20th century, technological advances such as radio, aircraft, and motorized vehicles allowed a commander to concentrate force at the *Schwerpunkt* so as to annihilate the opposition and achieve victory. During World War II each blitzkrieg campaign contained a *Schwerpunkt* that gave it meaning and substance, with doctrines of mobile warfare expounded by British military theorists J.F.C. Fuller and Sir Basil Liddell Hart providing the tactics necessary to translate the theory into action.

Once the strategic *Schwerpunkt* had been identified, the attack could commence, using the concept of *Kesselschlacht* ("cauldron battle"). A frontal attack would immobilize the enemy while forces on the flanks would execute a double envelopment, forming a pocket called a *Kessel* ("cauldron") around the enemy. Once surrounded, the opposing army, demoralized and with no chance of escape, would face the choice of annihilation or surrender.

Tested by the Germans during the Spanish Civil War in 1938 and against Poland in 1939, the blitzkrieg proved to be a formidable combination of land and air action. Germany's success with the tactic at the beginning of World War II hinged largely on the fact that it was the only country that had effectively linked its combined forces with radio communications. The use of mobility, shock, and locally concentrated firepower in a skillfully coordinated attack paralyzed an adversary's capacity to organize defenses, rather than attempting to physically overcome them, and then exploited that paralysis by penetrating to the adversary's rear areas and disrupting its whole system of communications and administration. The tactics, as employed by the Germans, consisted of a splitting thrust on a narrow front by combat groups using tanks, dive bombers, and motorized artillery to disrupt the main enemy battle position at the *Schwerpunkt*. Wide sweeps by armoured vehicles followed, establishing the *Kessel* that trapped and immobilized enemy forces. Those tactics were remarkably economical of both lives and matériel, primarily for the attackers but also, because of the speed and short duration of the campaign, among the victims.

Blitzkrieg tactics were used in the successful German invasions of Belgium, the Netherlands, and France in 1940, which saw audacious applications of air power and airborne infantry to overcome fixed fortifications that were believed by the defenders to be impregnable. The *Kesselschlacht* campaigns on the Eastern Front were staggering in scale, with *Kessels* that covered vast swathes of territory, enveloping hundreds of thousands of troops. Blitzkrieg tactics were also used by the German commander Erwin Rommel during the desert campaigns in North Africa.

After those initial German successes, the Allies adopted this form of warfare with great success, beginning with Stalingrad and subsequently used by commanders such as U.S. Gen. George Patton in the European operations of 1944. The Germans' last successful *Kessel* campaign was against the British paratroops at Arnhem, Netherlands, an encirclement that came to be known as the *Hexenkessel* ("witches' cauldron"). By the end of the war, Germany found itself defeated by the strategic (*Schwerpunkt*) and tactical (*Kesselschlacht*) concepts that had initially brought it such success. German armies were destroyed at Falaise in France, the Scheldt in the Netherlands, and the Bulge in Belgium and on the Eastern Front at Cherkasy (in modern Ukraine), Memel (now Klaipeda, Lithuania), and Halbe, Germany. The last great battle of World War II fought using blitzkrieg tactics was the Battle of Berlin (April 1945).

Later manifestations of blitzkrieg tactics were the combined air and ground attacks by Israeli forces on Syria and Egypt during the Six-Day War (June 1967) and the Israeli counterattacks and final counteroffensive of the Yom Kippur War (October 1973). The "left hook" flanking maneuver executed by U.S. Gen. Norman Schwarzkopf during the Persian Gulf War also utilized elements of blitzkrieg tactics, with a combined arms offensive that destroyed the Iraqi army in Kuwait in a period of just three days.

was invasion. They complied. All that remained to the new president in Prague, Emil Hácha, was the core region of Bohemia and Moravia. It was time, said Hácha with heavy sarcasm, "to consult our friends in Germany." There Hitler subjected the elderly, broken-spirited man to a tirade that brought tears, a fainting spell, and finally a signature on a "request" that Bohemia and Moravia be incorporated into the Reich. The next day, March 16, German units occupied Prague, and Czechoslovakia ceased to exist.

Technology, Strategy, and the Onset of Hostilities

The Anglo-French defection from east-central Europe doomed the balance of power of interwar Europe. That the Western powers were unwilling and unable to defend the balance was in part the product of inadequate military spending and planning over the course of the decade. Still, decisions were taken in the last 24 months of peace that would shape the course of World War II.

The central problem posed for all defense establishments was how to respond to the lessons of the 1914–18 stalemate. The British simply determined not to send an army to the Continent again, the French to turn their border into an impregnable fortress, and the Germans to perfect and synthesize the tactics and technologies of the last war into a dynamic new style of warfare: the Blitzkrieg ("lightning war"). Blitzkrieg was especially suited to a country whose geostrategic position made likely a war on two fronts and dictated an offensive posture: a Schlieffen solution made plausible by the internal-combustion engine.

REARMAMENT AND TACTICAL PLANNING

Whether or not Hitler actually planned for the type of war with which the general staff was experimenting is debatable. Perhaps he only made a virtue of necessity, for the Nazis had by no means created a full war economy in the 1930s. Since Blitzkrieg attacks by tank columns, motorized infantry, and aircraft permitted the

Workers assemble Bristol Blenheim bombers at a British aircraft factory.

defeat of enemies one by one with lightning speed, it required only "armament in width," not "armament in depth." This in turn allowed Hitler to mollify the German people with a "guns and butter" economy, with each new conquest providing the resources for the next. Blitzkrieg also allowed Hitler to conclude that he might successfully defy other Great Powers whose combined resources dwarfed those of Germany. After Munich, German rearmament accelerated. Hitler may have been right to launch his war as soon as possible, on the calculation that only by seizing the resources of the entire continent could the Reich prevail against the British Empire or the Soviet Union.

After Versailles the British government had established the Ten-Year Rule as a rationale for holding down military spending: Each year it was determined that virtually no chance existed of war breaking out over the next decade. In 1931 expenditures were cut to the bone in response to the worldwide financial crisis. The following year, in response to Japanese expansion, the Ten-Year Rule was abolished, but Britain did not make even a gesture toward rearmament until 1935. These were "the years the locust hath eaten," said Churchill. Understandably, British strategy fixed on the imperial threats from Japan and Italy and envisioned the dispatch of the Mediterranean fleet to Singapore. But Britain's defensive posture, budgetary limits, and underestimation of Japan's capabilities, especially in the air, made for a desultory buildup in battleships and cruisers rather than aircraft carriers. The British army in turn was tied up in garrisoning the empire; only two divisions were available for the Continent.

After March 1936 the Defence Requirements Committee recognized that home air defense must become Britain's top priority and commanded development of a high-speed, single-wing fighter plane. But two years passed before Sir Warren Fisher finally persuaded the Air Ministry to concentrate on fighter defense in its Scheme M, adopted in November 1938. At the time of Munich, therefore, the Royal Air Force possessed only two squadrons of Spitfires and Hurricanes, lacked oxygen masks sufficient to allow pursuit above 15,000 feet, and had barely begun deployment of that new wonder, radar. Only after Hitler's occupation of Prague was conscription reinstated (April 27, 1939) and a continental army of 32 divisions planned. Throughout the era of appeasement the British expected to resist Japan and come to terms with Germany. Instead, by dint of the mistaken choices in naval technology and the eleventh-hour attention to air defense, Britain would be humiliated by Japan and withstand Germany.

Of all the Great Powers, France most expected the next war to resemble the last and so came to rely on the doctrine of the continuous front, the Maginot Line, and the primacy of infantry and artillery. The Maginot Line was also a function of French demographic weakness vis-à-vis Germany, especially after military service was cut to one year in 1928. This siege mentality was the polar opposite of the French "cult of the attack" in 1914 and ensured that Colonel Charles de Gaulle's 1934 book depicting an all-mechanized army of the future would be ignored. As late as 1939 the French war council insisted that "no new method of warfare has been evolved since the termination of the Great War." Even though French military spending held steady through the Depression, France's army and air force were ill-designed and not deployed for offense or mobile defense, even if their aged and hidebound commanders had had the will to conduct them.

Soviet preparations and technical choices also presaged the defeats to come in the early years of the war. Communist doctrine decreed that matériel, not generalship, was decisive in war, and Stalin's Five-Year Plans concentrated on steel, technology, and weapons. Soviet planners also benefited from the work of some outstanding aviation designers, whose experimental planes broke world records and whose fighters performed well in the early days of the Spanish war. But Stalin's obsession with domestic security outweighed rational planning for national security. In 1937 Marshal Mikhail Tukhachevsky and his weapons research teams were liquidated or consigned to the gulag. Then Stalin ordered the 1936-vintage fighter planes into mass production at the very time the Germans were upgrading their Messerschmidts. The Soviets were sufficiently impressed by Douhet's theories to invest in heavy bombers that would be of marginal use against a Blitzkrieg and defenseless without fighter cover. Stalin's advisers also misunderstood the use of tanks, placing them in the front line rather than in mobile reserves. These mistakes almost spelled the death of Bolshevism in 1941.

Little need be said of Italian preparations. Italy's industrial base was so small, and its leaders so inept, that Mussolini had to order local Fascists to make a visual count of airplanes on fields around the country to contrive an estimate of his air strength. In August 1939, Ciano appealed to Mussolini not to join Hitler in unleashing war, given the deplorable state of Italian armed forces. This apprehensiveness was shared by the Italian generals and indeed by most military leaders of the 1930s. The Great War had revealed the vanity of planning, the vagaries of technical change, and the terrible cost of industrial war. In 1914 the generals had pushed for war while civilian leaders hung back; in the 1930s the roles were reversed. Only in Japan, which had won easy victories at little cost in 1914, did the military push for action.

POLAND AND SOVIET ANXIETY

Hitler's cynical occupation of Prague, giving the final lie to all his peaceful protestations after Munich, prompted much speculation about the identity of his next victim: Romania with its oil reserves, Ukraine, Poland, or even the "Germanic" Netherlands, which suffered an invasion scare in January? Chamberlain himself, offended in conscience and ego, attacked Hitler's mendacity and evident intention of dominating the continent by force. In a speech on March 17, 1939, he gave voice to the new conviction of "the man on the street" that Hitler could not be trusted and must be stopped. Three days later Hitler renewed his demand for a "corridor across the [Polish] Corridor" to East Prussia and restoration of Danzig to the Reich. On the 22nd he underscored his seriousness by forcing Lithuania to cede Memel (Klaipeda).

After 10 days of hand wringing, during which Colonel Beck repeated Poland's opposition to seeking help from Moscow, the British Cabinet declared a unilateral military guarantee of Polish security on March 31, solemnized in a bilateral treaty on April 6. It seemed an extraordinary turnaround in British policy: the apparent end of appeasement. In fact, it was a last desperate effort by Chamberlain to preserve appeasement and teach Hitler to settle foreign disputes by diplomacy, as at Munich, and not by force, as at Prague. But the pace of Fascist expansion was irreversible and even contagious. Mussolini had grown irritable over Hitler's succession of coups and his own junior-partner status, so Italy occupied Albania on April 7 and expelled its erstwhile client King Zog. Hitler, who reacted to the British guarantee with the oath, "I'll cook them a stew they'll choke on!" renounced his 1934 pact with Poland and the Anglo-German Naval Treaty on the 28th. Germany and Italy then turned their Axis into a military alliance known as the Pact of Steel on May 22.

How could Britain and France ever make good on their pledges to defend Poland? British planning called only for a naval blockade in the early stages of war, while the French (despite a promise to attack) contemplated no action beyond French soil. The answer was that the Polish guarantee was a military bluff unless the Red Army could somehow be enlisted. So finally, in the late spring of 1939, the Western allies went in search of collaboration with Moscow.

Stalin had witnessed events during the era of appeasement with growing suspicion and moved his pieces on the chessboard with deftness and cynicism. His overriding purpose was to deflect the thrusts of Germany and Japan elsewhere or—if the U.S.S.R. were forced to fight—make certain that the Western powers were likewise engaged. German reoccupation of the Rhineland had been a military setback, since it freed Germany for adventures to the east, but a diplomatic boon, since it enhanced the value of the Soviet alliance for France. The Anti-Comintern Pact had opened the terrible possibility for the Soviet Union of a war on two fronts, but it soon developed that Berlin and Tokyo were both expecting the other to stand guard over Russia while they pursued booty in central Europe and China respectively. Now Britain and France were promising to fight Hitler over Poland, thereby handing Stalin the choice of joining the Western powers in war or dealing separately with Germany to avoid conflict entirely. Fearing that war might unleash rebellion at home, Stalin chose to become the greatest appeaser of all.

It is often said that Munich forced Stalin to conclude that the Western powers were pushing Nazi Germany to the east and thus reluctantly to consider rapprochement with Hitler. But one might just as well interpret Litvinov's passionate pleas for collective security as a ploy to provoke conflict between Germany and the West while the U.S.S.R. huddled in safety behind its Polish buffer. The incident that made possible the union of the two dictators, as historian Adam Ulam has shown, was not Munich but the British guarantee of Poland. Before that act Stalin faced the prospect of an unopposed German march into Poland, whereupon the U.S.S.R. would be in mortal danger. After that act, Hitler could seize Poland only at the cost of war with the West, whereupon Hitler would need the U.S.S.R. as an ally. The British guarantee thus made Stalin the arbiter of Europe.

In a contest for Soviet friendship, however, the Allies were at a distinct disadvantage. All they could offer Stalin was the likelihood of war, albeit in alliance with them. On May 3, Stalin replaced Foreign Minister Litvinov, pro-Western and a Jew, with Vyacheslav Molotov—a clear signal of his willingness to improve relations with the Nazis. The Western powers accordingly stepped up their appeals to Moscow for an alliance, but they faced two lofty hurdles. First, Stalin demanded the right to occupy the Baltic states and portions of Romania. While Westerners could scarcely expect to enlist the Red Army in their cause without giving something in return, they could not justify turning free peoples over to Stalinist tyranny. Second, the Poles, as always, refused to invite the Red Army onto lands they had wrested from that same army just 18 years before. By July, Stalin was also demanding that a military convention precede the political one to ensure that he was not left in the lurch. Ironically, the only ploy likely to persuade Stalin of Western sincerity was a blunt threat that the West would not fight for Poland unless the U.S.S.R. participated.

German soldiers break down a barricade at the Polish border at the outbreak of World War II in 1939.

The Outbreak of War

Since the spring of 1939 the U.S.S.R. had been sending signals to Berlin that Hitler alternately acknowledged and ignored. His hatred for the Moscow regime was overcome, however, by the urgings of Ribbentrop and the unease of his generals. The Soviets, for their part, were again fighting heavy battles along the Manchurian border and were in need of security in Europe. Soviet bargaining power was enhanced by the fact that Hitler had a timetable: He had ordered the invasion of Poland by August 26. Negotiations dragged on from July 18 to August 21, when Hitler insisted that Stalin receive Ribbentrop and conclude their business two days hence. On Aug. 23, 1939, therefore, Ribbentrop and Molotov signed the German–Soviet Nonaggression Pact in Moscow, then raised their glasses as Stalin, the leader of world Communism, toasted the German people and their beloved Führer and vowed never to betray them. This nonagression pact was in fact a pact of aggression against Poland, which was to be partitioned, roughly along the old Curzon Line. Hitler also granted the U.S.S.R. a free hand in Finland, the Baltic states, and Bessarabia.

Hitler expected that his successful wooing of Russia would oblige Britain and France to withdraw their pledge to Poland. The free peoples were indeed shocked by the news from Moscow, but far from succumbing, they steeled their will to resist. The world situation, so cloudy since 1933, suddenly seemed clear, and scales fell from many eyes. The abstract and often effete ideological debate over democratic decadence and the relative merits of Fascism and Communism came suddenly to an end. Both vaunted ideologies now seemed so much lying propaganda, and their patrons so many gangsters. The day after the pact Chamberlain wrote to Hitler to warn that British resolve was as firm as ever, and on the 25th he signed a full alliance with Poland. British determination and the news that Italy was not ready for war prompted Hitler to delay his invasion a week in hopes of detaching Britain with promises of treaties and guarantees of the British Empire. When Chamberlain refused, Hitler demanded that a Polish plenipotentiary be sent to Berlin on August 30 to settle the matter of Danzig and the Polish Corridor. Should the Poles refuse, their obstinacy might give London an excuse to leave them to their fate. Colonel Beck, however, had seen the fate of Schuschnigg and Hácha, and he would not submit to a Hitlerian kidnapping or to another Munich. When Hitler's ultimatum expired, the German army staged a border incident and invaded Poland in force on the morning of Sept. 1, 1939. The British and French parliaments, confident that their governments had turned every stone in search of peace, declared war on Germany on September 3.

Hitler's War or Chamberlain's?

For two decades after 1939, German guilt for the outbreak of World War II seemed incontestable. The Nürnberg war-crimes trials in 1946 brought to light damning evidence of Nazi ambitions, preparations for war, and deliberate provocation of the crises over Austria, the Sudetenland, and Poland. Revelation of Nazi tyranny, torture, and genocide was a powerful deterrent to anyone in the West inclined to dilute German guilt. To be sure, there were bitter recriminations in France and Britain against those who had failed to stand up to Hitler, and the United States and the U.S.S.R. alike were later to invoke the lessons of the 1930s to justify Cold War policies: Appeasement only feeds the appetite of aggressors; there must be "no more Munichs." Nonetheless, World War II was undeniably Hitler's war, as the ongoing publication of captured German documents seemed to prove.

The British historian A.J.P. Taylor challenged the thesis of sole Nazi guilt in 1961, coincidently the same year in which Fritz Fischer revived the notion of German guilt for World War I. Taylor boldly suggested that Hitler's "ideology" was nothing more than the sort of nationalist ravings "which echo the conversation of any Austrian cafe or German beer-house"; that Hitler's ends and means resembled those of any "traditional German statesman"; and that the war came because Britain and France dithered between appeasement and resistance, leading Hitler to miscalculate and bring on the accident of September 1939. Needless to say, revisionism on a figure so odious as Hitler sparked vigorous rebuttal and debate. If Hitler had been a traditional statesman, then appeasement would have worked, said some. If the British had been consistent in appeasement—or resisted earlier—the war would not have happened, said others.

Fischer's theses on World War I were also significant, for, if Germany at that earlier time was bent on European hegemony and world power, then one could argue a continuity in German foreign policy from at least 1890 to 1945. Devotees of the "primacy of domestic policy" even made comparisons between Hitler's use of foreign policy to crush domestic dissent and similar practices under the Kaiser and Bismarck. But how, critics retorted, could one argue for continuity between the traditional imperialism of Wilhelmine Germany and the fanatical racial extermination of Nazi Germany after 1941? At bottom, Hitler was not trying to preserve traditional elites but to destroy the domestic and international order alike.

Soviet writers tried, without success, to draw a convincing causal chain between capitalist development and Fascism, but the researches of the British Marxist T.W. Mason exposed the German economic crisis of 1937, suggesting that the timing of World War II was partly a function of economic pressures.

Finally, Alan Bullock suggested a synthesis: Hitler knew where he wanted to go—his will was unbending—but as to how to get there he was flexible, an opportunist. Gerhard Weinberg's exhaustive study of the German documents then confirmed a neo-traditional interpretation to the effect that Hitler was bent on war and *Lebensraum* and that appeasement only delayed his gratification.

Publication of British and French documents, in turn, enabled historians to sketch a subtler portrait of appeasement. Chamberlain's reputation improved during the 1970s as American historians, conscious of U.S. overextension in the world and sympathetic to détente with the Soviets, came to appreciate the plight of Britain in the 1930s. Financial, military, and strategic rationalizations, however, could not erase the gross misunderstanding of the nature of the enemy that underlay appeasement. The British historian Anthony Adamthwaite concluded in 1984 that despite the accumulation of sources the fact remains that the appeasers' determination to reach agreement with Hitler blinded them to reality. If to understand is not to forgive, neither is it to give the past the odour of inevitability. Hitler wanted war, and Western and Soviet policies throughout the 1930s helped him to achieve it.

CHAPTER 3

THE WAR IN EUROPE, 1939–41

The German conquest of Poland in September 1939 was the first demonstration in war of the new theory of high-speed armoured warfare that had been adopted by the Germans when their rearmament began. Poland was a country all too well suited for such a demonstration. Its frontiers were immensely long—about 3,500 miles in all; and the stretch of 1,250 miles adjoining German territory had recently been extended to 1,750 miles in all by the German occupation of Bohemia-Moravia and of Slovakia so that Poland's southern flank became exposed to invasion—as the northern flank, facing East Prussia, already was. Western Poland had become a huge salient that lay between Germany's jaws.

It would have been wiser for the Polish army to assemble farther back, behind the natural defense line formed by the Vistula and San rivers, but that would have entailed the abandonment of some of the most valuable western parts of the country, including the Silesian coalfields and most of the main industrial zone, which lay west of the river barrier. The economic argument for delaying the German approach to the main industrial zone was heavily reinforced by Polish national pride and military overconfidence.

Forces and Resources of the European Combatants, 1939

In September 1939 the Allies, namely Great Britain, France, and Poland, were together superior in industrial resources, population, and military manpower, but the German army, or Wehrmacht, because of its armament, training, doctrine, discipline, and fighting spirit, was the most efficient and effective fighting force for its size in the world. The index of military strength in September 1939 was the number of divisions that each nation could mobilize. Against Germany's 100 infantry divisions and six armoured divisions, France had 90 infantry divisions in metropolitan France, Great Britain had 10 infantry divisions, and Poland had 30 infantry divisions, 12 cavalry brigades, and one armoured brigade (Poland had also 30 reserve infantry divisions, but these could not be mobilized quickly). A division contained from 12,000 to 25,000 men.

It was the qualitative superiority of the German infantry divisions and the number of their armoured divisions that made the difference in 1939. The firepower of a German infantry division far exceeded that of a French, British, or Polish division; the standard German division included 442 machine guns, 135 mortars, 72 antitank guns, and 24 howitzers. Allied divisions had a firepower only slightly greater than that of World War I. Germany had six armoured divisions in September 1939; the Allies, though they had a large number of tanks, had no armoured divisions at that time.

The six armoured, or panzer, divisions of the Wehrmacht comprised some 2,400 tanks. And though Germany would subsequently expand its tank forces during the first years of the war, it was not the number of tanks that Germany had (the Allies had almost as many in September 1939) but the fact of their being organized into divisions and operated as such that was to prove decisive. In accordance with the doctrines of General Heinz Guderian, the German tanks were used in massed formations in conjunction with motorized artillery to punch holes in the enemy line and to isolate segments of the enemy, which were then surrounded and captured by motorized

The War in Europe, 1939–41

German infantry divisions while the tanks ranged forward to repeat the process: Deep drives into enemy territory by panzer divisions were thus followed by mechanized infantry and foot soldiers. These tactics were supported by dive bombers that attacked and disrupted the enemy's supply and communications lines and spread panic and confusion in its rear, thus further paralyzing its defensive capabilities. Mechanization was the key to the German blitzkrieg, or "lightning war," so named because of the unprecedented speed and mobility that were its salient characteristics. Tested and well trained in maneuvers, the German panzer divisions constituted a force with no equal in Europe.

The German air force, or Luftwaffe, was also the best force of its kind in 1939. It was a ground-cooperation force designed to support the army, but its planes were superior to nearly all Allied types. In the rearmament period from 1935 to 1939 the production of German combat aircraft steadily mounted.

The standardization of engines and airframes gave the Luftwaffe an advantage over its opponents. Germany had an operational force of 1,000 fighters and 1,050 bombers in September 1939. The Allies actually had more planes in 1939 than Germany did, but their strength was made up of many different types, some of them obsolescent.

Great Britain, which was held back by delays in the rearmament program, was producing one modern fighter in 1939, the Hurricane. A higher-performance fighter, the Spitfire, was just coming into production and did not enter the air war in numbers until 1940.

The value of the French air force in 1939 was reduced by the number of obsolescent planes in its order of battle: 131 of the 634 fighters and nearly all of the 463 bombers. France was desperately trying to buy high-performance aircraft in the United States in 1939.

At sea the odds against Germany were much greater in September 1939 than in August 1914, since the Allies in 1939 had many more large surface warships than Germany had. At sea, however, there was to be no clash between the Allied and the German massed fleets but only the individual operation of German pocket battleships and commerce raiders.

The Campaign in Poland, 1939

When war broke out the Polish army was able to mobilize about 1,000,000 men, a fairly large number. The Polish army was woefully outmoded, however, and was almost completely lacking in tanks, armoured personnel carriers, and antitank and antiaircraft guns. Yet many of the Polish military leaders clung to the double belief that their preponderance of horsed cavalry was an important asset and that they could take the offensive against the German mechanized forces. They also tended to discount the effect of Germany's vastly superior air force, which was nearly 10 times as powerful as their own.

The unrealism of such an attitude was repeated in the Polish army's dispositions. Approximately one-third of Poland's forces were concentrated in or near the Polish Corridor (in northeastern Poland), where they were perilously exposed to a double envelopment—from East Prussia and the west combined. In the south, facing the main avenues of a German advance, the Polish forces were thinly spread. At the same time, nearly another one-third of Poland's forces were massed in reserve in the north-central part of the country, between Lódz and Warsaw, under the commander in chief Marshal Edward Rydz-Smigly. The Poles' forward concentration in general forfeited their chance of fighting a series of delaying actions, since their foot-marching army was unable to retreat to their defensive positions in the rear or to man them before being overrun by the invader's mechanized columns.

The War in Europe, 1939–41

The 40-odd infantry divisions employed by the Germans in the invasion counted for much less than their 14 mechanized or partially mechanized divisions: These consisted of six armoured divisions; four light divisions, consisting of motorized infantry (infantry wholly transported by trucks and personnel carriers) with two armoured units; and four motorized divisions. The Germans attacked with about 1,500,000 troops in all. It was the deep and rapid thrusts of these mechanized forces that decided the issue, in conjunction with the overhead pressure of the Luftwaffe, which wrecked the Polish railway system and destroyed most of the Polish air force before it could come into action. The Luftwaffe's terror-bombing of Polish cities, bridges, roads, rail lines, and power stations completed the disorganization of the Polish defenses.

Armoured German scout cars drive into Dirschau in September 1939.

On Sept. 1, 1939, the German attack began. Against northern Poland, General Fedor von Bock commanded an army group comprising General Georg von Küchler's 3rd Army, which struck southward from East Prussia, and General Günther von Kluge's 4th Army, which struck eastward across the base of the Corridor. Much stronger in troops and in tanks, however, was the army group in the south under General Gerd von Rundstedt, attacking from Silesia and from the Moravian and Slovakian border: General Johannes Blaskowitz's 8th Army, on the left, was to drive eastward against Lódz; General Wilhelm List's 14th Army, on the right, was to push on toward Kraków and to turn the Poles' Carpathian flank; and General Walther von Reichenau's 10th Army, in the centre, with the bulk of the group's armour, was to deliver the decisive blow with a northwestward thrust into the heart of Poland. By September 3, when Kluge in the north had reached the Vistula and Küchler was approaching the Narew River, Reichenau's armour was already beyond the Warta; two days later his left wing was well to the rear of Lódz and his right wing at Kielce; and by September 8 one of his armoured corps was in the outskirts of Warsaw, having advanced 140 miles in the first week of war. Light divisions on Reichenau's right were on the Vistula between Warsaw and Sandomierz by September 9, while List, in the south, was on the San above and below Przemysl. At the same time, the 3rd Army tanks, led by Guderian, were across the Narew attacking the line of the Bug River, behind Warsaw. All the German armies had made progress in fulfilling their parts in the great enveloping maneuver planned by General Franz Halder, chief of the general staff, and directed by General Walther von Brauchitsch, the commander in chief. The Polish armies were splitting up into uncoordinated fragments, some of which were retreating while others were delivering disjointed attacks on the nearest German columns.

On September 10 the Polish commander in chief, Marshal Edward Rydz-Smigly, ordered a general retreat to the southeast. The Germans, however, were by that time not only tightening their net around the Polish forces west of the Vistula (in the Lódz area and, still farther west, around Poznan) but also penetrating deeply into eastern Poland. The Polish defense was already reduced to random efforts by isolated bodies of troops when another blow fell: On Sept. 17, 1939, Soviet forces entered Poland from the east. The next day, the Polish government and high command crossed the Romanian frontier on their way into exile. The Warsaw garrison held out against the Germans until September 28, undergoing terror-bombings and artillery barrages that reduced parts of the city to rubble, with no regard for the civilian population. The last considerable fragment of the Polish army resisted until October 5; and some guerrilla fighting went on into the winter. The Germans took a total of 700,000 prisoners, and about 80,000 Polish soldiers escaped over neutral frontiers. Approximately 70,000 Polish soldiers were killed and more than 130,000 wounded during the battle, whereas the Germans sustained about 45,000 total casualties. Poland was conquered for partition between Germany and the U.S.S.R., the forces of which met and greeted each other on Polish soil. On September 28 another secret German–Soviet protocol modified the arrangements of August: All of Lithuania was to be a Soviet sphere of influence, not a German one, but the dividing line in Poland was changed in Germany's favour, being moved eastward to the Bug River.

The Baltic States and the Russo-Finnish War, 1939–40

Profiting quickly from its understanding with Germany, the U.S.S.R. on Oct. 10, 1939, constrained Estonia, Latvia, and

Lithuania to admit Soviet garrisons onto their territories. Approached with similar demands, Finland refused to comply, even though the U.S.S.R. offered territorial compensation elsewhere for the cessions that it was requiring for its own strategic reasons. Finland's armed forces amounted to about 200,000 troops in 10 divisions. The Soviets eventually brought about 70 divisions (about 1,000,000 men) to bear in their attack on Finland, along with about 1,000 tanks. Soviet troops attacked Finland on Nov. 30, 1939.

The invaders succeeded in isolating the little Arctic port of Petsamo in the far north but were ignominiously repulsed on all of the fronts chosen for their advance. On the Karelian Isthmus, the massive reinforced-concrete fortifications of Finland's Mannerheim Line blocked the Soviet forces' direct land route from Leningrad into Finland. The Soviet planners had grossly underestimated the Finns' national will to resist and the natural obstacles constituted by the terrain's numerous lakes and forests.

The Western powers exulted overtly over the humiliation of the Soviet Union. One important effect of Finland's early successes was to reinforce the tendency of both Hitler and the western democracies to underestimate the Soviet military capabilities. But in the meantime, the Soviet strategists digested their hard-learned military lessons.

On Feb. 1, 1940, the Red Army launched 14 divisions into a major assault on the Mannerheim Line. The offensive's weight was concentrated along a 10-mile sector of the line near Summa, which was pounded by a tremendous artillery bombardment. As the fortifications were pulverized, tanks and sledge-carried infantry advanced to occupy the ground while the Soviet air force broke up attempted Finnish counterattacks. After little more than a fortnight of this methodical process, a breach was made through the whole depth of the Mannerheim Line. Once the Soviets had forced a passage on the Karelian Isthmus, Finland's eventual collapse was certain. On March 6 Finland sued for peace, and a week later the Soviet terms were accepted: The Finns had to cede the entire Karelian Isthmus, Viipuri, and their part of the Rybachy Peninsula to the Soviets. The Finns had suffered about 70,000 casualties in the campaign, the Soviets more than 200,000.

The War in the West, September 1939–June 1940

During their campaign in Poland, the Germans kept only 23 divisions in the west to guard their frontier against the French, who had nearly five times as many divisions mobilized. The French commander in chief, General Maurice-Gustave Gamelin, proposed an advance against Germany through neutral Belgium and the Netherlands in order to have room to exercise his ponderous military machine. He was overruled, however, and French assaults on the 100-mile stretch of available front along the Franco-German frontier had barely dented the German defenses when the collapse of Poland prompted the recall of Gamelin's advanced divisions to defensive positions in the Maginot Line. From October 1939 to March 1940, successive plans were developed for counteraction in the event of a German offensive through Belgium—all of them based on the assumption that the Germans would come across the plain north of Namur, not across the hilly and wooded Ardennes. The Germans would indeed have taken the route foreseen by the French if Hitler's desire for an offensive in November 1939 had not been frustrated, on the one hand, by bad weather and, on the other, by the hesitations of his generals, but in March 1940 the bold suggestion of General Erich von Manstein that an offensive through the Ardennes should, in fact, be practicable for tank forces was adopted by Hitler, despite orthodox military opinion.

Meanwhile, Hitler's immediate outlook had been changed by considerations about Scandinavia. Originally he had intended to respect Norway's neutrality. Then rumours leaked out, prematurely, of British designs on Norway—as, in fact, Winston Churchill, first lord of the Admiralty, was arguing that mines should be laid in Norwegian waters to stop the export of Swedish iron ore from Gällivare to Germany through Norway's rail terminus and port of Narvik. The British Cabinet, in response to Churchill, authorized at least the preparation of a plan for a landing at Narvik; and in mid-December 1939 a Norwegian politician, Vidkun Quisling, leader of a pro-Nazi party, was introduced to Hitler. On Jan. 27, 1940, Hitler ordered plans for an invasion of Norway, for use if he could no longer respect Norway's neutrality.

After France's failure to interrupt the German conquest of Poland, the Western powers and the Germans were so inactive with regard to land operations that journalists began to speak derisively, over the next six months, of the "phony war." After the fall of Poland, while hope still existed that a repetition of World War I might be avoided, Hitler sought to persuade Britain to renege on its commitment to Poland's defense. In secret contacts and in his "Peace Address" to the Reichstag of October 6 he even hinted at the possibility of restoring a rump Polish state. The Chamberlain Cabinet, betrayed so often by Hitler, refused to acknowledge the demarches, however, and Hitler ordered preparations for an attack in the west by November 12. The army high command protested vigorously against a winter campaign, and bad weather did force a postponement first to January 1940 and then to the spring. Since the French and British were loath to take initiative, the Phony War dragged on.

At sea, however, the period was somewhat more eventful. German U-boats sank the British aircraft carrier *Courageous*

(September 17) and the battleship *Royal Oak* (October 14). The U-boats' main warfare, however, was against merchant shipping: They sank more than 110 vessels in the first four months of the war. Both the Germans and the British, meanwhile, were engaged in extensive mine laying.

In surface warfare at sea, the British were on the whole more fortunate than the Germans. A German pocket battleship in the Atlantic, the *Admiral Graf Spee* sank nine ships before coming to a tragic end: Having sustained and inflicted damage in an engagement with three British cruisers off the Río de la Plata on Dec. 13, 1939, she made off to Montevideo and obtained leave to spend four days there for repairs; the British mustered reinforcements for the two cruisers still capable of action after the engagement, namely the *Ajax* and the *Achilles*, and brought the *Cumberland* to the scene in time; but, on December 17, when the *Graf Spee* put to sea again, her crew scuttled her a little way out of the harbour before the fight could be resumed.

THE INVASION OF NORWAY

British plans for landings on the Norwegian coast in the third week of March 1940 were temporarily postponed. Prime Minister Neville Chamberlain, however, was by that time convinced that some aggressive action ought to be taken, and Paul Reynaud, who succeeded Édouard Daladier as France's premier on March 21, was of the same opinion. (Reynaud had come into office on the surge of the French public's demand for a more aggressive military policy and quicker offensive action against Germany.) It was agreed that mines should be laid in Norwegian waters and that the mining should be followed by the landing of troops at four Norwegian ports, Narvik, Trondheim, Bergen, and Stavanger.

Because of Anglo-French arguments, the date of the mining was postponed from April 5 to April 8. The postponement was catastrophic. Hitler had on April 1 ordered the German invasion of Norway to begin on April 9; so, when on April 8 the Norwegian government was preoccupied with earnest protest about the British mine laying, the German expeditions were well on their way.

On April 9, 1940, the major Norwegian ports from Oslo northward to Narvik (1,200 miles away from Germany's naval bases) were occupied by advance detachments of German troops. At the same time, a single parachute battalion (the first ever employed in warfare) took the Oslo and Stavanger airfields, and 800 operational aircraft overawed the Norwegian population. Norwegian resistance at Narvik, at Trondheim (the strategic key to Norway), at Bergen, at Stavanger, and at Kristiansand had been overcome very quickly, and Oslo's effective resistance to the seaborne forces was nullified when German troops from the airfield entered the city.

Simultaneously, along with their Norwegian enterprise, the Germans on April 9 occupied Denmark, sending troopships, covered by aircraft, into Copenhagen harbour and marching over the land frontier into Jutland. This occupation was obviously necessary for the safety of their communications with Norway.

Allied troops began to land at Narvik on April 14. Shortly afterward, British troops were landed also at Namsos and at Åndalsnes, to attack Trondheim from the north and from the south, respectively. The Germans, however, landed fresh troops in the rear of the British at Namsos and advanced up the Gudbrandsdal from Oslo against the force at Åndalsnes. By this time the Germans had about 25,000 troops in Norway. By May 2, both Namsos and Åndalsnes were evacuated by the British. The Germans at Narvik held out against five times as many British and French troops until May 27. By that time the German offensive in France had progressed to such an extent that the British could no longer afford any commitment in Norway, and the 25,000 Allied troops were evacuated from Narvik 10 days after their victory. The Norwegian king Haakon VII and his government left Norway for Britain at the same time. Hitler garrisoned Norway with about 300,000 troops for the rest of the war. By occupying Norway, Hitler had ensured the protection of Germany's supply of iron ore from Sweden and had obtained naval and air bases with which to strike at Britain if necessary.

What was to happen in Norway became a less important question for the Western powers when, on May 10, 1940, they were surprised by Hitler's long-debated stroke against them through the Low Countries.

THE INVASION OF THE LOW COUNTRIES AND FRANCE

France's 800,000-man standing army was thought at the time to be the most powerful in Europe. But the French had not progressed beyond the defensive mentality inherited from World War I, and they relied primarily on their Maginot Line for protection against a German offensive. The Maginot Line was an extremely well-developed chain of fortifications running from the Swiss frontier opposite Basel northward along the left bank of the Rhine and then northwestward no farther than Montmédy, near the Belgian frontier south of the Ardennes Forest. The line consisted of a series of giant pillboxes and other defensive installations constructed in depth, equipped with underground supply and communications facilities, and connected by rail lines, with all its heavy guns pointed east at the German frontier. Depending heavily on the line as a defense against German attack, the French had 41 divisions manning it or backing it, whereas only 39 divisions were watching the long stretch of frontier north of it, from Montmédy through the Ardennes and across Flanders to the English Channel.

In their plan for the invasion of France and the Low Countries, the Germans kept General Wilhelm von Leeb's Army Group C facing the Maginot Line so as to deter the French from diverting forces from it, while launching Bock's Army Group B into the basin of the Lower Maas River north of Liège and Rundstedt's Army Group A into the Ardennes. Army Group B comprised Küchler's 18th Army, with one armoured division and airborne support, to attack the Netherlands, and Reichenau's 6th, with two armoured divisions, to advance over the Belgian plain. These two armies would have to deal not only with the Dutch and Belgian armies but also with the forces that the Allies, according to their plan, would send into the Low Countries, namely two French armies and nine British divisions. Rundstedt's Army Group A, however, was much stronger, comprising as it did Kluge's 4th Army, List's 12th, and General Ernst Busch's 16th, with General Maximilian von Weichs's 2nd in reserve, besides a large armoured group under Paul Ludwig von Kleist and a smaller one under General Hermann Hoth, and amounting in all to 44 divisions, seven of them armoured, with 27 divisions in reserve. Army Group A thus amounted to more than 1,500,000 men and more than 1,500 tanks, and it would strike at the weak hinge of the Allies' wheel into Belgium—that is to say, at two French armies, General Charles Huntziger's 2nd and General André Corap's 9th, which together mustered only 12 infantry and four horsed cavalry divisions and stood, respectively, east and west of Sedan on the least-fortified stretch of the French frontier. Against this weak centre of the Allied line were thus massed nearly two-thirds of Germany's forces in the west and nearly three-quarters of its tank forces.

The Dutch army comprised 10 divisions and the equivalent of 10 more in smaller formations and thus totaled more than 400,000 men. It apparently had a good chance of withstanding the German invasion, since the attacking German army comprised only seven divisions, apart from the airborne forces it would use. The Dutch, however, had a wide front, a very sensitive and loosely settled rear, very few tanks, and no experience of modern warfare. On May 10, the German attack on the Netherlands began with the capture by parachutists of the bridges at Moerdijk, at Dordrecht, and at Rotterdam and with landings on the airfields around The Hague. On the same day, the weakly held Peel Line, south of the westward-turning arc of the Maas, was penetrated by the German land forces, and on May 11 the Dutch defenders fell back westward past Tilburg to Breda, with the consequence that the French 7th Army, under General Henri Giraud, whose leading forces had sped forward across Belgium over the 140 miles to Tilburg, fell back to Breda likewise. The German tanks thus had a clear road to Moerdijk, and by noon on May 12 they were in the outskirts of Rotterdam. North of the Maas, meanwhile, where the bulk of the Dutch defense was concentrated, the Germans achieved a narrow breach of the Geld Valley line on May 12, whereupon the Dutch, unable to counterattack, retreated to the "Fortress of Holland" Line protecting Utrecht and Amsterdam. Queen Wilhelmina and her government left the country for England on May 13, and the next day the Dutch commander in chief, General Henri Gerard Winkelman, surrendered to the Germans, who had threatened to bomb Rotterdam and Utrecht, as places in the front line of the fighting, if resistance continued. In fact, Rotterdam was bombed, after the capitulation, by 30 planes through a mistake in the Germans' signal communications.

The news of the German onslaught in the Low Countries, dismaying as it was to the Allies, had one effect that was to be of momentous importance to their fortunes: Chamberlain, whose halfhearted conduct of the war had been bitterly criticized in the House of Commons during the debate of May 7–8 on the campaign in Norway, resigned office in the evening of May 10 and was succeeded as prime minister by Churchill, who formed a coalition government.

For the first phase of the invasion of the Belgian plain north of Liège, Reichenau had four army corps, one armoured corps, and only 500 airborne troops, but he also had massive cooperation from the German Luftwaffe, whose dive bombers and fighters played a major role in breaking down the Belgian defenses. West of the Maastricht "appendix" of indefensible Dutch territory separating Belgium from Germany, the fortress of Eben Emael, immediately opposite Maastricht, and the line of the Albert Canal constituted the Belgians' foremost defensive position. On May 10 German airborne troops landed in gliders on the top of the fortress and on bridges over the canal. On May 11 the Belgian front was broken, the German tanks running on westward and some of the infantry turning southward to take Liège from the rear, while the Belgians made a general retreat to the Antwerp–Namur, or Dyle, Line. French and British divisions had just arrived on this Dyle Line, and General René Prioux's two tank divisions went out from it to challenge the German advance. After a big battle on May 14, however, Prioux's tanks had to retire to the consolidated Dyle Line, and on May 15, notwithstanding a successful defense against a German attack, Gamelin ordered the abandonment of the position, because events farther to the south had made it strategically untenable.

The chances for success of the German offensive against France hinged on a German advance through the hilly and dense Ardennes Forest, which the French considered to be impassable to tanks. But the Germans did succeed in moving

German troops ride through Paris after successfully occupying France.

their tank columns through that difficult belt of country by means of an amazing feat of staff work. While the armoured divisions used such roads through the forest as were available, infantry divisions started alongside them by using field and woodland paths and marched so fast across country that the leading ones reached the Meuse River only a day after the armoured divisions had.

The decisive operations in France were those of Rundstedt's Army Group A. Kleist's tanks on May 10 took only three hours to cover the 30 miles from the eastern border of independent Luxembourg to the southeastern border of Belgium, and on

May 11 the French cavalry divisions that had ridden forward into the Ardennes to oppose them were thrown back over the Semois River. By the evening of May 12 the Germans were across the Franco-Belgian frontier and overlooking the Meuse River. The defenses of this sector were rudimentary, and it was the least-fortified stretch of the whole French front. Worse still, the defending French 2nd and 9th armies had hardly any anti-tank guns or antiaircraft artillery with which to slow down the German armoured columns and shoot down their dive bombers. Such was the folly of the French belief that a German armoured thrust through the Ardennes was unlikely.

On May 13 Kleist's forces achieved a threefold crossing of the Meuse River. At Sedan wave after wave of German dive bombers swooped on the French defenders of the south bank. The latter could not stand the nerve-racking strain, and the German troops were able to push across the river in rubber boats and on rafts. The tremendous air bombardment was the decisive factor in the crossings. A thousand aircraft supported Kleist's forces, while only a few French aircraft intervened in a gallant but hopeless effort to aid their troops on the ground. Next day, after the tanks had been brought across, Guderian widened the Sedan bridgehead and beat off French counterattacks. On May 15 he broke through the French defenses into open country, turning westward in the direction of the English Channel. On May 16 his forces swept on west for nearly 50 miles. His superiors tried to put on the brake, feeling that such rapid progress was hazardous, but the pace of the German drive upset the French far more, and their collapse spread as Reinhardt's corps joined in the pressure. When more German tanks crossed the Meuse between Givet and Namur, the breach of the French front was 60 miles wide.

Driving westward down the empty corridor between the Sambre and the Aisne rivers, Guderian's tanks crossed the Oise

River on May 17 and reached Amiens two days later. Giraud, who on May 15 had superseded Corap in command of the French 9th Army, was thus frustrated in his desperate plan of checking the Germans on the Oise, and Kleist, meanwhile, by lining the Aisne progressively with tanks until the infantry came up to relieve them, was protecting the southwestern flank of the advance against the danger of a counteroffensive from the south. Indeed, when the Germans, on May 15, were reported to be crossing the Aisne River between Rethel and Laon, Gamelin told Reynaud that he had no reserves in that sector and that Paris might fall within two days' time. Thereupon Reynaud, though he postponed his immediate decision to move the government to Tours, summoned General Maxime Weygand from Syria to take Gamelin's place as commander in chief, but Weygand did not arrive until May 19.

Guderian's tanks were at Abbeville on May 20, and on May 22 he turned northward to threaten Calais and Dunkirk, while Reinhardt, swinging south of the British rear at Arras, headed for the same objectives, the remaining ports by which the British Expeditionary Force (BEF) could be evacuated.

THE EVACUATION FROM DUNKIRK

For the Allies, all communication between their northern and southern forces was severed by the arc of the westward German advance from the Ardennes to the Somme. The Allied armies in the north, having fallen back from the Dyle Line to the Escaut (Schelde), were being encircled, and already on May 19 the British commander, Viscount Gort, was considering the withdrawal of the BEF by sea. On May 21, however, to satisfy orders from London for more positive action, he launched an attack from Arras southward against the right flank of the Germans' corridor, but, though it momentarily alarmed the German high command, this small counterstroke lacked the armoured strength necessary for success. Meanwhile, Guderian's tanks had swept up past Boulogne and Calais and were crossing the canal defense line close to Dunkirk when, on May 24, an inexplicable order from Hitler not only stopped their advance but actually called them back to the canal line just as Guderian was expecting to drive into Dunkirk.

Dunkirk was now the only port left available for the withdrawal of the mass of the BEF from Europe, and the British Cabinet at last decided to save what could be saved. The British Admiralty had been collecting every kind of small craft it could find to help in removing the troops, and the British retreat to the coast now became a race to evacuate the troops before the Germans could occupy Dunkirk. Evacuation began on May 26 and became still more urgent the next day, when the Belgians, their right wing and their centre broken by Reichenau's advance, sued for an armistice. On May 27, likewise, bombing by the Luftwaffe put the harbour of Dunkirk out of use so that many of the thousands of men thronging the 10-mile stretch of beaches had to be ferried out to sea by petty craft pressed into service by the Royal Navy and manned largely by amateur seamen, though the harbour's damaged breakwater still offered a practicable exit for the majority.

By June 4, when the operation came to an end, 198,000 British and 140,000 French and Belgian troops had been saved, but virtually all of their heavy equipment had to be abandoned, and, of the 41 destroyers participating, six were sunk and 19 others damaged. The men who were saved represented a considerable part of the experienced troops possessed by Great Britain and were an inestimable gain to the Allies. The success of the near-miraculous evacuation from Dunkirk was due, on the one hand, to fighter cover by the Royal Air Force from the English coast and on the other to Hitler's fatal order of May 24 halting Guderian. That order had been made for several reasons, chiefly: Hermann

Göring, head of the Luftwaffe, had mistakenly assured Hitler that his aircraft alone could destroy the Allied troops trapped on the beaches at Dunkirk, and Hitler himself seems to have believed that Great Britain might accept peace terms more readily if its armies were not constrained into humiliating surrender. Three days passed before Walther von Brauchitsch, the German army commander in chief, was able to persuade Hitler to withdraw his orders and allow the German armoured forces to advance on Dunkirk. But they met stronger opposition from the British, who had had time to solidify their defenses, and almost immediately Hitler stopped the German armoured forces again, ordering them instead to move south and prepare for the attack on the Somme–Aisne line.

British and other Allied troops wade through the water to board ships at Dunkirk, France, in 1940.

The campaign in northern France was wound up by Küchler's forces, after both Guderian and Reichenau had been ordered southward. Altogether, the Germans had taken more than 1,000,000 prisoners in three weeks, at a cost of 60,000 casualties. Some 220,000 Allied troops, however, were rescued by British ships from France's northwestern ports (Cherbourg, Saint-Malo, Brest, and Saint-Nazaire), thus bringing the total of Allied troops evacuated to about 558,000.

There remained the French armies south of the Germans' Somme–Aisne front. The French had lost 30 divisions in the campaign so far. Weygand still managed to muster 49 divisions, apart from the 17 left to hold the Maginot Line, but against him the Germans had 130 infantry divisions as well as their 10 divisions of tanks. The Germans, after redisposing their units, began a new offensive on June 5 from their positions on the Somme. The French resisted stiffly for two days, but on June 7 the German tanks in the westernmost sector, led by Major General Erwin Rommel, broke through toward Rouen, and on June 9 they were over the Seine. On June 9 the Germans attacked on the Aisne: The infantry forced the crossings, and then Guderian's armour drove through the breach toward Châlons-sur-Marne before turning eastward for the Swiss frontier, thus isolating all the French forces still holding the Maginot Line.

ITALY'S ENTRY INTO THE WAR AND THE FRENCH ARMISTICE

Italy had been unprepared for war when Hitler attacked Poland, but if Benito Mussolini was to reap any positive advantages from partnership with Hitler it seemed that Italy would have to abandon its nonbelligerent stance before the Western democracies had been defeated by Germany singlehandedly. The obvious collapse of France convinced Mussolini that the time to implement his Pact of Steel with Hitler had come, and on June 10, 1940, Italy declared war against France and Great Britain. With about 30 divisions available on their Alpine frontier, the Italians delayed their actual attack on southeastern France until June 20, but it achieved little against the local defense. In any case, the issue in France had already been virtually settled by the victory of Italy's German ally.

Meanwhile, Reynaud had left Paris for Cangé, near Tours, and Weygand, after speaking frankly and despondently to Churchill at the Allied military headquarters at Briare on June 11, told Reynaud and the other ministers at Cangé on June 12 that the battle for France was lost and that a cessation of hostilities was compulsory. There was little doubt that he was correct in this estimate of the military situation: The French armies were now splitting up into fragments. Reynaud's government was divided between the advocates of capitulation and those who, with Reynaud, wanted to continue the war from French North Africa. The only decision that it could make was to move itself from Tours to Bordeaux.

The Germans entered Paris on June 14, 1940, and were driving still deeper southward along both the western and eastern edges of France. Two days later they were in the Rhône valley. Meanwhile, Weygand was still pressing for an armistice, backed by all the principal commanders. Reynaud resigned office on June 16, whereupon a new government was formed by Marshal Philippe Pétain, the revered and aged hero of the Battle of Verdun in World War I. In the night of June 16 the French request for an armistice was transmitted to Hitler. While discussion of the terms went on, the German advance went on too. Finally, on June 22, 1940, at Rethondes, the scene of the signing of the Armistice of 1918, the new Franco-German Armistice was signed. The Franco-Italian Armistice was signed on June 24. Both armistices came into effect early on June 25.

The Armistice of June 22 divided France into two zones: one to be under German military occupation and one to be left to the French in full sovereignty. The occupied zone comprised all northern France from the northwestern frontier of Switzerland to the Channel and from the Belgian and German frontiers to the Atlantic, together with a strip extending from the lower Loire southward along the Atlantic coast to the western end of

FREE FRENCH

In World War II (1939–45), the Free French (French Françaises Libres) were members of a movement for the continuation of warfare against Germany after the military collapse of Metropolitan France in the summer of 1940. Led by General Charles de Gaulle, the Free French were eventually able to unify most French resistance forces in their struggle against Germany.

On June 16, 1940, the government of France was constitutionally transmitted to Marshal Philippe Pétain, who had already decided that France must conclude an armistice with Germany. Two days later, a French army officer, General Charles de Gaulle, appealed by radio from London (whence he had fled on June 17) for a French continuation of the war against Germany. On June 28 de Gaulle was recognized by the British as the leader of Free France (as the nascent resistance movement was named), and from his base in London de Gaulle began to build up the Forces Françaises Libres, or Free French Forces. At first these consisted merely of French troops in England, volunteers from the French community resident in England since prewar times, and a few units of the French navy.

In the autumn of 1940 the French colonial territories of Chad, Cameroun, Moyen-Congo, French Equatorial Africa, and Oubangi-Chari (all in sub-Saharan Africa) rallied to de Gaulle's Free France, and the smaller French colonies in India and in the Pacific soon followed suit. A Free French military expedition in September 1940 to capture the important naval base of Dakar in French West Africa failed, however, and the base remained in the hands of French forces loyal to the national government that Pétain had set up in Vichy.

In 1941 Free French forces participated in British-controlled operations against Italian forces in Libya and Egypt, and that same year they joined the British in defeating the Vichy forces in Syria and Lebanon. In September de Gaulle created the Comité National Français (French National Committee), a Free French government-in-exile that was recognized by the Allied governments.

Despite these gains, the Free French remained a small force until 1942, by which time an underground anti-Nazi Résistance movement had sprung up in France. In his efforts to obtain the support of the Résistance, de Gaulle changed the name of his movement to Forces Françaises Combattantes (Fighting French Forces) and sent his emissary Jean Moulin to France to try to unify all the various Résistance groups in France under de Gaulle's leadership. Moulin came close to accomplishing this in May 1943 with his establishment of the Conseil Nationale de la Résistance (National Council of the Resistance).

The successful Anglo-American invasion of northwestern Africa in November 1942 resulted in the defection of most of the Vichy troops stationed there to the side of the Free French. De Gaulle then entered a power struggle with the Allied-backed commander in chief of the French forces in North Africa, General Henri Giraud. In June 1943 a Comité Français de Libération Nationale (French Committee of National Liberation) was constituted in Algiers, with Giraud and de Gaulle as its joint presidents. But de Gaulle soon outmaneuvered Giraud, whose resignation in the spring of 1944 left de Gaulle in supreme control of the entire French war effort outside of Metropolitan France. More and more Résistance groups were meanwhile acknowledging de Gaulle's leadership.

More than 100,000 Free French troops fought in the Anglo-American campaign in Italy in 1943, and, by the time of the Allied invasion of Normandy in June 1944, the Free French forces had swelled to more than 300,000 regular troops. They were almost wholly American equipped and supplied. In August 1944 the Free French 1st Army, under General Jean de Lattre de Tassigny, took part in the Allies' invasion of southern France, driving thence northeastward into Alsace before joining in the Western Allies' final thrust into Germany. In August 1944 the Résistance groups, now organized as Forces Françaises de l'Intérieur (French Forces of the Interior), mounted an anti-German insurrection in Paris, and the Free French 2nd Armoured Division under General Jacques-Philippe Leclerc drove into Paris to consummate the liberation. On Aug. 26, 1944, de Gaulle entered Paris in triumph.

the Pyrenees; the unoccupied zone comprised only two-fifths of France's territory, the southeast. The French navy and air force were to be neutralized, but it was not required that they be handed over to the Germans. The Italians granted very generous terms to the French: The only French territory that they claimed to occupy was the small frontier tract that their forces had succeeded in overrunning since June 20. Meanwhile, from June 18, General Charles de Gaulle, whom Reynaud had sent on a military mission to London on June 5, was broadcasting appeals for the continuance of France's war.

The collapse of France in June 1940 posed a severe naval problem to the British, because the powerful French navy still existed: Strategically, it was of immense importance to the British that these French ships not fall into German hands, since they would have tilted the balance of sea power decidedly in favour of the Axis—the Italian navy being now also at war with Britain. Mistrustful of promises that the French ships would be used only for "supervision and minesweeping," the British decided to immobilize them. Thus, on July 3, 1940, the British seized all French ships in British-controlled ports, encountering only nominal resistance. But when British ships appeared off Mers el-Kébir, near Oran on the Algerian coast, and demanded that the ships of the important French naval force there either join the Allies or sail out to sea, the French refused to submit, and the British eventually opened fire, damaging the battleship *Dunkerque*, destroying the *Bretagne*, and disabling several other vessels. Thereupon, Pétain's government, which on July 1 had installed itself at Vichy, on July 4 severed diplomatic relations with the British. In the eight following days, the constitution of France's Third Republic was abolished and a new French state created, under the supreme authority of Pétain himself. The few French colonies that rallied to General de Gaulle's Free French movement were strategically unimportant.

The Battle of Britain

With France conquered, Hitler could now turn his forces on Germany's sole remaining enemy: Great Britain, which was protected from the formidable German army by the waters of the English Channel. On July 16, 1940, Hitler issued a directive ordering the preparation and, if necessary, the execution of a plan for the invasion of Great Britain. But an amphibious invasion of Britain would only be possible, given Britain's large navy, if Germany could establish control of the air in the battle zone. To this end, the Luftwaffe chief, Göring, on August 2 issued the "Eagle Day" directive, laying down a plan of attack in which a few massive blows from the air were to destroy British air power and so open the way for the amphibious invasion, termed Operation "Sea Lion." Victory in the air battle for the Luftwaffe would indeed have exposed Great Britain to invasion and occupation. The victory by the Royal Air Force (RAF) Fighter Command blocked this possibility and, in fact, created the conditions for Great Britain's survival, for the extension of the war, and for the eventual defeat of Nazi Germany.

The forces engaged in the battle were relatively small. The British disposed some 600 frontline fighters to defend the country. The Germans made available about 1,300 bombers and dive bombers and about 900 single-engined and 300 twin-engined fighters. These were based in an arc around England from Norway to the Cherbourg Peninsula in northern coastal France. The preliminaries of the Battle of Britain occupied June and July 1940, the climax August and September, and the aftermath—the so-called Blitz—the winter of 1940–41. In the campaign, the Luftwaffe had no systematic or consistent plan of action: Sometimes it tried to establish a blockade by the destruction of British shipping and ports; sometimes, to destroy Britain's Fighter Command by combat and by the bombing of ground installations; and sometimes, to seek direct strategic results by attacks on London and other populous centres of industrial or political significance. The British, on the other hand, had prepared themselves for the kind of battle that in fact took place. Their radar early warning, the most advanced and the most operationally adapted system in the world, gave Fighter Command adequate notice of where and when to direct their fighter forces to repel German bombing raids. The Spitfire, moreover, though still in short supply, was unsurpassed as an interceptor by any fighter in any other air force.

The British fought not only with the advantage—unusual for them—of superior equipment and undivided aim but also against an enemy divided in object and condemned by circumstance and by lack of forethought to fight at a tactical disadvantage. The German bombers lacked the bomb-load capacity to strike permanently devastating blows and also proved, in daylight, to be easily vulnerable to the Spitfires and Hurricanes. Britain's radar, moreover, largely prevented them from exploiting the element of surprise. The German dive bombers were even more vulnerable to being shot down by British fighters, and long-range fighter cover was only partially available from German fighter aircraft, since the latter were operating at the limit of their flying range.

The German air attacks began on ports and airfields along the English Channel, where convoys were bombed and the air battle was joined. In June and July 1940, as the Germans gradually redeployed their forces, the air battle moved inland over the interior of Britain. On August 8 the intensive phase began, when the Germans launched bombing raids involving up to nearly 1,500 aircraft a day and directed them against the British fighter airfields and radar stations. In four actions, on August 8, 11, 12, and 13, the Germans lost 145 aircraft as against the British loss of 88. By late August the Germans had lost more than 600 aircraft, the RAF only 260, but the RAF was losing badly needed fighters and experienced pilots at too great a rate,

The War in Europe, 1939–41

and its effectiveness was further hampered by bombing damage done to the radar stations. At the beginning of September the British retaliated by unexpectedly launching a bombing raid on Berlin, which so infuriated Hitler that he ordered the Luftwaffe to shift its attacks from Fighter Command installations to London and other cities. These assaults on London, Coventry, Liverpool, and other cities went on unabated for several months. But already, by September 15, on which day the British believed, albeit incorrectly, that they had scored their greatest success by destroying 185 German aircraft, Fighter Command had demonstrated to the Luftwaffe that it could not gain air ascendancy over Britain. This was because British fighters were simply shooting down German bombers faster than German industry could produce them. The Battle of Britain was thus won, and the invasion of England was postponed indefinitely by Hitler. The

Smoke rises from the London Docklands after the first mass air raid on the British capital on Sept. 7, 1940.

British had lost more than 900 fighters but had shot down about 1,700 German aircraft.

During the following winter, the Luftwaffe maintained a bombing offensive, carrying out night-bombing attacks on Britain's larger cities. By February 1941 the offensive had declined, but in March and April there was a revival, and nearly 10,000 sorties were flown, with heavy attacks made on London. Thereafter German strategic air operations over England withered.

Central Europe and the Balkans, 1940–41

The continued resistance of the British caused Hitler once more to change his timetable. His great design for a campaign against the U.S.S.R. had originally been scheduled to begin about 1943—by which time he should have secured the German position on the rest of the European continent by a series of "localized" campaigns and have reached some sort of compromise with Great Britain. But in July 1940, seeing Great Britain still undefeated and the United States increasingly inimical to Germany, he decided that the conquest of the European part of the Soviet Union must be undertaken in May 1941 in order both to demonstrate Germany's invincibility to Great Britain and to deter the United States from intervention in Europe (because the elimination of the U.S.S.R. would strengthen the Japanese position in the Far East and in the Pacific). Events in the interval, however, were to make him change his plan once again.

While the invasion of the U.S.S.R. was being prepared, Hitler was much concerned to extend German influence across Slovakia and Hungary into Romania, the oil fields of which he was anxious to secure against Soviet attack and the military manpower of which might be joined to the forces of the German coalition. In May 1940 he obtained an oil and arms pact from Romania, but, when Romania, after being constrained by a Soviet ultimatum in June to cede Bessarabia and northern Bukovina to the U.S.S.R., requested a German military mission and a German guarantee of its remaining frontiers, Hitler refused to comply until the claims of other states against Romania had been met. Romania was compelled to cede southern Dobruja to Bulgaria on August 21 (an act that was formalized in the Treaty of Craiova on September 7), but its negotiations with Hungary about Transylvania were broken off on August 23. Since, if war had broken out between Romania and Hungary, the U.S.S.R. might have intervened and won control over the oil wells, Hitler decided to arbitrate immediately: By the Vienna Award of August 30, Germany and Italy assigned northern Transylvania, including the Szekler district, to Hungary, and Germany then guaranteed what was left of Romania. In the face of the Romanian nationalists' outcry against these proceedings, the king, Carol II, transferred his dictatorial powers to General Ion Antonescu on Sept. 4, 1940, and abdicated his crown in favour of his young son Michael two days later. Antonescu had already repeated the request for a German military mission, which arrived in Bucharest on October 12.

Though Hitler had apprised the Italian foreign minister, Galeazzo Ciano, of his intention to send a military mission to Romania, Ciano had not apprised Mussolini. So, since the latter's Balkan ambitions had been continually restrained by Hitler, particularly with regard to Yugoslavia, the sudden news of the mission annoyed him. On Oct. 28, 1940, therefore, having given Hitler only the barest hints of his project, Mussolini launched seven Italian divisions (155,000 men) from Albania into a separate war of his own against Greece.

The result was exasperating for Hitler. His ally's forces were not only halted by the Greeks, a few miles over the border, on

Nov. 8, 1940, but were also driven back by General Alexandros Papagos' counteroffensive of November 14, which was to put the Greeks in possession of one-third of Albania by mid-December. Moreover, British troops landed in Crete, and some British aircraft were sent to bases near Athens, whence they might have attacked the Romanian oil fields. Lastly, the success of the Greeks caused Yugoslavia and Bulgaria, who had hitherto been attentive to overtures from the Axis powers, to revert to a strictly neutral policy.

Anticipating Mussolini's appeal for German help in his "separate" or "parallel" war, Hitler in November 1940 drew Hungary, Romania, and Slovakia successively into the Axis, or Tripartite, Pact that Germany, Italy, and Japan had concluded on September 27, and he also obtained Romania's assent to the assembling of German troops in the south of Romania for an attack on Greece through Bulgaria. Hungary consented to the transit of these troops through its territory lest Romania take Hungary's place in Germany's favour and so be secured in possession of the Transylvanian lands left to it by the Vienna Award. Bulgaria, however, for fear of Soviet reaction, on the one hand, and of Turkish, on the other (Turkey had massed 28 divisions in Thrace when Italy attacked Greece), delayed its adhesion to the Axis until March 1, 1941. Only thereafter, on March 18, did the Yugoslav regent, Prince Paul, and his ministers Dragiša Cvetkovic and Aleksandar Cincar-Markovic agree to Yugoslavia's adhesion to the Axis.

Meanwhile, the German 12th Army had crossed the Danube from Romania into Bulgaria on March 2, 1941. Consequently, in accordance with a Greco-British agreement of February 21, a British expeditionary force of 58,000 men from Egypt landed in Greece on March 7, to occupy the Olympus–Vermion line. Then, on March 27, 1941, two days after the Yugoslav government's signature, in Vienna, of its adhesion to the Axis Pact, a group of Yugoslav army officers, led by General Dušan Simovic, executed a coup d'état in Belgrade, overthrowing the regency in favour of the 17-year-old king Peter II and reversing the former government's policy.

Almost simultaneously with the Belgrade coup d'état, the decisive Battle of Cape Matapan took place between the British and Italian fleets in the Mediterranean, off the Peloponnesian mainland northwest of Crete. Hitherto, Italo-British naval hostilities in the Mediterranean area since June 1940 had comprised only one noteworthy action: the sinking in November at the Italian naval base of Taranto of three battleships by aircraft from the British carrier *Illustrious*. In March 1941, however, some Italian naval forces, including the battleship *Vittorio Veneto*, with several cruisers and destroyers, set out to threaten British convoys to Greece, and British forces, including the battleships *Warspite*, *Valiant*, and *Barham* and the aircraft carrier *Formidable*, likewise with cruisers and destroyers, were sent to intercept them. When the forces met in the morning of March 28 off Cape Matapan, the *Vittorio Veneto* opened fire on the lighter British ships but was soon trying to escape from the engagement for fear of the torpedo aircraft from the *Formidable*. The battle then became a pursuit, which lasted long into the night. Finally, though the severely damaged *Vittorio Veneto* made good her escape, the British sank three Italian cruisers and two destroyers. The Italian navy made no more surface ventures into the eastern Mediterranean.

The German attack on Greece, scheduled for April 1, 1941, was postponed for a few days when Hitler, because of the Belgrade coup d'état, decided that Yugoslavia was to be destroyed at the same time. While Great Britain's efforts to draw Yugoslavia into the Greco-British defensive system were fruitless, Germany began canvasing allies for its planned invasion of Yugoslavia and Greece. Italy agreed to collaborate in the attack, and Hungary and Bulgaria agreed to send troops to occupy the territories that they coveted as soon as the Germans should have destroyed the Yugoslav state.

On April 6, 1941, the Germans, with 24 divisions and 1,200 tanks, invaded both Yugoslavia (which had 32 divisions) and Greece (which had 15 divisions). The operations were conducted in the same way as Germany's previous blitzkrieg campaigns. While massive air raids struck Belgrade, List's 12th Army drove westward and southward from the Bulgarian frontiers, Kleist's armoured group northwestward from Sofia, and Weichs's 2nd Army southward from Austria and from western Hungary. The 12th Army's advance through Skopje to the Albanian border cut communications between Yugoslavia and Greece in two days; Niš fell to Kleist on April 9, Zagreb to Weichs on April 10; and on April 11 the Italian 2nd Army (comprising 15 divisions) advanced from Istria into Dalmatia. After the fall of Belgrade to the German forces from bases in Romania (April 12), the remnant of the Yugoslav army—whose only offensive, in northern Albania, had collapsed—was encircled in Bosnia. Its capitulation was signed, in Belgrade, on April 17.

In Greece, meanwhile, the Germans took Salonika (Thessaloníki) on April 9, 1941, and then initiated a drive toward Ioánnina (Yannina), thus severing communication between the bulk of the Greek army (which was on the Albanian frontier) and its rear. The isolated main body capitulated on April 20, the Greek army as a whole on April 22. Two days later the pass of Thermopylae, defended by a British rear guard, was taken by the Germans, who entered Athens on April 27. All mainland Greece and all the Greek Aegean islands except Crete were under German occupation by May 11, the Ionian islands under Italian. The remainder of Britain's 50,000-man force in Greece was hastily evacuated with great difficulty after leaving all of their tanks and other heavy equipment behind.

The campaign against Yugoslavia brought 340,000 soldiers of the Yugoslav army into captivity as German prisoners of war. In the campaign against Greece the Germans took 220,000 Greek and 20,000 British or Commonwealth prisoners of war. The combined German losses in the Balkan campaigns were about 2,500 dead, 6,000 wounded, and 3,000 missing.

German airborne troops began to land in Crete on May 20, 1941, at Máleme, in the Canea-Suda area, at Réthimnon, and at Iráklion. Fighting, on land and on the sea, with heavy losses on both sides, went on for a week before the Allied commander in chief, General Bernard Cyril Freyberg of the New Zealand Expeditionary Force, was authorized to evacuate the island. The last defenders were overwhelmed at Réthimnon on May 31. The prisoners of war taken by the Germans in Crete numbered more than 15,000 British or Commonwealth troops, besides the Greeks taken. In battles around the island, German air attacks sank three light cruisers and six destroyers of the British Mediterranean fleet and damaged three battleships, one aircraft carrier, six light cruisers, and five destroyers.

Both the Yugoslav and the Greek royal governments went into exile on their armies' collapse. The Axis powers were left to dispose as they would of their conquests. Yugoslavia was completely dissolved: Croatia, the independence of which had been proclaimed on April 10, 1941, was expanded to form Great Croatia, which included Srem (Syrmia, the zone between the Sava and the Danube south of the Drava confluence) and Bosnia and Hercegovina; most of Dalmatia was annexed to Italy; Montenegro was restored to independence; Yugoslav Macedonia was partitioned between Bulgaria and Albania; Slovenia was partitioned between Italy and Germany; the Baranya triangle and the Backa went to Hungary; and the

Banat and Serbia were put under German military administration. Of the independent states, Great Croatia, ruled by Ante Pavelic's nationalist Ustaše ("Insurgents"), and Montenegro were Italian spheres of influence, although German troops still occupied the eastern part of Great Croatia. A puppet government of Serbia was set up by the Germans in August 1941.

While Bulgarian troops occupied eastern Macedonia and most of western Thrace, the rest of mainland Greece, theoretically subject to a puppet government in Athens, was militarily occupied by the Italians except for three zones, namely the Athens district, the Salonika district, and the Dimotika strip of Thrace, which the German conquerors reserved for themselves. The Germans also remained in occupation of Lesbos, Chios, Samos, Melos, and Crete.

CHAPTER 4
OTHER FRONTS, 1940–41

The contemporary course of events in the Balkans nullified the first great victory won by British land forces in World War II, which took place in North Africa. When Italy declared war against Great Britain in June 1940, it had nearly 300,000 men under Marshal Rodolfo Graziani in Cyrenaica (present-day Libya), to confront the 36,000 troops whom the British commander in chief in the Middle East, General Sir Archibald Wavell, had in Egypt to protect the North African approaches to the Suez Canal. Between these forces lay the Western Desert, in which the westernmost position actually held by the British was Mersa Matruh (Marsā Maṭrsūḥ), 120 miles east of the Cyrenaican frontier. The Italians in September 1940 occupied Sidi Barrani, 170 miles west of Mersa Matruh, but, after settling six divisions into a chain of widely separated camps, they did nothing more for weeks, and during that time Wavell received some reinforcements.

Egypt and Cyrenaica, 1940–Summer 1941

Wavell, whose command included not only Egypt but also the East African fronts against the Italians, decided to strike first in North Africa. On Dec. 7, 1940, some 30,000 men, under Major General Richard Nugent O'Connor, advanced westward, from Mersa Matruh, against 80,000 Italians, but, whereas the Italians at Sīdī Barrānī had only 120 tanks, O'Connor had 275. Having passed by night through a gap in the chain of forts, O'Connor's forces stormed three of the Italian camps, while the 7th

British soldiers raise the British flag over Benghazi after successfully capturing the town.

Armoured Division was already cutting the Italians' road of retreat along the coast to the west. On December 10 most of the positions closer to Sīdī Barrānī were overrun, and on December 11 the reserve tanks made a further enveloping bound to the coast beyond Buqbuq, intercepting a large column of retreating Italians. In three days the British had taken nearly 40,000 prisoners.

Falling back across the frontier into Cyrenaica, the remnant of the Italian forces from Sīdī Barrānī shut itself up in the fortress of Bardia (Bardīyah), which O'Connor's tanks speedily isolated. On Jan. 3, 1941, the British assault on Bardia began, and three days later the whole garrison of Bardia surrendered—45,000 men. The next fortress to the west, Tobruk (Ṭubruq), was assaulted on January 23 and captured the next day (30,000 more prisoners).

To complete their conquest of Cyrenaica, it remained for the British to take the port of Benghazi. On Feb. 3, 1941, however, O'Connor learned that the Italians were about to abandon Benghazi and to retreat westward down the coast road to Agheila (al- Uqaylah). Thereupon he boldly ordered the 7th Armoured Division to cross the desert hinterland and intercept the Italian retreat by cutting the coast road well to the east of Agheila. On February 5, after an advance of 170 miles in 33 hours, the British were blocking the Italians' line of retreat south of Beda Fomm (Baydā Fumm), and in the morning of February 6, as the main Italian columns appeared, a day of battle began. Though the Italians had, altogether, nearly four times as many cruiser tanks as the British, by the following morning 60 Italian tanks had been crippled, 40 more abandoned, and the rest of Graziani's army was surrendering in crowds. The British, only 3,000 strong and having lost only three of their 29 tanks, took 20,000 prisoners, 120 tanks, and 216 guns.

The British, having occupied Benghazi on February 6 and Agheila on February 8, could now have pushed on without hindrance to Tripoli, but the chance was foregone: The Greek government had accepted Churchill's reiterated offer of British troops to be sent to Greece from Egypt, which meant a serious reduction of British strength in North Africa.

The reduction was to have serious consequences, because on February 6, the very day of Beda Fomm, a young general, Erwin Rommel, had been appointed by Hitler to command two German mechanized divisions that were to be sent as soon as possible to help the Italians. Arriving in Tripolitania, Rommel decided to try an offensive with what forces he had. Against the depleted British strength, he was rapidly and brilliantly successful. After occupying Agheila with ease on March 24 and Mersa Bréga (Qasr al-Burayqah) on March 31, he resumed his advance on April 2—despite orders to stand still for two months—with 50 tanks backed by two new Italian divisions. The British evacuated Benghazi the next day and began a precipitate retreat into Egypt, losing great numbers of their tanks on the way (a large force of armour, surrounded at Mechili, had to surrender on April 7). By April 11 all Cyrenaica except Tobruk had been reconquered by Rommel's audacious initiative.

Tobruk, garrisoned mainly by the 9th Australian Division, held out against siege, and Rommel, though he defeated two British attempts to relieve the place (May and June 1941), was obliged to suspend his offensive on the Egyptian frontier, since he had overstretched his supply lines.

East Africa

Wavell, the success of whose North African strategy had been sacrificed to Churchill's recurrent fantasy of creating a Balkan front against Germany (Greece in 1941 was scarcely less disastrous for the British than the Dardanelles in 1915), nevertheless enjoyed one definitive triumph before Churchill, doubly chagrined at having lost Cyrenaica for Greece's sake and Greece for no advantage at all, removed him, in the summer of 1941, from his command in the Middle East. That triumph was the destruction of Italian East Africa and the elimination, thereby, of any threat to the Suez Canal from the south or to Kenya from the north.

In August 1940 Italian forces mounted a full-scale offensive and overran British Somaliland. Wavell, however, was already assured of the collaboration of the former Ethiopian emperor

Haile Selassie in raising the Ethiopians in patriotic revolt against the Italians, and, whereas in June he had disposed only of meagre resources against the 200,000 men and 325 aircraft under the Duca d'Aosta, Amedeo di Savoia, his troops in the Sudan were reinforced by two Indian divisions before the end of the year. After Haile Selassie and a British major, Orde Wingate, with two battalions of Ethiopian exiles, had crossed the Sudanese frontier directly into Ethiopia, General William Platt and the Indian divisions invaded Eritrea on Jan. 19, 1941 (the Italians had already abandoned Kassala), and, almost simultaneously, British troops from Kenya, under General Alan Cunningham, advanced into Italian Somaliland.

Platt's drive eastward into Eritrea was checked on February 5, at Keren, where the best Italian troops, under General Nicolangelo Carnimeo, put up a stiff defense facilitated by a barrier of cliffs. But when Keren fell on March 26, Platt's way to Asmara (Asmera), to Massawa (Mitsiwa), and then from Eritrea southward into Ethiopia was comparatively easy. Meanwhile, Cunningham's troops were advancing northward into Ethiopia, and on April 6 they entered the Ethiopian capital, Addis Ababa. Finally, the Duca d'Aosta was caught between Platt's column and Cunningham's, and at Amba Alaji, on May 20, he and the main body of his forces surrendered.

Iraq and Syria, 1940–41

In 1940 Prince ʿAbd al-Ilāh, regent of Iraq for King Fayṣal, had a government divided within itself about the war; he himself and his foreign minister, Nuri as-Said, were pro-British, but his prime minister, Rashid Ali al-Gailani, had pro-German leanings. Having resigned office in January 1941, Rashid Ali on April 3 seized power in Baghdad with help from some army officers and announced that the temporarily absent regent was deposed. The British, ostensibly exercising their right under the Anglo-Iraqi Treaty of 1930 to move troops across Iraqi territory, landed troops at Basra on April 19 and rejected Iraqi demands that these troops be sent on into Palestine before any further landings. Iraqi troops were then concentrated around the British air base at Ḥabbānīyah, west of Baghdad, and on May 2 the British commander there opened hostilities, lest the Iraqis should attack first. Having won the upper hand at Ḥabbānīyah and been reinforced from Palestine, the British troops from the air base marched on Baghdad, and on May 30 Rashid Ali and his friends took refuge in Iran. 'Abd al-Ilāh was reinstated as regent; Nuri became prime minister; and the British military presence remained to uphold them.

German military supplies for Rashid Ali were dispatched too late to be useful to him, but they reached Iraq via Syria, whose high commissioner, General H.-F. Dentz, was a nominee of the Vichy government of France. Lest Syria and Lebanon should fall altogether under Axis control, the British decided to intervene there. Consequently, Free French forces, under General Georges Catroux, with British, Australian, and Indian support, were sent into both countries from Palestine on June 8, 1941, and a week later British forces invaded Syria from Iraq. Dentz's forces put up an unexpectedly stiff resistance, particularly against the Free French, but were finally obliged to capitulate: An armistice was signed at Acre on July 14. By an arrangement of July 25 the Free French retained territorial command in Syria and Lebanon subject to strategic control by the British.

The Beginning of Lend-Lease

On June 10, 1940, when Italy entered the war on the German side and when the fall of France was imminent, U.S. president Franklin D. Roosevelt declared that the United States would "extend to the opponents of force the material resources of this nation." After France fell, he pursued this policy by aiding the British in their struggle against Germany. Roosevelt arranged for the transfer of surplus American war matériel to the British under various arrangements, including the exchange of 50 old American destroyers for certain British-held Atlantic bases, and he facilitated the placing of British orders for munitions in the United States. The British decided to rely on the United States unreservedly and without regard to their ability to pay. By December 1940 they had already placed orders for war matériel that were far more than they could possibly muster the dollar exchange to finance.

Churchill suggested the concept of lend-lease to Roosevelt in December 1940, proposing that the United States provide war matériel, foodstuffs, and clothing to the democracies (and particularly to Great Britain). Roosevelt assented, and a bill to achieve this purpose was passed by the Congress in early 1941. The Lend-Lease Act not only empowered the president to transfer defense matériel, services, and information to any foreign government whose defense he deemed vital to that of the United States but also left to his discretion what he should ask in return. An enormous grant of power, it gave Roosevelt virtually a free hand to pursue his policy of matériel aid to the "opponents of force." Congress appropriated funds generously, amounting to almost $13,000,000,000 by November 1941. Other countries besides Britain began receiving lend-lease aid by this time, including China and the Soviet Union. From the time of the German invasion of the U.S.S.R., Roosevelt had been clearly determined to aid the Soviet Union, but the American public's suspicions of Communism delayed his declaring that country eligible for lend-lease until November 1941. American deliveries of aircraft, tanks, and other supplies to the U.S.S.R. began shortly thereafter.

The Atlantic and the Mediterranean, 1940–41

At the outbreak of World War II, the primary concerns of the British navy were to defend Great Britain from invasion and to retain command of the ocean trading routes, both in order to protect the passage of essential supplies of food and raw materials for Britain and to deny the trading routes to the Axis powers, thus drawing tight once again the blockade that had proved so successful during World War I. Britain had adequate forces of battleships, aircraft carriers, cruisers, and other ships to fulfill these tasks.

The German navy's role was to protect Germany's coasts, to defend its sea communications and to attack those of the Allies, and to support land and air operations. These modest goals were in keeping with Germany's position as the dominant

A German U-boat glides through the English Channel.

CONVOY SYSTEM

Convoys consist of vessels sailing under the protection of an armed escort. Originally, convoys of merchant ships were formed as a protection against pirates. Since the 17th century, neutral powers have claimed the "right of convoy"; that is, immunity from search for neutral merchant vessels sailing under the convoy of a warship of the neutral. England, the dominant naval power, refused to recognize this right. Among states recognizing the right of convoy were the United States, Austria, and France. Great Britain deviated from its position only during the Crimean War in order to harmonize its practice with that of its French ally.

In the Declaration of London, 1909, the principal powers, including Great Britain, recognized and formalized the right of neutral convoy. The London declaration failed to enter into force, however. During World War I the right of convoy was invoked on only one or two occasions.

Convoys were to serve a totally different purpose during World War I—the protection of British merchant shipping against German surface raiders and submarines. The German practice of proclaiming as war zones large areas of the high seas and waging unrestricted submarine war on belligerent and neutral commercial shipping left the British no alternative to the practice of consolidating merchant vessels into large, protected groups, or convoys. The advantage of using convoys was that defenseless merchant vessels no longer need traverse the high seas alone and unprotected but could travel in groups large enough to justify the allocation of scarce destroyers and other patrol vessels to escort them across the Atlantic. These warships, whose guns, torpedoes, and depth charges were more than a match for any submarine, would form a protective screen or cordon around the central core of merchant vessels. In order to come within striking distance of the merchant ships, the German submarines would themselves come under the deadly guns of the escort ships.

Although the convoy system was not adopted in World War I until losses of British merchant ships became catastrophic in 1917, it then quickly proved effective.

During World War II the convoy system was developed to its fullest extent, and it played a decisive role in achieving victory against the formidable German submarine fleet formed to prey on Allied shipping. The new use of sonar, air escorts, specially designed rescue ships, and voice radio communications permitted convoys to be more easily coordinated and afforded greater protection against the new German tactics of marshalling U-boats into "wolf packs" of 8 or even 20 submarines that would intercept convoys and attack them at night en masse. The effectiveness of the convoy system during World War II can be seen in the fact that of the approximately 2,700 Allied and neutral merchant vessels sunk by submarines, less than 30 percent were torpedoed while sailing in convoy, while 60 percent were unescorted and the rest were stragglers from convoys. From 1939 to 1942, 4,435 Allied and neutral ships were lost from all causes, including U-boats. From 1943, when the convoy system became fully operational, only 1,452 Allied and neutral ships were lost. Conversely, the failure of the Imperial Japanese Navy to develop an effective convoy system led to the almost total destruction of the Japanese merchant marine by U.S. submarines from 1943 to 1945.

land-based power in continental Europe. Germany's main naval weapon during the war was to be the submarine, or U-boat, with which it attacked Allied shipping much as it had in World War I.

German control of the Biscay ports after the fall of France in June 1940 provided the U-boats with bases from which they could infest the Atlantic without having to pass either through the Channel or around the north of the British Isles at the end of every sortie. Thenceforward, so long as naval escorts for outgoing convoys from the British Isles could go only 200 or 300 miles out to sea before having to turn back to escort incoming convoys, the U-boats had a very wide field for free-ranging activity: Sinkings rose sharply from 55,580 tons in May 1940 to 352,407 tons in October, achieved mainly by solitary attacks by single U-boats at night. But the beginning of lend-lease and the freeing of British warships after the German invasion threat waned enabled the British to escort their convoys for 400 miles by October 1940 and halfway across the Atlantic by April 1941. Since air cover for shipping could also be provided from the British Isles, from Canada, and from Iceland, the Atlantic space left open to the U-boats was reduced by May 1941 to a width of only 300 miles. Moreover, British surface vessels had the ASDIC (Anti-Submarine Detection Investigation Committee) device to detect submerged U-boats. By the spring of 1941, under the guidance of Admiral Karl Dönitz, the U-boat commanders were changing their tactic of individual operation to one of wolf-pack attacks: Groups of U-boats, disposed in long lines, would rally when one of them by radio signaled a sighting and overwhelm the convoy by weight of numbers. Between July and December 1941 the German U-boat strength was raised from 65 to more than 230.

Furthermore, the German surface fleet became more active against Allied seaborne trade. Six armed German raiders disguised as merchantmen, with orders to leave convoys alone and to confine their attacks to unescorted ships, roamed the oceans with practical impunity from the spring of 1940 and had sunk 366,644 tons of shipping by the end of the year. German battleships—the *Admiral Scheer*, the *Admiral Hipper*, the *Scharnhorst*, and the *Gneisenau*—one after another began similar raiding operations, with considerable success, from October

1940, and in May 1941 a really modern battleship, the *Bismarck*, and a new cruiser, the *Prinz Eugen*, put out to sea from Germany. The *Bismarck* and the *Prinz Eugen*, however, were located by British reconnaissance in the North Sea near Bergen, and an intensive hunt for them was immediately set in motion. Tracked from a point northwest of Iceland by two British cruisers, the two German ships were engaged on May 24 by the battle cruiser *Hood* and by the new battleship *Prince of Wales*, and, though the *Hood* was sunk, the *Bismarck*'s fuel supply was put out of action so that its commander, Admiral Günther Lütjens, decided to make for the French coast. Separating from the *Prinz Eugen* (which escaped), the *Bismarck* threw off her pursuers early on May 25 but was sighted again the next day some 660 miles west of Brest. Paralyzed by torpedo aircraft from the *Ark Royal*, it was bombarded by the *King George V*, the *Rodney*, and the *Dorsetshire* on May 27 and sank.

In the Mediterranean the year 1941 ended with some naval triumphs for the Axis: U-boats torpedoed the *Ark Royal* on November 13 and the *Barham* 12 days later; Italian frogmen, entering the harbour of Alexandria, on December 19 crippled the battleships *Queen Elizabeth* and *Valiant*; and two British cruisers and a destroyer were also sunk in Mediterranean waters in December.

German Strategy, 1939–42

German strategy in World War II is wholly intelligible only if Hitler's far-reaching system of power politics and his racist ideology are borne in mind. Since the 1920s his program had been first to win power in Germany proper, next to consolidate Germany's domination over Central Europe, and then to raise Germany to the status of a world power by two stages: (1) the building up of a continental empire embracing all Europe, including the European portion of the Soviet Union, and (2) the attainment for Germany of equal rank with the British Empire, Japan, and the United States—the only world powers to be left after the elimination of France and the U.S.S.R.—through the acquisition of colonies in Africa and the construction of a strong fleet with bases on the Atlantic. In the succeeding generation Hitler foresaw a decisive conflict between Germany and the United States, during which he hoped that Great Britain would be Germany's ally.

The conquest of the European part of the Soviet Union, which in Hitler's calendar was dated approximately for 1943–45, was to be preceded, he thought, by short localized campaigns elsewhere in Europe to provide a strategic shield and to secure Germany's rear for the great expedition of conquest in the East, which was also bound up with the extermination of the Jews. The most important of the localized campaigns would be that against France. While this European program remained unfulfilled, it was imperative to avoid any world war, since only after the German Reich had come to dominate the whole European continent would it have the economic base and the territorial extent that were prerequisite for success in a great war, especially against maritime world powers.

Hitler had always contemplated the overthrow of the Soviet regime, and though he had congratulated himself on the German-Soviet Nonaggression Pact of 1939 as a matter of expediency, anti-Bolshevism had remained his most profound emotional conviction. His feelings had been stirred up afresh by the Soviet occupation of the Baltic states and of Bessarabia and northern Bukovina in June 1940 and by the consequent proximity of Soviet forces to the Romanian oil fields on which Germany depended. Hitler became acutely suspicious of the intentions of the Soviet leader, Joseph Stalin, and he began to feel that he could not afford to wait to complete the subjugation of western Europe before dealing with the Soviet Union. Hitler and his generals had originally scheduled the invasion of the U.S.S.R. for mid-May 1941, but the unforeseen necessity of invading Yugoslavia and Greece in April of that year had forced them to postpone the Soviet campaign to late June. The swiftness of Hitler's Balkan victories enabled him to keep to this revised timetable, but the five weeks' delay shortened the time for carrying out the invasion of the U.S.S.R. and was to prove the more serious because in 1941 the Russian winter would arrive earlier than usual. Nevertheless, Hitler and the heads of the Oberkommando des Heeres (OKH, or German Army High Command), namely the army commander in chief Walther von Brauchitsch and the army general staff chief Franz Halder, were convinced that the Red Army could be defeated in two or three months, and that, by the end of October, the Germans would have conquered the whole European part of Russia and Ukraine west of a line stretching from Archangel to Astrakhan. The invasion of the Soviet Union was given the code name "Operation Barbarossa."

Invasion of the Soviet Union, 1941

For the campaign against the Soviet Union, the Germans allotted almost 150 divisions containing a total of about 3,000,000 men. Among these were 19 panzer divisions, and in total the "Barbarossa" force had about 3,000 tanks, 7,000 artillery pieces, and 2,500 aircraft. It was in effect the largest and most powerful invasion force in human history. The Germans' strength was further increased by more than 30 divisions of Finnish and Romanian troops.

The Soviet Union had twice or perhaps three times the number of both tanks and aircraft as the Germans had, but their aircraft were mostly obsolete. The Soviet tanks were about equal to those of the Germans, however. A greater hindrance to Hitler's chances of victory was that the German intelligence

German troops ride into the Soviet Union as part of the launch of Operation Barbarossa.

service underestimated the troop reserves that Stalin could bring up from the depths of the U.S.S.R. The Germans correctly estimated that there were about 150 divisions in the western parts of the U.S.S.R. and reckoned that 50 more might be produced. But the Soviets actually brought up more than 200 fresh divisions by the middle of August, making a total of 360. The consequence was that, though the Germans succeeded in shattering the original Soviet armies by superior technique, they then found their path blocked by fresh ones. The effects of the miscalculations were increased because much of August was wasted while Hitler and his advisers were having long arguments as to what course they should follow after their initial victories. Another factor in the Germans' calculations was purely political, though no less mistaken; they believed that within three to six months of their invasion, the Soviet regime would collapse from lack of domestic support.

The German attack on the Soviet Union was to have an immediate and highly salutary effect on Great Britain's situation. Until then Britain's prospects had appeared hopeless in the eyes of most people except the British themselves, and the government's decision to continue the struggle after the fall of France and to reject Hitler's peace offers could spell only slow suicide unless relief came from either the United States or the U.S.S.R. Hitler brought Great Britain relief by turning eastward and invading the Soviet Union just as the strain on Britain was becoming severe.

On June 22, 1941, the German offensive was launched by three army groups under the same commanders as in the invasion of France in 1940: On the left (north), an army group under Leeb struck from East Prussia into the Baltic states toward Leningrad; on the right (south), another army group, under Rundstedt, with an armoured group under Kleist, advanced from southern Poland into Ukraine against Kiev, whence it was to wheel southeastward to the coasts of the Black Sea and the Sea of Azov; and in the centre, north of the Pripet Marshes, the main blow was delivered by Bock's army group, with one armoured group under Guderian and another under Hoth, thrusting northeastward at Smolensk and Moscow.

The invasion along a 1,800-mile front took the Soviet leadership completely by surprise and caught the Red Army in an unprepared and partially demobilized state. Piercing the northern border, Guderian's tanks raced 50 miles beyond the frontier on the first day of the invasion and were at Minsk, 200 miles beyond it, on June 27. At Minsk they converged with Hoth's tanks, which had pierced the opposite flank, but Bock's infantry could not follow up quickly enough to complete the encirclement of the Soviet troops in the area; Though 300,000 prisoners were taken in the salient, a large part of the Soviet forces was able to escape to the east. The Soviet armies were clumsily handled and frittered their tank strength away in piecemeal action like that of the French in 1940. But the isolated Soviet troops fought with a stubbornness that the French had not shown, and their resistance imposed a brake by continuing to block road centres long after the German tide had swept past them. The result was similar when Guderian's tanks, having crossed the Dnieper River on July 10, entered Smolensk six days later and converged with Hoth's thrust through Vitebsk: 200,000 Soviet prisoners were taken, but some Soviet forces were withdrawn from the trap to the line of the Desna, and a large pocket of resistance lay behind the German armour. By mid-July, moreover, a series of rainstorms were turning the sandy Russian roads into clogging mud, over which the wheeled vehicles of the German transport behind the tanks could make only very slow progress. The Germans also began to be hampered by the scorched earth policy adopted by the retreating Soviets. The Soviet troops burned crops, destroyed bridges, and evacuated factories in the face of the German advance. Entire steel and munitions plants in the westernmost portions of the U.S.S.R. were dismantled and shipped by rail to the east, where they were put back into production. The Soviets also destroyed or evacuated most of their rolling stock (railroad cars), thus depriving the Germans of the use of the Soviet rail system, since Soviet railroad track was of a different gauge than German track and German rolling stock was consequently useless on it.

Nevertheless, by mid-July the Germans had advanced more than 400 miles and were only 200 miles from Moscow. They still had ample time to make decisive gains before the onset of winter, but they lost the opportunity, primarily because of arguments throughout August between Hitler and the OKH about the destination of the next thrusts thence:

Whereas the OKH proposed Moscow as the main objective, Hitler wanted the major effort to be directed southeastward, through Ukraine and the Donets Basin into the Caucasus, with a minor swing northwestward against Leningrad (to converge with Leeb's army group).

In Ukraine, meanwhile, Rundstedt and Kleist had made short work of the foremost Soviet defenses, stronger though the latter had been. A new Soviet front south of Kiev was broken by the end of July, and in the next fortnight the Germans swept down to the Black Sea mouths of the Bug and Dnieper rivers—to converge with Romania's simultaneous offensive. Kleist was then ordered to wheel northward from Ukraine, Guderian southward from Smolensk, for a pincer movement around the Soviet forces behind Kiev, and by the end of September the claws of the encircling movement had caught 520,000 men. These gigantic encirclements were partly the fault of inept Soviet high commanders and partly the fault of Stalin, who as commander in chief stubbornly overrode the advice of his generals and ordered his armies to stand and fight instead of allowing them to retreat eastward and regroup in preparation for a counteroffensive.

Winter was approaching, and Hitler stopped Leeb's northward drive on the outskirts of Leningrad. He ordered Rundstedt and Kleist, however, to press on from the Dnieper toward the Don and the Caucasus, and Bock was to resume the advance on Moscow.

Bock's renewed advance on Moscow began on Oct. 2, 1941. Its prospects looked bright when Bock's armies brought off a great encirclement around Vyazma, where 600,000 more Soviet troops were captured. That left the Germans momentarily with an almost clear path to Moscow. But the Vyazma battle had not been completed until late October; the German troops were tired, the country became a morass as the weather got worse, and fresh

Soviet forces appeared in the path as they plodded slowly forward. Some of the German generals wanted to break off the offensive and to take up a suitable winter line. But Bock wanted to press on, believing that the Soviets were on the verge of collapse, while Brauchitsch and Halder tended to agree with his view. As that also accorded with Hitler's desire, he made no objection. The temptation of Moscow, now so close in front of their eyes, was too great for any of the topmost leaders to resist. On December 2 a further effort was launched, and some German detachments penetrated into the suburbs of Moscow, but the advance as a whole was held up in the forests covering the capital. The stemming of this last phase of the great German offensive was partly due to the effects of the Russian winter, whose subzero temperatures were the most severe in several decades. In October and November a wave of frostbite cases had decimated the ill-clad German troops, for whom provisions of winter clothing had not been made, while the icy cold paralyzed the Germans' mechanized transport, tanks, artillery, and aircraft. The Soviets, by contrast, were well clad and tended to fight more effectively in winter than did the Germans. By this time German casualties had mounted to levels that were unheard of in the campaigns against France and the Balkans; by November the Germans had suffered about 730,000 casualties.

In the south, Kleist had already reached Rostov-on-Don, gateway to the Caucasus, on November 22, but had exhausted his tanks' fuel in doing so. Rundstedt, seeing the place to be untenable, wanted to evacuate it but was overruled by Hitler. A Soviet counteroffensive recaptured Rostov on November 28, and Rundstedt was relieved of his command four days later. The Germans, however, managed to establish a front on the Mius River—as Rundstedt had recommended.

As the German drive against Moscow slackened, the Soviet commander on the Moscow front, General Georgy Konstantinovich Zhukov, on December 6 inaugurated the first great counteroffensive with strokes against Bock's right in the Elets (Yelets) and Tula sectors south of Moscow and against his centre in the Klin and Kalinin sectors to the northwest. Levies of Siberian troops, who were extremely effective fighters in cold weather, were used for these offensives. There followed a blow at the German left, in the Velikie Luki sector, and the counteroffensive, which was sustained throughout the winter of 1941–42, soon took the form of a triple convergence toward Smolensk.

These Soviet counteroffensives tumbled back the exhausted Germans, lapped around their flanks, and produced a critical situation. From generals downward, the invaders were filled with ghastly thoughts of Napoleon's retreat from Moscow. In that emergency Hitler forbade any retreat beyond the shortest possible local withdrawals. His decision exposed his troops to awful sufferings in their advanced positions facing Moscow, for they had neither the clothing nor the equipment for a Russian winter campaign, but if they had once started a general retreat it might easily have degenerated into a panic-stricken rout.

The Red Army's winter counteroffensive continued for more than three months after its December launching, though with diminishing progress. By March 1942 it had advanced more than 150 miles in some sectors. But the Germans maintained their hold on the main bastions of their winter front—such towns as Schlüsselburg, Novgorod, Rzhev, Vyazma, Bryansk, Orël (Oryol), Kursk, Kharkov, and Taganrog—despite the fact that the Soviets had often advanced many miles beyond these bastions, which were in effect cut off. In retrospect, it became clear that Hitler's veto on any extensive withdrawal worked out in such a way as to restore the confidence of the German troops and probably saved them from a widespread collapse. Nevertheless, they paid a heavy price indirectly for that rigid defense. One immediate handicap was that the strength of the Luftwaffe was drained in the prolonged effort to maintain supplies by air, under winter conditions, to the garrisons of these more or less isolated bastion towns. The tremendous strain of that winter campaign, on armies which had not been prepared for it, had other serious effects. Before the winter ended, many German divisions were reduced to barely a third of their original strength, and they were never fully built up again.

The German plan of campaign had begun to miscarry in August 1941, and its failure was patent when the Soviet counteroffensive started. Nevertheless, having dismissed Brauchitsch and appointed himself army commander in chief in December, Hitler persisted in overruling the tentative opposition of the general staff to his strategy.

The first three months of the German–Soviet conflict produced cautious rapprochements between the U.S.S.R. and Great Britain and between the U.S.S.R. and the United States. The Anglo-Soviet agreement of July 12, 1941, pledged the signatory powers to assist one another and to abstain from making any separate peace with Germany. On Aug. 25, 1941, British and Soviet forces jointly invaded Iran, to forestall the establishment of a German base there and to divide the country into spheres of occupation for the duration of the war, and late in September—at a conference in Moscow—Soviet, British, and U.S. representatives formulated the monthly quantities of supplies, including aircraft, tanks, and raw materials, that Great Britain and the United States should try to furnish to the Soviet Union.

The critical situation on the Eastern Front did not deter Hitler from declaring Germany to be at war with the United States on Dec. 11, 1941, after the Japanese attack on the U.S., British, and Dutch positions in the Pacific and in the Far East, since this extension of hostilities did not immediately commit the German land forces to any new theatre but at the same time had the merit of entitling the German navy to intensify the war at sea.

The War in the Pacific, 1938–41

In 1931–32 the Japanese had invaded Manchuria (Northeast China) and, after overcoming ineffective Chinese resistance there, had created the Japanese-controlled puppet state of Manchukuo. In the following years the Nationalist government of China, headed by Chiang Kai-shek, temporized in the face of Japanese military and diplomatic pressures and instead waged an internal war against the Chinese Communists, led by Mao Zedong, who were based in Shensi Province in north-central China. Meanwhile, the Japanese began a military buildup in North China proper, which in turn stimulated the formation of a unified resistance by the Nationalists and the Communists.

THE WAR IN CHINA, 1937–41

Overt hostilities between Japan and China began after the Marco Polo Bridge incident of July 7, 1937, when shots were exchanged between Chinese and Japanese troops on the outskirts of Peking. Open fighting broke out in that area, and in late July the Japanese captured the Peking-Tientsin area. Thereupon full-scale hostilities began between the two nations. The Japanese landed near Shanghai, at the mouth of the Yangtze River, and took Shanghai in November and the Chinese capital, Nanking, in December 1937. Chiang Kai-shek moved his government to Han-k'ou (one of the Wu-han cities), which lay 435 miles west of Shanghai along the Yangtze. The Japanese also pushed southward and westward from the Peking area into Hopeh and Shansi provinces. In 1938 the Japanese launched several ambitious military campaigns that brought them deep into the heart of central China. They advanced to the northeast and west from Nanking, taking Suchow and occupying the Wu-han cities. The Nationalists were forced to move their government to Chungking in Szechwan Province, about 500 miles west of the Wu-han cities. The Japanese also occupied Canton and several other coastal cities in South China in 1938.

Nationalist Chinese resistance to these Japanese advances was ineffective, primarily because the Nationalist leadership was still more interested in holding their forces in reserve for a future struggle with the Communists than in repelling the Japanese. By contrast, the Communists, from their base in north-central China, began an increasingly effective guerrilla war against the Japanese troops in Manchuria and North China. The Japanese needed large numbers of troops to maintain their hold on the immense Chinese territories and populations they controlled. Of the 51 infantry divisions making up the Japanese army in 1941, 38 of them, comprising about 750,000 men, were stationed in China (including Manchuria).

JAPANESE POLICY, 1939–41

When war broke out in Europe in September 1939, the Japanese, despite a series of victorious battles, had still not brought their war in China to an end: On the one hand, the Japanese strategists had made no plans to cope with the guerrilla warfare pursued by the Chinese; on the other, the Japanese commanders in the field often disregarded the orders of the supreme command at the Imperial headquarters and occupied more Chinese territory than they had been ordered to take. Half of the Japanese army was thus still tied down in China when the commitment of Great Britain and France to war against Germany opened up the prospect of wider conquests for Japan in Southeast Asia and in the Pacific. Japan's military ventures in China proper were consequently restricted rather more severely henceforth.

The German victories over the Netherlands and France in the summer of 1940 further encouraged the Japanese premier, Prince Konoe, to look southward at those defeated powers' colonies and also, of course, at the British and U.S. positions in the Far East. The island archipelago of the Dutch East Indies (now Indonesia) along with French Indochina and British-held Malaya contained raw materials (tin, rubber, petroleum) that were essential to Japan's industrial economy, and if Japan could seize these regions and incorporate them into the empire, it could make itself virtually self-sufficient economically and thus become the dominant power in the Pacific Ocean. Since Great Britain, singlehandedly, was confronting the might of the Axis in Europe, the Japanese strategists had to reckon, primarily, with the opposition of the United States to their plans for territorial aggrandizement. When Japanese troops entered northern Indochina in September 1940 (in pursuance of an agreement extorted in August from the Vichy government of France), the United States uttered a protest. Germany and Italy, by contrast, recognized Japan as the leading power in the Far East by concluding with it the Tripartite, or Axis, Pact of Sept. 27, 1940: Negotiated by Japanese foreign minister Matsuoka Yosuke, the pact pledged its signatories to come to one another's help in the event of an attack "by a power not already engaged in war." Japan also concluded a neutrality pact with the U.S.S.R. on April 13, 1941.

On July 2, 1941, the Imperial Conference decided to press the Japanese advance southward even at the risk of war with Great Britain and the United States, and this policy was pursued even when Matsuoka was relieved of office a fortnight later. On July 26, in pursuance of a new agreement with Vichy France, Japanese forces began to occupy bases in southern Indochina.

This time the United States reacted vigorously, not only freezing Japanese assets under U.S. control but also imposing an embargo on supplies of oil to Japan. Dismay at the embargo drove the Japanese naval command, which had hitherto been more moderate than the army, into collusion with the army's extremism. When negotiations with the Dutch of Indonesia for an alternative supply of oil produced no satisfaction, the Imperial Conference on September 6, at the high command's insistence, decided that war must be undertaken against the United States and Great Britain unless an understanding with the United States could be reached in a few weeks' time.

General Tojo Hideki, who succeeded Konoe as premier in mid-October 1941, continued the already desperate talks. The United States, however, persisted in making demands that Japan could not concede: renunciation of the Tripartite Pact (which would have left Japan diplomatically isolated); the withdrawal of Japanese troops from China and from Southeast Asia (a humiliating retreat from an overt commitment of four years' standing); and an open-door regime for trade in China. When Cordell Hull, the U.S. secretary of state, on Nov. 26, 1941, sent an abrupt note to the Japanese bluntly requiring them to evacuate China and Indochina and to recognize no Chinese regime other than that of Chiang Kai-shek, the Japanese could see no point in continuing the talks.

Since peace with the United States seemed impossible, Japan set in motion its plans for war, which would now necessarily be waged not only against the United States but also against Great Britain (the existing war effort of which depended on U.S. support and the Far Eastern colonies of which lay within the orbit of the projected Japanese expansion) and against the Dutch East Indies (the oil of which was essential to Japanese enterprises, even apart from geopolitical considerations).

The evolving Japanese military strategy was based on the peculiar geography of the Pacific Ocean and on the relative weakness and unpreparedness of the Allied military presence in that ocean. The western half of the Pacific is dotted with many islands, large and small, while the eastern half of the ocean is, with the exception of the Hawaiian Islands, almost devoid of landmasses (and hence of usable bases). The British, French, American, and Dutch military forces in the entire Pacific region west of Hawaii amounted to only about 350,000 troops, most of them lacking combat experience and being of disparate nationalities. Allied air power in the Pacific was weak and consisted mostly of obsolete planes. If the Japanese, with their large, well-equipped armies that had been battle-hardened in China, could quickly launch coordinated attacks from their existing bases on certain Japanese-mandated Pacific islands, on Formosa (Taiwan), and from Japan itself, they could overwhelm the Allied forces, overrun the entire western Pacific Ocean as well as Southeast Asia, and then develop those areas' resources to their own military-industrial advantage. If successful in their campaigns, the Japanese planned to establish a strongly fortified defensive perimeter extending from Burma in the west to the southern rim of the Dutch East Indies and northern New Guinea in the south and sweeping around to the Gilbert and Marshall islands in the southeast and east. The Japanese believed that any American and British counteroffensives against this perimeter could be repelled, after which those nations would eventually seek a negotiated peace that would allow Japan to keep her newly won empire.

Until the end of 1940 the Japanese strategists had assumed that any new war to be waged would be against a single enemy. When it became clear, in 1941, that the British and the Dutch as well as the Americans must be attacked, a new and daring war plan was successfully sponsored by the commander in chief of the Combined Fleet, Admiral Yamamoto Isoroku.

Yamamoto's plan prescribed two operations, together involving the whole strength of his navy, which was composed of the following ships: 10 battleships, six regular aircraft carriers, four auxiliary carriers, 18 heavy cruisers, 20 light cruisers, 112 destroyers, 65 submarines, and 2,274 combat planes. The first operation, to which all six regular aircraft carriers, two battleships, three cruisers, and 11 destroyers were allocated, was to be a surprise attack, scheduled for December 7 (December 8 by Japanese time), on the main U.S. Pacific Fleet in its base at Pearl Harbor in the Hawaiian Islands. The rest of the Japanese navy was to support the army in the "Southern Operation": 11 infantry divisions and seven tank regiments, assisted by 795 combat planes, were to undertake two drives, one from Formosa through the Philippines, the other from French Indochina and Hainan Island through Malaya, so as to converge on the Dutch East Indies, with a view to the capture of Java as the culmination of a campaign of 150 days—during which, moreover, Wake Island, Guam, the Gilbert Islands, and Burma should also have been secured as outer bastions, besides Hong Kong.

PEARL HARBOR AND THE JAPANESE EXPANSION, TO JULY 1942

In accordance with Yamamoto's plan, the aircraft carrier strike force commanded by Admiral Nagumo Chuichi sailed eastward undetected by any U.S. reconnaissance until it had reached a point 275 miles north of Hawaii. From there, on Sunday, Dec. 7, 1941, a total of about 360 aircraft, composed of dive bombers, torpedo bombers, and a few fighters, was launched in two waves in the early morning at the giant U.S. naval base at Pearl Harbor. The base at that time was accommodating 70 U.S. fighting ships, 24 auxiliaries, and some 300

A U.S. battleship sinks during the Pearl Harbor attack.

planes. The Americans were taken completely by surprise, and all eight battleships in the harbour were hit (though six were eventually repaired and returned to service); three cruisers, three destroyers, a minelayer, and other vessels were damaged; more than 180 aircraft were destroyed and others damaged (most while parked at airfields); and more than 2,330 troops were killed and over 1,140 wounded. Japanese losses were comparatively small. The Japanese attack failed in one crucial respect, however; the Pacific Fleet's three aircraft carriers were at sea at the time of the attack and escaped harm, and these were to become the nucleus of the United States' incipient

THE "BACK DOOR TO WAR" THEORY

Was there a "back door" to World War II, as some revisionist historians have asserted? According to this view, President Franklin D. Roosevelt, inhibited by the American public's opposition to direct U.S. involvement in the fighting and determined to save Great Britain from a Nazi victory in Europe, manipulated events in the Pacific in order to provoke a Japanese attack on the U.S. naval base at Pearl Harbor on Dec. 7, 1941, thereby forcing the United States to enter the war on the side of Britain.

Although there is no question that Roosevelt was concerned about public support for entering the war, this was not because he thought that he could not obtain a declaration without it—in late 1941, before the Pearl Harbor attack, he had enough votes in Congress to pass a formal declaration of war. Rather, according to most historians, his concern was that Americans would not be able to sustain such an enormous effort, with all its sacrifice of blood and treasure, unless they were united in the spirit of a moral crusade. Accordingly, in his major foreign policy decisions regarding the war in Europe in 1940–41, he was careful not to commit the country to greater involvement in the fighting than public opinion would support. The draft, the destroyer-bases exchange, the lend-lease program, convoying, and economic sanctions against Japan were all undertaken with Roosevelt's belief that the public regarded them as vital to American national security. Contrary to the revisionist view, most historians regard these incremental decisions not as attempts to drag the country into the war but rather as efforts by Roosevelt to exercise all other options, in keeping with his deep reluctance to enter the fighting without the firm support of the American public.

Although Roosevelt did admit to Winston Churchill and Soviet leader Joseph Stalin that it would have been difficult to gain public support for war without the Japanese attack, nevertheless, according to most historians, he actually tried to avoid a war with Japan throughout 1941, fearing that it would limit America's aid to Britain and lengthen the struggle against Germany. For example, in a discussion of the American embargo on Japan at a cabinet meeting on Nov. 7, 1941, he said that the administration should "strain every nerve to satisfy and keep on good relations" with Japanese negotiators. He told Secretary of State Cordell Hull not to let the talks "deteriorate and break up if you can possibly help it. Let us make no move of ill will. Let us do nothing to precipitate a crisis."

Roosevelt and his advisers did foresee a Japanese military action on December 6–7. Nevertheless, most historians agree that they did not know where the attack would come. Intercepted Japanese diplomatic and military messages indicated an attack somewhere, but information suggesting that the target would be British, Dutch, or French possessions in Southeast Asia obscured other information suggesting Pearl Harbor. Moreover, as most historians point out, it is implausible to think that Roosevelt, a former assistant secretary of the navy, would have exposed so much of the U.S. fleet to destruction at Pearl Harbor had he known an assault was coming. If his only purpose was to use a Japanese attack to bring the United States into the war, he could have done so with the loss of just a few destroyers and some airplanes. In fact, he was genuinely surprised by the target, if not the timing, of the Japanese attack. According to one scholar, Roberta Wohlstetter, this was partly the consequence of a tendency among U.S. military leaders to see the fleet in Hawaii as a deterrent rather than a target. It was also the result of a failure by U.S. military intelligence to measure Japanese capabilities accurately: The Americans did not believe that Japanese air and naval forces could mount a successful attack on U.S. bases in Hawaii.

Most historians believe that there was no back door to war and no conspiracy to trick the American public into a conflict

> it did not wish to fight in either Europe or Asia. American involvement in World War II, they argue, was the consequence of the country's rise to global power and the resulting need to combat aggressive, undemocratic regimes that were hostile to American institutions and to the survival of the United States as a free country. However, the controversy has continued to be relevant in American political debate. Despite suggestions that Congress was validating the theory, its defense authorization bill in 2000 included a provision that would absolve Admiral Husband Kimmel and General Walter Short, the military commanders at Pearl Harbor, of any blame for Japan's attack, declaring that they were not "provided necessary and critical intelligence that would have alerted them to prepare for the attack."

naval defense in the Pacific. Pearl Harbor's shore installations and oil-storage facilities also escaped damage. The Pearl Harbor attack, unannounced beforehand by the Japanese as it was, unified the American public and swept away any remaining support for American neutrality in the war. On December 8 the U.S. Congress declared war on Japan with only one dissenting vote.

On the day of the attack, December 8 by local time, Formosa-based Japanese bombers struck Clark and Iba airfields in the Philippines, destroying more than 50 percent of the U.S. Army's Far East aircraft, and, two days later, further raids destroyed not only more U.S. fighters but also Cavite Naval Yard, likewise in the Philippines. Part of the U.S. Asiatic Fleet, however, had already gone south in November, and the surviving major ships and bomber aircraft, which were vulnerable for lack of fighter protection, were withdrawn in the next fortnight to safety in bases in Java and Australia.

Japanese forces began to land on the island of Luzon in the Philippines on December 10. The main assault, consisting of the bulk of one division, was made at Lingayen Gulf, 100 miles north-northwest of Manila, on December 22, and a second large landing took place south of Manila two days later. Manila itself fell unopposed to the Japanese on Jan. 2, 1942, but by that time the U.S. and Filipino forces under General Douglas MacArthur were ready to hold Bataan Peninsula (across the bay from Manila) and Corregidor Island (in the bay). The Japanese attack on Bataan was halted initially, but it was reinforced in the following eight weeks. MacArthur was ordered to Australia on March 11, leaving Bataan's defense to Lieutenant General Jonathan M. Wainwright. The latter and his men surrendered on April 9; Corregidor fell in the night of May 5–6; and the southern Philippines capitulated three days later.

Japanese bombers had already destroyed British air power at Hong Kong on Dec. 8, 1941, and the British and Canadian defenders surrendered to the ground attack from the Kowloon Peninsula (the nearest mainland) on December 25. To secure their flank while pushing southward into Malaya, the Japanese also occupied Bangkok on December 9 and Victoria Point in southernmost Burma on December 16. The Japanese landings in Malaya, from December 8 onward, accompanied as they were by air strikes, overwhelmed the small Australian and Indian forces, and the British battleship *Prince of Wales* and the battle cruiser *Repulse*, sailing from Singapore to cut Japanese communications, were sunk by Japanese aircraft on December 10. By the end of January 1942, two Japanese divisions, with air and armoured support, had occupied all Malaya except Singapore Island. In Burma, meanwhile, other Japanese troops had taken Moulmein and were approaching Rangoon and Mandalay.

On the eastern perimeter of the war zone, the Japanese had bombed Wake Island on December 8, attempted to capture it on December 11, and achieved a landing on December 23, quickly subduing the garrison. Guam had already fallen on December 10. Having also occupied Makin and Tarawa in the Gilbert Islands in the first days of the war, the Japanese successfully attacked Rabaul, the strategic base on New Britain (now part of Papua New Guinea), on Jan. 23, 1942.

A unified American–British–Dutch–Australian Command, ABDACOM, under Wavell, responsible for holding Malaya, Sumatra, Java, and the approaches to Australia, became operative on Jan. 15, 1942, but the Japanese had already begun their advance on the oil-rich Dutch East Indies. They occupied Kuching (December 17), Brunei Bay (January 6), and Jesselton (January 11), on the northern coast of Borneo, as well as Tarakan Island (off northeastern Borneo) and points on Celebes. Balikpapan (on Borneo's east coast) and Kendari (in southeastern Celebes) fell to the Japanese on January 24, 1942, Amboina on February 4, Makasar City (in southwestern Celebes) on February 8, and Bandjarmasin (in southern Borneo) on February 16. Bali was invaded on February 18, and by February 24 the Japanese were also in possession of Timor.

THE FALL OF SINGAPORE

Meanwhile, on February 8 and 9, three Japanese divisions had landed on Singapore Island, and on February 15 they forced the 90,000-strong British, Australian, and Indian garrison there, under Lieutenant General A.E. Percival, to surrender. Singapore was the major British base in the Pacific and had been regarded as unassailable due to its strong seaward defenses. The Japanese took it with comparative ease by advancing down the Malay Peninsula and then assaulting the base's landward side, which the British had left inadequately defended. On February 13, moreover, Japanese paratroopers had landed at Palembang in Sumatra, which fell to an amphibious assault three days later.

When ABDACOM was dissolved on Feb. 25, 1942, only Java remained to complete the Japanese program of conquest. The Allies' desperate attempt to intercept the Japanese invasion fleet was defeated in the seven-hour Battle of the Java Sea on February 27, in which five Allied warships were lost and only one Japanese destroyer damaged. The Japanese landed at three points on Java on February 28 and rapidly expanded their beachheads. On March 9 the 20,000 Allied troops in Java surrendered. In the Indian Ocean, the Japanese captured the Andaman Islands on March 23 and began a series of attacks on British shipping. After the failure of ABDACOM, the U.S.–British Combined Chiefs of Staff placed the Pacific under the U.S. Joint Chiefs' strategic direction. MacArthur became supreme commander of the Southwest Pacific Area, which comprised the Dutch East Indies (less Sumatra), the Philippines, Australia, the Bismarck Archipelago, and the Solomons, and Admiral Chester W. Nimitz became commander in chief of the Pacific Ocean Areas, which comprised virtually every area not under MacArthur. Their missions were to hold the U.S.–Australia line of communications, to contain the Japanese within the Pacific, to support the defense of North America, and to prepare for major amphibious counteroffensives.

Japan's initial war plans were realized with the capture of Java. But despite their military triumphs, the Japanese saw no indication that the Allies were ready for a negotiated peace. On the contrary, it seemed evident that an Allied counterstroke was in the making. The U.S. Pacific Fleet bombed the Marshall Islands on Feb. 1, 1942, Wake Island on February 23, and Marcus Island (between Wake and Japan) on March 1. These moves, together with the bombing of Rabaul on February 23 and the establishment of bases in Australia and a line of communications across the South Pacific, made the Japanese decide to expand so as to cut the Allied line of communications to Australia. They planned to occupy New Caledonia, the Fiji Islands, and Samoa and also to seize eastern New Guinea, whence they would threaten Australia from an air base to be established at Port Moresby. They planned also to capture Midway Island in the North Pacific and to establish air bases in the Aleutians. In pursuance of this new program, Japanese troops occupied Lae and Salamaua in New Guinea and Buka in the Solomon Islands in March 1942 and Bougainville in the Solomons and the Admiralty Islands (north of New Guinea) early in April.

Something to raise the Allies' morale was achieved on April 18, 1942, when 16 U.S. bombers raided Tokyo—though they did little real damage except to the Japanese government's prestige. Far more important were the consequences of the U.S. intelligence services' detection of Japanese plans to seize Port Moresby and Tulagi (in the southern Solomons). Had these two places fallen, Japanese aircraft could have dominated the Coral Sea. In the event, after U.S. aircraft on May 3, 1942, had interfered with the Japanese landing on Tulagi, U.S. naval units, with aircraft, challenged the Japanese ships on their circuitous detour from Rabaul to Port Moresby. On May 5 and 6 the opposing carrier groups sought each other out, and the four-day Battle of the Coral Sea ensued. On May 7 planes from the Japanese carriers sank a U.S. destroyer and an oil tanker, but U.S. planes sank the Japanese light carrier *Shoho* and a cruiser, and the next day, though Japanese aircraft sank the U.S. carrier *Lexington* and damaged the carrier *Yorktown*, the large Japanese carrier *Shokaku* had to retire crippled. Finally, the Japanese lost so many planes in the battle that their enterprise against Port Moresby had to be abandoned.

Despite the mixed results of the Battle of the Coral Sea, the Japanese continued with their plan to seize Midway Island. Seeking a naval showdown with the remaining ships of the U.S. Pacific Fleet and counting on their own numerical superiority to secure a victory, the Japanese mustered four heavy and three light aircraft carriers, two seaplane carriers, 11 battleships, 15 cruisers, 44 destroyers, 15 submarines, and miscellaneous small vessels. The U.S. Pacific Fleet had only three heavy carriers, eight cruisers, 18 destroyers, and 19 submarines, though there were some 115 aircraft in support of it. The Americans, however, had the incomparable advantage of knowing the intentions of the Japanese in advance, thanks to the U.S. intelligence services' having broken the Japanese navy's code and deciphered key radio transmissions. In the ensuing Battle of Midway, the Japanese ships destined to take Midway Island were attacked while still 500 miles from their target by U.S. bombers on June 3. The Japanese carriers were still able to launch their aircraft against Midway early on June 4, but in the ensuing battle, waves of carrier- and Midway-based U.S. bombers sank all four of the Japanese heavy carriers and one heavy cruiser. Appalled by this disaster, the Japanese began to retreat in the night of June 4–5. Though the U.S. carrier *Yorktown* was sunk by torpedo on June 6, Midway was saved from invasion. In the Aleutians, the Japanese bombed Dutch Harbor effectively and on June 7 occupied Attu and Kiska.

The Battle of Midway was probably the turning point of the war in the Pacific, for Japan lost its first-line carrier strength and most of its navy's best trained pilots. Henceforth, the naval strengths of the Japanese and of the Allies were virtually equal. Having lost the strategic initiative, Japan canceled its plans to invade New Caledonia, Fiji, and Samoa.

THE CHINESE FRONT AND BURMA, 1941–42

Japan's entry into war against the Western Allies had its repercussions in China. Chiang Kai-shek's government on Dec. 9, 1941, formally declared war not only against Japan (a formality long overdue) but also, with political rather than military intent, against Germany and Italy. Three Chinese armies were rushed to the Burmese frontier, since the Burma Road was the only land route whereby the Western Allies could send supplies to the Nationalist Chinese government. On Jan. 3, 1942, Chiang was recognized as supreme Allied commander for the China theatre of war, and a U.S. general, Joseph W. Stilwell, was sent to him to be his chief of staff. In the first eight weeks after Pearl Harbor, however, the major achievement of the Chinese was the definitive repulse, on Jan. 15, 1942, of a long-sustained Japanese drive against Ch'ang-sha, on the Canton–Han-k'ou railway.

Thereafter, Chiang and Stilwell were largely preoccupied by efforts to check the Japanese advance into Burma. By mid-March 1942 two Chinese armies, under Stilwell's command, had crossed the Burmese frontier, but before the end of the month the Chinese force defending Toungoo, in central Burma between Rangoon and Mandalay, was nearly annihilated by the more soldierly Japanese. British and Indian units in Burma fared scarcely better, being driven into retreat by the enemy's numerical superiority both in the air and on the ground. On April 29 the Japanese took Lashio, the Burma Road's southern terminus, thus cutting the supply line to China and turning the Allies' northern flank. Under continued pressure, the British and Indian forces in the following month fell back through Kalewa to Imphal (across the Indian border), while most of the Chinese retreated across the Salween River into China. By the end of

1942 all of Burma was in Japanese hands, China was effectively isolated (except by air), and India was exposed to the danger of a Japanese invasion through Burma.

Since the U.S. bombers that raided Tokyo on April 18 flew on to Chinese airfields, particularly to those in Chekiang (the coastal province south of Shanghai), the Japanese reacted by launching a powerful offensive to seize those airfields. By the end of July they had generally achieved their objectives.

CHAPTER 5

DEVELOPMENTS FROM AUTUMN 1941 TO AUTUMN 1943

Within a year after American entry into the war Axis power crested and began to ebb, for critical battles were fought in 1942 in every major theatre. The year also saw the forging of a Grand Alliance among the United States, Britain, and the U.S.S.R. and the first sign of disagreement on strategy and war aims. After Pearl Harbor, Churchill requested an immediate conference with Roosevelt.

Allied Strategy and Controversies, 1940–42

In the year following the collapse of France in June 1940, British strategists, relying as they could on supplies from the nonbelligerent United States, were concerned first with home defense, second with the security of the British positions in the Middle East, and third with the development of a war of attrition against the Axis powers, pending the buildup of adequate forces for an invasion of the European continent. For the United States, President Roosevelt's advisers, from November 1940, based their strategic plans on the "Europe first" principle; that is to say, if the United States became engaged in war simultaneously against Germany, Italy, and Japan, merely defensive operations should be conducted in the Pacific (to protect at least the Alaska–Hawaii–Panama triangle) while an offensive was being mounted in Europe.

Japan's entry into the war terminated the nonbelligerency of the United States. The three weeks' conference, named Arcadia, that Roosevelt, Churchill, and their advisers opened in Washington, D.C., on Dec. 22, 1941, reassured the British about U.S. maintenance of the "Europe first" principle and also produced two plans: a tentative one, code-named "Sledgehammer," for the buildup of an offensive force in Great Britain, in case it should be decided to invade France, and another, code-named "Super-Gymnast," for combining a British landing behind the German forces in Libya (already planned under the code name "Gymnast") with a U.S. landing near Casablanca on the Atlantic coast of Morocco. The same conference furthermore created the machinery of the Combined Chiefs of Staff, where the British Chiefs of Staff Committee was to be linked continuously, through delegates in Washington, D.C., with the newly established U.S. Joint Chiefs of Staff Organization, so that all aspects of the war could be studied in concert. It was on Jan. 1, 1942, during the Arcadia Conference, that the Declaration of the United Nations was signed in Washington, D.C., as a collective statement of the Allies' war aims in sequel to the Atlantic Charter.

Meanwhile, Churchill became anxious to do something to help the embattled Soviets—who were clamouring for the United States and Britain to invade continental Europe so as to take some of the German pressure off the Eastern Front. Roosevelt was no less conscious than Churchill of the fact that the Soviet Union was bearing by far the greatest burden of the war against Germany, and this consideration inclined him to listen to the arguments of his Joint Chiefs of Staff Organization for a change of plan. After some hesitation, he sent his

Developments from Autumn 1941 to Autumn 1943

confidant Harry Hopkins and his army chief of staff General George C. Marshall to London in April 1942 to suggest the scrapping of "Super-Gymnast" in favour of "Bolero," namely the concentration of forces in Great Britain for a landing in Europe (perhaps at Brest or at Cherbourg) in the autumn; then "Roundup," an invasion of France by 30 U.S. and 18 British divisions, could follow in April 1943. The British agreed but soon began to doubt the practicability of mounting an amphibious invasion of France at such an early date.

Attempts to conclude an Anglo-Soviet political agreement were renewed without result, but a 20-year Anglo-Soviet alliance was signed on May 26, 1942, and, though Churchill warned the Soviet foreign minister, Vyacheslav Mikhaylovich Molotov, not to expect an early second front in Europe, Molotov seemed gratified by what he was told about Anglo-U.S. plans.

Visiting Roosevelt again in the latter part of June 1942, Churchill at Hyde Park, New York, and in Washington, D.C., pressed for a revised and enlarged joint operation in North Africa before the end of the year, instead of a buildup for the invasion of France, but the U.S. Joint Chiefs resolutely upheld the latter plan. After further debate and disagreement, in July the U.S. Joint Chiefs yielded at last to British obstinacy in favour of a North African enterprise: It was decided that "Torch," as this combined Anglo-U.S. operation came to be called, should begin the following autumn.

Already, on July 17, 1942, Churchill had had to notify Stalin that convoys of Allied supplies to northern Russia must be suspended because of German submarine activity on the Arctic sea route (on June 2 a convoy from Iceland had lost 23 out of 34 vessels). Consequently, it was more awkward to inform Stalin that there would be no second front in Europe before 1943. In mid-August 1942, when Churchill went to Moscow to break the news, Stalin raged against the retreat from the plan for a second front in Europe but had to admit the military logic of "Torch."

Libya and Egypt, Autumn 1941–Summer 1942

In the Western Desert, a major offensive against Rommel's front was undertaken on Nov. 18, 1941, by the British 8th Army, commanded by Cunningham under the command in chief of Wavell's successor in the Middle East, General Sir Claude Auchinleck. The offensive was routed. General Neil Methuen Ritchie took Cunningham's place on November 25, still more tanks were brought up, and a fortnight's resumed pressure constrained Rommel to evacuate Cyrenaica and to retreat to Agedabia. There, however, Rommel was at last, albeit meagrely, reinforced, and, after repulsing a British attack on December 26, he prepared a counteroffensive. When the British still imagined his forces to be hopelessly crippled, he attacked on Jan. 21, 1942, and, by a series of strokes, drove the 8th Army back to the Gazala–Bir Hakeim line, just west of Tobruk.

Both sides were subsequently further reinforced. Then, on the night of May 26–27, Rommel passed around Ritchie's southern flank with his three German divisions and two Italian ones, leaving only four Italian divisions to face the Gazala line. Though at first Rommel did some damage to the British tanks as they came into action piecemeal from a weak position, he failed to break through to the coast behind Gazala. In a single day one-third of Rommel's tank force was lost, and, after another unsuccessful effort to reach the coast, he decided, on May 29, to take up a defensive position.

The new German position, aptly known as the Cauldron, seemed indeed to be perilously exposed, and throughout the

Developments from Autumn 1941 to Autumn 1943

first days of June the British attacked it continually from the air and from the ground, imagining that Rommel's armour was caught at last. The British tanks, however, persisted in making direct assaults in small groups against the Cauldron and were beaten off with very heavy losses, and Rommel, meanwhile, secured his rear and his line of supply by overwhelming several isolated British positions to the south.

Whereas in May 1942 the British had had 700 tanks, with 200 more in reserve, against Rommel's 525, by June 10 their present armoured strength was reduced, through their wasteful tactics against the Cauldron, to 170, and most of the reserve was exhausted. Suddenly then, on June 11, Rommel struck eastward, to catch most of the remaining British armour in the converging fire of two panzer divisions. By nightfall on June 13 the British had barely 70 tanks left, and Rommel, with some 150 still fit for action, was master of the battlefield.

British troops fire heavy artillery at Tobruk during a night campaign against Rommel's forces.

The British on June 14 began a precipitate retreat from the Gazala line toward the Egyptian frontier. A garrison of 33,000 men, however, with an immense quantity of matériel, was left behind in Tobruk—on the retention of which Churchill characteristically and most unfortunately insisted in successive telegrams from London. Rommel's prompt reduction of Tobruk, achieved on June 21, 1942, was felt by Great Britain as a national disaster second only to the loss of Singapore, and 80 percent of the transport with which Rommel chased the remnant of the 8th Army eastward consisted of captured British vehicles.

At this point Auchinleck relieved Ritchie of his command and in a realistic and soldierly way ordered a general British retreat back to the Alamein area. By June 30 the German tanks were pressing against the British positions between el-Alamein (al-'Alamayn) and the Qattara Depression, some 60 miles west of Alexandria, after an advance of more than 350 miles from Gazala. Hitler and Mussolini could expect that within a matter of days Rommel would be the master of Egypt.

The ensuing First Battle of el-Alamein, which lasted throughout July 1942, marked the end of the German hopes of a rapid victory. Rommel's troops, having come so far and so fast, were exhausted; their first assaults failed to break the defense rallied by Auchinleck; and they were also subjected to disconcerting counterstrokes. At this point, the respite that Rommel had to grant to his men gave Auchinleck time to bring up reinforcements. By the end of July Rommel knew that it was he rather than Auchinleck who was now on the defensive.

Auchinleck had saved Egypt by halting Rommel's invasion, but his counterattacks had not driven it back. Early in August, when Churchill arrived in Cairo to review the situation, Auchinleck insisted on postponing the resumption of

Developments from Autumn 1941 to Autumn 1943

the offensive until September so that his new forces could be properly acclimatized and trained for desert warfare. Impatient of this delay, Churchill removed Auchinleck from the command in chief in the Middle East and gave the post to General Sir Harold Alexander, while the command of the 8th Army was transferred eventually (after the sudden death of Churchill's first nominee) to General Bernard Law Montgomery. Paradoxically, Montgomery postponed the resumption of the offensive even longer than Auchinleck had desired.

While the British in the course of August raised their strength in armour at the front to some 700 tanks, Rommel received only meagre reinforcement in the shape of infantry. He had, however, about 200 gun-armed German tanks and also 240 Italian tanks (of an obsolete model). With this armament, in the night of Aug. 30–31, 1942, he launched a fresh attack, intending to capture by surprise the minefields on the southern sector of the British front and then to drive eastward with his armour for some 30 miles before wheeling north into the 8th Army's supply area on the coast. In the event, the minefields proved unexpectedly deep, and by daybreak Rommel's spearhead was only eight miles beyond them. Delayed on their eastward drive and already under attack from the air, the two German panzer divisions of the Afrika Korps had to make their wheel to the north at a much shorter distance from the breach than Rommel had planned. Their assault thus ran mainly into the position held by the British 22nd Armoured Brigade, to the southwest of the ridge 'Alam al-Halfa'. Shortage of fuel on the German side and reinforced defense on the British, together with intensification of the British bombing, spelled the defeat of the offensive, and Rommel on September 2 decided to make a gradual withdrawal.

The Germans' Summer Offensive in Southern Russia, 1942

The German plan to launch another great summer offensive crystallized in the early months of 1942. Hitler's decision was influenced by his economists, who mistakenly told him that Germany could not continue the war unless it obtained petroleum supplies from the Caucasus. Hitler was the more responsive to such arguments because they coincided with his belief that another German offensive would so drain the Soviet Union's manpower that the U.S.S.R. would be unable to continue the war. His thinking was shared by his generals, who had been awed by the prodigality with which the Soviets squandered their troops in the fighting of 1941 and the spring of 1942. By this time at least 4,000,000 Soviet troops had been killed, wounded, or captured, while German casualties totaled only 1,150,000.

In the early summer of 1942 the German southern line ran from Orël southward east of Kursk, through Belgorod, and east of Kharkov down to the loop of the Soviet salient opposite Izyum, beyond which it veered southeastward to Taganrog, on the northern coast of the Sea of Azov. Before the Germans were ready for their principal offensive, the Red Army in May started a drive against Kharkov, but this premature effort actually served the Germans' purposes, since it not only preempted the Soviet reserves but also provoked an immediate counterstroke against its southern flank, where the Germans broke into the salient and reached the Donets River near Izyum. The Germans captured 240,000 Soviet prisoners in the encirclement that followed. In May also the Germans drove the Soviet defenders of the Kerch Peninsula out of Crimea, and on June 3 the Germans began an assault against Sevastopol, which, however, held out for a month.

Developments from Autumn 1941 to Autumn 1943

The Germans' crossing of the Donets near Izyum on June 10, 1942, was the prelude to their summer offensive, which was launched at last on June 28: Field Marshal Maximilian von Weichs's Army Group B, from the Kursk–Belgorod sector of the front, struck toward the middle Don River opposite Voronezh, whence General Friedrich Paulus' 6th Army was to wheel southeastward against Stalingrad (Volgograd), and List's Army Group A, from the front south of Kharkov, with Kleist's 1st Panzer Army, struck toward the lower Don to take Rostov and to thrust thence northeastward against Stalingrad as well as southward into the vast oil fields of Caucasia. Army Group B swept rapidly across a 100-mile stretch of plain to the Don and captured Voronezh on July 6. The 1st Panzer Army drove 250 miles from its starting line and captured Rostov on July 23. Once his forces had reached Rostov, Hitler decided to split his troops so that they could both invade the rest of the Caucasus and take the important industrial city of Stalingrad on the Volga River, 220 miles northeast of Rostov. This decision was to have fatal consequences for the Germans, since they lacked the resources to successfully take and hold both of these objectives.

Maikop (Maykup), the great oil centre 200 miles south of Rostov, fell to Kleist's right-hand column on August 9, and Pyatigorsk, 150 miles east of Maikop, fell to his centre on the same day, while the projected thrust against Stalingrad, in the opposite direction from Rostov, was being developed. Shortage of fuel, however, slowed the pace of Kleist's subsequent southeastward progress through the Caucasian mountains, and, after forcing a passage over the Terek River near Mozdok early in September, he was halted definitively just south of that river. From the end of October 1942 the Caucasian front was stabilized, but the titanic struggle for Stalingrad, draining manpower that might have won victory for the Germans in Caucasia, was to rage on, fatefully, for three more months. Already, however, it was evident that Hitler's new offensive had fallen short of its objectives, and the scapegoat this time was Halder, who was superseded by Kurt Zeitzler as chief of the army general staff.

The Allies' First Decisive Successes

In the Pacific, the naval Battle of Midway in June, the landing of U.S. forces on Guadalcanal in August, and the creation of an "island-hopping" strategy against Japan's sudden and far-flung empire similarly blunted the string of the Axis' early victories. Meanwhile, General Douglas MacArthur rallied Allied forces in Australia in anticipation of fulfilling his departing promise to the Filipinos: "I shall return." A Japanese invasion force landed near Gona at the southeastern end of New Guinea in July 1942 and drove Australian troops back to within 32 miles of Port Moresby. But MacArthur executed a series of landings behind the Japanese and secured the entire Papuan coast by late January 1943. Thenceforth Japan, too, went on the strategic defensive.

THE PACIFIC AND OTHER FRONTS, JULY 1942–MAY 1943

On July 2, 1942, the U.S. Joint Chiefs of Staff ordered limited offensives in three stages to recapture the New Britain–New Ireland–Solomons–eastern New Guinea area: first, the seizure of Tulagi and of the Santa Cruz Islands, with adjacent positions; second, the occupation of the central and northern Solomons and of the northeast coast of New Guinea; third, the seizure of Rabaul and of other points in the Bismarck Archipelago.

U.S. Marines charge onto shore on Guadalcanal in the first major Pacific offensive by Allied forces.

On July 6 the Japanese landed troops on Guadalcanal, one of the southern Solomons, and began to construct an air base. The Allied high command, fearing further Japanese advances southeastward, sped into the area to dislodge the enemy and to obtain a base for later advances toward Japan's main base in the theatre, Rabaul. The U.S. 1st Marine Division poured ashore on August 7 and secured Guadalcanal's airfield, Tulagi's harbour, and neighbouring islands by dusk on August 8—the Pacific war's first major Allied offensive. During the night of August 8–9, Japanese cruisers and destroyers, attempting to hold Guadalcanal, sank four U.S. cruisers, themselves sustaining one cruiser sunk and one damaged and later sunk. On August 23–25, in the Battle of the Eastern Solomons, the Japanese lost a light carrier, a destroyer, and a submarine and sustained damage to a cruiser and to a seaplane carrier but sank an Allied destroyer and crippled a cruiser. On August 31 another U.S. carrier was disabled, and on September 15 Japanese submarines sank the carrier *Wasp* and damaged a battleship. Meanwhile, more than 6,000 Japanese reinforced their Guadalcanal garrison, attacking the Marines' beachhead on August 20–21 and on September 12–14. On September 18 some U.S. reinforcements arrived, and mid-October saw about 22,000 Japanese ranged against 23,000 U.S. troops. The sea battles of Cape Esperance and of the Santa Cruz Islands—in which two Japanese cruisers and two destroyers were sunk and three carriers and two destroyers damaged in return for the loss of one U.S. carrier and two destroyers, besides damage to six other Allied ships—thwarted an attempt to reinforce further the Japanese ground troops, whose attack proved a failure (October 20–29).

After October, Allied strength was built up. Another Japanese attempt at counter-reinforcement led to the naval Battle of Guadalcanal, fought on November 13–15: It cost Japan two battleships, three destroyers, one cruiser, two submarines, and 11 transports and the Allies (now under Admiral William F. Halsey) two cruisers and seven destroyers sunk and one battleship and one cruiser damaged. Only 4,000 Japanese troops out of 12,500 managed to reach land, without equipment, and on November 30 eight Japanese destroyers, attempting to land more troops, were beaten off in the Battle of Tassafaronga, losing one destroyer sunk and one crippled, at an Allied cost of one cruiser sunk and three damaged.

By Jan. 5, 1943, Guadalcanal's Allied garrison totaled 44,000, against 22,500 Japanese. The Japanese decided to evacuate the position, carrying away 12,000 men in early February in daring destroyer runs. In ground warfare Japanese losses were more than 24,000 for the Guadalcanal campaign, Allied losses about 1,600 killed and 4,250 wounded (figures that ignore the higher number of casualties from disease). On February 21, U.S. infantry began occupying the Russell Islands, to support advances on Rabaul.

Earlier, before Allied plans to secure eastern New Guinea had been implemented, the Japanese had landed near Gona on the north coast of Papua (the southeastern extremity of the great island) on July 24, 1942, in an attempt to reach Port Moresby overland, via the Kokoda Trail. Advanced Japanese units from the north, despite Australian opposition, had reached a ridge 32 miles from Port Moresby by mid-September. Then, however, they had to withdraw exhausted to Gona and to nearby Buna, where there were some 7,500 Japanese assembled by November 18. The next day U.S. infantry attacked them there. Each side was subsequently reinforced, but the Australians took Gona on December 9 and the Americans Buna village on December 14. Buna government station fell to the Allies on Jan. 2, 1943, Sanananda on January 18, and all Japanese resistance in Papua ceased on January 22.

The retaking of Guadalcanal and Papua ended the Japanese drive south, and communications with Australia and New Zealand were now secure. Altogether, Papua cost Japan nearly 12,000 killed and 350 captured. Allied losses were 3,300 killed and 5,500 wounded. Allied air forces had played a particularly important role, interdicting Japanese supply lines and transporting Allied supplies and reinforcements.

Japan, having lost Guadalcanal, fought henceforth defensively, with worsening prospects. Its final effort to reinforce the Lae–Salamaua position in New Guinea from the stronghold of Rabaul was a disaster: In the Battle of the Bismarck Sea, on March 2–4, 1943, the Japanese lost four destroyers and eight transports, and only 1,000 of the 7,000 troops reached their destination. On March 25 the Japanese army and navy high commands agreed on a policy of strengthening the defense of strategic points and of counterattacking wherever possible, priority being given to the defense of the remaining Japanese positions in New Guinea, with secondary emphasis on the Solomon Islands. In the following three weeks, however, the Allies improved their own position in New Guinea, and Japanese intervention was confined to air attacks. Before the end of April, moreover, the Japanese navy sustained a disaster: The guiding genius of the Japanese war effort, Yamamoto, was sent late in March to command the forces based on Rabaul but was killed in an American air ambush on a flight to Bougainville.

Developments of the Allies' war against Japan also took place outside the southwest Pacific area. British forces in the summer of 1942 invaded Vichy French-held Madagascar. A renewed British offensive in September 1942 overran the island; hostilities ceased on November 5, and a Free French administration of Madagascar took office on Jan. 8, 1943. In the North Pacific, meanwhile, the United States had decided to expel the Japanese from the Aleutians. Having landed forces on Adak in August 1942, they began air attacks against Kiska and Attu from Adak the next month and from Amchitka also in the following January, while a naval blockade prevented the Japanese from reinforcing their garrisons. Finally, U.S. troops, bypassing Kiska, invaded Attu on May 11, 1943—to kill most of the island's 2,300 defenders in three weeks of fighting. The Japanese then evacuated Kiska. Bases in the Aleutians thenceforth facilitated the Allies' bombing of the Kuril Islands.

BURMA, AUTUMN 1942–SUMMER 1943

On the Burmese front the Allies found they could do little to dislodge the Japanese from their occupation of that country, and what little the Allies did attempt proved abortive. Brigadier

General Orde Wingate's "Chindits," which were long-range penetration groups depending on supplies from the air, crossed the Chindwin River in February 1943 and were initially successful in severing Japanese communications on the railroad between Mandalay and Myitkyina. But the Chindits soon found themselves in unfavourable terrain and in grave danger of encirclement, and so they made their way back to India.

In May 1943, however, the Allies reorganized their system of command for Southeast Asia. Vice Admiral Lord Louis Mountbatten was appointed supreme commander of the South East Asia Command (SEAC), and Stilwell was appointed deputy to Mountbatten. Stilwell at the same time was chief of staff to Chiang Kai-shek. The British–Indian forces destined for Burma meanwhile constituted the 14th Army, under Lieutenant General William Slim, whose operational control Stilwell agreed to accept. Shortly afterward, Auchinleck succeeded Wavell as commander in chief in India.

MONTGOMERY'S BATTLE OF EL-ALAMEIN AND ROMMEL'S RETREAT, 1942–43

While Churchill was still chafing in London about his generals' delay in resuming the offensive in Egypt, Montgomery waited for seven weeks after 'Alam al-Halfa' in order to be sure of success. He finally chose to begin his attack in the night of Oct. 23–24, 1942, when there would be moonlight for the clearing of gaps in the German minefields.

By mid-October the British 8th Army had 230,000 men and 1,230 gun-armed tanks ready for action, while the German–Italian forces numbered only 80,000 men, with only 210 tanks of comparable quality ready, and in air support the British enjoyed a superiority of 1,500 to 350. Allied air and submarine attacks on the Axis supply lines across the Mediterranean, moreover, had prevented Rommel's army from receiving adequate replenishments of fuel, ammunition, and food, and Rommel himself, who had been ill before 'Alam al-Halfa', was convalescing in Austria.

The British launched their infantry attack at el-Alamein at 10:00 PM on Oct. 23, 1942, but found the German minefields harder to clear than they had foreseen. Two days later, however, some of those tanks were deploying six miles beyond the original front. When Rommel, ordered back to Africa by Hitler, reached the front in the evening of October 25, half of the Germans' available armour was already destroyed. Nevertheless, the impetus of the British onslaught was stopped the next day, when German antitank guns took a heavy toll of armour trying to deepen the westward penetration. In the night of October 28 Montgomery turned the offensive northward from the wedge, but this drive likewise miscarried. In the first week of their offensive the British lost four times as many tanks as the Germans but still had 800 available against the latter's remaining 90.

When Montgomery switched the British line of attack back to its original direction, early on Nov. 2, 1942, Rommel was no longer strong enough to withstand him. After expensive resistance throughout the daytime, he ordered a retreat to Fūka (Fūkah), but in the afternoon of November 3 the retreat was fatally countermanded by Hitler, who insisted that the Alamein position be held. The 36 hours wasted in obeying this long-distance instruction cost Rommel his chance of making a stand at Fūka: When he resumed his retreat, he had to race much farther back to escape successive British attempts to intercept him on the coast road by scythelike sweeps from the south. A fortnight after resuming his withdrawal from el-Alamein, Rommel was 700 miles to the west, at the traditional backstop of Agheila. As the British took their time to mount their attacks, he fell back farther by stages: after three weeks, 200 miles to

Buerat ("al-Bu-'ayraī"); after three more weeks, in mid-January 1943, the whole distance of 350 miles past Tripoli to the Mareth Line within the frontiers of Tunisia. By that time the Axis position in Tunisia was being battered from the west, through the execution of "Torch."

STALINGRAD AND THE GERMAN RETREAT, SUMMER 1942–FEBRUARY 1943

The German 4th Panzer Army, after being diverted to the south to help Kleist's attack on Rostov late in July 1942, was redirected toward Stalingrad a fortnight later. Stalingrad was a large industrial city producing armaments and tractors; it stretched for 30 miles along the banks of the Volga River. By the end of August the 4th Army's northeastward advance against the city was converging with the eastward advance of the 6th Army, under General Friedrich Paulus, with 330,000 of the German army's finest troops. The Red Army, however, put up the most determined resistance, yielding ground only very slowly and at a high cost as the 6th Army approached Stalingrad. On August 23 a German spearhead penetrated the city's northern suburbs, and the Luftwaffe rained incendiary bombs that destroyed most of the city's wooden housing. The Soviet 62nd Army was pushed back into Stalingrad proper, where, under the command of General Vasily I. Chuikov, it made a determined stand. Meanwhile, the Germans' concentration on Stalingrad was increasingly draining reserves from their flank cover, which was already strained by having to stretch so far—400 miles on the left (north), as far as Voronezh, 400 again on the right (south), as far as the Terek River.

By mid-September the Germans had pushed the Soviet forces in Stalingrad back until the latter occupied only a nine-mile-long strip of the city along the Volga, and this strip was only two or three miles wide. The Soviets had to supply their troops by barge and boat across the Volga from the other bank. At this point Stalingrad became the scene of some of the fiercest and most concentrated fighting of the war; streets, blocks, and individual buildings were fought over by many small units of troops and often changed hands again and again. The city's remaining buildings were pounded into rubble by the unrelenting close combat. The most critical moment came on October 14, when the Soviet defenders had their backs so close to the Volga that the few remaining supply crossings of the river came under German machine-gun fire. The Germans, however, were growing dispirited by heavy losses, by fatigue, and by the approach of winter.

A huge Soviet counteroffensive, planned by generals G.K. Zhukov, A.M. Vasilevsky, and Nikolay Nikolayevich Voronov, was launched on Nov. 19–20, 1942, in two spearheads, north and south of the German salient whose tip was at Stalingrad. The twin pincers of this counteroffensive struck the flanks of the German salient at points about 50 miles north and 50 miles south of Stalingrad and were designed to isolate the 250,000 remaining men of the German 6th and 4th armies in the city. The attacks quickly penetrated deep into the flanks, and by November 23 the two prongs of the attack had linked up about 60 miles west of Stalingrad; the encirclement of the two German armies in Stalingrad was complete. The German high command urged Hitler to allow Paulus and his forces to break out of the encirclement and rejoin the main German forces west of the city, but Hitler would not contemplate a retreat from the Volga River and ordered Paulus to "stand and fight." With winter setting in and food and medical supplies dwindling, Paulus' forces grew weaker. In mid-December Hitler allowed one of the most talented German commanders, Field Marshal Erich von Manstein, to form a special army corps to rescue Paulus' forces by fighting its way eastward, but Hitler refused to let Paulus fight his way westward at the same time in order to link up with Manstein. This fatal decision doomed Paulus' forces, since the main German forces now simply lacked the reserves needed to break through the Soviet encirclement singlehandedly. Hitler exhorted the trapped German forces to fight to the death, but on Jan. 31, 1943, Paulus surrendered; 91,000 frozen, starving men (all that was left of the 6th and 4th armies) and 24 generals surrendered with him.

Besides being the greatest battle of the war, Stalingrad proved to be the turning point of the military struggle between Germany and the Soviet Union. The battle used up precious German reserves, destroyed two entire armies, and humiliated the prestigious German war machine. It also marked the increasing skill and professionalism of a group of younger Soviet generals who had emerged as capable commanders, chief among whom was Zhukov.

Meanwhile, early in January 1943, only just in time, Hitler acknowledged that the encirclement of the Germans in Stalingrad would lead to an even worse disaster unless he extricated his forces from the Caucasus. Kleist was therefore ordered to retreat, while his northern flank of 600 miles was still protected by the desperate resistance of the encircled Paulus. Kleist's forces were making their way back across the Don at Rostov when Paulus at last surrendered. Had Paulus surrendered three weeks earlier (after seven weeks of isolation), Kleist's escape would have been impossible.

Even west of Rostov there were threats to Kleist's line of retreat. In January, two Soviet armies, the one under General Nikolay Fyodorovich Vatutin, the other under General Filipp Ivanovich Golikov, had crossed the Don upstream from Serafimovich and were thrusting southwestward to the Donets between Kamensk and Kharkov: Vatutin's forces, having crossed the Donets at Izyum, took Lozovaya Junction on February 11, Golikov's took Kharkov five days later. Farther to the north, a third Soviet army, under General Ivan Danilovich Chernyakhovsky, had initiated a drive westward from Voronezh on February 2 and had retaken Kursk on February 8. Thus, the Germans had to retreat from all the territory they had taken in their great summer offensive in 1942. The Caucasus returned to Soviet hands.

A sudden thaw supervened to hamper the Red Army's transport of supplies and reinforcements across the swollen courses of the great rivers. With the momentum of the Soviet counteroffensive thus slowed, the Germans made good their retreat to the Dnepr along the easier routes of the Black Sea littoral and were able, before the end of February 1943, to mount a counteroffensive of their own.

THE INVASION OF NORTHWEST AFRICA, NOVEMBER–DECEMBER 1942

When the U.S. and British strategists had decided on "Torch" (Allied landings on the western coast of North Africa) late in July 1942, it remained to settle the practical details of the operation. The purpose of "Torch" was to hem Rommel's forces in between U.S. troops on the west and British troops to the east. After considerable discussion, it was finally agreed that landings, under the supreme command of Major General Dwight D. Eisenhower, should be made on November 8 at three places in the vicinity of Casablanca on the Atlantic coast of Morocco and on beaches near Oran and near Algiers itself on the Mediterranean coast of Algeria. The amphibious landings would involve a total of about 110,000 troops, most of them Americans.

The conciliation of the French on whose colonial territory the landings would be made was a more delicate matter. All of

Allied troops land on a beach near Algiers during Operation Torch, on Nov. 8, 1942.

French North Africa was still loyal to the Vichy government of Marshal Pétain, with which the United States, unlike Great Britain, was still formally maintaining diplomatic relations. Thus, the French commander in chief in Algeria, General Alphonse Juin, and his counterpart in Morocco, General Charles-Auguste Noguès, were subordinate to the supreme commander of all Vichy's forces, namely Admiral Jean-François Darlan. American diplomats and generals tried to gain these officers' collaboration with the Allies in the landings, for it was vital to try to avoid a situation in which Vichy French troops put up armed resistance to the landings at the beaches.

The U.S.-British landings at Algiers began on November 8 and were met by little French resistance. The simultaneous landings near Oran met stiffer resistance, and on November 9 the whole U.S. plan of operations was dislocated by a French counterattack on the Arzew beachhead. Around Casablanca the U.S. landings were accomplished without difficulty, but resistance developed when the invaders tried to expand their beachheads. On November 10, however, the fighting was called off, and next day the French authorities in Morocco concluded an armistice with the Americans.

The landing in Algiers, meanwhile, was complicated by the fact that Darlan himself was in the city at the time. The situation was muddled, with some French troops loyal to Pétain while others backed de Gaulle and the anti-Vichy French general whom the Allies were sponsoring in North Africa, Henri Giraud.

On Nov. 11, 1942, in reaction to the Allied landings, German and Italian forces overran southern France, the metropolitan territory hitherto under Pétain's immediate authority. This event helped induce Noguès and the other French commanders in Algeria to assent to Darlan's proposals for a working agreement with the Allies, including recognition of Giraud as military commander in chief of the French forces. Concluded on November 13, the agreement was promptly endorsed by Eisenhower. French West Africa, including Senegal, with the port of Dakar, likewise followed Darlan's lead. The Germans, however, by mining the exit from the harbour of Toulon, forestalled plans for the escape of the main French fleet from metropolitan France to North Africa: On November 27, the French crews scuttled their ships to avoid capture. On Dec. 24, 1942, Darlan was assassinated; both Royalist and Gaullist circles in North Africa had steadfastly objected to him on political grounds. Giraud thereupon took his place, for a time, as French high commissioner in North Africa.

TUNISIA, NOVEMBER 1942–MAY 1943

Axis troops had begun to arrive in Tunisia as early as Nov. 9, 1942, and were reinforced in the following fortnight until they numbered about 20,000 combat troops (which were subsequently heavily reinforced by air). Thus, when the British general Kenneth Anderson, designated to command the invasion of Tunisia from the west with the Allied 1st Army, started his offensive on November 25, the defense was unexpectedly strong. By December 5 the 1st Army's advance was checked a dozen miles from Tunis and from Bizerte. Further reinforcements enabled Colonel General Jürgen von Arnim, who assumed the command in chief of the Axis defense in Tunisia on December 9, to expand his two bridgeheads in Tunisia until they were merged into one. Germany and Italy had won the race for Tunis but were henceforth to succumb to the lure of retaining their prize regardless of the greater need of conserving their strength for the defense of Europe.

After Rommel had fallen back from Libya to the Mareth Line in mid-January 1943, two German armies, Arnim's and Rommel's, were holding the north and the south of the eastern littoral both against Anderson's 1st Army attacking from the west and against Montgomery's 8th from the southeast. Rommel judged that a counterstroke should be delivered first against the Allies in the west. Accordingly, on February 14 the Axis forces delivered a major attack against U.S. forces between the Fāʾid Pass in the north and Gafsa in the south. West of Fāʾid, the 21st Panzer Division, under General Heinz Ziegler, destroyed 100 U.S. tanks and drove the Americans back 50 miles. In the Kasserine Pass, however, the Allies put up some stiffer opposition.

When on February 19 Rommel received authority to continue his attack, he was ordered to advance not against Tébessa but northward from Kasserine against Thala—where, in fact, Alexander was expecting him. Having overcome the stubborn U.S. resistance in the Kasserine Pass on February 20, the Germans entered Thala the next day, only to be expelled a few hours later by Alexander's reserve troops. His chance having been forfeited, Rommel began a gradual withdrawal on February 22.

The delays ensuing from the frustration of Rommel's stroke against the 1st Army reduced the effectiveness of his stroke against the 8th. Whereas on Feb. 26, 1943, Montgomery had had only one division facing the Mareth Line, he quadrupled his strength in the following week, massing 400 tanks and 500 antitank guns. Rommel's attack, on March 6, was brought to an early halt, and 50 German tanks were lost. A sick man and a disappointed soldier, Rommel relinquished his command.

The Allied 1st Army resumed the offensive on March 17, with attacks by the U.S. II Corps, under General George Patton, on the roads through the mountains, with the aim of cutting the Afrika Korps' line of retreat up the coast to Tunis, but these attacks were checked by the Germans in the passes. In the night of March 20–21, however, the British 8th Army launched a frontal assault on the Mareth Line, combined with an outflanking movement by the New Zealand Corps toward el-Hamma (al-Ḥammah) in the Germans' rear, and a few days later, seeing the frontal assault to have failed, Montgomery switched the main weight of his attack to the flank. Threatened with encirclement, the Germans decided to abandon the Mareth Line, which the 8th Army occupied on March 28, but the German defenses at el-Hamma held out long enough to enable the rest of the Afrika Korps to retreat without much loss to a new line on the Wādī al-'Akārīt, north of Gabès. The new line, however, was breached by the 8th Army on April 6, and, meanwhile, the Americans were also advancing on the Axis troops' rear from Gafsa. By the following morning the Afrika Korps was retreating rapidly northward along the littoral toward Tunis, and by April 11 it had joined hands with Arnim's forces for the defense of a 100-mile perimeter stretching around Tunis and Bizerte (Banzart).

Thanks to the rapidity of the Afrika Korps' retreat from Wādī al-ʿAkārīt, the German high command had an opportunity to withdraw its forces from the rump of Tunisia to Sicily, but it chose instead to defend the indefensible rump. The defenders indeed withstood the converging assaults that the 8th and 1st armies delivered against the perimeter from April 20 to April 23, but on May 6 a concentrated attack by Allied artillery, aircraft, infantry, and tanks was launched on the two-mile front of the Medjerda (Majardah) Valley leading to Tunis, and on May 7 the city fell to the leading British armoured forces, while the Americans and the French almost simultaneously captured Bizerte. At the same time, the Germans' line of retreat into the Cap Bon Peninsula was severed by an armoured division's swift turn southeastward from Tunis. A general collapse of the German resistance followed, the Allies taking more than 250,000 prisoners, including 125,000 German troops and Arnim himself. North Africa had been cleared of Axis forces and was now completely in Allied hands. Its capture ensured the safety of Allied shipping and naval movements throughout the Mediterranean, and North Africa would serve as a base for future Allied operations against Italy itself.

THE ATLANTIC, THE MEDITERRANEAN, AND THE NORTH SEA, 1942–45

The year 1942 was, on the whole, a favourable one for the German U-boats. First, the U.S. entry into the war entitled them to infest the U.S. coast of the North Atlantic, and it was not until the middle of the year that the Allies' introduction of the convoy system from the Caribbean northward constrained the raiders to go so far afield as the waters between Brazil and West Africa. Second, U-tankers were developed; i.e., large converted U-boats equipped to provide fuel, torpedoes, and other supplies to U-boats operating in remote waters. In the course of 1942, the U-boats sank more than 6,266,000 tons of shipping, and, since in the same period their operational strength rose from 91 to 212, it seemed conceivable that they might soon score their desired target of 800,000 tons of sinkings per month.

March 1943 saw the climax of the U-boats' good fortune: Their strength rose to 240; they sank in that single month 627,377 tons of shipping; and, in the greatest convoy battle of the war, when 20 of them attacked two convoys merged into one, they sank 21 ships (141,000 tons) out of 77 with the loss of only one of their own number. The anticlimax followed, thanks to five developments of the Allies' counteraction: "Support groups" were reintroduced; aircraft carriers became progressively available for escorts; more and more long-range Liberator aircraft began to cover the convoys offshore; ships were equipped with a radar set of very short wavelength, the probing of which was undetectable to the U-boats; and a regular offensive against U-boats on their transit routes was launched from the air (56 were destroyed in April–May 1943). The U-boats sank 327,943 tons in April, 264,852 in May, only 95,753 in June 1943, and for the rest of the war monthly totals were less than 100,000 tons except in July and September 1943 and in March 1944.

Late in 1944 the U-boats were equipped with the snorkel breathing tube, which provided them with the necessary oxygen to recharge their batteries under water and so converted them from submersible torpedo boats into almost complete submarines virtually undetectable to radar. About the same time a new model of U-boat, with greater underwater speed and endurance, came into operation. These improvements came too late, however, because the Allies' surface and air resources for the protection of the convoys were already overwhelming.

Developments from Autumn 1941 to Autumn 1943

AIR WARFARE, 1942–43

Early in 1942 the RAF bomber command, headed by Sir Arthur Harris, began an intensification of the Allies' growing strategic air offensive against Germany. These attacks, which were aimed against factories, rail depots, dockyards, bridges, and dams and against cities and towns themselves, were intended to both destroy Germany's war industries and to deprive its civilian population of their housing, thus sapping their will to continue the war. The characteristic feature of the new program was its emphasis on area bombing, in which the centres of towns would be the points of aim for nocturnal raids.

Already in March 1942 an exceptionally destructive bombing raid, using the Germans' own incendiary method, had been made on Lübeck, and intensive attacks were also made on Essen (site of the Krupp munitions works) and other Ruhr

An American B-17 bomber flies over the German city of Hamburg during an air raid.

towns. In the night of May 30–31 more than 1,000 bombers were dispatched against Cologne, where they did heavy damage to one-third of that city's built-up area. Such operations, however, became highly expensive to the bomber command, particularly because of the defense put up by the German night fighter force. Interrupted for two months during which the bombers concentrated their attention on U-boat bases on the Bay of Biscay, the air offensive against Germany was resumed in March 1943. In the following 12 months, moreover, its resources were to be increased formidably so that by March 1944 the bomber command's average daily operational strength had risen to 974 from about 500 in 1942. These numbers helped the RAF to concentrate effectively against major industrial targets, such as those in the Ruhr. The phases of the resumed offensive were: (1) the Battle of the Ruhr, from March to July 1943, comprising 18,506 sorties and costing 872 aircraft shot down and 2,126 damaged, its most memorable operation being that of the night of May 16–17, when the Möhne Dam in the Ruhr Basin and the Eder Dam in the Weser Basin were breached, (2) the Battle of Hamburg, from July to November 1943, comprising 17,021 sorties and costing 695 bombers lost and 1,123 damaged but, nevertheless, thanks in part to the new Window antiradar and "H2S" radar devices, achieving an unprecedented measure of devastation, since four out of its 33 major actions, with a little help from minor attacks, killed about 40,000 people and drove nearly 1,000,000 from their homes, and (3) the Battle of Berlin, from November 1943 to March 1944, comprising 20,224 sorties but costing 1,047 bombers lost and 1,682 returned damaged and achieving, on the whole, less devastation than the Battle of Hamburg.

    The U.S. 8th Air Force, based in Great Britain, also took part in the strategic offensive against Germany from January 1943. Its bombers, Flying Fortresses (B-17s) and Liberators

CASABLANCA CONFERENCE

In the wake of Operation "Torch," Roosevelt and Churchill met at Casablanca (January 1943) to determine strategy for the coming year. Once again Roosevelt conciliated Churchill, agreeing to put off opening a second front in France in favour of more modest operations against Sicily, Italy, and the "soft underbelly" of Europe after the liberation of North Africa. General George Marshall and Admiral Ernest King succeeded in winning approval for offensives in Burma and the southwest Pacific. The French rivals, de Gaulle and Giraud, were persuaded at least to feign unity and later to create a French Committee of National Liberation under their joint chairmanship (May 1943). But the main event was Roosevelt's parting announcement that "peace can come to the world only by the total elimination of German and Japanese military power... (which) means unconditional surrender." This surprise declaration was not spontaneous, as Roosevelt claimed; it was a considered signal to Stalin of Allied resolve, especially necessary after General Eisenhower's ignominious "Darlan deal." But it also rashly committed the United States to a power vacuum, rather than a balance of power, in postwar Europe and may have discouraged Germans from attempting to oust Hitler in hopes of escaping utter defeat.

Stalin's reaction to Casablanca was predictably sour. In March he expressed great anxiety about repeated postponement of the second front in France. On the other hand, the Battle of Stalingrad had more or less assured eventual Soviet victory. Would it not have served Soviet interests more to delay the Allied presence in Europe as long as possible? It is likely that Stalin's continued pressure for a second front was a function of his perennial fears for internal Soviet security. Stalin may have wanted to recapture his lost ground, especially Ukraine, as quickly as possible lest anti-Soviet movements take hold there or in neighbouring countries.

(B-24s), attacked industrial targets in daylight. They proved, however, to be very vulnerable to German fighter attack whenever they went beyond the range of their own escort of fighters—that is to say, farther than the distance from Norfolk to Aachen: The raid against the important ball-bearing factory at Schweinfurt, for instance, on Oct. 14, 1943, lost 60 out of the 291 bombers participating, and 138 of those that returned were damaged. Not until December 1943 was the P-51B (Mustang III) brought into operation with the 8th Air Force—a long-range fighter that portended a change in the balance of air power. The Germans, meanwhile, continued to increase their production of aircraft and, in particular, of their highly successful fighters.

CASABLANCA AND TRIDENT, JANUARY–MAY 1943

To decide what should be done after victory in North Africa, Roosevelt and Churchill, with their advisers, met at Casablanca in mid-January 1943. After long argument, it was eventually agreed that Sicily should be the next Axis area to be taken, in July. For the war against Japan, it was decided that two offensive operations should be undertaken: MacArthur should move toward the Japanese base at Rabaul, on the island of New Britain, and convergent movements on Burma should be made by the British from the mainland of India and by the Americans from the sea. Politically, the Casablanca Conference owes its importance to the fact that, at its end, Roosevelt publicly announced a demand for the unconditional surrender of Germany, Italy, and Japan.

Only four months after Casablanca it became necessary to hold another Anglo-U.S. conference. In mid-May 1943, Roosevelt, Churchill, and their advisers met, in Washington, D.C., for the conference code-named Trident. There the Sicilian project was effectively confirmed, and the date May 1, 1944, was prescribed—definitively in the U.S view, provisionally in the British—for the landing of 29 divisions in France, but the question whether the conquest of Sicily should be followed, as the British proposed, by an invasion of Italy was left unsettled.

THE EASTERN FRONT, FEBRUARY–SEPTEMBER 1943

The German counteroffensive of February 1943 threw back the Soviet forces that had been advancing toward the Dnepr River on the Izyum sector of the front, and by mid-March the Germans had retaken Kharkov and Belgorod and reestablished a front on the Donets River. Hitler also authorized the German forces to fall back, in March, from their advanced positions facing Moscow to a straighter line in front of Smolensk and Orël. Finally, there was the existence of the large Soviet bulge, or salient, around Kursk, between Orël and Belgorod, which extended for about 150 miles from north to south and protruded 100 miles into the German lines. This salient irresistibly tempted Hitler and Zeitzler into undertaking a new and extremely ambitious offensive instead of remaining content to hold their newly shortened front.

Hitler concentrated all efforts on this offensive without regard to the risk that an unsuccessful attack would leave him without reserves to maintain any subsequent defense of his long front. The Germans' increasing difficulty in building up their forces with fresh drafts of men and equipment was reflected in the increased delay that year in opening the summer offensive. Three months' pause followed the close of the winter campaign.

By contrast, the Red Army had improved much since 1942, both in quality and in quantity. The flow of new equipment had greatly increased, as had the number of new divisions, and its numerical superiority over the Germans was now about 4 to 1. Better still, its leadership had improved with experience: Generals and junior commanders alike had become more skilled tacticians. That could already be discerned in the summer of 1943, when the Soviets waited to let the Germans lead off and commit themselves deeply to an offensive, and so stood well-poised to exploit the Germans' loss of balance in lunging.

The German offensive against the Kursk salient was launched on July 5, 1943, and into it Hitler threw 20 infantry divisions and 17 armoured divisions having a total of about 3,000 tanks. But the German tank columns got entangled in the deep minefields that the Soviets had laid, forewarned by the long preparation of the offensive. The Germans advanced only 10–30 miles, and no large bag of Soviet prisoners was taken, since the Red Army had withdrawn their main forces from the salient before the German attack began. After a week of effort the German armoured divisions were seriously reduced by the well-prepared Soviet antitank defenses in the salient. On July 12, as the Germans began to pull out, the Soviets launched a counteroffensive upon the German positions in the salient and met with great success, taking Orël on August 5. By this time the Germans had lost 2,900 tanks and 70,000 men in the Battle of Kursk, which was the largest tank battle in history. The Soviets continued to advance steadily, taking Belgorod and then Kharkov. In September the Soviet advance was accelerated, and by the end of the month the Germans in Ukraine had been driven back to the Dnepr.

THE SOUTHWEST AND SOUTH PACIFIC, JUNE–OCTOBER 1943

A Pacific military conference held in Washington, D.C., in March 1943 produced a new schedule of operations calling

Developments from Autumn 1941 to Autumn 1943

for the development of some counterattacks against the Japanese. The reduction of the threat from the large Japanese naval base at Rabaul, by encirclement if not by the capture of that stronghold, was a primary objective for MacArthur.

Between June 22 and June 30, 1943, two U.S. regiments invaded Woodlark and Kiriwina islands (northeast of the tip of Papua), whence aircraft could range over not only the Coral Sea but also the approaches to Rabaul and to the Solomons. At the same time, U.S. and Australian units advanced from Buna along the coast of New Guinea toward Lae and Salamaua, while other Australian forces simultaneously advanced from Wau in the hinterland, and in the night of June 29–30, U.S. forces secured Nassau Bay as a base for further advances against the same positions.

U.S. landings on New Georgia and on Rendova in the Solomons, however, also made in the night of June 29–30, provoked the Japanese into strong counteraction: Between July 5 and July 16, in the battles of Kula Gulf and of Kolombangara, the Allies lost one cruiser and two destroyers and had three more cruisers crippled, and the Japanese, though they lost a cruiser and two destroyers, were able to land considerable reinforcements (from New Britain). Only substantial counter-reinforcement secured the New Georgia group of islands for the Allies, who, moreover, began on August 15 to extend their operation to the island of Vella Lavella also. In the last two months of the struggle, which ended with the Japanese evacuation of Vella Lavella on October 7, the Japanese sank an Allied destroyer and crippled two more but lost a further six of their own, and their attempt to defend the Solomon Islands cost them 10,000 lives, as against the Americans' 1,150 killed and 4,100 wounded.

Meanwhile, U.S. planes on August 17–18 had attacked Japanese bases at Wewak (on the New Guinea coast far to the west of Lae) and destroyed more than 200 aircraft there. On September 4 an Australian division landed near Lae, and the next day U.S. paratroops dropped at Nadzab, above Lae on the Markham River, where they were soon joined by an Australian airborne division. Salamaua fell to the Allies on September 12, Lae on September 16, and Finschhafen, on the Huon Peninsula behind Lae, on October 2. On Sept. 30, 1943, the Japanese made a new policy decision: A last defense line was to be established from western New Guinea and the Carolines to the Marianas by spring 1944, to be held at all costs, and also to be used as a base for counterattacks.

CHAPTER 6
THE FINAL SOLUTION

Hitler's racist ideology and his brutal conception of power politics caused him to pursue certain aims in those European countries conquered by the Germans in the period 1939–42. Hitler intended that those western and northern European areas in which civil administrations were installed—the Netherlands and Norway—would at some later date become part of the German Reich, or nation. Those countries left by Germany under military administration (which originally had been imposed everywhere), such as France and Serbia, would eventually be included more loosely in a German-dominated European bloc. Poland and the Soviet Union, on the other hand, were to be a colonial area for German settlement and economic exploitation.

Without regard to these distinctions, the SS, the elite corps of the Nazi Party, possessed exceptional powers throughout German-dominated Europe and in the course of time came to perform more and more executive functions, even in those countries under military administration. Similarly, the powers that Hitler gave to his chief labour commissioner, Fritz Sauckel, for the compulsory enrollment of foreign workers into the German armaments industry were soon applied to the whole of German-dominated Europe and ultimately turned 7,500,000 people into forced or slave labourers. Above all, however, there was the Final Solution of the "Jewish question" as ordered by Hitler, which meant the physical extermination of the Jewish people throughout Europe wherever German rule was in force or where German influence was decisive.

Changes in Policy

The Final Solution—that is to say the step beyond half-measures such as the concentration of Poland's Jews into overcrowded ghettos—was introduced concurrently with Germany's preparations for the military campaign against the Soviet Union, since Hitler believed that the annihilation of the Communists entailed not only the extermination of the Soviet ruling class but also what he believed to be its "biological basis"—the millions of Jews in western Russia and Ukraine. Accordingly, with the start of the invasion of the Soviet Union in 1941, special mobile killing squads began systematically shooting the Jewish population on conquered Soviet territory in the rear of the advancing German armies; in a few months, up to the end of 1941, they had killed about 1,400,000 people. Meanwhile, plans were made in 1941 to

German SS troops round up Jews at a railway station where they would be shipped to concentration camps.

WANNSEE CONFERENCE

The Wannsee Conference was a meeting of Nazi officials on Jan. 20, 1942, in the Berlin suburb of Wannsee to plan the "final solution" (Endlösung) to the so-called "Jewish question" (Judenfrage). On July 31, 1941, Nazi leader Reichsmarschall Hermann Göring had issued orders to Reinhard Heydrich, SS (Nazi paramilitary corps) leader and Gestapo (Secret Police) chief, to prepare a comprehensive plan for this "final solution." The Wannsee Conference, held six months later, was attended by 15 Nazi senior bureaucrats led by Heydrich and including Adolf Eichmann, chief of Jewish affairs for the Reich Central Security Office.

The conference marked a turning point in Nazi policy toward the Jews. An earlier idea, to deport all of Europe's Jews to the island of Madagascar, off of Africa, was abandoned as impractical in wartime. Instead, the newly planned final solution would entail rounding up all Jews throughout Europe, transporting them eastward, and organizing them into labour gangs. The work and living conditions would be sufficiently hard as to fell large numbers by "natural diminution"; those that survived would be "treated accordingly."

The men seated at the table were among the elite of the Reich. More than half of them held doctorates from German universities. They were well informed about the policy toward Jews. Each understood that the cooperation of his agency was vital if such an ambitious, unprecedented policy was to succeed.

Among the agencies represented were the Department of Justice, the Foreign Ministry, the Gestapo, the SS, the Race and Resettlement Office, and the office in charge of distributing Jewish property. Also at the meeting was a representative of the General Government, the Polish occupation administration, whose territory included more than 2 million Jews. The head of Heydrich's office for Jewish affairs, Adolf Eichmann, prepared the conference notes.

World War II

Heydrich himself introduced the agenda:

Another possible solution of the [Jewish] problem has now taken the place of emigration—i.e., evacuation of the Jews to the east... Such activities are, however, to be considered as provisional actions, but practical experience is already being collected which is of greatest importance in relation to the future final solution of the Jewish problem.

The men needed little explanation. They understood that "evacuation to the east" was a euphemism for concentration camps and that the "final solution" was to be the systematic murder of Europe's Jews, which is now known as the Holocaust. The final protocol of the Wannsee Conference never explicitly mentioned extermination, but, within a few months after the meeting, the Nazis installed the first poison-gas chambers in Poland in what came to be called extermination camps. Responsibility for the entire project was put in the hands of Heinrich Himmler and his SS and Gestapo.

similarly exterminate the Jews of central and western Europe. At the Wannsee Conference of Nazi and SS chiefs in January 1942, it was agreed that those Jews would be deported and sent to camps in eastern Poland where they would be killed en masse or made to work as slave labourers until they perished. In the period from May 1942 to September 1944 more than 4,200,000 Jews were killed in such death camps as Auschwitz (Oswiecim), Treblinka, Belzec, Chelmno, Majdanek, and Sobibor. About 5,700,000 Jews died in the course of the Final Solution.

While Hitler destined the Jews in his empire to physical extermination, he regarded the Slavs, principally the Poles and the Russians, as "subhumans" who were to be subjected to continual decimation and used as a pool of cheap labour, that is to say, reduced to slavery. Poland became the training ground for this purpose. Upon the German conquest of Poland in 1939, Hitler ordered the SS to kill a large proportion of the Polish intelligentsia. A reign of terror against the nationalistic-minded Polish ruling classes began, and by the war's end a total of 3,000,000 Poles (in addition to 3,000,000 Polish Jews) had been killed. Hitler further willed that the whole mass of Slavs and Balts in the occupied portions of the Soviet Union should be indiscriminately subjected to German domination and should be economically exploited without hindrance or compassion. In the event, Ukraine was the major area subject to economic exploitation and also became the main source of slave labour. When the German armies first entered Ukraine in July 1941, many Ukrainians had welcomed the Germans as their liberators from Stalinist terror and collectivization. But this goodwill soon turned to resentment as the Germans requisitioned large quantities of grain from the farms, forcibly deported several million Ukrainians for work in Germany, and engaged in brutal reprisals against civilians for acts of resistance or sabotage.

These inhumane occupation policies were practiced to a greater or lesser extent in all the countries occupied by the Germans, and the result was the beginning in 1940–41 of armed, underground resistance movements in those countries. Underground resistance was especially effective in the Soviet Union because it functioned behind fronts on which the German armies were still engaged in battle with the Red Army. The Soviet Partisans, as they were called, could thus covertly receive arms, equipment, and direction from the Soviet forces at the front itself. Soviet Partisans, like the members of other nations' Resistance movements, harassed and disrupted German military and economic activities by blowing up ammunition dumps and communications and transport facilities, sabotaging factories, ambushing small German units, and gathering military intelligence for use by the Allied armies. By 1944 the Resistance organizations in the Soviet Union, Poland, Yugoslavia, France, and Greece had grown quite large and were holding down many German divisions that were badly needed at the battlefront. In eastern Europe and Yugoslavia, the Resistance came to control large tracts of land in more inaccessible areas such as forests, mountain ranges, and swamplands. Some Resistance organizations, such as the Partisans in Yugoslavia and the National Liberation Movement in Greece, were Communist ones, while others, such as the Maquis in France and the Home Army in Poland, comprised people of many different political persuasions, though they were invariably anti-Fascists.

The German occupation authorities' attempts to eradicate the Resistance in most cases merely fanned the flames, due to the Germans' use of indiscriminate reprisals against civilians. It is generally agreed that by 1944 the Germans had earned the overwhelming antipathy of most of the people in the occupied nations of Europe. It should be noted, however, that the German occupation was in general far harsher in eastern Europe and the Balkans than in western Europe. In the Soviet Union, Poland, Yugoslavia, and Greece, a process of Resistance guerrilla warfare and Nazi reprisals began in 1941 and rose to a crescendo in 1943–44 as the fury of Nazi racism resulted in a war of annihilation upon the Slavic peoples.

Nazi Anti-Semitism and the Origins of the Holocaust

Even before the Nazis came to power in Germany in 1933, they had made no secret of their anti-Semitism. As early as 1919, Adolf Hitler had written, "Rational anti-Semitism,

NÜRNBERG LAWS

The Nürnberg Laws were two race-based measures depriving Jews of rights, designed by Adolf Hitler and approved by the Nazi Party at a convention in Nürnberg on September 15, 1935. One, the Reichsbürgergesetz (German: "Law of the Reich Citizen"), deprived Jews of German citizenship, designating them "subjects of the state." The other, the Gesetz zum Schutze des Deutschen Blutes und der Deutschen Ehre ("Law for the Protection of German Blood and German Honour"), usually called simply the Blutschutzgesetz ("Blood Protection Law"), forbade marriage or sexual relations between Jews and "citizens of German or kindred blood." These measures were among the first of the racist Nazi laws that culminated in the Holocaust.

Under these laws, Jews could not fly the German flag and were forbidden "to employ in domestic service female subjects of German or kindred blood who are under the age of 45 years." The first supplementary decree of November 14, 1935—one of 13 ordinances elaborating these laws—defined Jews as persons with at least one Jewish grandparent and declared explicitly that "a Jew cannot be a citizen of the Reich. He cannot exercise the right to vote; he cannot occupy public office." The other enactments completed the process of Jewish segregation. Before long Jewish passports were stamped with a red "J" (for Jude; "Jew"), and Jews were compelled to adopt "Jewish" names. Jewish communities were deprived of their legal status by the decree of March 28, 1938, and steps were taken to exclude Jews completely from the practice of medicine.

This racial definition meant that Jews were persecuted not for their religious beliefs and practices but for a so-called racial identity transmitted irrevocably through the blood of their ancestors. These laws resolved the question of definition and set a legal precedent. The Nazis later imposed the Nürnberg Laws on territories they occupied. The laws also provided a model for the treatment and eventual genocide of the Roma (Gypsies).

> Although the Nürnberg Laws divided the German nation into Germans and Jews, neither the term *Jew* nor the phrase *German or kindred blood* was defined. Because the laws contained criminal provisions for noncompliance, the bureaucrats had the urgent task of spelling out what the words meant. Two basic Jewish categories were established. A full Jew was anyone with three Jewish grandparents. That definition was fairly simple. Defining part-Jews—*Mischlinge* ("mongrels")—was more difficult, but they were eventually divided into two classes. First-degree *Mischlinge* were people who had two Jewish grandparents but did not practice Judaism and did not have a Jewish spouse. Second-degree *Mischlinge* were those who had only one Jewish grandparent.
>
> The efforts to prove one's non-Jewish ancestry generated a new cottage industry employing hordes of "licensed family researchers," offering their services to anxious Germans afraid of a skeleton in the family closet. These efforts also involved the Health Ministry and church offices, which had to provide birth and baptismal certificates.

however, must lead to systematic legal opposition…Its final objective must unswervingly be the removal of the Jews altogether." In *Mein Kampf* ("My Struggle"; 1925–27), Hitler further developed the idea of the Jews as an evil race struggling for world domination. Nazi anti-Semitism was rooted in religious anti-Semitism and enhanced by political anti-Semitism. To this the Nazis added a further dimension: racial anti-Semitism. Nazi racial ideology characterized the Jews as *Untermenschen* (German: "subhumans"). The Nazis portrayed Jews as a race and not a religious group. Religious anti-Semitism could be resolved by conversion, political anti-Semitism by expulsion. Ultimately, the logic of Nazi racial anti-Semitism led to annihilation.

The Final Solution

When Hitler came to power legally on Jan. 30, 1933, as the head of a coalition government, his first objective was to consolidate power and to eliminate political opposition. The assault against the Jews began on April 1 with a boycott of Jewish businesses. A week later the Nazis dismissed Jews from the civil service, and by the end of the month, the participation of Jews in German schools was restricted by a quota. On May 10, thousands of Nazi students, together with many professors, stormed university libraries and bookstores in 30 cities throughout Germany to remove tens of thousands of books written by non-Aryans and those opposed to Nazi ideology. The books were tossed into bonfires in an effort to cleanse German culture of "un-Germanic" writings. A century earlier, Heinrich Heine—a German poet of Jewish origin—had said, "Where one burns books, one will, in the end, burn people." In Nazi Germany, the time between the burning of Jewish books and the burning of Jews was eight years.

As discrimination against Jews increased, German law required a legal definition of a Jew and an Aryan. Promulgated at the annual Nazi Party rally in Nürnberg on Sept. 15, 1935, the Nürnberg Laws—the Law for the Protection of German Blood and German Honour and the Law of the Reich Citizen—became the centerpiece of anti-Jewish legislation and a precedent for defining and categorizing Jews in all German-controlled lands. Marriage and sexual relations between Jews and citizens of "German or kindred blood" were prohibited. Only "racial" Germans were entitled to civil and political rights. Jews were reduced to subjects of the state. The Nürnberg Laws formally divided Germans and Jews, yet neither the word German nor the word Jew was defined. That task was left to the bureaucracy. Two basic categories were established in November: Jews—those with at least three Jewish grandparents—and *Mischlinge* ("mongrels," or "mixed breeds")—people with one or two Jewish grandparents. Thus, the definition of a Jew was primarily based not on the identity an individual affirmed or the religion he practiced but on his ancestry. Categorization was the first stage of destruction.

Responding with alarm to Hitler's rise, the Jewish community sought to defend their rights as Germans. For those Jews who felt themselves fully German and who had patriotically fought in World War I, the Nazification of German society was especially painful. Zionist activity intensified. "Wear it with pride," journalist Robert Wildest wrote in 1933 of the Jewish identity the Nazis had so stigmatized. Martin Buber led an effort at Jewish adult education, preparing the community for the long journey ahead. Rabbi Leo Baeck circulated a prayer for Yom Kippur (the Day of Atonement) in 1935 that instructed Jews how to behave: "We bow down before God; we stand erect before man." Yet while few, if any, could foresee its eventual outcome, the Jewish condition was increasingly perilous and expected to get worse.

By the late 1930s there was a desperate search for countries of refuge. Those who could get visas and qualify under stringent quotas emigrated to the United States. Many went to Palestine, where the small Jewish community was willing to receive refugees. Still others sought refuge in neighbouring European countries. Most countries, however, were unwilling to receive large numbers of refugees.

Responding to domestic pressures to act on behalf of Jewish refugees, U.S. President Franklin D. Roosevelt convened, but did not attend, the Évian Conference on resettlement, in Évian-les-Bains, France, in July 1938. In his invitation to government leaders, Roosevelt specified that they would not have to change laws or spend government funds; only philanthropic funds would be used for resettlement. The result was that little was attempted, and less accomplished.

The Final Solution

From Kristallnacht to the "Final Solution"

On the evening of Nov. 9, 1938, carefully orchestrated anti-Jewish violence "erupted" throughout the Reich, which since March had included Austria. Over the next 48 hours rioters burned or damaged more than 1,000 synagogues and ransacked and broke the windows of more than 7,500 businesses. The Nazis arrested some 30,000 Jewish men between the ages of 16 and 60 and sent them to concentration camps. Police stood by as the violence—often the action of neighbours, not strangers—occurred. Firemen were present not to protect the synagogues but to ensure that the flames did not spread to adjacent "Aryan" property. The pogrom was given a quaint name: Kristallnacht ("Crystal Night," or "Night of Broken Glass"). In its aftermath, Jews lost the illusion that they had a future in Germany.

On Nov. 12, 1938, Field Marshal Hermann Göring convened a meeting of Nazi officials to discuss the damage to the

Pedestrians view a Jewish store in Berlin that was damaged during Kristallnacht.

German economy from pogroms. The Jewish community was fined one billion Reichsmarks. Moreover, Jews were made responsible for cleaning up the damage. German Jews, but not foreign Jews, were barred from collecting insurance. In addition, Jews were soon denied entry to theatres, forced to travel in separate compartments on trains, and excluded from German schools. These new restrictions were added to earlier prohibitions, such as those barring Jews from earning university degrees, from owning businesses, or from practicing law or medicine in the service of non-Jews. The Nazis would continue to confiscate Jewish property in a program called "Aryanization." Göring concluded the November meeting with a note of irony: "I would not like to be a Jew in Germany!"

NON-JEWISH VICTIMS OF NAZISM

While Jews were the primary victims of Nazism as it evolved and were central to Nazi racial ideology, other groups were victimized as well—some for what they did, some for what they refused to do, and some for what they were.

Political dissidents, trade unionists, and Social Democrats were among the first to be arrested and incarcerated in concentration camps. Under the Weimar government, centuries-old prohibitions against homosexuality had been overlooked, but this tolerance ended violently when the SA (Storm Troopers) began raiding gay bars in 1933. Homosexual intent became just cause for prosecution. The Nazis arrested German and Austrian male homosexuals—there was no systematic persecution of lesbians—and interned them in concentration camps, where they were forced to wear special yellow armbands and later pink triangles. Jehovah's Witnesses were a problem for the Nazis because they refused to swear allegiance to the state, register for the draft, or utter the words "Heil Hitler." As a

The Final Solution

result, the Nazis imprisoned many of the roughly 20,000 Witnesses in Germany. Germans of African descent—many of whom, called "Rhineland bastards" by the Nazis, were the offspring of German mothers and French colonial African troops who had occupied the Rhineland after World War I—were also persecuted by the Nazis. Although their victimization was less systematic, it included forced sterilization and, often, internment in concentration camps. The Nazis also singled out the Roma (Gypsies). They were the only other group that the Nazis systematically killed in gas chambers alongside the Jews.

In 1939 the Germans initiated the T4 Program—framed euphemistically as a "euthanasia" program—for the murder of mentally retarded, physically disabled, and emotionally disturbed Germans who departed from the Nazi ideal of Aryan supremacy. The Nazis pioneered the use of gas chambers and mass crematoria under this program.

Following the invasion of Poland, German occupation policy especially targeted the Jews but also brutalized non-Jewish Poles. In pursuit of *Lebensraum* ("living space"), Germany sought systematically to destroy Polish society and nationhood. The Nazis killed Polish priests and politicians, decimated the Polish leadership, and kidnapped the children of the Polish elite, who were raised as "voluntary Aryans" by their new German "parents." Many Poles were also forced to perform hard labour on survival diets, deprived of property and uprooted, and interned in concentration camps.

NAZI EXPANSION AND THE FORMATION OF GHETTOS

Paradoxically, at the same time that Germany tried to rid itself of its Jews via forced emigration, its territorial expansions kept bringing more Jews under its control. Germany annexed

Austria in March 1938 and the Sudetenland (now in the Czech Republic) in September 1938. It established control over the Protectorate of Bohemia and Moravia (now in the Czech Republic) in March 1939. When Germany invaded Poland on Sept. 1, 1939, the "Jewish question" became urgent. When the division of Poland between Germany and the Soviet Union was complete, more than two million more Jews had come under German control. For a time, the Nazis considered shipping the Jews to the island of Madagascar, off the southeast coast of Africa. But as the seas became a war zone and the resources required for such a massive deportation scarce, they discarded the plan as impractical.

On Sept. 21, 1939, Reinhard Heydrich ordered the establishment of the Judenräte ("Jewish Councils"), comprising up to 24 men—rabbis and Jewish leaders. Heydrich's order made these councils personally responsible in "the literal sense of the term" for carrying out German orders. When the Nazis sealed the Warsaw Ghetto, the largest of German-occupied Poland's 400 ghettos, in the fall of 1940, the Jews—then 30 percent of Warsaw's population—were forced into 2.4 percent of the city's area. The ghetto's population reached a density of over 200,000 persons per square mile (77,000 per square km) and 9.2 per room. Disease, malnutrition, hunger, and poverty took their toll even before the first bullet was fired.

For the German rulers, the ghetto was a temporary measure, a holding pen for the Jewish population until a policy on its fate could be established and implemented. For the Jews, ghetto life was the situation under which they thought they would be forced to live until the end of the war. They aimed to make life bearable, even under the most trying circumstances. When the Nazis prohibited schools, they opened clandestine schools. When the Nazis banned religious life, it persisted in hiding. The Jews used humour as a means of defiance, so too song. They resorted to arms only late in the Nazi assault.

Historians differ on the date of the decision to murder Jews systematically, the so-called "final solution to the Jewish question." There is debate about whether there was one central decision or a series of regional decisions in response to local conditions, but in either case, when Germany attacked the Soviet Union, its former ally, in June of 1941, the Nazis began the systematic killing of Jews.

The Einsatzgruppen

Entering conquered Soviet territories alongside the Wehrmacht (the German armed forces) were 3,000 men of the Einsatzgruppen ("deployment groups"), special mobile killing units. Their task was to murder Jews, Soviet commissars, and Roma in the areas conquered by the army. Alone or with the help of local police, native anti-Semitic populations, and accompanying Axis troops, the Einsatzgruppen would enter a town, round up their victims, herd them to the outskirts of the town, and shoot them. They killed Jews in family units. Just outside Kiev, Ukraine, in the valley of Babi Yar, an Einsatzgruppe killed 33,771 Jews on Sept. 28–29, 1941. In the Rumbula Forest outside the ghetto in Riga, Latvia, 25,000–28,000 Jews died on November 30 and December 8–9. Beginning in the summer of 1941, Einsatzgruppen killed more than 70,000 Jews at Ponary, outside Vilna (now Vilnius) in Lithuania. They slaughtered 9,000 Jews, half of them children, at the Ninth Fort adjacent to Kovno (now Kaunas), Lithuania, on October 28.

The mass shootings continued unabated, with a first wave and then a second. When the killing ended in the face of a Soviet counteroffensive, special units returned to dig up the dead and burn their bodies to destroy the evidence of the crimes. It is estimated that the Einsatzgruppen killed more than one million people, most of whom were Jews.

Historians are divided about the motivations of the members of Einsatzgruppen. Christopher Browning describes them as ordinary men in extraordinary circumstances in which conformity, peer pressure, careerism, obedience to orders, and group solidarity gradually overcame moral inhibitions. Daniel Goldhagen sees them as "willing executioners," sharing Hitler's vision of genocidal anti-Semitism and finding their tasks unpleasant but necessary. Both concur that no Einsatzgruppe member faced punishment if he asked to be excused. Individuals had a choice whether to participate or not. Almost all chose to become killers.

Extermination Camps

In early 1942 the Nazis built extermination camps at Treblinka, Sobibor, and Belzec in Poland, per the decisions made at the Wannsee Conference. The death camps were to be the essential instrument of the "final solution." The Einsatzgruppen had traveled to kill their victims. With the extermination camps, the process was reversed. The victims traveled by train, often in cattle cars, to their killers. The extermination camps became factories producing corpses, effectively and efficiently, at minimal physical and psychological cost to German personnel. Assisted by Ukrainian and Latvian collaborators and prisoners of war, a few Germans could kill tens of thousands of prisoners each month. At Chelmno, the first of the extermination camps, the Nazis used mobile gas vans. Elsewhere, they built permanent gas chambers linked to the crematoria where bodies were burned. Carbon monoxide was the gas of choice at most

An inmate of a concentration camp at Gusen, Austria, suffers from starvation.

camps. Zyklon-B, an especially lethal killing agent, was employed primarily at Auschwitz and later at other camps.

Auschwitz, perhaps the most notorious and lethal of the concentration camps, was actually three camps in one: a prison camp (Auschwitz I), an extermination camp (Auschwitz II–Birkenau), and a slave-labour camp (Auschwitz III–Buna-Monowitz). Upon arrival, Jewish prisoners faced what was called a Selektion. A German doctor presided over the selection of pregnant women, young children, the elderly, handicapped, sick, and infirm for immediate death in the gas chambers. As necessary, the Germans selected able-bodied prisoners for forced labour in the factories adjacent to Auschwitz where one German company, IG Farben, invested 700,000 million Reichsmarks in 1942 alone to take advantage of forced labour. Deprived of adequate food, shelter, clothing, and medical care, these prisoners were literally worked to death. Periodically, they would face another Selektion. The Nazis would transfer those unable to work to the gas chambers of Birkenau.

While the death camps at Auschwitz and Majdanek used inmates for slave labour to support the German war effort, the extermination camps at Belzec, Treblinka, and Sobibor had one task alone: killing. At Treblinka, a staff of 120, of whom only 30 were SS (the Nazi paramilitary corps), killed some 750,000 to 900,000 Jews during the camp's 17 months of operation. At Belzec, German records detail a staff of 104, including about 20 SS, who killed some 600,000 Jews in less than 10 months. At Sobibor, they murdered about 250,000. These camps began operation during the spring and summer of 1942, when the ghettos of German-occupied Poland were filled with Jews. Once they had completed their missions—murder by gassing, or "resettlement in the east," to use the language of the Wannsee protocols—the Nazis closed the camps. There were six extermination camps, all in German-occupied Poland, among the thousands of concentration and slave-labour camps throughout German-occupied Europe.

The word Holocaust is derived from the Greek *holokauston*, a translation of the Hebrew word *'olah*, meaning a burnt sacrifice offered whole to God. This word was chosen because in the ultimate manifestation of the Nazi killing program—the extermination camps—the bodies of the victims were consumed whole in crematoria and open fires. The impact of the Holocaust varied from region to region and from year to year in the 21 countries that were directly affected. Nowhere was the Holocaust more intense and sudden than in Hungary. What took place over several years in Germany occurred over 16 weeks in Hungary. Entering the war as a German ally, Hungary had persecuted its Jews but not

The Final Solution

permitted their deportation. After Germany invaded Hungary on March 19, 1944, this situation changed dramatically. By mid-April the Nazis had confined Jews to ghettos. On May 15, deportations began, and over the next 55 days, the Nazis deported some 438,000 Jews from Hungary to Auschwitz on 147 trains.

Policies differed widely among Germany's Balkan allies. In Romania it was primarily the Romanians themselves who slaughtered the country's Jews. Toward the end of the war, however, when the defeat of Germany was all but certain, the Romanian government found more value in living Jews who could be held for ransom or used as leverage with the West. Bulgaria permitted the deportation of Jews from neighbouring Thrace and Macedonia, but government leaders faced stiff opposition to the deportation of native Bulgarian Jews.

German-occupied Denmark rescued most of its own Jews by spiriting them to Sweden by sea in October 1943. This was possible partly because the German presence in Denmark was relatively small. Moreover, while anti-Semitism in the general population of many other countries led to collaboration with the Germans, Jews were an integrated part of Danish culture. Under these unique circumstances, Danish humanitarianism flourished.

In France, Jews under Fascist Italian occupation in the southeast fared better than the Jews of Vichy France, where collaborationist French authorities and police provided essential support to the understaffed German forces. The Jews in those parts of France under direct German occupation fared the worst. Although allied with Germany, the Italians did not participate in the Holocaust until Germany occupied northern Italy after the overthrow of the Fascist leader, Benito Mussolini.

Throughout German-occupied territory the situation of Jews was desperate. They had meagre resources and few allies and faced impossible choices. A few people came to their rescue, often at the risk of their own lives. Swedish diplomat Raoul Wallenberg arrived in Budapest on July 9, 1944, in an effort to save Hungary's sole remaining Jewish community. Over the next six months, he worked with other neutral diplomats, the Vatican, and Jews themselves to prevent the deportation of these last Jews. Elsewhere, Le Chambon-sur-Lignon, a French Huguenot village, became a haven for 5,000 Jews. In Poland, where it was illegal to aid Jews and where such action was punishable by death, the Zegota (Council for Aid to Jews) rescued a similar number of Jewish men, women, and children. Financed by the Polish government in exile and involving a wide range of clandestine political organizations, the Zegota provided hiding places, financial support, and forged identity documents.

Some Germans, even some Nazis, dissented from the murder of the Jews and came to their aid. The most famous was Oskar Schindler, a Nazi businessman, who had set up operations using involuntary labour in German-occupied Poland in order to profit from the war. Eventually, he moved to protect his Jewish workers from deportation to extermination camps. In all occupied countries, there were individuals who came to the rescue of Jews, offering a place to hide, some food, or shelter for days, weeks, or even for the duration of the war. Most of the rescuers did not see their actions as heroic but felt bound to the Jews by a common sense of humanity. Israel later recognized rescuers with honorary citizenship and commemoration at Yad Vashem, Israel's memorial to the Holocaust.

Although the Germans killed victims from several groups, the Holocaust is primarily associated with the murder of the Jews. Only the Jews were targeted for total annihilation, and their elimination was central to Hitler's vision of the "New Germany." The intensity of the Nazi campaign against the Jews continued unabated to the very end of the war and at points even took priority over German military efforts.

When the war ended, Allied armies found between seven and nine million displaced persons living outside their own countries. More than six million people returned to their native lands, but more than one million refused repatriation. Some had collaborated with the Nazis and feared retaliation. Others feared persecution under the new Communist regimes. For the Jews, the situation was different. They had no homes to return to. Their communities had been shattered, their homes destroyed or occupied by strangers, and their families decimated and dispersed. First came the often long and difficult physical recuperation from starvation and malnutrition, then the search for loved ones lost or missing, and finally the question of the future.

Upon liberating the camps, many Allied units were so shocked by what they saw that they meted out spontaneous punishment to some of the remaining SS personnel. Others were arrested and held for trial. The most famous of the postwar trials occurred in 1945–46 at Nürnberg, the former site of Nazi Party rallies. There, the International Military Tribunal tried 22 major Nazi officials for war crimes, crimes against the peace, and a new category of crimes: crimes against humanity. This new category encompassed "murder, extermination, enslavement, deportation, and other inhumane acts committed against any civilian population... persecution on political, racial, or religious grounds... whether or not in violation of the domestic laws of the country where perpetrated." After the first trials, 185 defendants were divided into 12 groups, including physicians responsible for medical experimentation (but not so-called euthanasia), judges who preserved the facade of legality for Nazi crimes, Einsatzgruppe leaders, commandants of concentration camps, German generals, and business leaders who profited from slave labour. The defendants made up, however, a miniscule fraction of those who had perpetrated the crimes. In the eyes of many, their trials were a desperate, inadequate, but necessary effort to restore a semblance of justice in the aftermath of so great a crime. The Nürnberg trials established the precedent, later enshrined by international convention, that crimes against humanity are punishable by an international tribunal.

CHAPTER 7

DEVELOPMENTS FROM AUTUMN 1943 TO SUMMER 1944

Hitler's greatest strategic disadvantage in opposing the Allies' imminent reentry into Europe lay in the immense stretch of Germany's conquests, from the west coast of France to the east coast of Greece. It was difficult for him to gauge where the Allies would strike next. The Allies' greatest strategic advantage lay in the wide choice of alternative objectives and in the powers of distraction they enjoyed through their superior sea power. Hitler, while always having to guard against a cross-Channel invasion from England's shores, had cause to fear that the Anglo-American armies in North Africa might land anywhere on his southern front between Spain and Greece.

Sicily and the Fall of Mussolini, July–August 1943

Having failed to save its forces in Tunisia, the Axis had only 10 Italian divisions of various sorts and two German panzer units stationed on the island of Sicily at midsummer 1943. The Allies, meanwhile, were preparing to throw some 478,000 men into the island—150,000 of them in the first three days of the invasion. Under the supreme command of Alexander, Montgomery's British 8th Army and Patton's U.S. 7th Army were to be landed on two stretches of beach 40 miles long, 20 miles distant from one another, the British in the southeast of the island, the Americans in the south. The Allies' air superiority in the Mediterranean theatre was so great by this time—more than 4,000 aircraft against some 1,500 German and Italian ones—that the Axis bombers had been withdrawn from Sicily in June to bases in north-central Italy.

On July 10 Allied seaborne troops landed on Sicily. The coastal defenses, manned largely by Sicilians unwilling to turn their homeland into a battlefield for the Germans' sake, collapsed rapidly enough. The British forces had cleared the whole southeastern part of the island in the first three days of the invasion. The Allies' drive toward Messina then took the form of a circuitous movement by the British around Mount Etna in combination with an eastward drive by the Americans, who took Palermo, on the western half of the northern coast, on July 22. Meanwhile, the German armoured strength in Sicily had been reinforced.

After the successive disasters sustained by the Axis in Africa, many of the Italian leaders were desperately anxious to make peace with the Allies. The invasion of Sicily, representing an immediate threat to the Italian mainland, prompted them to action. On the night of July 24–25, 1943, when Mussolini revealed to the Fascist Grand Council that the Germans were thinking of evacuating the southern half of Italy, the majority of the council voted for a resolution against him, and he resigned his powers. On July 25 the king, Victor Emmanuel III, ordered the arrest of Mussolini and entrusted Marshal Pietro Badoglio with the formation of a new government. The new government entered into secret negotiations with the Allies, despite the presence of sizable German forces in Italy.

A few days after the fall of Mussolini, Field Marshal Albert Kesselring, the German commander in chief in Italy, decided

Developments from Autumn 1943 to Summer 1944

that the Axis troops in Sicily must be evacuated; the local Italian commander thought so too. While rearguard actions held up the Allies at Adrano (on the western face of Mount Etna) and at Randazzo (to the north), 40,000 Germans and 60,000 Italian troops were safely withdrawn across the Strait of Messina to the mainland, mostly in the week ending on Aug. 16, 1943—the day before the Allies' entry into Messina.

The Allies sustained about 22,800 casualties in their conquest of Sicily. The Axis powers suffered about 165,000 casualties, of whom 30,000 were Germans.

The Quadrant Conference (Quebec I)

The success of the Sicilian operation and the fall of Mussolini converted the American military and political leadership into supporters of a campaign in Italy. Furthermore, Lieutenant General Sir Frederick Morgan, who after Casablanca had been designated chief of staff to the Supreme Allied Commander (COSSAC), produced a detailed and realistic plan for the long-envisaged invasion of France from Great Britain, thus enabling the U.S. strategists to calculate more precisely how much of the Allies' resources were needed for that purpose and how much could be spared for operations in the Mediterranean and for the Pacific. With regard to the Pacific, plans sponsored by Admiral Nimitz for operations against the Gilbert and Marshall islands apart from the enterprise against Rabaul were approved early in August 1943.

The new turn of strategical thought necessitated a new Anglo-U.S. conference, which took place in Quebec in mid-August 1943 and was code-named "Quadrant." After vigorous debate, the question of the timing of "Overlord" was eventually left open, but it was agreed that the strength of the assault force should exceed the original estimate by 25 percent, that the cross-Channel landing should be supported by a landing in southern France, and that a U.S. officer should be in command of "Overlord." It was also decided that a new Southeast Asia theatre of war should be organized, under British command.

The Allies' Invasion of Italy and the Italian Volte-Face, 1943

From Sicily, the Allies had a wide choice of directions for their next offensive. Calabria, the "toe" of Italy, was the nearest and most obvious possible destination, and the "shin" was also vulnerable, and the "heel" was also very attractive. The two army corps of Montgomery's 8th Army crossed the Strait of Messina and landed on the "toe" of Italy on Sept. 3, 1943, but, though the initial resistance was practically negligible, they made only very slow progress, as the terrain, with only two good roads running up the coasts of the great Calabrian "toe" prevented the deployment of large forces. On the day of the landing, however, the Italian government at last agreed to the Allies' secret terms for a capitulation. It was understood that Italy would be treated with leniency in direct proportion to the part that it would take, as soon as possible, in the war against Germany. The capitulation was announced on September 8.

The landing on the "shin" of Italy, at Salerno, just south of Naples, was begun on September 9, by the mixed U.S.–British 5th Army, under U.S. General Mark Clark. Transported by 700 ships, 55,000 men made the initial assault, and 115,000 more followed up. At first they were faced only by the German 16th Panzer Division, but Kesselring, though he had only eight weak divisions to defend all southern and central Italy, had had time to plan since the fall of Mussolini and had been expecting a blow at the "shin." His counterstroke made the success of the Salerno landing precarious for six days, and it was not until October 1 that the 5th Army entered Naples.

British troops assemble captured German soldiers after the Allied offensive at Salerno.

By contrast, the much smaller landing on the "heel" of Italy, which had been made on September 2 (the day preceding the invasion of the "toe"), took the Germans by surprise. Notwithstanding the paucity of its strength in men and in equipment, the expedition captured two good ports, Taranto and Brindisi, in a very short time, but it lacked the resources to advance promptly. Nearly a fortnight passed before another small force was landed at Bari, the next considerable port north of Brindisi, to push thence unopposed into Foggia.

It was the threat to their rear from the "heel" of Italy and from Foggia that had induced the Germans to fall back from their positions defending Naples against the 5th Army. When the Italian government, in pursuance of a Badoglio–Eisenhower agreement of September 29, declared war against Germany on Oct. 13, 1943, Kesselring was already receiving reinforcements and consolidating the German hold on central and northern Italy. The 5th Army was checked temporarily on the Volturno

KATYN MASSACRE

The Katyn Massacre was the mass execution of Polish military officers by the Soviet Union during World War II. The discovery of the massacre precipitated the severance of diplomatic relations between the Soviet Union and the Polish government-in-exile in London.

After Nazi Germany and the Soviet Union concluded their Nonaggression Pact of 1939 and Germany invaded Poland from the west, Soviet forces occupied the eastern half of Poland. As a consequence of this occupation, tens of thousands of Polish military personnel fell into Soviet hands and were interned in prison camps inside the Soviet Union. But after the Germans invaded the Soviet Union (June 1941), the Polish government-in-exile (located in London) and the Soviet government agreed to cooperate against Germany, and a Polish army on Soviet territory was to be formed. The Polish general Wladyslaw Anders began organizing this army, but when he requested that 15,000 Polish prisoners of war whom the Soviets had once held at camps near Smolensk be transferred to his command, the Soviet government informed him in December 1941 that most of those prisoners had escaped to Manchuria and could not be located.

The fate of the missing prisoners remained a mystery. Then on April 13, 1943, the Germans announced that they had discovered mass graves of Polish officers in the Katyn forest near Smolensk, in western Russian S.F.S.R. A total of 4,443 corpses were recovered that had apparently been shot from behind and then piled in stacks and buried. Investigators identified the corpses as the Polish officers who had been interned at a Soviet prison camp near Smolensk and accused the Soviet authorities of having executed the prisoners in May 1940. In response to these charges, the Soviet government claimed that the Poles had been engaged in construction work west of Smolensk in 1941 and the invading German army had killed them after overrunning that area in August

1941. But both German and Red Cross investigations of the Katyn corpses then produced firm physical evidence that the massacre took place in early 1940, at a time when the area was still under Soviet control.

The Polish government-in-exile in London requested that the International Committee of the Red Cross examine the graves and also asked the Soviet government to provide official reports on the fates of the remaining missing prisoners. The Soviet government refused these demands, and on April 25, 1943, the Soviets broke diplomatic relations with the Polish government in London. The Soviets then set about establishing a Polish government-in-exile composed of Polish communists.

The Katyn Massacre left a deep scar in Polish-Soviet relations during the remainder of the war and afterward. For Poles, Katyn became a symbol of the many victims of Stalinism. Although a 1952 U.S. congressional inquiry concluded that the Soviet Union had been responsible for the massacre, Soviet leaders insisted for decades that the Polish officers found at Katyn had been killed by the invading Germans in 1941. This explanation was accepted without protest by successive Polish communist governments until the late 1980s, when the Soviet Union allowed a noncommunist coalition government to come to power in Poland. In March 1989 this government officially shifted the blame for the Katyn Massacre from the Germans to the Soviet secret police, the NKVD. In 1992 the Russian government released documents proving that the Soviet Politburo and the NKVD had been responsible for the massacre and cover-up and revealing that there may have been more than 20,000 victims. In 2000 a memorial was opened at the site of the killings in Katyn.

On April 7, 2010, Russian Prime Minister Vladimir Putin joined Polish Prime Minister Donald Tusk at a ceremony commemorating the massacre, marking the first time that a Russian leader had taken part in such a commemoration. Three days later, on April 10, a plane carrying Polish Pres. Lech Kaczynski to another commemoration ceremony crashed near Smolensk and the Katyn site, killing Kaczynski, his wife, the head of the national security bureau, the president of the national bank, the army chief of staff, and a number of other Polish government officials.

In November 2010 the State Duma (the lower house of the Russian Federal Assembly) officially declared that Joseph Stalin and other Soviet leaders were responsible for ordering the execution of the Polish officers at Katyn.

River, only 20 miles north of Naples, then more lastingly on the Garigliano River, while the 8th Army, having made its way from Calabria up the Adriatic coast, was likewise held on the Sangro River. Autumn and midwinter passed without the Allies' making any notable impression on the Germans' Gustav Line, which ran for 100 miles from the mouth of the Garigliano through Cassino and over the Apennines to the mouth of the Sangro.

The Western Allies and Stalin: Cairo and Tehran, 1943

Relations between the Western Allies and the U.S.S.R. were still delicate. Besides their inability to satisfy Soviet demands for convoys of supplies and for an early invasion of France, the Americans and the British were embarrassed by the discrepancy between their political war aims and Stalin's.

The longest-standing difference was about Poland. While Poles were still fighting on the Allies' side and acknowledging the authority of General Wladyslaw Sikorski's London-based Polish government in exile, Stalin was trying to get the Allies to consent to the U.S.S.R.'s retention, after the

Developments from Autumn 1943 to Summer 1944

war, of all the territory taken from Poland by virtue of the German–Soviet pacts of 1939. On Jan. 16, 1943, the Soviet government announced that Poles from the border territories in dispute were being treated as Soviet citizens and drafted into the Red Army. On April 25, the Soviet government severed relations with the London Poles, and Moscow subsequently began to build up its own puppet government for postwar Poland.

Besides the quarrel over Poland, the Western Allies and the U.S.S.R. were also at variance with regard to the postwar fate of other European states still under German domination, but the Americans and the British were really more interested in maintaining the Soviet war effort against Germany than in insisting, at the risk of offense to Stalin, on the detailed application of their own loudly but vaguely enunciated war aims.

Sextant, the conference of Nov. 22–27, 1943, for which Churchill, Roosevelt, and Chiang Kai-shek met in Cairo, was, on Roosevelt's insistence, devoted mainly to discussing plans for a British–U.S.–Chinese operation in northern Burma. Little was produced by Sextant except the Cairo Declaration, published on December 1, a further statement of war aims. It prescribed inter alia that Japan was to surrender all Pacific islands acquired since 1914, to retrocede Manchuria, Formosa, and the Pescadores to China, and to give up all other territory "taken by violence and greed," and, in addition, it was stipulated that Korea was in due course to become independent.

From Cairo, Roosevelt and Churchill went to Tehran, to meet Stalin at the Eureka conference of November 28–December 1. Stalin renewed the Soviet promise of military intervention against Japan, but he primarily wanted an assurance that "Overlord" (the invasion of France) would indeed take place in 1944. Reassured about this by Roosevelt, he declared that the Red Army would attack simultaneously on the Eastern Front. On the political plane, Stalin now demanded the Baltic coast of East Prussia for the U.S.S.R. as well as the territories annexed in 1939–40. The main communique of the conference was accompanied by a joint declaration guaranteeing the postwar restoration of Iran. Returning to Cairo, Roosevelt and Churchill spent six more days, December 2–7, in staff talks to compose their differences on strategy. They finally agreed that "Overlord" (with Eisenhower in command) should have first claim on resources.

German Strategy, from 1943

From late 1942 German strategy, every feature of which was determined by Hitler, was solely aimed at protecting the still very large area under German control—most of Europe and part of North Africa—against a future Soviet onslaught on the Eastern Front and against future Anglo-U.S. offensives on the southern and western fronts. The Germans' vague hopes that the Allies would shrink from such costly tasks or that the "unnatural" coalition of Western capitalism and Soviet Communism would break up before achieving victory were disappointed, so Hitler, in accordance with his dictum that "Germany shall either be a world power or not be at all," consciously resolved to preside over the downfall of the German nation. He gave inflexible orders whereby whole armies were made to stand their ground in tactically hopeless positions and were forbidden to surrender under any circumstances. The initial success of this strategy in preventing a German rout during the Soviet winter counteroffensive of 1941–42 had blinded Hitler to its impracticability in the very different military circumstances on the Eastern Front by 1943, by which time the Germans simply lacked sufficient numbers of troops to defend an extremely long front against

Developments from Autumn 1943 to Summer 1944

much more numerous Soviet forces. (By December 1943 the 3,000,000 German troops there were opposed by about 5,500,000 Soviet troops.)

The strategy of keeping his armies stationary was made easier for Hitler by the complete ascendancy he had achieved over his generals, who disputed with Hitler only at the risk of losing their commands or worse. Frequent changes were made in the command of the various army groups and armies, with the result that during 1943–44 most of the talented commanders who had been associated with Germany's past successes were removed, and everyone who was suspected of a critical attitude at headquarters was silenced.

From late 1943 on, Hitler's strategy, which from a political standpoint remains inexplicable to most Western historians, was to strengthen the German forces in western Europe at the expense of those on the Eastern Front. In view of the danger of the great Anglo-U.S. invasion of western Europe that seemed imminent by early 1944, the loss of some part of his eastern conquests evidently seemed to Hitler to be less serious. Hitler continued to insist on the primacy of the war in the west after the start of the Allied invasion of northern France in June 1944, and while his armies made strenuous efforts to contain the Allied bridgehead in Normandy for the next two months, Hitler accepted the annihilation of the German Army Group Centre on the Eastern Front by the Soviet summer offensive (from June 1944), which brought the Red Army in a few weeks' time to the Vistula River and the borders of East Prussia. But the Western Front likewise crumbled in a few weeks, whereupon the Allies advanced to Germany's western borders. Then, still adhering to his guiding principle, Hitler assembled on the Western Front all that was left of his forces there and tried to drive the British and Americans back in what became known as the Battle of the Bulge. This campaign had some successes but meant that Germany's last battleworthy units were used on the Western Front while the Red Army, heavily outnumbering the remaining German troops in the east, resumed its drive on the eastern frontiers of Germany and reached the Oder River by the end of January 1945.

The Eastern Front, October 1943–April 1944

By the end of the first week of October 1943, the Red Army had established several bridgeheads on the right bank of the Dnieper River. Then, while General N.F. Vatutin's drive against Kiev was engaging the Germans' attention, General Ivan Stepanovich Konev suddenly pushed so far forward from the Kremenchug bridgehead (more than halfway downstream between Kiev and Dnepropetrovsk) that the German forces within the great bend of the Dnieper to the south would have been isolated if Manstein had not stemmed the Soviet advance just in time to extricate them. By early November the Red Army had reached the mouth of the Dnieper also, and the Germans in Crimea were isolated. Kiev, too, fell to Vatutin on November 6, and Zhitomir, 80 miles to the west, and Korosten, north of Zhitomir, fell in the next 12 days. Farther north, however, the Germans, who had already fallen back from Smolensk to a line covering the upper Dnieper, repelled with little difficulty five rather predictable Soviet thrusts toward Minsk in the last quarter of 1943.

Vatutin's forces from the Zhitomir–Korosten sector advanced westward across the prewar Polish frontier on Jan 4, 1944, and, though another German flank attack, by troops drawn from adjacent fronts, slowed them down, they had reached Lutsk, 100 miles farther west, a month later. Vatutin's

Developments from Autumn 1943 to Summer 1944

left wing, meanwhile, wheeled southward to converge with Konev's right so that 10 German divisions were encircled near Korsun, on the Dnieper line south of Kiev. Vainly trying to save those 10 divisions, the Germans had to abandon Nikopol, in the Dnieper bend far to the south, with its valuable manganese mines.

March 1944 saw a triple thrust by the Red Army: Zhukov, succeeding to Vatutin's command, drove southwest toward Tarnopol, to outflank the Germans on the upper stretches of the southern Bug River. General Rodion Yakovlevich Malinovsky, in the south, advanced across the mouth of the latter river from that of the Dnieper; and between them Konev, striking over the central stretch of the Bug, reached the Dniester, 70 miles ahead, and succeeded in crossing it. When Zhukov had crossed the upper Prut River and Konev was threatening Iasi on the Moldavian stretch of the river, the Carpathian Mountains were the only natural barrier remaining between the Red Army and the Hungarian Plain. German troops occupied Hungary on March 20, since Hitler suspected that the Hungarian regent, Admiral Miklós Horthy, might not resist the Red Army to the utmost.

A German counterstroke from the Lwów area of southern Poland against Zhukov's extended flank early in April not only put an end to the latter's overhasty pressure on the Tatar (Yablonitsky) Pass through the Carpathians but also made possible the withdrawal of some of the German forces endangered by the Red Army's March operation. Konev, too, was halted in front of Iasi, but his left swung southward down the Dniester to converge with Malinovsky's drive on Odessa. That great port fell to the Red Army on April 10. On May 9 the Germans in Crimea abandoned Sevastopol, caught as they were between Soviet pincers from the mainland north of the isthmus and from the east across the Strait of Kerch.

At the northern end of the Eastern Front, a Soviet offensive in January 1944 had been followed by an orderly German retreat from the fringes of the long-besieged Leningrad area to a shorter line exploiting the great lakes farther to the south. The retreat was beneficial to the Germans but sacrificed their land link with the Finns, who now found themselves no better off than they had been in 1939–40. Finland in February 1944 sought an armistice from the U.S.S.R., but the latter's terms proved unacceptable.

The War in the Pacific, October 1943– August 1944

Considering that it might be necessary for them to invade Japan proper, the Allies drew up new plans in mid-1943. The main offensive, it was decided, should be from the south and from the southeast, through the Philippines and through Micronesia (rather than from the Aleutians in the North Pacific or from the Asian mainland). While occupation of the Philippines would disrupt Japanese communications with the East Indian isles west of New Guinea and with Malaya, the conquest of Micronesia, from the Gilberts by way of the Marshalls and Carolines to the Marianas, would not only offer the possibility of drawing the Japanese into a naval showdown but also win bases for heavy air raids on the Japanese mainland prior to invasion.

For the approach to the Philippines, it was prerequisite, on the one hand, to complete the encirclement of Rabaul, thereby nullifying the threat from the Japanese positions in the Solomon Islands and in the Bismarck Archipelago (New Britain, New Ireland, etc.) and, on the other, to reduce the Japanese hold on western New Guinea. Great emphasis, however, was put on the advance across the central Pacific through Micronesia, to be begun via the Gilberts.

THE ENCIRCLEMENT OF RABAUL

Allied moves to isolate the large Japanese garrison on Rabaul proceeded by land and air. The encirclement of Rabaul by land began during October and November 1943 with the capture by New Zealand troops of the Treasury Islands in the Solomons and was accompanied on November 1 by a U.S. landing at Empress Augusta Bay on the west of Bougainville. U.S. reinforcements subsequently repulsed Japanese counter-attacks in December, when they sank two destroyers, and in March 1944, when they killed almost 6,000 men. What remained of the Japanese garrison on Bougainville was no longer capable of fighting, though it did not surrender until the end of the war.

Continuing the approach to Rabaul, U.S. troops landed on December 15 at Arawe on the southwestern coast of New Britain, thereby distracting Japanese attention from Cape Gloucester, on the northwestern coast, where a major landing was made on December 26. By Jan. 16, 1944, the airstrip at Cape Gloucester had been captured and defense lines set up. Talasea, halfway to Rabaul, fell in March 1944. The conquest of western New Britain secured Allied control of the Vitiaz and Dampier straits between that island and New Guinea.

By constructing air bases on each island that they captured, the Allies systematically blocked any westward movement that the Japanese might have made: New Zealand troops took the Green Islands southeast of New Guinea on February 15, and U.S. forces invaded Los Negros in the Admiralty Islands on February 29 and captured Manus on March 9.

With the fall of the Emirau Islands on March 20, the Allies' stranglehold on Rabaul and Kavieng was practically complete so that they could thenceforth disregard the 100,000 Japanese immobilized there.

WESTERN NEW GUINEA

Before they could push northward to the Philippines, the Allies had to subdue Japanese-held western New Guinea. U.S. troops took Saidor, on the Huon Peninsula, on Jan. 2, 1944, and established an air base there, and the Australians took Sio, to the east of Saidor, on January 16. Then reinforcements were landed at Mindiri, west of Saidor, on March 5, and Australian infantry began to move westward up the coast, to take Bogadjim, Madang, and Alexishafen.

Bypassing Hansa Bay (which was eventually captured on June 15) and Wewak, whither the Japanese had retreated, the Allies, on April 22, 1944, made two simultaneous landings at Hollandia: Having in the past weeks already destroyed 300 Japanese planes, they captured the airfields there in four days' time. In the following months Hollandia was converted into a major base and command post for the Southwest Pacific area. The Allies also took Aitape, on the coast east of Hollandia, and held it against counterattacks by more than 200,000 Wewak-based Japanese during July and August. Biak, the isle guarding the entrance to Geelvink Bay, west of Hollandia, was invaded by U.S. troops on May 27, 1944, but the Japanese defense of it was maintained until early August. Though westernmost New Guinea fell likewise to the Allies in August 1944, the Japanese garrison at Wewak held out until May 10, 1945.

THE CENTRAL PACIFIC

Though the U.S. Joint Chiefs of Staff envisaged no major offensive westward across the Pacific toward Formosa until mid-1944, they nevertheless decided to launch a limited offensive in the central Pacific in 1943, hoping thereby both

Developments from Autumn 1943 to Summer 1944

to speed the pace of the war and to draw the Japanese away from other areas. Accordingly, Nimitz' central Pacific forces invaded the Gilberts on Nov. 23, 1943. Makin fell easily, but well-fortified Japanese defenses on Tarawa cost the U.S. Marines 1,000 killed and 2,300 wounded. Japanese losses in the Gilberts totaled about 8,500 men.

Having been forced to cede the Gilberts, the Japanese elected next to defend the Marshalls, in order both to absorb Allied forces and to strain the latters' extended lines of supply. Nimitz subjected Kwajalein Atoll, which he chose first to attack, to so heavy a preliminary bombardment that the U.S. infantry could land on it on Jan. 31, 1944, and U.S. forces moved on to Enewetak on February 17.

In support of the landings on the Marshalls, the U.S. fleet on Feb. 17, 1944, started a series of day and night attacks against the Japanese base at Truk in the Caroline Islands, where they destroyed some 300 aircraft and 200,000 tons of merchant shipping. Henceforth, the Allies could confidently ignore Truk and bypass it.

The Allies' next objective, for which they required more than 500 ships and 125,000 troops, was to reduce the Mariana Islands, lying 1,000 miles from Enewetak and 3,500 miles from Pearl Harbor. Against this threat, after the destruction at Truk, the Japanese hastily drew up a new defense plan, "Operation A," relying on their remaining 1,055 land-based aircraft in the Marianas, in the Carolines, and in western New Guinea and on timely and decisive intervention by a sea force, which should include nine aircraft carriers with 450 aircraft. But in the spring of 1944 the Japanese air strength was still further depleted, and, moreover, on March 31 the sponsor of the plan, Admiral Koga Mineichi (Yamamoto's successor), and his staff were killed in an air disaster. When, on June 15, two U.S. Marine divisions went ashore on Saipan Island in the

U.S. Marines advance against Japanese positions on Saipan in 1944.

Marianas, the 30,000 Japanese defenders put up so fierce a resistance that an army division was needed to reinforce the Marines. Using the same defensive tactics as on other small islands, the Japanese had fortified themselves in underground caves and bunkers that afforded protection from American artillery and naval bombardment. Notwithstanding this, the Japanese defenders were gradually compressed into smaller and smaller pockets, and they themselves ended most organized resistance with a suicidal counterattack on July 7, the largest of its kind during the war.

   The loss of Saipan was such a disaster for Japan that when the news was announced in Tokyo the prime minister, Tojo Hideki, and his entire cabinet resigned. To realists in the Japanese high command, the loss of the Marianas spelled the ultimate loss of the war, but no one dared say so. Tojo's cabinet was succeeded by that of General Koiso

Developments from Autumn 1943 to Summer 1944

Kuniaki, which was pledged to carrying on the fight with renewed vigour.

Air power enthusiasts have called the conquest of Saipan "the turning point of the war in the Pacific," for it enabled the United States to establish air bases there for the big B-29 bombers, which had been developed for the specific purpose of bombing Japan. The first flight of 100 B-29s took off from Saipan on Nov. 24, 1944, and bombed Tokyo, the first bombing raid on the Japanese capital since 1942.

While the Japanese were still resisting on Saipan, the Japanese Combined Fleet, under Admiral Ozawa Jisaburo, was approaching from Philippine and East Indian anchorages, in accordance with "Operation A," to challenge the U.S. 5th Fleet, under Admiral Raymond Spruance. Ozawa, with only nine aircraft carriers against 15 for the United States, was obviously inferior in naval power, but he counted heavily on help from land-based aircraft on Guam, Rota, and Yap. The encounter, which took place west of the Marianas and is known as the Battle of the Philippine Sea, has been called the greatest carrier battle of the war. It began on June 19 when Ozawa sent 430 planes in four waves against Spruance's ships. The result was a disaster for the Japanese. U.S. airmen shot down more than 300 planes and sank two carriers, and as the Japanese fleet retreated northward toward Okinawa it lost another carrier and almost 100 more planes. The United States lost about 130 planes. The hasty and incomplete training of the Japanese pilots and the inadequate armour plating of their planes were decisive factors in the numerous aerial combats of this battle, which was ultimately of more strategic importance than the fall of Saipan. Nimitz's forces could thereafter occupy other major islands in the Marianas: Guam on July 21 and Tinian on July 24. The Marianas cost the Japanese 46,000 killed or captured, the Americans only 4,750 killed.

The Burmese Frontier and China, November 1943–Summer 1944

For the dry season of 1943–44 both the Japanese and the Allies were resolved on offensives in Southeast Asia. On the Japanese side, Lieutenant General Kawabe Masakazu planned a major Japanese advance across the Chindwin River, on the central front, in order to occupy the plain of Imphal and to establish a firm defensive line in eastern Assam. The Allies, for their part, planned a number of thrusts into Burma: Stilwell's NCAC forces, including his three Chinese divisions and "Merrill's Marauders" (U.S. troops trained by Wingate on Chindit lines), were to advance against Mogaung and Myitkyina, while Slim's 14th Army was to launch its XV Corps southeastward into Arakan and its IV Corps eastward to the Chindwin. Because the Japanese had habitually got the better of advanced British forces by outflanking them, Slim formulated a new tactic to ensure that his units would stand against attack in the forthcoming campaign, even if they should be isolated: They were to know that, when ordered to stand, they could certainly count both on supplies from the air and on his use of reserve troops to turn the situation against the Japanese attackers.

On the southern wing of the Burmese front, the XV Corps's Arakan operation, launched in November 1943, had achieved most of its objectives by the end of January 1944. When the Japanese counterattack surrounded one Indian division and part of another, Slim's new tactic was brought into play, and the Japanese found themselves crushed between the encircled Indians and the relieving forces.

The Japanese crossing of the Chindwin into Assam, on the central Burmese front, when the fighting in Arakan was dying down, played into Slim's hands, since he could now profit from the Allies' superiority in aircraft and in tanks. The Japanese

Developments from Autumn 1943 to Summer 1944

were able to approach Imphal and to surround Kohima, but the British forces protecting these towns were reinforced with several Indian divisions that were taken from the now-secure Arakan front. With air support, Slim's reinforced forces now defended Imphal against multiple Japanese thrusts and outflanking movements until, in mid-May 1944, he was able to launch two of his divisions into an offensive eastward, while still containing the last bold effort of the Japanese to capture Imphal. By June 22 the 14th Army had averted the Japanese menace to Assam and won the initiative for its own advance into Burma. The Battle of Imphal–Kohima cost the British and Indian forces 17,587 casualties (12,600 of them sustained at Imphal), the Japanese forces 30,500 dead (including 8,400 from disease) and 30,000 wounded.

On the northern Burmese front, Stilwell's forces were already approaching Mogaung and Myitkyina before the southern crisis of Imphal–Kohima, and the subsidiary Chindit operation against Indaw was going well ahead when, on March 24, 1944, Wingate himself was killed in an air crash. Meanwhile, Chiang Kai-shek was constrained by U.S. threats of a suspension of lend-lease to finally authorize some action by the 12 divisions of his Yunnan Army, which on May 12, 1944, with air support, began to cross the Salween River westward in the direction of Myitkyina, Bhamo, and Lashio. Myitkyina airfield was taken by Stilwell's forces, with "Merrill's Marauders," on May 17, Mogaung was taken by the Chindits on June 26, and finally Myitkyina itself was taken by Stilwell's Chinese divisions on August 3. All of northwest and much of northern Burma was now in Allied hands.

In China proper, a Japanese attack toward Ch'ang-sha, begun on May 27, won control not only of a further stretch of the north–south axis of the Peking–Han-K'ou railroad but also of several of the airfields from which the Americans had been bombing the Japanese in China and were intending to bomb them in Japan.

A mortar crew on the Gustav Line, January 1944.

The Italian Front, 1944

The Allies' northward advance up the Italian peninsula to Rome was still blocked by Kesselring's Gustav Line, which was hinged on Monte Cassino. To bypass that line, the Allies landed some 50,000 seaborne troops, with 5,000 vehicles, at Anzio, only 33 miles south of Rome, on Jan. 22, 1944. The landing surprised the Germans and was met, at first, with very little opposition, but, instead of driving on over the Alban Hills to Rome at once, the force at Anzio spent so much time consolidating its position there that Kesselring was able, with his reserves, to develop a powerful counteroffensive against it on February 3. The beachhead was thereby reduced to a very

Developments from Autumn 1943 to Summer 1944

shallow dimension, while the defenses at Monte Cassino held out unimpaired against a new assault by Clark's 5th Army.

For a final effort against the Gustav Line, Alexander decided to shift most of the 8th Army, now commanded by Major General Sir Oliver Leese, from the Adriatic flank of the peninsula to the west, where it was to strengthen the 5th Army's pressure around Monte Cassino and on the approaches to the valley of the Liri (headstream of the Garigliano). The combined attack, which was started in the night of May 11–12, 1944, succeeded in breaching the German defenses at a number of points between Cassino and the coast. Thanks to this victory, the Americans could push forward up the coast, while the British entered the valley and outflanked Monte Cassino, which fell to a Polish corps of the 8th Army on May 18. Five days later, the Allies' force at Anzio struck out against the investing Germans (whose strength had been diminished in order to reinforce the Gustav Line), and by May 26 it had achieved a breakthrough. When the 8th Army's Canadian Corps penetrated the last German defenses in the Liri Valley, the whole Gustav Line began to collapse.

Concentrating all available strength on his left wing, Alexander pressed up from the south to effect a junction with the troops thrusting northward from Anzio. The Germans in the Alban Hills could not withstand the massive attack. On June 5, 1944, the Allies entered Rome. The propaganda value of their occupying the Eternal City, Mussolini's former capital, was offset, however, by an unforeseen strategical reality: Kesselring's forces retreated not in the expected rout but gradually, to the line of the Arno River; Florence, 160 miles north of Rome, did not fall to the Allies until August 13; and by that time the Germans had made ready yet another chain of defenses, the Gothic Line, running from the Tyrrhenian coast midway between

Pisa and La Spezia, over the Apennines in a reversed S curve, to the Adriatic coast between Pesaro and Rimini.

Alexander might have made more headway against Kesselring's new front if some of his forces had not been subtracted, in August 1944, for the American-sponsored but eventually unnecessary invasion of southern France ("Operation Anvil," finally renamed "Dragoon"). As it was, the 8th Army, switched back from the west to the Adriatic coast, achieved only an indecisive breakthrough toward Rimini. After this September offensive, the autumn rains set in, to make even more difficult Alexander's indirect movements, against Kesselring's resolute opposition, toward the mouth of the Po River.

CHAPTER 8

DEFEAT OF THE AXIS POWERS

The German army high command had long been expecting an Allied invasion of northern France but had no means of knowing where precisely the stroke would come: While Rundstedt, commander in chief in the west, thought that the landings would be made between Calais and Dieppe (at the narrowest width of the Channel between England and France), Hitler prophetically indicated the central and more westerly stretches of the coast of Normandy as the site of the attack, and Rommel, who was in charge of the forces on France's Channel coast, finally came around to Hitler's opinion. The fortifications of those stretches were consequently improved, but Rundstedt and Rommel still took different views about the way in which the invasion should be met: While Rundstedt recommended a massive counterattack on the invaders after their landing, Rommel, fearing that Allied air supremacy might interfere fatally with the adequate massing of the German forces for such a counterattack, advocated instead immediate action on the beaches against any attempted landing. The Germans had 59 divisions spread over western Europe from the Low Countries to the Atlantic and Mediterranean coasts of France, but approximately half of this number was static, and the remainder included only 10 armoured or motorized divisions.

World War II

The Allied Invasions of Western Europe, June–November 1944

Postponed from May, the Western Allies' "Operation Overlord," their long-debated invasion of northern France, took place on June 6, 1944—the war's most celebrated D-Day—when 156,000 men were landed on the beaches of Normandy between the Orne estuary and the southeastern end of the Cotentin Peninsula: 83,000 British and Canadian troops on the eastern beaches, 73,000 Americans on the western. Under Eisenhower's supreme direction and Montgomery's immediate command, the invading forces initially comprised the Canadian 1st Army (Lieutenant General Henry Duncan Graham Crerar); the British 2nd Army (Lieutenant General Sir Miles Dempsey); and the British 1st and 6th airborne divisions, the U.S. 1st

Reserve troops of the Canadian 3rd Division come ashore at Bernières, at the Nan sector of Juno Beach, on D-Day.

Army, and the U.S. 82nd and 101st airborne divisions (all under Lieutenant General Omar N. Bradley).

By 9:00 AM on D-Day the coastal defenses were generally breached, but Caen, which had been scheduled to fall on D-Day and was the hinge of an Allied advance, held out until July 9, the one panzer division already available there on June 6 having been joined the next day by a second. Though the heavy fighting at Caen attracted most of the German reserves, the U.S. forces in the westernmost sector of the front likewise met a very stubborn resistance. But when they had taken the port of Cherbourg on June 26 and proceeded to clear the rest of the Cotentin, they could turn southward to take Saint-Lô on July 18.

The Allies could not have made such rapid progress in northern France if their air forces had not been able to interfere decisively with the movement of the German reserves. Allied aircraft destroyed most of the bridges over the Seine River to the east and over the Loire to the south. The German reserves thus had to make long detours in order to reach the Normandy battle zone and were so constantly harassed on the march by Allied strafing that they suffered endless delays and only arrived in driblets. And even where reserves could have been brought up, their movement was sometimes inhibited by hesitation and dissension on the Germans' own side. Hitler, though he had rightly predicted the zone of the Allies' landings, came to mistakenly believe, after D-Day, that a second and larger invasion was to be attempted east of the Seine and so was reluctant to allow reserves to be moved westward over that river. He also forbade the German forces already engaged in Normandy to retreat in time to make an orderly withdrawal to new defenses.

Rundstedt, meanwhile, was slow in obtaining Hitler's authority for the movement of the general reserve's SS panzer corps from its position north of Paris to the front, and Rommel, though he made prompt use of the forces at hand, had been absent from his headquarters on D-Day itself, when a forecast of rough weather had seemed to make a cross-Channel invasion unlikely. Subsequently, Rundstedt's urgent plea for permission to retreat provoked Hitler, on July 3, to appoint Günther von Kluge as commander in chief in the west in Rundstedt's place, and Rommel was badly hurt on July 17, when his car crashed under attack from Allied planes.

There was something else, besides the progress of the Allies, to demoralize the German commanders—the failure and the aftermath of a conspiracy against Hitler. Alarmed at the calamitous course of events and disgusted by the crimes of the Nazi regime, certain conservative but anti-Nazi civilian dignitaries and military officers had formed themselves into a secret opposition, with Karl Friedrich Goerdeler (a former chief mayor of Leipzig) and Colonel General Ludwig Beck (a former chief of the army general staff) among its leaders. From 1943 this opposition canvased the indispensable support of the active military authorities with some notable success: General Friedrich Olbricht (chief of the General Army Office) and several of the serving commanders, including Rommel and Kluge, became implicated to various extents. Apart from General Henning von Tresckow, however, the group's most dynamic member was Colonel Graf Claus von Stauffenberg, who as chief of staff to the chief of the army reserve from July 1, 1944, had access to Hitler. Finally, it was decided to kill Hitler and to use the army reserve for a coup d'état in Berlin, where a new regime under Beck and Goerdeler should be set up. On July 20, therefore, Stauffenberg left a bomb concealed in a briefcase in the room where Hitler was conferring at his headquarters in East Prussia. The bomb duly exploded, but Hitler survived, and the coup in Berlin miscarried. The Nazi reaction was savage: Besides 200 immediately implicated conspirators, 5,000 people who were more remotely linked with the plot or were altogether unconnected with it were put to death. Kluge committed suicide on August 17, Rommel on October 14. Fear permeated and paralyzed the German high command in the weeks that followed.

On July 31, 1944, the Americans on the Allies' right, newly supported by the landing of the U.S. 3rd Army under Patton, broke through the German defenses at Avranches, the gateway from Normandy into Brittany. On August 7 a desperate counterattack by four panzer divisions from Mortain, east of Avranches, failed to seal the breach, and American tanks poured southward through the gap and flooded the open country beyond. Though some of the U.S. forces were then swung southwestward in the hope of seizing the Breton ports in pursuance of the original prescription of "Overlord" and though some went on in more southerly directions toward the crossings of the Loire, others were wheeled eastward—to trap, in the Falaise "pocket," a large part of the German forces retreating southward from the pressure of the Allies' left at Caen. The Americans' wide eastward flanking maneuver after the breakout speedily produced a general collapse of the German position in northern France.

Meanwhile, more and more Allied troops were being landed in Normandy. On August 1, two army groups were constituted: the 21st (comprising the British and Canadian armies) under Montgomery, and the 12th (for the Americans) under Bradley. By the middle of August an eastward wheel wider than that which had cut off the Falaise pocket had brought the Americans to Argentan, southeast of Falaise and level with the British and Canadian advance on the left (north) of the Allies' front so that a concerted drive eastward could now be launched, and on August 19 a U.S. division successfully crossed the Seine at Mantes-Gassicourt. Already on August 17 the Americans on the Loire had taken Orléans. The clandestine French Resistance in Paris rose against the Germans on August 19, and a French division under General Jacques Leclerc, pressing forward from Normandy, received the surrender of the German forces there and liberated the city on August 25.

The German forces would have had ample time to pull back to the Seine River and to form a strong defensive barrier line there had it not been for Hitler's stubbornly stupid orders that there should be no withdrawal. It was his folly that enabled the Allies to liberate France so quickly. The bulk of the German armoured forces and many infantry divisions were thrown into the Normandy battle and kept there by Hitler's "no withdrawal" orders until they collapsed and a large part of them were trapped. The fragments were incapable of further resistance, and their retreat (which was largely on foot) was soon outstripped by the British and American mechanized columns. More than 200,000 German troops were taken prisoner in France, and 1,200 German tanks had been destroyed in the fighting. When the Allies approached the German border at the beginning of September, after a sweeping drive from Normandy, there was no organized resistance to stop them from driving on into the heart of Germany.

Meanwhile, "Operation Dragoon" (formerly "Anvil") was launched on Aug. 15, 1944, when the U.S. 7th Army and the French 1st Army landed on the French Riviera, where there were only four German divisions to oppose them. While the Americans drove first into the Alps to take Grenoble, the French took Marseille on August 23 and then advanced eastward through France up the Rhône Valley, to be rejoined by the Americans north of Lyon early in September. Both armies then moved swiftly northeastward into Alsace.

In the north, however, some discord had arisen among the Allied commanders after the crossing of the Seine. Whereas

Montgomery wanted to concentrate on a single thrust northeastward through Belgium into the heavily industrialized Ruhr Valley (an area vital to Germany's war effort), the U.S. generals argued for continuing to advance eastward through France on a broad front, in accordance with the pre-invasion plan. Eisenhower, by way of compromise, decided on August 23 that Montgomery's drive into Belgium should have the prior claim on resources until Antwerp should have been captured but that thereafter the pre-invasion plan should be resumed.

Consequently, Montgomery's 2nd Army began its advance on August 29, entered Brussels on September 3, took Antwerp, with its docks intact, on September 4, and went on, three days later, to force its way across the Albert Canal. The U.S. 1st Army, meanwhile, supporting Montgomery on the right, had taken Namur on the day of the capture of Antwerp and was nearing Aachen. Far to the south, however, Patton's U.S. 3rd Army, having raced forward to take Verdun on August 31, was already beginning to cross the Moselle River near Metz on September 5, with the obvious possibility of achieving a breakthrough into Germany's economically important Saarland. Eisenhower, therefore, could no longer devote a preponderance of supplies to Montgomery at Patton's expense.

Montgomery nevertheless attempted a thrust to cross the Rhine River at Arnhem, the British 1st Airborne Division being dropped ahead there to clear the way for the 2nd Army, but the Germans were just able to check the thrust, thus isolating the parachutists, many of whom were taken prisoner. By this time, indeed, the German defense was rapidly stiffening as the Allies approached the German frontiers: The U.S. 1st Army spent a month grinding down the defenses of Aachen, which fell at last on October 20 (the first city of pre-war Germany to be captured by the Western Allies), and the 1st Canadian Army, on the left of the British 2nd, did not clear the Schelde estuary west of Antwerp, including Walcheren Island, until early November. Likewise, Patton's 3rd Army was held up before Metz.

The Allies' amazing advance of 350 miles in a few weeks was thus brought to a ha In early September the U.S. and British forces had had a combined superiority of 20 to 1 in tanks and 25 to 1 in aircraft over the Germans, but by November 1944 the Germans still held both the Ruhr Valley and the Saarland, after having been so near collapse in the west in early September that one or the other of those prizes could have easily been taken by the Allies. The root of the Allied armies' sluggishness in September was that none of their top planners had foreseen such a complete collapse of the Germans as occurred in August 1944. They were therefore not prepared, mentally or materially, to exploit it by a rapid offensive into Germany itself. The Germans thus obtained time to build up their defending forces in the west, with serious consequences both for occupied Europe and the postwar political situation of the Continent.

The Eastern Front, June–December 1944

After a successful offensive against the Finns on the Karelian Isthmus had culminated in the capture of Viipuri (Vyborg) on June 20, 1944, the Red Army on June 23 began a major onslaught on the Germans' front in Belorussia. The attackers' right wing took the bastion town of Vitebsk (Vitebskaya) and then wheeled southward across the highway from Orsha to Minsk; their left wing, under General Konstantin Konstantinovich Rokossovsky, broke through just north of the Pripet Marshes and then drove forward for 150 miles in a week, severing the highway farther to the west, between Minsk and Warsaw. Minsk itself fell to the Red Army on July 3, and, though the Germans extricated a large part of their forces from the Soviet enveloping movement, the Soviet tanks raced ahead, bypassing any attempts to block their path, and were deep into Lithuania and northeastern Poland by mid-July. Then the Soviet forces south of the Pripet Marshes struck too, capturing Lwów and pushing across the San River. This increase of pressure on the Germans enabled Rokossovsky's mobile columns to thrust still farther westward: They reached the Vistula River, and one of them, on July 31, even penetrated the suburbs of Warsaw. The Polish underground in Warsaw thereupon rose in revolt against the Germans and briefly gained control of the city. But three SS armoured divisions arrived to suppress the revolt in Warsaw, and the Soviet Red Army stood idly by across the Vistula while the Germans crushed the insurrection. Although the Soviet halt outside Warsaw was a purposeful move, it is true that the unprecedented length and speed of the Red Army's advance—450 miles in five weeks—had overstrained the Soviet communications. The halt on the Vistula was to last six months.

On August 20, however, two Soviet thrusts were launched in another direction—against the German salient in Bessarabia. A new government came to power in Romania on August 23 and not only suspended hostilities against the U.S.S.R. but also, on August 25, declared war against Germany. This long, premeditated volte-face opened the way for three great wheeling movements by the Red Army's left wing through the vast spaces of southeastern and central Europe: southwestward across Bulgaria, where they met no opposition; westward up the Danube Valley and over the Yugoslav frontier; and northwestward through the Carpathians into Transylvania. The Germans could only try to hold the threatened centres of communication long enough for the withdrawal of their forces from Greece and from southern Yugoslavia. Belgrade fell to a concerted action by the Red Army and Tito's Partisan forces on

Oct. 20, 1944, and a rapid drive from the Transylvanian sector into the Hungarian Plain brought Soviet forces up to the suburbs of Budapest on November 4. Budapest, however, was stubbornly defended: By the end of the year, it was enveloped but still holding out.

At the northern end of the Eastern Front, Finland had capitulated early in September, and the following weeks saw a series of scythelike strokes by the Red Army against the German forces remaining in Estonia, Latvia, and Lithuania. By mid-October the remnants of those forces were cornered in Courland, but the subsequent Soviet attempt to break through from Lithuania into East Prussia was repelled.

Air Warfare, 1944

The Allies' strategic air offensive against Germany began to attain its maximum effectiveness in the opening months of 1944. Both the U.S. air forces concerned, namely, the 8th in England and the 15th in Italy, were increased in numbers and improved in technical proficiency. By the end of 1943 the 8th Bomber Command alone could mount attacks of 700 planes, and early in 1944 regular 1,000-bomber attacks became possible. Even more important was the arrival in Europe of effective long-range fighters, chief of which, the P-51 Mustang, was capable of operating at maximum bomber range. The U.S. fighters could now get the better of the Luftwaffe in the air over Germany so that whereas 9.1 percent of bombers going out had been lost and 45.6 percent damaged in October 1943, the corresponding figures were only 3.5 percent and 29.9 percent in February 1944, though in that very month a massive and very difficult attack at extreme range had been made on the German aircraft industry. Carl Spaatz, commanding general of the U.S.

Strategic Air Forces in Europe, in May 1944 initiated an offensive against Germany's synthetic-oil production—an offensive that was to become more and more harmful to the German war effort after the loss of Romania's oil fields to the Soviet Union. Meanwhile, the Luftwaffe's resistance dwindled almost to nothing as its fighter plane production dropped and most of its remaining trained pilots died in aerial combat.

The RAF Bomber Command launched nearly 10,000 sorties in March 1944 and dropped some 27,500 tons of bombs, about 70 percent of this effort being concentrated on Germany, but in the following months its offensive was largely diverted to the intensive preparation and, later, to the support of the Allied landings in France. Nevertheless, it joined usefully in the U.S. offensive against German oil production, continued to play its part in the Battle of the Atlantic, and also assumed the task of bombing the launching ramps of the Germans' "V" missiles. By early 1945, the unending Allied bombing and strafing raids on bridges, roads, rail facilities, locomotives, and supply columns had paralyzed the German transportation system.

The "V" missiles, flying bombs and long-range rockets, were the new weapons on which Hitler had vainly been counting to reduce Great Britain to readiness for peace. His faith in them had indeed been a major motive for his insistence on holding the sites, in northernmost France, from which they were initially to be aimed at London. The V-1 missiles were first launched on June 13, 1944, mostly from sites in the Pas-de-Calais; the V-2 missiles were launched a few months later, on September 8, from sites in the Netherlands (after the Allies' occupation of the Pas-de-Calais on their way to Belgium). The V-2 offensive was maintained until March 1945.

Allied Policy and Strategy: Octagon (Quebec II) and Moscow, 1944

The progress of the Soviet armies toward central and southeastern Europe made it all the more urgent for the Western Allies to come to terms with Stalin about the fate of the "liberated" countries of eastern Europe. London had already proposed to Moscow in May 1944 that Romania and Bulgaria should be zones for Soviet military operation, Yugoslavia and Greece—whose royalist governments in exile were under British protection—for British, and Roosevelt had approved this proposition in June.

The Soviet Union had in February 1944 sent a military mission to Josip Tito's Communist Partisans in Yugoslavia (the Partisans had become the sole Yugoslavian recipients, since the Tehran Conference, of Western aid, though their royalist rivals, the Chetniks, were not publicly disavowed by Churchill until May 25). Along with this, a would-be government of Greece had been set up in March by the EAM (National Liberation Front), which was a Communist movement controlling a military organization, the ELAS (National Popular Liberation Army), in opposition to the EDES (Greek Democratic National Army), which was loyal to the British-backed government in exile. The Polish question, moreover, was still unresolved, and in July the Soviets established, at Lublin, a Committee of National Liberation independent of the London Poles. In Romania, despite the government's change of side in August, the Soviets proceeded to disband the Romanian Army, and early in September they declared war on Bulgaria, invaded that country, and sponsored a Communist revolution there.

With this background, Churchill and Roosevelt met again for their second Quebec Conference, code-named "Octagon," which lasted from September 11 to 16. The most important decision made at the conference was that Roosevelt and Churchill together approved the European Advisory Commission's scheme for the division of defeated Germany into U.S., British, and Soviet zones of occupation (the southwest, the northwest, and the east, respectively) and also the radical plan elaborated by the U.S. secretary of the treasury, Henry Morgenthau, Jr., for turning Germany "into a country primarily agricultural and pastoral" without "war-making industries." The Morgenthau Plan, however, was subsequently revoked.

The next conference of the Allies was held in Moscow Oct. 9–20, 1944, between Churchill and Stalin, with U.S. ambassador W. Averell Harriman also present at most of their talks. Disagreement persisted over Poland. Stalin, however, consented readily to Churchill's provisional suggestion for zones of influence in southeastern Europe: The U.S.S.R. should be preponderant in Romania and in Bulgaria, the Western powers in Greece, and Western and Soviet influences should counterbalance one another evenly in Yugoslavia and in Hungary. The timing of the next Western and Soviet offensives against Germany was also agreed, and some accord was reached about the scale of the eventual Soviet participation in the war against Japan.

The Philippines and Borneo, from September 1944

On July 27–28, 1944, Roosevelt had approved MacArthur's argument that the next objective in the Pacific theatre of the war should be the Philippine Archipelago (which was comparatively near to the already conquered New Guinea). The initial steps toward the Philippines were taken almost simultaneously, in mid-September 1944: MacArthur's forces from New Guinea seized Morotai, the northeasternmost isle of the Moluccas, which was on the direct route to Mindanao, southernmost landmass of the Philippines, and Nimitz's fleet from the east landed troops in the Palau Islands.

Already by mid-September the Americans had discovered that the Japanese forces were unexpectedly weak not only on Mindanao but also on Leyte, the smaller island north of the Surigao Strait. With this knowledge they decided to bypass Mindanao and to begin their invasion of the Philippines on Leyte. On Oct. 17–18, 1944, American forces seized offshore islets in Leyte Gulf, and on October 20 they landed four divisions on the east coast of Leyte.

The threat to Leyte was the signal for the Japanese to put into effect their recently formulated plan "Sho-Go" ("Operation Victory"), whereby the Allies' next attempts at invasion were to be countered by concerted air attacks. Though in the case of Leyte the Japanese army and navy air forces in the immediate theatre numbered only 212 planes, it was hoped that the dispatch of four carriers under Vice Admiral Ozawa, with 106 planes, southward from Japanese waters would lure the U.S. aircraft carriers away from Leyte Gulf and that the suicidal "kamikaze" tactics of the Japanese airmen would save the situation. (Kamikaze pilots deliberately crashed their bomb-armed planes into enemy ships.) At the same time, however, a Japanese naval force from Singapore was to sail to Brunei Bay and there split itself into two groups that would converge on Leyte Gulf from the north and from the southwest: The stronger group, under Vice Admiral Kurita Takeo, would enter the Pacific through the San Bernardino Strait between the Philippine islands of Samar and Luzon; the other, under Vice Admiral Nishimura Teiji, would pass through the Surigao Strait.

Kurita's fleet (five battleships, 12 cruisers, 15 destroyers) lost two of its heavy cruisers to U.S. submarine attack on

October 23, when it was off Palawan, and one of the mightiest of Japan's battleships, the *Musashi*, was sunk by aerial attack the next day. On October 25, however, Kurita made his way unopposed through the San Bernardino Strait, since the commander of the U.S. 3rd Fleet, Admiral Halsey, had diverted his main strength toward the bait dangled by Ozawa farther to the north. Three groups of U.S. escort carriers, met by Kurita on his way toward Leyte Gulf, suffered heavy damage, but, meanwhile, Nishimura's fleet (two battleships, one heavy cruiser, four destroyers) had been detected on its way to the Surigao Strait and, on its entry into Leyte Gulf in the early hours of October 25, had been practically annihilated by the U.S. 7th Fleet. Kurita consequently turned back from his rendezvous in Leyte Gulf, and the Japanese defeat in the war's greatest naval confrontation was sealed by Ozawa's losses to Halsey: all of his four carriers, together with a light cruiser and two destroyers. The Japanese navy's "Sho-Go" as it transpired in the Battle of Leyte Gulf had not only failed to inflict serious damage on the Americans but had resulted in serious losses for the Japanese. These losses amounted to three battleships, one large aircraft carrier, three light carriers, six heavy cruisers, four light cruisers, and 11 destroyers, while the United States lost only one light carrier, two escort carriers, and three destroyers. The battle reduced the Japanese navy to vestigial strength and cleared the way for the U.S. occupation of the Philippines.

Defeat in the gulf, however, did not prevent the Japanese from landing reinforcements on the west coast of Leyte. They put up so stubborn a resistance that the Americans themselves had to be reinforced before Ormoc fell on Dec. 10, 1944; it was not before December 25 that the Americans could claim control of all Leyte—though there was still some mopping up to be done. Altogether, the defense of Leyte cost the Japanese some 75,000 combatants killed or taken prisoner.

From Leyte the Americans proceeded first, on December 15, to the invasion of Mindoro, the largest of the islands immediately south of Luzon. Kamikaze counterattacks made this conquest more costly, and they were to be continued after the Americans had surprised the Japanese by landing, on Jan. 9, 1945, at Lingayen Gulf on the west coast of Luzon itself, the most important island of the Philippines. The local Japanese commander, Lieutenant General Yamashita Tomoyuki, with no hope of reinforcement, opted for tying the enemy forces down as long as possible by a static defense in three mountainous sectors—west, northwest, and east of the Central Plains behind Manila.

Manila itself was also strongly defended by the Japanese. One U.S. corps, however, was approaching it from Lingayen over the Central Plains; a second corps was landed at Subic Bay, at the northern end of the Bataan Peninsula, on Jan. 29, 1945, to make contact with the former corps at Dinalupihan a week later; and troops made an amphibious landing at Nasugbu, south of Manila Bay, on January 31. Manila was then invested, and during the siege the bay was cleared by the occupation of the southern tip of Bataan Peninsula on February 15 and by the reduction of Corregidor Island in the following fortnight. On March 3 Manila fell at last to the Americans.

The Japanese resistance on Luzon continued in the mountains, and east of Manila it went on until mid-June 1945. Mindanao, meanwhile, was likewise being reduced. A U.S. division landed at Zamboanga, on the southwestern peninsula, on March 10, 1945, and a corps began the occupation of the core of the island on April 17.

The last phase of the U.S. campaign in the Philippines coincided with the opening of the reconquest of Borneo from the Japanese, chiefly by Australian forces. Tarakan Island, off the northeast coast, was invaded on May 1; Brunei on the northwest coast was invaded on June 10; and Balikpapan, on the east coast far to the south of Tarakan, was attacked on July 1. The subsequent collapse of the Japanese defenses around Balikpapan deprived Japan of the oil supplies of southern Borneo.

Burma and China, October 1944–May 1945

Chiang Kai-shek's demand for the recall of the talented but abrasive Stilwell was satisfied in October 1944, and some reorganization of the Allies' commands in Southeast Asia followed. While Lieutenant General Daniel Sultan took Stilwell's place, Major General A.C. Wedemeyer became commander of U.S. forces in the China theatre and Sir Oliver Leese commander of the land forces under Mountbatten.

On the northern wing of the Burma front, a three-pronged drive by NCAC forces southward from Myitkyina to the Irrawaddy River had been planned by Stilwell. Launched under Sultan, the triple drive was at first only partially successful: The right took Indaw and Katha early in December and effected a junction with Slim's British 14th Army, and the centre reached Shwegu, across the river, but the left, though it took Bhamo, was checked 60 miles west of Wan-t'ing. Sultan thereupon decided to push farther southward, both on the right against Kyaukme, on the Burma Road northeast of Mandalay, and on the left against Wan-t'ing. Threatened with envelopment, the Japanese fell back from Wan-t'ing, which Sultan's troops promptly occupied. Convoys up the Burma Road from Wan-t'ing to K'un-ming were resumed on Jan. 18, 1945.

For central Burma, meanwhile, Slim had thought, after his victory at Imphal, that he must immediately seize the crossings of the Chindwin River at Sittaung and at Kalewa and then advance southward against Mandalay itself. He did indeed effect the Chindwin crossings, but in mid-December 1944 he saw that the Japanese were in any case going to withdraw altogether to the left bank of the Irrawaddy. Thereupon, he changed his plan: His objective should rather be Meiktila, which lay east of the Irrawaddy and was a vital centre of Japanese communications between Mandalay and Rangoon to the south. To conceal his new intention, he allowed one of the corps already directed against Mandalay to continue its eastward advance, but the other corps was surreptitiously moved over a circuitous route of 300 miles southward to Pakokku, which lay south of the Chindwin–Irrawaddy confluence and northwest of Meiktila. While the crossing of the Irrawaddy by the former corps on both sides of Mandalay distracted the attention of the Japanese, the latter corps took Meiktila on March 3, 1945, and held it against fierce counterattacks. Mandalay fell 10 days later, and the whole area was under the 14th Army's control by the end of the month. When the action was over, two Japanese armies had lost one-third of their fighting strength.

It remained for Slim to capture the Burmese capital, Rangoon. Allied ground forces advanced on Rangoon along two routes from the north: One corps, having moved down the Sittang Valley east of the Irrawaddy, took Pegu; the other, moving down the river, took Prome (Pye). The monsoon, however, was imminent, and to forestall it a small combined operation was undertaken: Parachute troops were dropped at Elephant Point, on the coast south of Rangoon, on May 1, 1945, and an Indian division, landing at Rangoon itself the next day, took the city without opposition, just when the monsoon rains were beginning to fall. The recapture of Burma was essentially complete with the taking of Rangoon.

The German Offensive in the West, Winter 1944–45

Hitler still hoped to drive the Allies back and still adhered to his principle of concentrating on the war in the west. Late in 1944, therefore, he assembled on the Western Front all the manpower that had become available as a consequence of his second "total mobilization": A decree of October 18 had raised a *Volkssturm*, or "home guard," for the defense of the Third Reich, conscripting all able-bodied men between the ages of 16 and 60 years.

In mid-November all six Allied armies on the Western Front had launched a general offensive, but, though the French 1st Army and the U.S. 7th had reached the Rhine River in Alsace, there were only small gains on other sectors of the front. Meanwhile, the German defense was being continuously strengthened with hastily shifted reserves and with freshly raised forces, besides the troops that had managed to make their way back from France. The German buildup along the front was by now progressing faster than that of the Allies, despite Germany's great inferiority of material resources. In mid-December 1944 the Germans gave the Allied armies a shock by launching a sizable counteroffensive. The Germans amassed 24 divisions for the attack. Under the overall command of the reinstated Rundstedt, this attack was to be delivered through the wooded hill country of the Ardennes against the weakest sector of the U.S.-manned front, between Monschau (southwest of Aachen) and Echternach (northwest of Trier). While the 5th Panzer Army on the left, under the talented commander General Hasso von Manteuffel, with its own left flank covered by the German 7th Army, was to wheel northwestward after the breakthrough and to cross the Meuse River of Namur in a drive on Brussels, the 6th Panzer Army on the right, under SS General Sepp Dietrich, was to wheel more sharply northward against the Allies' important supply port of Antwerp. Thus, it was hoped, the British and Canadian forces at the northern end of the front could be cut off from their supplies and crushed, while the U.S. forces to the south were held off by the German left.

The offensive was prepared with skill and secrecy and was launched on Dec. 16, 1944, at a time when mist and rain would minimize the effectiveness of counteraction from the air. The leading wedge of the attack by eight German armoured divisions along a 75-mile front took the Allies by surprise, and the 5th Panzer Army, which achieved the deeper penetration, reached points within 20 miles of the crossings of the Meuse River at Givet and at Dinant. U.S. detachments, however, stood firm, albeit outflanked, at Bastogne and at other bottlenecks in the Ardennes, and there followed what is popularly remembered as the Battle of the Bulge. By December 24 the German drive had narrowed but deepened, having penetrated about 65 miles into the Allied lines along a 20-mile front. But by this time the Allies had begun to respond. Montgomery, who had taken charge of the situation in the north, swung his reserves southward to forestall the Germans on the Meuse. Bradley, commanding the Allied forces south of the German wedge, sent his 3rd Army under Patton to the relief of Bastogne, which was accomplished on December 26. The weather cleared, and as many as 5,000 Allied aircraft began to bomb and strafe the German forces and their supply system. During Jan. 8–16, 1945, the German attackers were compelled to withdraw, lest the salient that they had driven into the Allied front be cut off in its turn. Though their abortive offensive inflicted much damage and upset the Allies' plans, the Germans spent too much of their strength on it and thereby forfeited whatever chance they had had of maintaining prolonged resistance later. The Germans sustained 120,000 casualties and the Americans sustained about 75,000 in the Battle of the Bulge.

The Soviet Advance to the Oder, January–February 1945

At the end of 1944 the Germans still held the western half of Poland, and their front was still 200 miles east of where it had been at the start of the war in 1939. The Germans had checked the Soviets' summer offensive and had established a firm line along the Narew and Vistula rivers southward to the Carpathians, and in October they repelled the Red Army's attempted thrust into East Prussia. Meanwhile, however, the Soviet left, moving up from the eastern Balkans, had been gradually pushing around through Hungary and Yugoslavia in a vast flanking movement, and the absorption of German forces in opposing this side-door approach detracted considerably from the Germans' capacity to maintain their main Eastern and Western fronts.

The Soviet high command was now ready to exploit the fundamental weaknesses of the German situation. Abundant supplies for their armies had been accumulated at the railheads. The mounting stream of American-supplied trucks had by this time enabled the Soviets to motorize a much larger proportion of their infantry brigades and thus, with the increasing production of their own tanks, to multiply the number of armoured and mobile corps for a successful breakthrough.

Before the end of December ominous reports were received by Guderian—who, in this desperately late period of the war, had been made chief of the German general staff. German army intelligence reported that 225 Soviet infantry divisions and 22 armoured corps had been identified on the front between the Baltic and the Carpathians, assembled to attack. But when Guderian presented the report of these massive Soviet offensive preparations, Hitler refused to believe it, exclaiming: "It's the biggest imposture since Genghis Khan! Who is responsible for producing all this rubbish?"

If Hitler had been willing to stop the Ardennes counteroffensive in the west, troops could have been transferred to the Eastern Front, but he refused to do so. At the same time he refused Guderian's renewed request that the 30 German divisions now isolated in Courland (on the Baltic seacoast in Lithuania) should be evacuated by sea and brought back to reinforce the gateways into Germany. As a consequence, Guderian was left with a mobile reserve of only 12 armoured divisions to back up the 50 weak infantry divisions stretched out over the 700 miles of the main front.

The Soviet offensive opened on Jan. 12, 1945, when Konev's armies were launched against the German front in southern Poland, starting from their bridgehead over the Vistula River near Sandomierz. After it had pierced the German defense and produced a flanking menace to the central sector, Zhukov's armies in the centre of the front bounded forward from their bridgeheads nearer Warsaw. That same day, January 14, Rokossovsky's armies also joined in the offensive, striking from the Narew River north of Warsaw and breaking through the defenses covering this flank approach to East Prussia. The breach in the German front was now 200 miles wide.

On Jan. 17, 1945, Warsaw was captured by Zhukov, after it had been surrounded, and on January 19 his armoured spearheads drove into Lódz. That same day Konev's spearheads reached the Silesian frontier of prewar Germany. Thus, at the end of the first week the offensive had been carried 100 miles deep and was 400 miles wide—far too wide to be filled by such scanty reinforcements as were belatedly provided.

The crisis made Hitler renounce any idea of pursuing his offensive in the west, but, despite Guderian's advice, he switched the 6th Panzer Army not to Poland but to Hungary in an attempt to relieve Budapest. The Soviets could thus continue their advance through Poland for two more weeks. While Konev's spearheads crossed the Oder River in the vicinity of Breslau

(Wroclaw) and thus cut Silesia's important mineral resources off from Germany, Zhukov made a sweeping advance in the centre by driving forward from Warsaw, past Poznan, Bydgoszcz, and Torun, to the frontiers of Brandenburg and of Pomerania. At the same time Rokossovsky pushed on, through Allenstein (Olsztyn), to the Gulf of Danzig, thus cutting off the 25 German divisions in East Prussia. To defend the yawning gap in the centre of the front, Hitler created a new army group and put Heinrich Himmler in command of it with a staff of favoured SS officers. Their fumbling helped to clear the path for Zhukov, whose mechanized forces by Jan. 31, 1945, were at Küstrin, on the lower Oder, only 40 miles from Berlin.

Zhukov's advance now came to a halt. Konev, however, could still make a northwesterly sweep down the left bank of the middle Oder, reaching Sommerfeld, 80 miles from Berlin, on February 13, and the Neisse River two days later. The Germans' defense benefited from being driven back to the straight and shortened line formed by the Oder and Neisse rivers. This front, extending from the Baltic coast to the Bohemian frontier, was less than 200 miles long. The menace of the Soviets' imminent approach to Berlin led Hitler to decide that most of his fresh drafts of troops must be sent to reinforce the Oder; the way was thus eased for the crossing of the Rhine River by the American and British armies.

On Feb. 13, 1945, the Soviets took Budapest, the defense of which had entailed the Germans' loss of Silesia.

Yalta

Roosevelt's last meeting with Stalin and Churchill took place at Yalta, in Crimea, Feb. 4–11, 1945. The conference is chiefly remembered for its treatment of the Polish problem: The Western Allied leaders, abandoning their support of the Polish government in London, agreed that the Lublin committee—already recognized as the provisional government of Poland by the Soviet masters of the country—should be the nucleus of a provisional government of national unity, pending free elections. But while they also agreed that Poland should be compensated in the west for the eastern territories that the U.S.S.R. had seized in 1939, they declined to approve the Oder–Neisse line as a frontier between Poland and Germany, considering that it would put too many Germans under Polish rule. For the rest of "liberated Europe" the Western Allied leaders obtained nothing more substantial from Stalin than a declaration prescribing support for "democratic elements" and "free elections" to produce "governments responsive to the will of the people."

For Germany the conference affirmed the project for dividing the country into occupation zones, with the difference that the U.S. zone was to be reduced in order to provide a fourth zone, for the French to occupy. Roosevelt and Churchill,

(From left) *Winston Churchill, Franklin Roosevelt, and Joseph Stalin meet at the Yalta Conference in 1945.*

THE LAST BIG THREE SUMMIT

The Yalta conference was a last chance to forestall the disintegration of the Big Three's alliance upon victory or, conversely, for the British and Americans to take firm measures against Soviet control in eastern Europe. Roosevelt was now mortally ill and exhausted by the strenuous journey. Controversy later raged over his decision to attend the conference at all, his eagerness to conciliate Stalin, and the sinister presence in his entourage of Communist agent Alger Hiss. Postwar critics would charge that Roosevelt had been duped at Yalta and had "sold out" eastern Europe to the Communists. Doubtless if Churchill's advice had been followed, the policy of trust might have given way to one of hard bargaining and clear haggling over boundaries and governments in Europe and Asia. But in fact there was little the Western powers could have done to frustrate Stalin other than threatening a new world war. Nor could Churchill and Roosevelt have openly relinquished any liberated states to Stalin without abrogating the principles on which the war had been fought and alienating the millions of U.S. voters of eastern European descent. As for Asia, the United States was yet facing a campaign that might cost hundreds of thousands of American lives. Purchasing Soviet help against Japan seemed both realistic and humane. Roosevelt could not predict that the atomic bomb would render Soviet aid superfluous.

Of the three great allies Britain was the weakest and most interested in restoring a balance of power in Europe. Churchill, a keen critic of Bolshevism since 1919, had lobbied all throughout the summer of 1944 for an Italian campaign in hopes that the Allies might reach the Danube before the Red Army, and in October he had made the "spheres of influence" deal with Stalin. But the war map—and Roosevelt's unwillingness to strain the alliance—defeated all these tactics. On the eve of Yalta, Churchill wondered whether "the end of this war may well prove to be more disappointing than was the last." American war aims, by contrast, were nebulous to nonexistent, except for a reprise of Wilsonian internationalism. There is little evidence of economic motives in U.S. policy and, incredibly, no contingency plans for a breakdown in relations with the U.S.S.R. While Roosevelt feared another American retreat into isolationism, he also believed in the possibility of a postwar Great Power condominium. He was prepared to show Stalin that the Anglo-Saxons were not ganging up on him and wanted Soviet participation in a United Nations Organization. But Stalin pursued the old-fashioned way of postwar security: military and political control of eastern Europe to create a buffer for the U.S.S.R. and to ensure Soviet domination over its own repressed nationalities.

At the Yalta Conference, Big Three unity seemed intact, but only because the participants resorted to vagueness or postponements on the most explosive issues. A joint European Advisory Commission, it was decided, would divide Germany into occupation zones, with the Soviet zone extending to the Elbe and a French zone carved out of the Anglo-American spheres. Berlin would likewise be placed under four-power control. The Western Allies repudiated the extreme plans broached at Quebec for the pastoralization of Germany and favoured German industrial recovery under international control. But the Soviets insisted on the right to strip Germany of $20,000,000,000 worth of machinery and raw materials. The issue was assigned to a reparations commission. As for the political future of Germany, Stalin revived earlier Big Three talk of breaking Germany into several states, but the Western Allies now perceived the danger of further Balkanization in central Europe in light of Soviet power. This matter, too, was left for study.

however, had already discarded the Morgenthau Plan for the postwar treatment of Germany, and Yalta found no comprehensive formula to replace it. The three leaders simply pledged themselves to furnish the defeated Germans with the necessities for survival; to "eliminate or control" all German industry that could be used for armaments; to bring major war criminals to trial; and to set up a commission in Moscow for the purpose of determining what reparation Germany should pay.

The German Collapse, Spring 1945

Before their ground forces were ready for the final assault on Germany, the Western Allies intensified their aerial bombardment. This offensive culminated in a series of five attacks on Dresden, launched by the RAF with 800 aircraft in the night of Feb. 13–14, 1945, and continued by the U.S. 8th Air Force with 400 aircraft in daylight on February 14, with 200 on February 15, with 400 again on March 2, and, finally, with 572 on April 17. The motive of these raids was allegedly to promote the Soviet advance by destroying a centre of communications important to the German defense of the Eastern Front, but, in fact, the raids achieved nothing to help the Red Army militarily and succeeded in obliterating the greater part of one of the most beautiful cities of Europe and in killing up to 25,000 people.

The main strength of the ground forces being built up meanwhile for the crossing of the Rhine was allotted to Montgomery's armies on the northern sector of the front. Meanwhile, some of the U.S. generals sought to demonstrate the abilities of their own less generously supplied forces. Thus, Patton's 3rd Army reached the Rhine at Coblenz (Koblenz) early in March, and, farther downstream, General Courtney H. Hodges' 1st Army seized the bridge over the Rhine at Remagen south of Bonn and actually crossed the river, while, still farther downstream, Lieutenant General William H. Simpson's 9th Army reached the Rhine near Düsseldorf. All three armies were ordered to mark time until Montgomery's grand assault was ready, but, meanwhile, they cleared the west bank of the river, and eventually, in the night of March 22–23, the 3rd Army crossed the Rhine at Oppenheim, between Mainz and Mannheim, almost unopposed.

At last, in the night of March 23–24, Montgomery's attack by 25 divisions was launched across a stretch—30 miles long—of the Rhine near Wesel after a stupendous bombardment by more than 3,000 guns and waves of attacks by bombers. Resistance was generally slight, but Montgomery would not sanction a further advance until his bridgeheads were consolidated into a salient 20 miles deep. Then the Canadian 1st Army, on the left, drove ahead through the Netherlands, the British 2nd went northeastward to Lübeck and to Wismar on the Baltic, and the U.S. armies swept forward across Germany, fanning out to reach an arc that stretched from Magdeburg (9th Army) through Leipzig (1st) to the borders of Czechoslovakia (3rd) and of Austria (7th and French 1st).

Guderian had tried to shift Germany's forces eastward to hold the Red Army off, but Hitler, despite his anxiety for Berlin, still wished to commit the 11th and 12th armies—formed from his last reserves—to driving the Western Allies back over the Rhine and, on March 28, replaced Guderian with General Hans Krebs as chief of the general staff.

The dominant desire of the Germans now, both troops and civilians, was to see the British and American armies sweep eastward as rapidly as possible to reach Berlin and occupy as much of the country as possible before the Soviets overcame the Oder line. Few of them were inclined to assist Hitler's purpose of obstruction by self-destruction. On March 19 (the eve of the Rhine crossing), Hitler had issued an order declaring that "the battle should be conducted without consideration for our own population." His regional commissioners were instructed to destroy "all industrial plants, all the main electricity works, waterworks, gas works" together with "all food and clothing stores" in order to create "a desert" in the Allies' path. When his minister of war production, Albert Speer, protested against this drastic order, Hitler retorted: "If the war is lost, the German nation will also perish. So there is no need to consider what the people require for continued existence." Appalled at such callousness, Speer was shaken out of his loyalty to Hitler: He went behind Hitler's back to the army and industrial chiefs and persuaded them, without much difficulty, to evade executing Hitler's decree. The Americans and the British, driving eastward from the Rhine, met little opposition and reached the Elbe River 60 miles from Berlin, on April 11. There they halted.

On the Eastern Front, Zhukov enlarged his bridgehead across the Oder early in March. On their far left the Soviets reached Vienna on April 6, and on the right they took Königsberg on April 9. Then, on April 16, Zhukov resumed the offensive in conjunction with Konev, who forced the crossings of the Neisse; this time the Soviets burst out of their bridgeheads, and within a week they were driving into the suburbs of Berlin. Hitler chose to stay in his threatened capital, counting on some miracle to bring salvation and clutching at such straws as the news of the death of Roosevelt on April 12. By April 25 the armies of Zhukov and Konev had completely encircled Berlin, and on the same day they linked up with the Americans on the Elbe River.

Isolated and reduced to despair, Hitler married his mistress, Eva Braun, during the night of April 28–29, and on April 30 he committed suicide with her in the ruins of the Chancellery, as the advancing Soviet troops were less than a half mile from his bunker complex; their bodies were hurriedly cremated in the garden. The "strategy" of Hitler's successor, Dönitz, was one of capitulation and of saving as many as possible of the westward-fleeing civilians and of his German troops from Soviet hands. During the interval of surrender, 1,800,000 German troops (55 percent of the Army of the East) were transferred into the British–U.S. area of control.

On the Italian front, the Allied armies had long been frustrated by the depletion of their forces for the sake of other enterprises, but early in 1945 four German divisions were transferred from Kesselring's command to the Western Front, and in April the thin German defenses in Italy were broken by an Allied attack. A surrender document that had been signed on April 29 (while Hitler was still alive) finally brought the fighting to a conclusion on May 2.

The surrender of the German forces in northwestern Europe was signed at Montgomery's headquarters on Lüneburg Heath on May 4, and a further document, covering all the

A crowd in London celebrates VE day after the German surrender.

German forces, was signed with more ceremony at Eisenhower's headquarters at Reims, in the presence of Soviet as well as U.S., British, and French delegations. At midnight on May 8, 1945, the war in Europe was officially over.

Potsdam

The last inter-Allied conference of World War II, code-named "Terminal," was held at the suburb of Potsdam, outside ruined Berlin, from July 17 to Aug. 2, 1945. It was attended by the Soviet, U.S., and British heads of government and foreign ministers: respectively, Stalin and Molotov; President Harry S. Truman (Roosevelt's successor) and James F. Byrnes; and Churchill and Anthony Eden, the last-named pair being replaced by Clement Attlee and Ernest Bevin after Great Britain's change of government following a general election.

Operations against Japan were discussed, and the successful testing of an atomic bomb in the United States was divulged to Stalin. Pending the Soviet entry into the war against Japan, a declaration was issued on July 26 calling on Japan to surrender unconditionally and forecasting the territorial spoliation of the empire and the military occupation of Japan proper as well as the prosecution of war criminals, yet still promising that the Japanese people would not be enslaved or the nation destroyed.

Time was spent discussing the peace settlement and its procedure. Stalin induced Truman and Attlee to consent provisionally to the Soviet Union's demands that it should take one-third of Germany's naval and merchant fleet; have the right to exact reparations from its occupied zones of Germany and of Austria and also from Finland, Hungary, Romania, and even Bulgaria; and should furthermore receive a percentage of reparation from the Western-occupied zones. The total amounts of all these exactions were, however, to be determined at a later date.

There was a profound disagreement at the conference about the Balkan areas occupied by the Red Army in which representatives of the Western powers were allowed little say, and about the area east of the Oder–Neisse line, all of which the Soviets had arbitrarily put under Polish administration. The Western statesmen protested at these lone-handed arrangements but perforce accepted them.

The End of the Japanese War, February–September 1945

While the campaign for the Philippines was still in progress, U.S. forces were making great steps in the direct advance toward their final objective, the Japanese homeland. Aerial bombardment was, of course, the prerequisite of the projected invasion of Japan—which was to begin, it was imagined, with landings on Kyushu, the southernmost of the major Japanese islands.

IWO JIMA AND THE BOMBING OF TOKYO

With U.S. forces firmly established in the Mariana Islands, the steady long-range bombing of Japan by B-29s under the command of General Curtis E. LeMay continued throughout the closing months of 1944 and into 1945. But it was still 1,500 miles from Saipan to Tokyo, a long flight even for the B-29s. Strategic planners therefore fixed their attention on the little volcanic island of Iwo Jima in the Bonin Islands, which lay about halfway between the Marianas and Japan. If Iwo Jima could be eliminated as a Japanese base, the island could then be immensely valuable as a base for U.S. fighter planes defending the big bombers.

Defeat of the Axis Powers

The Japanese were determined to hold Iwo Jima. As they had done on other Pacific islands, they had created underground defenses there, making the best possible use of natural caves and the rough, rocky terrain. The number of Japanese defenders on the island, under command of Lieutenant General Kuribayashi Tadamichi, was more than 20,000.

Day after day before the actual landing the island was subjected to intense bombardment by naval guns, by rockets, and by air strikes using napalm bombs. But the results fell far short of expectations. The Japanese were so well protected that no amount of conventional bombing or shelling could knock them out. U.S. Marines landed on Iwo Jima on Feb. 19, 1945, and encountered an obstinate resistance. Meanwhile, kamikaze counterattacks from the air sank the light carrier *Bismarck Sea* and damaged other ships, and, though the U.S. flag was planted on Mount Suribachi on February 23, the isle was not finally secured until March 16. Iwo Jima had cost the lives of 6,000 Marines, as well as the lives of nearly all the Japanese defenders, but in the next five months more than 2,000 B-29 bombers were able to land on it.

Meanwhile, a new tactic had been found for the bombing of Japan from bases in the Marianas. Instead of high-altitude strikes in daylight, which had failed to do much damage to the industrial centres attacked, low-level strikes at night, using napalm firebombs, were tried, with startling success. The first, in the night of March 9–10, 1945, against Tokyo, destroyed about 25 percent of the city's buildings (most of them flimsily built of wood and plaster), killed more than 80,000 people, and made 1,000,000 homeless. This result indicated that Japan might be defeated without a massive invasion by ground troops, and so similar bombing raids on such major cities as Nagoya, Osaka, Kobe, Yokohama, and Toyama followed. Japan literally was being bombed out of the war.

OKINAWA

Plans for invasion, however, were not immediately discarded. Okinawa, largest of the Ryukyu Islands strung out northeastward from Taiwan, had been regarded as the last stepping-stone to be taken toward Kyushu, which was only 350 miles away from it. It had therefore been subjected to a series of air raids from October 1944, culminating in March 1945 in an attack that destroyed hundreds of Japanese planes, but there were still at least 75,000 Japanese troops on the island, commanded by Lieutenant General Ushijima Mitsuru. The invasion of Okinawa was, in fact, to be the largest amphibious operation mounted by the Americans in the Pacific war.

Under the overall command of Nimitz, with Admiral Raymond Spruance in charge of the actual landings and with Lieutenant General Simon Bolivar Buckner, Jr., commanding the ground forces, the operation began with the occupation of the Kerama Islets, 15 miles west of Okinawa, on March 26, 1945. Five days later a landing was made on Keise-Jima, whence artillery fire could be brought to bear on Okinawa itself. Then, on April 1, some 60,000 U.S. troops landed on the central stretch of Okinawa's west coast, seizing two nearby airfields and advancing to cut the island's narrow waist. Koiso's government in Tokyo resigned on April 5, and the U.S.S.R. on the same day refused to renew its treaty of nonaggression with Japan.

The first major counterattack on Okinawa by the Japanese, begun on April 6, involved not only 355 kamikaze air raids but also the *Yamato*, the greatest battleship in the world (72,000 tons, with nine 18.1-inch [460-millimetre] guns), which was sent out on a suicidal mission with only enough fuel for the single outward voyage and without sufficient air cover. The Japanese hoped the *Yamato* might finish off the

Allied fleet after the latter had been weakened by kamikaze attacks. In the event, the *Yamato* was hit repeatedly by bombs and torpedoes and was sunk on April 7. Equally suicidal was a new Japanese weapon, *baka*, which claimed its first victim, the U.S. destroyer *Abele*, off Okinawa on April 12. *Baka* was a rocket-powered glider crammed with explosives, which was towed into range by a bomber and was then released to be guided by its solitary pilot into the chosen target for their mutual destruction.

The U.S. ground forces invading Okinawa met little opposition on the beaches because Ushijima had decided to offer his main resistance inland, out of range of the enemy's naval guns. In the southern half of the island this resistance was bitterest: It lasted until June 21, and Ushijima killed himself the next day. The campaign for Okinawa was ended officially on July 2. For U.S. troops it had been the longest and bloodiest Pacific campaign since Guadalcanal in 1942. Taking the island had cost the Americans 12,000 dead and 36,000 wounded, with 34 ships sunk and 368 damaged, and the Japanese losses exceeded 100,000 dead.

On April 3, 1945, two days after the first landing on Okinawa, the U.S. command in the Pacific was reorganized: MacArthur was henceforth to be in command of all army units and also in operational control of the U.S. Marines for the invasion of Japan; Nimitz was placed in command of all navy units.

HIROSHIMA AND NAGASAKI

Throughout July 1945 the Japanese mainlands, from the latitude of Tokyo on Honshu northward to the coast of Hokkaido, were bombed just as if an invasion was about to be launched. In fact, something far more sinister was in hand, as the Americans were telling Stalin at Potsdam.

In 1939 physicists in the United States had learned of experiments in Germany demonstrating the possibility of nuclear fission and had understood that the potential energy might be released in an explosive weapon of unprecedented power. On Aug. 2, 1939, Albert Einstein had warned Roosevelt of the danger of Nazi Germany's forestalling other states in the development of an atomic bomb. Eventually, the U.S. Office of Scientific Research and Development was created in June 1941 and given joint responsibility with the war department in the Manhattan Project to develop an atomic bomb. After four years of intensive and ever-mounting research and development efforts, an atomic device was set off on July 16, 1945, in a desert area near Alamogordo, New Mexico, generating an explosive power equivalent to that of more than 15,000 tons of TNT. Thus the atomic bomb was born. Truman, the new U.S. president, calculated that this monstrous weapon might be used to defeat Japan in a way less costly of U.S. lives than a conventional invasion of the Japanese homeland. Japan's unsatisfactory response to the Allies' Potsdam Declaration decided the matter. On Aug. 6, 1945, an atomic bomb carried from Tinian Island in the Marianas in a specially equipped B-29 was dropped on Hiroshima, at the southern end of Honshu: The combined heat and blast pulverized everything in the explosion's immediate vicinity, generated fires that burned almost 4.4 square miles completely out, and immediately killed some 70,000 people (the death toll passed 100,000 by the end of the year). A second bomb, dropped on Nagasaki on August 9, killed between 35,000 and 40,000 people, injured a like number, and devastated 1.8 square miles.

THE JAPANESE SURRENDER

News of Hiroshima's destruction was only slowly understood in Tokyo. Many members of the Japanese government did not appreciate the power of the new Allied weapon until after the Nagasaki

THE DECISION TO USE THE ATOMIC BOMB

Less than two weeks after being sworn in as president, Harry S. Truman received a long report from Secretary of War Henry L. Stimson. "Within four months," it began, "we shall in all probability have completed the most terrible weapon ever known in human history." Truman's decision to use the atomic bomb on Hiroshima and Nagasaki resulted from the interplay of his temperament and several other factors, including his perspective on the war objectives defined by his predecessor, Franklin D. Roosevelt, the expectations of the American public, an assessment of the possibilities of achieving a quick victory by other means, and the complex American relationship with the Soviet Union. Although in later decades there was considerable debate about whether the bombings were ethically justified, virtually all of America's political and military leadership, as well as most of those involved in the atomic bomb project, believed at the time that Truman's decision was correct.

During World War I, Truman commanded a battery of close-support 75mm artillery pieces in France and personally witnessed the human costs of intense front-line combat. After returning home, he became convinced that he probably would have been killed if the war had lasted a few months longer. At least two of his World War I comrades had lost sons in World War II, and Truman had four nephews in uniform. His firsthand experience with warfare clearly influenced his thinking about whether to use the atomic bomb.

A second factor in Truman's decision was the legacy of Roosevelt, who had defined the nation's goal in ending the war as the enemy's "unconditional surrender," a term coined to reassure the Soviet Union that the Western allies would fight to the end against Germany. It was also an expression of the American temperament; the United States was accustomed to winning wars and dictating the peace. On May 8, 1945, Germany surrendered unconditionally to great rejoicing in the Allied countries. The hostility of the American public toward Japan was even more intense and demanded an unambiguous total victory in the Pacific. Truman was acutely aware that the country—in its fourth year of total war—also wanted victory as quickly as possible.

A skilled politician who knew when to compromise, Truman respected decisiveness. Meeting with Anthony Eden, the British foreign secretary, in early May, he declared: "I am here to make decisions, and whether they prove right or wrong I am going to make them," an attitude that implied neither impulsiveness nor solitude. After being presented with Stimson's report, he appointed a blue-ribbon "Interim Committee" to advise him on how to deal with the atomic bomb. Headed by Stimson and James Byrnes, whom Truman would soon name secretary of state, the Interim Committee was a group of respected statesmen and scientists closely linked to the war effort. After five meetings between May 9 and June 1, it recommended use of the bomb against Japan as soon as possible and rejected arguments for advance warning. Clearly in line with Truman's inclinations, the recommendations of the Interim Committee amounted to a prepackaged decision.

At the Potsdam Conference in Germany in mid-July, Truman met with British Prime Minister Winston Churchill (who was succeeded near the end of the conference by Clement Attlee) and Soviet leader Joseph Stalin. From Truman's perspective, the conference had two purposes: to lay the groundwork for rebuilding postwar Europe and to secure Soviet participation in the war against Japan. On July 16, the day before the conference opened, Truman received word that the first atomic bomb had been successfully tested in the New Mexico desert. He shared the information fully with Churchill (Britain was a partner in the development of the bomb) but simply told Stalin that the United States had created a powerful new weapon. Stalin—who had detailed knowledge of the project through espionage—feigned indifference. He also reaffirmed an earlier pledge to attack Japanese positions in Manchuria no later than mid-August. Truman, apparently uncertain that the bomb alone could compel surrender, was elated. Revisionist historians would later argue that the bomb was used in the hope of securing Japan's surrender before the Soviet Union could enter the Pacific War.

On Aug. 9, 1945, the United States dropped a plutonium-fueled atomic bomb over the Japanese port of Nagasaki.

attack. Meanwhile, on August 8, the U.S.S.R. had declared war against Japan. The combination of these developments tipped the scales within the government in favour of a group that had, since the spring, been advocating a negotiated peace. On August 10 the Japanese government issued a statement agreeing to accept the surrender terms of the Potsdam Declaration on the understanding that the emperor's position as a sovereign ruler would not be prejudiced. In their reply the Allies granted Japan's request that the emperor's sovereign status be maintained, subject only to their supreme commander's directives. Japan accepted this proviso on August 14, and the emperor Hirohito urged his people to accept the decision to surrender. It was a bitter pill to swallow, though, and every effort was made to persuade the Japanese to accept the defeat that they had come to regard as unthinkable. Even princes of the Japanese Imperial house were dispatched to deliver the emperor's message in person to distant Japanese army forces in China and in Korea, hoping thus to mitigate the shock. A clique of diehards nevertheless attempted to assassinate the new prime minister, Admiral Suzuki Kantaro, but by September 2, when the formal surrender ceremonies took place, the way had been smoothed.

Truman designated MacArthur as the Allied powers' supreme commander to accept Japan's formal surrender, which was solemnized aboard the U.S. flagship *Missouri* in Tokyo Bay: The Japanese foreign minister, Shigemitsu Mamoru, signed the document first, on behalf of the emperor and his government. He was followed by General Umezu Yoshijiro on behalf of the Imperial General Headquarters. The document was then signed by MacArthur, Nimitz, and representatives of the other Allied powers. Japan concluded a separate surrender ceremony with China in Nanking on Sept. 9, 1945. With this last formal surrender, World War II came to an end.

CHAPTER 9
COSTS AND AFTERMATH OF THE WAR

The statistics on World War II casualties are inexact. Only for the United States and the British Commonwealth can official figures showing killed, wounded, prisoners, or missing for the armed forces be cited with any degree of assurance. For most other nations, only estimates of varying reliability exist. Statistical accounting broke down in both Allied and Axis nations when whole armies were surrendered or dispersed. Guerrilla warfare, changes in international boundaries, and mass shifts in population vastly complicated postwar efforts to arrive at accurate figures even for the total dead from all causes.

Killed, Wounded, Prisoners, or Missing

Civilian deaths from land battles, aerial bombardment, political and racial executions, war-induced disease and famine, and the sinking of ships probably exceeded battle casualties. These civilian deaths are even more difficult to determine, yet they must be counted in any comparative evaluation of national losses. There are no reliable figures for the casualties of the Soviet Union and China, the two countries in which casualties were undoubtedly greatest. Mainly for this reason, estimates of total dead in World War II vary anywhere from 35,000,000 to

60,000,000—a statistical difference of no small import. Few have ventured even to try to calculate the total number of persons who were wounded or permanently disabled.

However inexact many of the figures, their main import is clear. The heaviest proportionate human losses occurred in eastern Europe where Poland lost perhaps 20 percent of its prewar population, Yugoslavia and the Soviet Union around 10 percent. German losses, of which the greater proportion occurred on the Eastern Front, were only slightly less severe. The nations of western Europe, however great their suffering from occupation, escaped with manpower losses that were hardly comparable with those of World War I. In East Asia, the victims of famine and pestilence in China are to be numbered in the millions, in addition to other millions of both soldiers and civilians who perished in battle and bombardment.

Human and Material Cost

There can be no real statistical measurement of the human and material cost of World War II. The money cost to governments involved has been estimated at more than $1,000,000,000,000, but this figure cannot represent the human misery, deprivation, and suffering, the dislocation of peoples and of economic life, or the sheer physical destruction of property that the war involved.

EUROPE

The Nazi overlords of occupied Europe drained their conquered territories of resources to feed the German war machine. Industry and agriculture in France, Belgium, the Netherlands, Denmark, and Norway were forced to produce to meet German needs with a resulting deprivation of their own peoples. Italy, though at first a German ally, fared no better. The resources of the occupied territories in eastern Europe were even more ruthlessly exploited. Millions of able-bodied men and women were drained away to perform forced labour in German factories and on German farms. The whole system of German economic exploitation was enforced by cruel and brutal methods, and the guerrilla resistance it aroused was destructive in itself and provoked German reprisals that were even more destructive, particularly in Poland, Yugoslavia, and the occupied portions of the Soviet Union.

Great Britain, which escaped the ravages of occupation, suffered heavily from the German aerial blitz of 1940–41 and later from V-bombs and rockets. On the other side, German cities were leveled by Allied bombers, and in the final invasion of Germany from both east and west there was much retaliatory devastation, destruction, and pillage.

The destruction of physical plant was immense and far exceeded that of World War I, when it was largely confined to battle areas. France estimated the total cost at an amount equivalent to three times the total French annual national income. Belgium and the Netherlands suffered damage roughly in similar proportions to their resources. In Great Britain about 30 percent of the homes were destroyed or damaged, in France, Belgium, and the Netherlands about 20 percent. Agriculture in all the occupied countries suffered heavily from the destruction of facilities and farm animals, the lack of machinery and fertilizers, and the drain on manpower. Internal transport systems were completely disrupted by the destruction or confiscation of railcars, locomotives, and barges and the bombing of bridges and key rail centres. By 1945 the economies of the continental nations of western Europe were in a state of virtually complete paralysis.

In eastern Europe the devastation was even worse. Poland reported 30 percent of its buildings destroyed, as well as 60 percent of its schools, scientific institutions, and public administration facilities, 30–35 percent of its agricultural property, and 32 percent of its mines, electrical power, and industries. Yugoslavia reported 20.7 percent of its dwellings destroyed. In the battlegrounds of the western portion of the Soviet Union, the destruction was even more complete. In Germany itself, the U.S. Strategic Bombing Survey found that in 49 of the largest cities, 39 percent of the dwelling units were destroyed or seriously damaged. Central business districts had generally been reduced to rubble, leaving only suburban rings standing around a destroyed core.

Millions throughout Europe were rendered homeless. There were an estimated 21,000,000 refugees, more than half of them "displaced persons" who had been deported from their homelands to perform forced labour. Other millions who had remained at home were physically exhausted by five years of strain, suffering, and undernourishment. The roads of Europe were swamped by refugees all through 1945 and into 1946 as more than 5,000,000 Soviet prisoners of war and forced labourers returned eastward to their homeland and more than 8,000,000 Germans fled or were evacuated westward out of the Soviet-occupied portions of Germany. Millions of other persons of almost every European nationality also returned to their own countries or emigrated to new homes in other lands.

THE FAR EAST

The devastation of World War II in China was inflicted on a country that was already suffering from the economic ills of overpopulation, underdevelopment, and a half-century of war, political disunity, and unrest. The territory occupied by Japanese forces was roughly equivalent to that occupied by the Axis in Europe and the period of occupation was longer. That area of China unoccupied by the Japanese was virtually cut off from the outside world after the Japanese conquest of Burma in early 1942, and its economy continually tottered on the brink of collapse. In both areas, famines, epidemics, and civil unrest were recurrent, much farmland was flooded, and millions of refugees fled their homes, some several times. Cities, towns, and villages were laid waste by aerial bombardment and marching armies. The transportation system, poor to begin with, was thoroughly disrupted. Most of the limited number of hospitals and health institutions in China were destroyed or lost.

In India famine was recurrent, and the Indian economy was severely strained to support the burden the Allied military authorities placed upon it. The Philippines suffered from three years of Japanese occupation and exploitation and from the destruction wrought in the reconquest of the islands by the Americans in 1944–45. The harbour at Manila was wrecked by the retreating Japanese, and many portions of the city were demolished by bombardment.

In Japan the U.S. Strategic Bombing Survey found the damage to urban centres comparable to that in Germany. In the aggregate, 40 percent of the built-up areas of 66 Japanese cities was destroyed, and approximately 30 percent of the entire urban population of Japan lost their homes and many of their possessions. Hiroshima and Nagasaki suffered the peculiar and lasting damage done by atomic explosion and radiation.

Postwar Developments

A significant postwar development was the decline of British power. Soon after the war Britain began to give up its empire. World War I had produced a few new states as eastern European empires crumbled. World War II sounded the death knell for global empires. The immediate postwar period saw the reemergence into full independence of several great civilizations that the age of imperialism had placed under generations of European tutelage. These reborn countries had taken to heart the doctrines of European diplomacy. With the zeal of new converts, they were, in many ways, more insistent on the concepts of sovereignty, territorial integrity, and noninterference in internal affairs than their former colonial masters now were.

In 1947, after a long struggle for independence, Indians formed two proudly assertive but mutually antagonistic states, India and Pakistan. In the same year Britain turned over the Palestine problem to the United Nations. In 1948 the State of Israel was created. The states and principalities of the Arab world resumed their independence and then insisted, over the objections of their former colonial masters, on exercising full sovereignty throughout their own territories, as Egypt did with respect to the Suez Canal. Anti-imperialist sentiment soon made colonialism globally unacceptable.

For more than a year after the war the United States had problems that many foreign nations took for signs of weakness. Members of the armed forces demanded their release. By 1947 the army was down from its war peak of more than 8 million soldiers to a peacetime strength of about 1 million. Congress passed the nation's second peacetime draft law in 1948. There were also many shortages of consumer goods. Widespread labour troubles resulted in damaging strikes. Dissatisfaction with conditions brought a sweeping Republican victory in the 1946 congressional elections.

THE MARSHALL PLAN

One of the causes of World War II was the collapse of the European economy. To avoid a repeat of this situation and to create a strong economy that would enable Europeans to resist Communist aggression, the United States decided to aid European recovery.

The United States feared that the poverty, unemployment, and dislocation of the post-World War II period were reinforcing the appeal of Communist parties to voters in western Europe. On June 5, 1947, in an address at Harvard University, Secretary of State George C. Marshall advanced the idea of a European self-help program to be financed by the United States. On the basis of a unified plan for western European economic reconstruction presented by a committee representing 16 countries, the U.S. Congress authorized the establishment of the European Recovery Program, which was signed into law by President Harry S. Truman on April 3, 1948. Aid was originally offered to almost all the European countries, including those under military occupation by the Soviet Union. The Soviets early on withdrew from participation in the plan, however, and were soon followed by the other eastern European nations under their influence. This left the following countries to participate in the plan: Austria, Belgium, Denmark, France, Greece, Iceland, Ireland, Italy, Luxembourg, the Netherlands, Norway, Portugal, Sweden, Switzerland, Turkey, the United Kingdom, and western Germany.

Under Paul G. Hoffman, the Economic Cooperation Administration (ECA), a specially created bureau, distributed over the next four years some $13 billion worth of economic aid, helping to restore industrial and agricultural production, establish financial stability, and expand trade. Direct grants accounted for the vast majority of the aid, with the remainder in the form of loans. To coordinate the European participation, 16 countries, led by the United Kingdom and France, established the Committee of European Economic Cooperation to suggest a four-year recovery program. This organization was later replaced by the permanent Organisation for European

Economic Co-operation (OEEC), to which West Germany was ultimately admitted.

The Marshall Plan was very successful. The western European countries involved experienced a rise in their gross national products of 15 to 25 percent during this period. The plan contributed greatly to the rapid renewal of the western European chemical, engineering, and steel industries. Truman extended the Marshall Plan to less-developed countries throughout the world under the Point Four Program, initiated in 1949. The plan laid the foundations for the European Economic Union (Common Market). The Soviets refused to allow the eastern European nations under their control to participate.

WAR TRIALS AND PEACE TREATIES

In August 1945 the United States, Britain, the Soviet Union, and France wrote a charter for an Allied War Crimes Commission. The court established by the commission met at Nürnberg, Germany. It called before it 22 leading Nazis. In October 1946 the court sentenced most of the defendants. Ten of them were hanged. Seven were imprisoned, and three were acquitted. Others were sentenced later.

The British, Norwegians, and French also held separate war criminal trials. In Japan after V-J Day General MacArthur set up an army commission to try war criminals. Hundreds were executed, and thousands more were put in prison.

Delegates from 21 member countries of the United Nations met in Paris on July 29, 1946, to draft treaties with Italy, Hungary, Bulgaria, Romania, and Finland. Representatives of the United States, Britain, the Soviet Union, and France signed the treaties in Paris on Feb. 10, 1947. Each treaty provided that border fortifications were to be limited to those needed to keep internal security. Guarantees were given against racial discrimination and the rebirth of fascist governments. The Balkan treaties provided for free navigation of the Danube.

THE PROBLEM OF GERMANY

At Potsdam in 1945 Allied leaders set up a temporary administration for Germany. The country was divided into American, British, French, and Soviet occupation zones. The American, British, and French zones together made up the western two-thirds of Germany, while the Soviet zone comprised the eastern third. Control of Berlin, in the Soviet zone, was divided between the Soviet Union and the Western powers. Later, in 1961, the city would be physically partitioned by a concrete and barbed-wire wall.

The victors were determined that Germany should not regain the industrial strength necessary for war. Wiping out all German industry, however, would have been disastrous. Western Europe depended on Germany for coal and heavy metal products. In return Germany normally bought huge quantities of foodstuffs from its neighbours.

The Allied powers also had to settle on a form of German government. The United States and Britain favoured a federal type, with most matters entrusted to German states (Länder) and a federal government to deal with national matters such as currency. The Soviet Union preferred a strong central government with political parties directly represented so that Communists could dominate. France wanted a very loose federation, with international control of the Ruhr.

Representatives of the four powers convened in Moscow in 1947 to discuss treaties for Germany and Austria. Because of the postwar weakness of Britain and France, the conference was chiefly a contest between the United States and the Soviet Union.

NÜRNBERG TRIALS

The Nürnberg (also Nuremberg) trials were series of trials held in Nürnberg, Germany, in 1945–46, in which former Nazi leaders were indicted and tried as war criminals by the International Military Tribunal. The indictment lodged against them contained four counts: (1) crimes against peace (i.e., the planning, initiating, and waging of wars of aggression in violation of international treaties and agreements), (2) crimes against humanity (i.e., exterminations, deportations, and genocide), (3) war crimes (i.e., violations of the laws of war), and (4) "a common plan or conspiracy to commit" the criminal acts listed in the first three counts.

The authority of the International Military Tribunal to conduct these trials stemmed from the London Agreement of August 8, 1945. On that date, representatives from the United States, Great Britain, the Soviet Union, and the provisional government of France signed an agreement that included a charter for an international military tribunal to conduct trials of major Axis war criminals whose offenses had no particular geographic location. Later 19 other nations accepted the provisions of this agreement. The tribunal was given the authority to find any individual guilty of the commission of war crimes (counts 1–3 listed above) and to declare any group or organization to be criminal in character. If an organization was found to be criminal, the prosecution could bring individuals to trial for having been members, and the criminal nature of the group or organization could no longer be questioned. A defendant was entitled to receive a copy of the indictment, to offer any relevant explanation to the charges brought against him, and to be represented by counsel and confront and cross-examine the witnesses.

The tribunal consisted of a member plus an alternate selected by each of the four signatory countries. The first session, under the presidency of Gen. I.T. Nikitchenko, the

Soviet member, took place on Oct. 18, 1945, in Berlin. At this time, 24 former Nazi leaders were charged with the perpetration of war crimes, and various groups (such as the Gestapo, the Nazi secret police) were charged with being criminal in character. Beginning on Nov. 20, 1945, all sessions of the tribunal were held in Nürnberg under the presidency of Lord Justice Geoffrey Lawrence (later Baron Trevethin and Oaksey), the British member.

After 216 court sessions, on Oct. 1, 1946, the verdict on 22 of the original 24 defendants was handed down. (Robert Ley committed suicide while in prison, and Gustav Krupp von Bohlen und Halbach's mental and physical condition prevented his being tried.) Three of the defendants were acquitted: Hjalmar Schacht, Franz von Papen, and Hans Fritzsche. Four were sentenced to terms of imprisonment ranging from 10 to 20 years: Karl Dönitz, Baldur von Schirach, Albert Speer, and Konstantin von Neurath. Three were sentenced to life imprisonment: Rudolf Hess, Walther Funk, and Erich Raeder. Twelve of the defendants were sentenced to death by hanging. Ten of them—Hans Frank, Wilhelm Frick, Julius Streicher, Alfred Rosenberg, Ernst Kaltenbrunner, Joachim von Ribbentrop, Fritz Sauckel, Alfred Jodl, Wilhelm Keitel, and Arthur Seyss-Inquart—were hanged on Oct. 16, 1946. Martin Bormann was tried and condemned to death in absentia, and Hermann Göring committed suicide before he could be executed.

In rendering these decisions, the tribunal rejected the major defenses offered by the defendants. First, it rejected the contention that only a state, and not individuals, could be found guilty of war crimes; the tribunal held that crimes of international law are committed by men and that only by punishing individuals who commit such crimes can the provisions of international law be enforced. Second, it rejected the argument that the trial and adjudication were ex post facto. The tribunal responded that such acts had been regarded as criminal prior to World War II.

Nazi officials sit together in the dock during the Nürnberg proceedings for war crimes at the Palace of Justice.

The Soviet Union demanded $10 billion in reparations from Germany in 20 years. The United States rejected this proposal on the grounds that the money could be made available only if the United States supplied an equivalent sum to support the Germans. If the reparations were to be paid without such support, it would greatly hamper Germany's economic recovery. The conference ended with no agreement. Later meetings also failed. Then, in June 1948, the Soviet Union blockaded the roads and railways to Berlin in an attempt to force the United States, Britain, and France out of the city.

The Western powers responded by supplying western Berlin with food, fuel, and medicine from outside by air. This airlift kept life going in western Berlin for 11 months, until the Soviet Union lifted the blockade in May 1949. In that same month the Western powers organized their occupation zones into a new nation called the Federal Republic of Germany, commonly known as West Germany. The Soviet Union then established its zone as the German Democratic Republic, or East Germany. When the Soviet Union continued to block a German peace treaty the United States in 1952 ratified a "peace contract" with West Germany. Germany would not be reunited as a nation until 1990.

THE PROBLEMS OF AUSTRIA AND TRIESTE

The postwar split between the Soviet Union and the West was also illustrated in Austria. After the war Austria was divided into four areas of occupation—American, British, French, and Soviet—with Vienna under the control of all four powers. In 1955, after repeated disagreements about terms, a peace treaty was signed in Vienna. Soviet and Allied occupation forces were withdrawn.

Another postwar trouble spot in Europe was Trieste. In 1945 the city and surrounding territory were divided into two zones—Zone A (including Trieste) was occupied by British and United States forces, Zone B by the Yugoslavs. The Italian peace treaty of 1947 established the Free Territory of Trieste under the jurisdiction of the United Nations. Conflicts between Yugoslavia and Italy over their claims to the territory continued, however. In an agreement signed by the two countries in 1954, Trieste and most of Zone A were given to Italy while Yugoslavia received Zone B and some added territory.

Meanwhile the increased threat of Communism in Europe led to the formation of new pacts among the free nations. In 1949 ten nations of western Europe joined with the United States and Canada in establishing the North Atlantic Treaty Organization (NATO). Three years later the European Defense Community was founded. This group received NATO support.

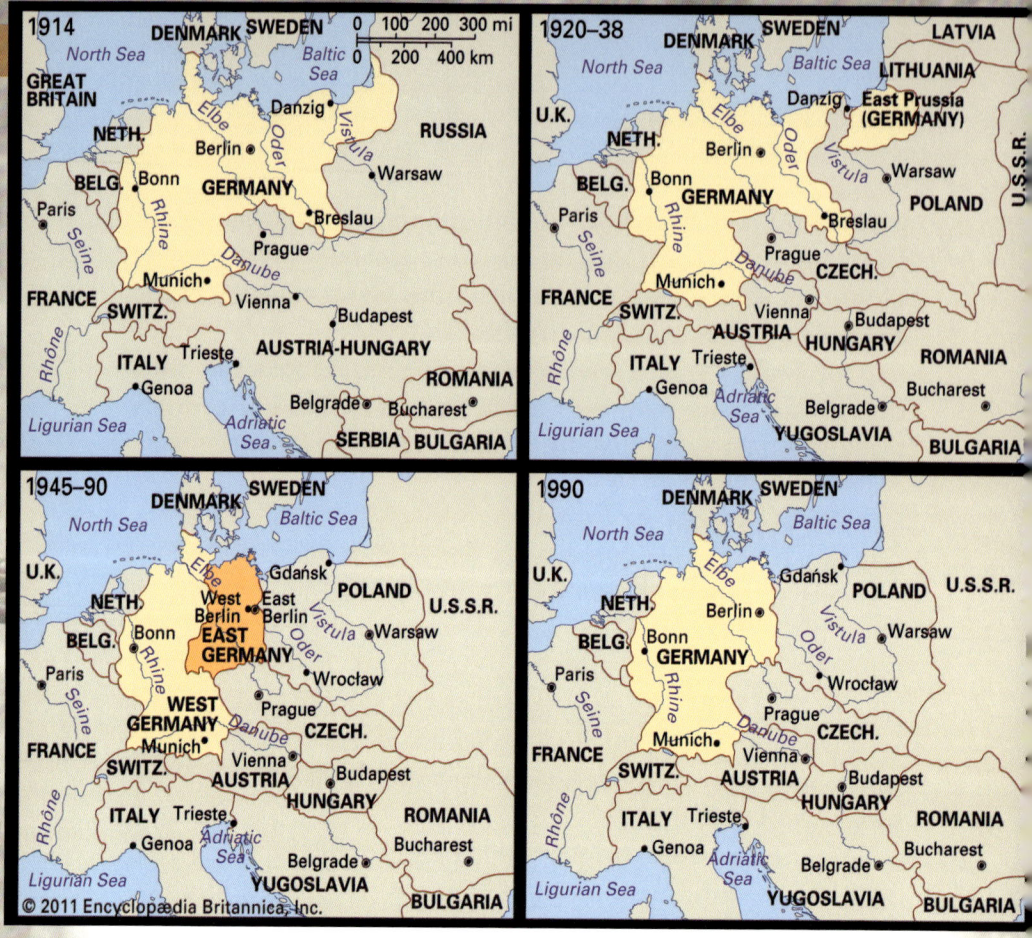

These maps depict changes in Germany's territory and internal status from 1914 to 1990.

POSTWAR PROBLEMS IN ASIA

In the Far East Communist military aggression created a new balance of power before the World War II peace treaty with Japan could be signed. On the Asia mainland Chinese Communist forces routed the armies of Nationalist China (1946–49). Mao Zedong, the Chinese Communist leader, proclaimed the People's Republic of China and allied it with the Soviet Union. This made China the strongest military power in the Far East. The defeated Nationalist forces, headed by Chiang Kai-shek, fled to the island of Taiwan.

The successful Communist revolution in China set the pattern for Communist revolts in other Asian countries. In Malaya and the Philippines rebels waged campaigns of terrorism that lasted for a number of years. In Indochina Communist forces attacked French-supported Vietnam. They forced the French to partition Vietnam.

After World War II Korea was occupied in the north by the Soviet Union and in the south by the United States. When the Republic of Korea was established in the south, most of the United States forces withdrew. In 1950 Communist forces from North Korea and China invaded the new republic. Thus the increasing tensions in eastern Asia had finally exploded into warfare.

Japan struggled to rebuild itself after its crushing defeat. During this time all efforts by the Allies to frame a peace treaty were blocked by the Soviet Union's disagreements with the United States. Finally, in 1951, the United States sponsored a treaty that was endorsed by Japan and 48 other nations. The Chinese signatory—the Nationalist government—signed in 1952. Negotiations between Japan and the Soviet Union continued until 1956, when a peace treaty was finally signed.

BUILDUP TO THE COLD WAR

After World War II in 1945, western Europe was economically exhausted and militarily weak (the Western Allies had rapidly and drastically reduced their armies at the end of the war), and newly powerful Communist parties had arisen in France and Italy. By contrast, the Soviet Union had emerged from the war with its armies dominating all the states of central and eastern Europe, and by 1948 Communists under Moscow's sponsorship had consolidated their control of the governments of those countries and suppressed all non-Communist political activity. What became known as the Iron Curtain, a term popularized by Winston Churchill, had descended over central and eastern Europe. Further, wartime cooperation between the Western Allies and the Soviets had completely broken down.

The world became divided into two tight blocs, one dominated by the United States and one by the Soviet Union, with a fragile nonaligned movement (mostly of newly independent countries) lying precariously in between. The Cold War took place under the threat of nuclear catastrophe and gave rise to two major alliances—NATO, led by the United States, and the Warsaw Pact, led by the Soviet Union—along with a conventional and nuclear arms race, endless disarmament negotiations, much conference diplomacy, many summits, and periodic crisis management.

Conclusion

War once again broke out over nationality conflicts in east-central Europe, provoked in part by a German drive for continental hegemony, and it expanded, once again, into a global conflict whose battle zones touched the waters or heartlands of almost every continent. The total nature of World War II surpassed that of 1914–18 in that civilian populations not only contributed to the war effort but also became direct targets of aerial attack. Moreover, in 1941 the Nazi regime unleashed a war of extermination against Slavs, Jews, and other elements deemed inferior by Hitler's ideology, while Stalinist Russia extended its campaign of terror against the Ukrainians to the conquered Poles. The Japanese-American war in the Pacific also assumed at times the brutal aspect of a war between races. This ultimate democratization of warfare eliminated the age-old distinction between combatants and non-combatants and ensured that total casualties in World War II would greatly exceed those of World War I and that civilian casualties would exceed the military.

Once again the European war devolved into a contest between a German-occupied Mitteleuropa and a peripheral Allied coalition. But this time Italy abandoned neutrality for the German side, and the Soviet Union held out in the east, while France collapsed in the west. Hence Soviet dictator Joseph Stalin took France's place in meetings of the "Big Three," together with U.S President Franklin Roosevelt and British prime minister Winston Churchill. The Japanese chose to remain neutral vis-à-vis the U.S.S.R., while the Grand Alliance of anti-Fascist states simmered with conflicts over strategy and war aims. World War II, therefore, comprised several parallel or overlapping wars, while the war in Europe became a kind of three-way struggle among the forces of democracy, Nazism, and Communism. As soon as German and Japanese power were effaced, the conflicts among the victors burst into the open and gave birth to the Cold War. World War II completed the destruction of the old Great Power system, prepared the disintegration of Europe's overseas empires, and submerged Europe itself into a world arena dominated by the Soviet Union and the United States.

Glossary

amphibious Done by soldiers who are brought to land in special boats; carried out by land and sea forces acting together.

Anschluss Political or economic union of one government or territory with another; especially, the political union of Austria with Germany, achieved through annexation by Adolf Hitler in 1938.

Aryan Of or relating to a hypothetical ethnic type illustrated by or descended from early speakers of Indo-European languages; used in Nazism to designate a supposed master race of non-Jewish Caucasians usually having Nordic features.

arms race A situation in which countries that are enemies each try to build or collect weapons faster than the other can.

atom bomb A bomb whose violent explosive power is due to the sudden release of energy resulting from the splitting of nuclei of a heavy chemical element (as plutonium or uranium) by neutrons in a very rapid chain reaction.

balkanization To break up (as a region or group) into smaller and often hostile units.

bridgehead Any area that an army takes from an enemy and from which it can move forward to make an attack.

Cold War The nonviolent conflict between the United States and the former U.S.S.R. after 1945.

collective security The maintenance by common action of the security of all members of an association of nations.

détente An ending of unfriendly or hostile relations between countries.

euthanasia Act or practice of painlessly putting to death persons suffering from painful and incurable disease or incapacitating physical disorder or allowing them to die by withholding treatment or withdrawing artificial life-support measures.

Fascism A political philosophy, movement, or regime (as that of the Fascisti) that exalts nation and often race above the individual and that stands for a centralized autocratic government headed by a dictatorial leader, severe economic and social regimentation, and forcible suppression of opposition.

lend-lease The transfer of goods and services to an ally to aid in a common cause with payment made by a return of the original items or their use in the cause or by a similar transfer of other goods and services.

matériel Equipment and supplies used by soldiers.

panzer A German tank of World War II.

parliamentarism A system of government in which a group of people are responsible for making the laws.

plebiscite A vote by the people of an entire country or district to decide on some issue, such as choice of a ruler or government, option for independence or annexation by another power, or a question of national policy.

pogrom The organized killing of many helpless people usually because of their race or religion.

putsch A secretly plotted and suddenly executed attempt to overthrow a government.

reparations Payment in money or materials by a nation defeated in war. After World War I, reparations to the Allied powers were required of Germany by the Treaty of Versailles.

social Darwinism A sociological theory that sociocultural advance is the product of intergroup conflict and competition and the socially elite classes (as those possessing wealth and power) possess biological superiority in the struggle for existence.

social democracy A political movement that uses principles of democracy to change a capitalist country to a socialist one.

tariff Tax levied upon goods as they cross national boundaries, usually by the government of the importing country.

totalitarian Of or relating to a political regime based on subordination of the individual to the state and strict control of all aspects of the life and productive capacity of the nation especially by coercive measures (as censorship and terrorism).

tribunal A kind of court that has authority in a specific area.

Bibliography

The literature on World War II is vast and ever-growing. Nonfiction books range from popular overviews to multivolume official histories to scholarly analyses of single campaigns or social issues. In addition, numerous motion-picture and television documentaries are available as video recordings.

Surveys

Good histories of the war include Andrew Roberts, *The Storm of War* (2009); Williamson Murray and Allan R. Millett, *A War to Be Won: Fighting the Second World War* (2000); Gerhard L. Weinberg, *A World At Arms: A Global History of World War II* (1994); John Keegan, *The Second World War* (1990, reissued 1997); Mark Calvocoressi, Guy Wint, and John Pritchard, *Total War*, rev. 2nd ed., 2 vol. (1995); and B.H. Liddell Hart, *History of the Second World War* (1970, reissued 1999).

Documentaries

The classic documentary, organized around original film footage and interviews with key individuals still living at the time, is the massive 32-hour series *The World at War* (1974), produced by Jeremy Isaacs and narrated by Sir Laurence Olivier for Thames Television, in cooperation with the Imperial War Museum. American perspectives are given in *World War II with Walter Cronkite*, a multipart series first broadcast by CBS-TV in 1982, and *America Goes to War* (1998), a series on the "home front" produced by Questar Inc. and narrated by another CBS journalist, Eric Sevareid. In addition, the Arts and Entertainment Television Network has produced outstanding biographical documentaries of World War II personalities, including every major political figure and numerous military leaders such as Douglas MacArthur, Bernard Montgomery, Chester Nimitz, George Patton, and Georgy Zhukov.

Scholarly Views

The origins of the war are explored in Joachim Remak, *The Origins of the Second World War* (1976); Donald Cameron Watt, *How War Came: The Immediate Origins of the Second World War, 1938–1939* (1989); and Akira Iriye, *The Origins of the Second World War in Asia and the Pacific* (1987).

Specific campaigns of the European theatre are the focus of Richard Hough and Denis Richards, *The Battle of Britain: The Greatest Air Battle of World War II* (1989); Richard Overy, *Russia's War* (1997, reissued 1999); Carlo D'Este, *Bitter Victory: The Battle for Sicily, July–August 1943* (1988, reprinted 1991); John Keegan, *Six Armies in Normandy,* new ed. (1994); Trevor N. Dupuy, David L. Bongard, and Richard C. Anderson, *Hitler's Last Gamble: The Battle of the Bulge, December 1944–January 1945* (1994); and John Toland, *The Last 100 Days: The Tumultuous and Controversial Story of the Final Days of WW II in Europe* (1965, reissued 2003).

Outstanding treatments of the war in the Pacific from the Japanese point of view include Saburo Ienaga, *The Pacific War, 1931–1945* (1978), and Akira Iriye, *Power and Culture: The Japanese-American War, 1941–1945* (1981). The American perspective is found in John Costello, *The Pacific War,* rev. ed. (1985), and Ronald H. Spector, *Eagle Against the Sun: The American War with Japan,* new ed. (2000).

Naval history is treated in Paul S. Dull, *A Battle History of the Imperial Japanese Navy, 1941–1945* (1978), and John Prados, *Combined Fleet Decoded: The Secret History of American Intelligence and the Japanese Navy in World War II* (1995, reissued 2001). The war under the waves is detailed in the following books on submarines by Clay Blair: *Silent Victory: The U.S. Submarine War Against Japan* (1975, reissued 2001); *Hitler's U-Boat War: The Hunters, 1939–1942* (1996, reissued 2000); and *Hitler's U-Boat War: The Hunted, 1942–1944* (1998, reissued 2000). The air war has likewise received special attention, including Richard J. Overy, *The Air War, 1939–1945* (1980, reissued 1991); Michael S. Sherry, *The Rise of American Air Power: The Creation of Armageddon* (1987); and Geoffrey Perret, *Winged Victory: The Army Air Forces in World War II* (1993, reissued 1997).

There is a vast literature on the war's cultural and social aspects. The racial dimensions of World War II are the subject of John Dower, *War Without Mercy* (1986, reprinted with corrections, 1993). Stories of the home front are well told in Angus Calder, *The People's War: Britain, 1939–1945* (1969, reissued 1992); Susan M. Hartmann, *The Home Front and Beyond: American Women in the 1940s* (1982, reissued 1995); John Barber and Mark Harrison, *The Soviet Home Front, 1941–1945* (1991); and Ben-Ami Shillony, *Politics and Culture in Wartime Japan* (1981, reissued 2001).

Decisions concerning the atomic bomb and the end of war in the Pacific are outlined in scores of books, many published in 1994 and 1995 as the world marked the 50th anniversary of the atomic bombings of Hiroshima and Nagasaki. In some ways, Herbert Feis, *The Atomic Bomb and the End of World War II*, rev. ed. (1966, reissued 1970), remains the standard. Competing views of this important aspect of the war are given in Gar Alperovitz, *The Decision to Use the Atomic Bomb and the Architecture of an American Myth* (1995), and Richard Frank, *Downfall: The End of the Imperial Japanese Empire* (1999, reissued 2001).

Official Histories

In the half-century following the war, Her Majesty's Stationery Office (now known as The Stationery Office) published scores of books under the general title "History of the Second World War." These include F.H. Hinsley et al., *British Intelligence in the Second World War*, 5 vol. (1981–90); S.W. Roskill, *War at Sea 1939–1945*, 3 vol. in 4 (1954–61); and L.F. Ellis et al., *Victory in the West*, 2 vol. (1960–68). The standard for U.S. official histories, published by the Office of the Chief of Military History, is *The United States Army in World War II*, 75 vol. (1944–86), also known as the "Green Books." Other U.S. histories include Samuel Eliot Morison, *History of United States Naval Operations in World War II*, 15 vol. (1947–62, reissued 2001), and Wesley Craven and James Cate (eds.), *The Army Air Forces in World War II*, 7 vol. (1948–58, reissued 1983). Militärgeschictliches Forschungsamt (Armed Forces Historical Research Office), *Das Deutsche Reich und der Zweite Weltkrieg*, 10 vol. (1979–), is the official German history; the volumes are being published in English under the title *Germany and the Second World War* (1990–).

Index

A

Abyssinia, 20, 38, 40–41, 44, 45, 50, 53, 118–119
Addis Ababa, 44, 119
Admiral Graf Spree (battleship), 89
Admiral Hipper (battleship), 125
Admiral Scheer (battleship), 125
Africa
    Allied invasion of northwest Africa, 172–174
    British in, 115–120
    desert warfare in, 115–118, 156, 159
    and East Africa, 118–119
    Italian invasion of Africa, 38, 40–41
    prisoners of war, 116–117, 177
Afrika Korps, 159, 176–177
air warfare, 179–180, 181, 242–243
Alamein, Battle of el-, 158, 167–169
Albania, 72, 109–113
Aleutian Islands, 149, 150, 166, 222
Algeria, 104, 172–174
Allies
    and initial victories, 162–180, 182–186
    invasion of Italy, 212–213, 216, 230–232
    invasion of western Europe, 234–240
    policies of, 244
    strategies and controversies (1940–42), 153–156
Alsace, 103, 238, 251
Anschluss, 24, 36, 57
Anti-Comintern Pact, 43–44, 73
Anvil, Operation, 232, 238
Anzio, 230–231
appeasement policy, 44–46, 55, 76–78
Arcadia Conference, 154
Ark Royal (aircraft carrier), 126
Atlantic, Battle of the, 243
atomic bomb, 257, 263, 268, 269–271, 277
Auschwitz, 190, 203, 204, 205
Australia, 120, 145, 149, 162, 165, 185, 186, 224
Austria
    Allied invasion, of 260
    postwar problems, 285–286
    union with Germany, 24, 54–57
Axis Pact, 72, 104, 110, 138, 153, 233–269

B

B-17 (Flying Fortress), 180
B-24 (Liberator), 182
"Back Door to War" Theory, 143–145
Barbarossa, Operation, 128–129
Barham (battleship), 111, 126
Bataan Peninsula, 146, 248
Beck, Józef, 35
Beer Hall Putsch, 32
Belgium
    Allied liberation of, 239, 243
    German invasion of, 65–66,

Index

91–95
  neutrality of, 44, 87
  postwar, 279
Belgrade, 111–112, 241–242
Belorussia, 240
Belzec, 204
Benghazi, 117–118
Bergen, 89, 90, 126
Berlin, 75–76, 255, 258, 260–261, 281, 283, 284
Berlin, Battle of, 66, 107, 180
Bismarck (battleship), 126
Bismarck Sea, Battle of, 165–166
Blitz, the, 105–107, 275
Blitzkrieg ("lightning war"), 64–66, 67–68, 81, 112
Britain
  air bombardment of, 105–108
  appeasement policy, 44–46, 55, 76–77
  colonies of, 118–120
  declaration of war against Germany, 76
  rearmament of, 69–70, 81–82
Britain, Battle of, 105–108
British Expeditionary Force (BEF), 97, 110
British Somaliland, 118
Brüning, Heinrich, 29–30
Bulge, Battle of the, 220, 252
Burma, 140, 141, 146, 151–152, 166–167, 228–229, 249–250, 277

C

Canadian Army, 146, 231, 234, 237, 239, 252, 260
Cape Matapan, Battle of, 111
Casablanca Conference, 181, 182–183
casualties of war, 273–277
Caucasus, 132, 133, 160, 161, 171, 172
Chamberlain, Neville, 44, 55, 57–58, 59–60, 61–63, 71, 72, 75, 76–78, 89, 94
Chiang Kai-shek, 25, 51–53, 136, 139, 151, 167, 217, 229, 249, 287
China
  Chinese front, 151–152
  Communist Revolution in, 136, 286, 287
  Japanese aggression in, 50–53
  Japanese invasion of, 136–137
  Nationalists, 136–137, 151, 286–287
  and puppet government, 136
  resistance, 136–137
Churchill, Winston, 45, 60, 62, 69, 88, 94, 117, 118, 121, 153–155, 158–159, 167, 182, 217–218, 244–245, 255–258, 263, 288–289
Cold War, 287–288, 290
Cologne, 180
communists, 29–30, 36, 38–39, 192, 207, 215, 244, 257, 279, 281, 287–288
concentration camps, 203, 204, 207, 208
conferences (Allied)
  Arcadia Conference, 154
  Casablanca Conference, 181, 182, 211
  Potsdam Conference, 263–264, 270
  Quadrant Conference, 211–212
  Quebec Conference, 244–245
  Sextant Conference, 217
  Tehran Conference, 244
  Trident Conference, 182

Yalta Conference, 255–259
convoy system, 123–124
Coral Sea, Battle of, 149–150
Courageous (ship), 88
Crete, 110–114
Crimea, 160, 220, 221
Cyrenaica, 115–118, 156
Czechoslovakia, 42, 54–55, 57–63, 260

D

D-Day invasion, 234–240
Dunkirk, 97–100
Dutch Army, 92–94, 140, 144, 147
Dutch East Indies, 138–141, 147, 148

E

Eastern Front, 65–66, 135–136, 183–184, 218–222, 240–242, 254, 259, 261, 274
Eastern Solomons, Battle of, 163–166
Egypt 115–118, 156–159, 167
Eichmann, Adolf, 189
Einsatzgruppen, 201–202
Einstein, Albert, 268
Eisenhower, Dwight D., 172, 174, 181, 218, 234–235, 239, 263
English Channel, 46, 92, 105, 106
Estonia, 85–87, 242
Eureka Conference, 217
extermination camps, 202–208

F

Fiji Islands, 149
Final Solution, 187–208
Finland, 75, 86–87, 222, 242, 268, 280
Formidable (battleship), 111
Four-Power Pact, 34–35

France
  colonies of, 102, 138, 141, 166
  conquest of, 101, 104
  declaration of war against Germany, 76
  Free French, 102–103, 104, 120, 166
  German invasion of, 91–104
  Vichy, 102–103, 104, 120, 138, 166, 173, 174
Franco, Francisco, 46–48
Free French, 102–103, 104, 120, 166
French Resistance, 102, 238

G

Galeazzo, Ciano, 43, 109
Gamelin, Maurice-Gustave, 42, 87, 94, 97
Gaulle, Charles de, 70, 102–103, 104, 174, 181
Geneva Disarmament Conference, 28
German Navy, 122, 124–126
Germany
  and air war over Britain, 105–108
  Allied occupation of, 281, 284–285
  defeat of, 259–263
  and failure of the German Republic, 29
  invasion of Central Europe, 108–114
  invasion of Czechoslovakia, 57–58
  invasion of the Soviet Union, 128–136, 160–162
  invasion of western Europe, 91–97
  postwar, 281, 284–285
  rearmament of, 67–68, 81–82

Index

strategy of (1939–42), 126–128
strategy of (1943), 218–220
union with Austria, 54–57
Western offensive (1944–45), 251–252
Gestapo (Secret Police), 63, 189–190, 283
ghettos, 199–201
Giraud, Henry, 93, 97, 103, 174, 181
Gneisenau (battleship), 125
Good Neighbor Policy, 49
Göring, Hermann, 54, 55, 61, 99, 105, 189, 197–198, 283
Great Depression, 20, 21–23, 25, 27, 29, 35, 48, 50, 70
Greece
    German invasion of, 110–114, 128
    government in exile, 244
    Italian invasion of, 109
    postwar, 279
    resistance in, 192, 241
Guadalcanal, 162–165, 267
Guam, 141, 147, 227
Guderian, Heinz, 80, 84, 96, 97–100, 130–132, 253–254, 260

H

Hácha, Emil, 66, 76
Hamburg, Battle of, 180
Hess, Rudolph, 31, 283
Himmler, Heinrich, 190, 255
Hindenburg, Paul von, 29, 30
Hirohito (Emperor of Japan), 272
Hiroshima, 267–268, 269, 277
Hitler, Adolf
    assassination attempt on, 236–237
    last days of, 261–262
    and Mussolini, 21, 36–37, 71–72
    and Nazi rallies, 30
    and rise to power, 29
Hoare-Laval Plan, 41
Holocaust, 190, 192, 193, 204, 205, 206
Hoover, Herbert, 24, 27, 50
Hungary, 63, 108–110, 112, 113, 204, 205, 221, 254, 253, 254, 263, 280

I

Imphal-Kohima, Battle of, 229
Iraq, 119–120
Italian front, 230–232, 262
Italian Somaliland, 119
Italy
    Allied invasion of, 212–213, 216
    declaration of war against Germany, 213
    invasion of Abyssinia, 40–41, 45
    invasion of France, 100
    Sicily, 209–211
Iwo Jima, 264–267

J

Japan
    attack on Pearl Harbor, 141–142, 145–149
    and end of the war, 264–272
    invasion of China, 50–53
    and military expansion, 141–142, 145–147
    and policy (1939–41), 137–140
    surrender of, 268, 272
Java, 141, 145, 146, 148
Java Sea, Battle of, 148
Jews
    and anti-Semitism, 31, 33, 192, 194, 201–202, 205

and the "final solution," 187–208
forced deportations of, 189, 190, 191, 204–207
and ghettos, 199–201
and the Holocaust, 190, 192, 193, 204, 205, 206
and Judenräte ("Jewish Councils"), 200

K

kamikaze, 246, 248, 265–267
Katyn Massacre, 214–216
Kiev, 130, 132, 201, 220–221
Kimmel, Husband, 145
Kowloon Peninsula, 146
Kristallnacht ("Night of Broken Glass"), 197–198
Kursk, Battle of, 184
Kwantung Army, 25–26

L

Latvia, 85–87, 201, 242
Lausanne Conference, 24–25
League of Nations, 25–28
Lebensraum ("living space"), 32, 34, 56, 78, 199
Lend-Lease Act, 120–121, 143, 229
Leningrad, 86, 130, 132, 222
Lexington (aircraft carrier), 149
Leyte Gulf, Battle of, 247–249
Lingayen Gulf, 146, 248
Lithuania, 85–86, 201, 241–242
London Economic Conference, 28
London Naval Conference, 27
Luftwaffe, 45, 62, 81, 83, 94, 98, 99, 105, 107, 108, 169, 242–243
Luzon, 146, 246, 248

M

MacArthur, Douglas, 146, 148, 162, 182, 185, 245, 267, 272, 280, 295
Maginot Line, 35, 70, 87, 91–92, 100
Majdanek, 190, 204
Manchuria, 20, 25–26, 51, 63, 136–137, 214, 217, 271
Manhattan Project, 268
Manila, 146, 248, 277
Mannerheim Line, 86
Mao Zedong, 51, 136, 286
Marshall Plan, 278–280
Mein Kampf ("My Struggle"), 30, 32–34, 194
Messina, 210–211, 212
Midway, Battle of, 150, 162
Midway Island, 149, 150
Mineichi, Koga, 225
Minsk, 130, 220, 240
Molotov, Vyacheslav, 74, 75, 155, 263
Montgomery, Bernard Law, 159, 167, 168, 175, 176, 237, 239, 252, 259, 260
Moscow, 34–35, 39, 72–75, 130–135, 155, 183, 244–245, 259, 281, 287
Munich Agreement, 57–58, 61–63, 66–67
Mussolini, Benito
fall of, 209–211, 212
and Hitler, 21, 36–37, 71–72
and Italian aggression, 40–41
rise to power, 41

N

Nagasaki, 267–268, 269, 277
Nanking, 25, 52–53, 136, 272
Naples, 212, 213, 216
Narvik, 88–91
naval warfare, 177–178
Nazis
and anti-Semitism, 192,

Index

194–196
and the "final solution," 187, 188, 189, 190, 197, 201, 202
and non-Jewish victims, 198–199
and the Nürnberg laws, 193–194
rise of, 29–31, 33–34, 196
Netherlands, The, 65–66, 71, 87, 92–94, 187, 243, 260, 274, 275, 279
New Britain, 147, 162, 182, 185, 222–223
New Caledonia, 149, 150
New Guinea, 140, 147, 149, 162, 165, 166, 185–186, 222–225, 245
Nimitz, Chester, W., 148, 211, 225, 227, 246, 266–267, 272
Nonagression Pact, 75
North Atlantic Treaty Organization (NATO), 285, 288
Norway, 88–91, 94, 105, 187, 274, 279
Nürnberg, 54, 58, 195, 207, 280
Nürnberg laws, 193–194, 195
Nürnberg trials, 76, 208, 282–283

O

Okinawa, 227, 266–267
Operation A, 17–18
Overlord, Operation, 211–212, 217–218, 234, 237

P

Pacific, war in, 162–166, 184–186, 222–227
Pacific Fleet, 141, 142, 148, 150
Pact of Steel, 72, 100
Papagos, Alexandros, 110
peace treaties, 280–281
Pearl Harbor, 141–142, 143–145, 151, 153, 225
Pétain, Marshal, 101, 102, 104, 173–174
Philippine Sea, Battle of, 227
Pius XI (Pope), 35
Poland
and army, 82–83
casualties in, 274–276
extermination camps in, 202, 206
German invasion of, 79, 82–85
government-in-exile, 214–215
and Jews, 188, 190, 191, 199
and Katyn Massacre, 214–216
resistance in, 192
Soviet advance in, 253–255
Potsdam Conference, 263–264
Potsdam Declaration, 272
Prince of Wales (battleship), 126, 146
Prinz Eugen (cruiser), 126

Q

Quadrant Conference, 211–212
Quebec Conference, 244–245
Quisling, Vidkun, 88

R

Rabaul, 223
radar, 69, 106–107, 178
Reichstag, 29, 30, 88
Repulse (battle cruiser), 146
resistance movements, 136–137, 191–192, 238, 241
Rhineland, 42–43, 54, 73, 199
Ribbentrop, Joachim von, 54–55, 75, 283
Roma (Gypsies), 193, 199
Romania, 71, 74, 85, 108–112, 127–128, 132, 205, 241, 243–245, 263, 280
Rommel, Erwin, 65, 100, 117–118,

156, 159, 167–168, 175–176, 233, 236, 237
Roosevelt, Franklin, 49, 50, 52–53, 58, 120–121, 143–144, 153–155, 181, 182, 196, 217–218, 244–245, 255, 257–258, 261, 263
Rotterdam, 93
Royal Air Force (RAF), 81, 105–108, 235, 243, 259
Royal Navy, 98, 105, 122
Royal Oak (ship), 89
Ruhr, Battle of, 180
Russo-Finnish War, 85–87

S

Salerno, 212
Salonika, 112, 114
Samoa, 149, 150
Scharnhorst (battleship), 125
Sea Lion, Operation, 105
Serbia, 114, 187
Sextant Conference, 217
Shoho (light carrier), 149
Shokaku (aircraft carrier), 149
Sicily, 181, 182–183, 209–211, 212
Singapore, 146, 147–148, 158, 246
Sino-Japanese War, 51–52
Sikorski, Wladyslaw, 216–218
slave labour, 187, 190–191, 203, 204, 208
Slovakia, 79, 84, 108, 110
Smolensk, 130–134, 183, 214–215, 220
Sobibor, 190, 202, 204
Solomon Islands, 148–149, 162–163, 166, 185, 222, 223
Soviet Union
    declaration of war against Germany, 241
    declaration of war against Japan, 272
    and the Eastern Front (1943–1944), 220–222
    German invasion of (1941), 128–136, 259–261
    and preparations for war, 70–71
    and Red Army, 74, 86, 128, 130, 134, 160, 169, 183–184, 217–221, 240–241, 264
    and summer offensive, (1942), 160–162
Spain, 46–48, 50, 53, 56
Spanish Civil War, 46–48
Speer, Albert, 261, 283
Spitfire (aircraft), 81, 106
Stalin, Joseph, 36, 39, 47, 54, 62–63, 70–75, 127, 132, 143, 155, 161, 181, 215–218, 244, 245, 255–258, 270
Stalingrad, 161, 169–172
Stimson Doctrine, 26, 52
Storm Troopers (SA), 198
Stresa Front, 40–42, 44
Sudetenland, 59–60, 61, 76, 200
Suez Canal, 115, 118
Syria, 40–41, 66, 97, 119–120, 178

T

T-4 Program, 199
Tassafaronga, Battle of, 164–165
Tehran Conference, 244
Ten-Year Rule, 69
Terminal, 263
Tito, Josip, 241–242, 244
Tobruk, 117, 118, 156–158
Tojo Hideki, 139, 226
Tokyo, 26, 51, 73, 149, 152, 226, 227, 264–268, 272
Torch, Operation, 155–156, 169, 172, 181
Treblinka, 190, 202, 204
Trident Conference, 182

Index

Trieste, 285–286
Tripoli, 117, 169
Truman, Harry, 263, 268, 269–271, 272, 279, 280
Tunisia, 174–177
Turkey, 110, 279

U

U-boats, 88–89, 124, 125, 126, 177–178, 180
Ukraine, 34, 39, 71, 128, 130, 132, 184, 188, 191, 201
United States
    and the atomic bomb, 257, 263, 268, 269–271, 277
    declaration of war, 143, 145
    and European recovery, 278–280
    Good Neighbor Policy, 49
    isolationism, 48–50

V

Valiant (battleship), 111, 126
Versailles, Treaty of, 20, 29, 38, 45, 55
Vichy, France, 102–103, 104, 120, 138, 166, 173, 174
Victory, Operation, 246
Vittorio Veneto (battleship), 111
V-J Day, 280
"V" missiles, 243

W

Wake Island, 141, 147, 148
Wannsee Conference, 189–190, 202, 204
Warsaw, 82, 84–85, 240–241, 253–255, 288
Wasp (aircraft carrier), 164
Wavell, Archibald, 115, 118, 147, 156, 167
Weimar Republic, 29–31, 34–35, 38, 198
Western Desert, 115, 156
Wilson, Woodrow, 45
World War I, 22, 24, 26, 77, 91, 101, 122, 123–124, 199, 274, 275,

Y

Yalta Conference, 255–259
Yugoslavia, 38, 109–113, 128, 192, 241, 244, 245, 253, 274–276, 285

Z

Zhukov, Konstantinovich, 133, 170, 171, 221, 254, 255, 261
Zyklon–B, 203

Photo Credits

Cover, p. 3 (top) © iStockphoto.com/George Cairns; cover, p. 3 (bottom) © iStockphoto.com/Avid Creative, Inc.; p. 12 Carol M. Highsmith's America/Library of Congress, Washington, D.C. (C-DIG-highsm- 04950); p. 23 Popperfoto/Getty Images; p. 31 Central Press/Hulton Archive/Getty Images; p. 37 Photos.com/Jupiterimages; p. 43 Hulton Archive/Getty Images; p. 52 © Pictures from History/The Image Works; pp. 58, 83, 129 ullstein bild/Getty Images; p. 68 Keystone-France/Gamma-Keystone/Getty Images; p. 74 Library of Congress, Washington, D.C.; p. 95 Henry Guttmann/Hulton Archive/Getty Images; p. 99 Photos.com/Thinkstock; p. 107 New Times Paris Bureau Collection/USIA/NARA; pp. 116, 163 © AP Images; p. 122 © akg-images/The Image Works; pp. 142, 173 National Archives, Washington, D.C.; pp. 157, 213, 230 Mondadori Portfolio/Getty Images; p. 179 © Manchester Daily Express/SSPL/The Image Works; p. 188 Time Life Pictures/The LIFE Picture Collection/Getty Images; p. 197 Universal Images Group/Getty Images; p. 203 T4c Sam Gilbert—Records of the Office of the Chief Signal Officer/U.S. National Archives and Records Administration (111-SC- 264918); pp. 226, 271 U.S. Department of Defense; p. 234 National Archives of Canada, photo by Gilbert Milne; neg. no. PA137013; p. 256 U.S. Army Photo; p. 262 Universal History Archive/Universal Images Group/Getty Images; p. 284 Galerie Bilderwelt/Hulton Archive/Getty Images; p. 286 Encyclopædia Britannica, Inc.; back cover and interior pages background image ©iStockphoto.com/Vallarie Enriquez